PRAISE FOR TIFFANY CLARE
and her captivating novels . . .

"Tiffany Clare writes a swoon-worthy romance filled with rich details and vivid characters. Any readers wishing for a bold and sweeping historical romance need look no further—Tiffany Clare is a treasure of an author!"
—Lisa Kleypas, *New York Times* bestselling author

The Secret Desires of a Governess

"With its irrepressible heroine, deliciously dark and dangerous hero, and suitably atmospheric setting, Clare's latest impeccably written novel cleverly references the classic gothic romances of Victoria Holt and Madeleine Brent, while at the same time incorporating plenty of the steamy passion and lush sensuality found in today's brand of sexy historical romances."
—*Booklist*

"With its brooding hero and dark backdrop Clare brings an updated gothic twist to her latest novel. By incorporating the themes and red herrings of a classic Victoria Holt or Daphne du Maurier, she entices readers to keep turning the pages to uncover the mystery and savor the highly sensual romance."
—*RT Book Reviews*

"This is an entertaining throwback to the Victoria Holt legendary Gothic tales as Tiffany Clare employs all the elements from the innocent female, to the foreboding castle to the brooding hero inside a romantic suspense thriller. Abby and Elliot are terrific lead characters while the support cast, espe̶c̶i̶a̶l̶l̶y̶ ̶t̶h̶e̶ ̶v̶i̶l̶l̶a̶g̶e̶rs, and her fam̶ ̶ance."
—*Review*

"[*The Seduction of His Wife*] will draw you in. . . .You'll find yourself riveted."

—*Night Owl Reviews* (Top Pick)

"Tiffany Clare has penned another superb and masterfully crafted romance. *The Seduction of His Wife* has all that I love in a book: humor, suspense, sigh-inducing romance, and fan-your-face, sizzling sex scenes. Ms. Clare's first book, *The Surrender of a Lady*, was a bold and daring story, and her latest book is equally as entertaining. If you've never read a Tiffany Clare book, run to your nearest bookstore. You don't know what you're missing!"

—*Romance Dish*

The Surrender of a Lady

"A unique, unforgettable, sensual love story sweeping from the harems of the east to staid Victorian ballrooms. Watch out for this sizzling new talent to rise to the top."

—*RT Book Reviews*

"Exotic, bold and captivating. Tiffany Clare's rich, sensual prose is delightful indulgence!"

—Alexandra Hawkins, author of *All Night with a Rogue*

"Dazzling, daring, and different! Exotic and erotic! *The Surrender of a Lady* will have you turning the pages until you finish, no matter how late it gets. Tiffany Clare is a brilliant new talent in historical romance."

—Anna Campbell, author of *Midnight's Wild Passion*

Also by Tiffany Clare

Midnight Temptations with a Forbidden Lord

Wicked Nights with a Proper Lady

The Secret Desires of a Governess

The Seduction of His Wife

The Surrender of a Lady

The Scandalous Duke Takes a Bride

TIFFANY CLARE

St. Martin's Paperbacks

This is a work of fiction. All of the characters, organizations, and events portrayed in this novel are either products of the author's imagination or are used fictitiously.

THE SCANDALOUS DUKE TAKES A BRIDE

Copyright © 2014 by Tiffany Clare.

All rights reserved.

For information address St. Martin's Press, 175 Fifth Avenue, New York, NY 10010.

ISBN: 978-1-250-00804-6

Printed in the United States of America

St. Martin's Paperbacks edition / March 2014

St. Martin's Paperbacks are published by St. Martin's Press, 175 Fifth Avenue, New York, NY 10010.

10 9 8 7 6 5 4 3 2 1

This book is for my readers. You e-mailed me and asked for Jez's story shortly after the first book in the series was released. This story is for you.

Acknowledgments

There is a lot that goes into writing a book. Time, sweat, crying, swearing, tearing up of pages to restart something that just doesn't work. I won't lie, this book was especially difficult to write, and I think that was partly because I could relate to Jez's larger than life personality. Though she was my most difficult character to write, she is my favorite heroine because of her determination and refusal to back down to anyone, even while facing her worst fears, which means I had to get her right on the page for my readers.

I could not have written this book and turned it into the story it is without my editor's, Monique Patterson's, brilliance. You always see the one thing missing that will turn the story around and make it a gazillion times better.

Elyssa, what is there to say? I think you read this book as many times as I did. Thank you for the e-mails, the crits, the long phone calls strategizing this book that was so important for me to get right. Jez has been a long time coming. And though we doubted me even pulling it off, I think after the torture I put her through, she turned out just fine with Hayden at her side.

Chapter 1

The rumors this writer has heard about the most sought-after bachelor in all of England. And what wicked things this particular man has committed. . . . Could you suspend belief if I accused a certain duke of engaging in acts only a commoner would participate in?

Mayfair Chronicles, May 1846

"Hold, Miller." When the valet dodged around a tall stack of crates on the dock, Hayden, the Duke of Alsborough, had no choice but to punch out the blunt end of his cane to knock the man to the ground. Hayden roughly pulled Miller up the rest of the way.

Dazed but still determined to escape, Miller stood on wobbly legs and threw out a fist that glanced off Hayden's left shoulder. The feeble hit was ineffective and only angered Hayden further.

He returned the blow, striking the valet square in the face and knocking him back another step. The man teetered to the right before falling like a sack laden with rocks to the cobbled road. He tried to scramble backward on his hands and feet, but his shoulders came up against a wall.

For two days Hayden had searched for this man. There was no way in hell he would give Miller the opportunity to run now that he had finally caught up to him. He unsheathed the blade from his cane and pointed it at the valet's neck, a mere inch from piercing his pale skin. It took everything in him to hold back and not bury it deep into Miller's throat.

"We've been over this," Hayden reminded him, the sharp edge of his temper spilling out in his words. "You came here willingly not an hour ago on the presumption that you would be leaving London. *Tonight*."

He exacted enough pressure to the valet's throat, just above his rumpled cravat—it would only take the flick of Hayden's wrist to end the other man's life should he run again.

Miller laughed, the sound gurgled and broken as he spat out a wad of blood next to Hayden's boot. When Miller grinned, a gaping hole at the front of his mouth oozed more blood where his tooth had been knocked out. "You're no better than me, Duke."

"That's where you're wrong," Hayden said.

Hayden stared at the one man who threatened the only person who mattered to him, the only woman he'd ever truly loved. Though he'd only been tossed out of his master's house a week past, Miller's dark hair stood on end greasy with dirt, and stubble covered his jaw and neck. He also sported a black eye that Hayden had not been the one to deliver.

"You'll leave or the outcome will look like child's play compared to what I've already done to you."

Miller shook his head, a sinister smile curling his lips. "You're mistaken to think you have any hold over me."

"Oh, I assure you I do. Should you choose to stay in England, you will live to regret that decision before the day is through." Slowly, Hayden removed the blade from the man's jugular.

The valet wiped his dirty sleeve across his mouth as he stood on unsteady feet, following the tip of Hayden's blade as though they were in the midst of some macabre dance of death.

"Why did you do it?" That was the one question Hayden wanted answered most.

"She's got no right to the fortune. I told my lordship I'd do anything he saw fit done." Miller spat and wiped his sleeve across his mouth again, smearing blood across his cheek. "You're too late to change the outcome. His Lordship would have divorced her were he still alive."

Hayden glared at the valet and took a threatening step forward. Jessica had every right to the fortune she'd married into. Hell, Hayden didn't know a person more deserving of a decent life, one that she'd been deprived of since the ill-fated day her father gave her to Fallon. Divorce seemed drastic, even for the old earl—and on what grounds?

Divorce was risky. The valet was lying. He had to be.

"Why are you here, Duke? Hushing up a bit of dirty work? Protecting that whore's reputation, or at least what's left of it?" The valet sneered. "You aristocrats are all the same, thinking your secrets are so precious. Especially Lady Jessica's. We both know she's no better than a trollop."

Hayden looked at the glint of steel in his hand. He could end all of Jessica's problems right now. But what kind of man would that make him? He lowered his blade long enough to sock Miller in the face again. The valet shook his head, dazed.

Hayden pulled away, cracking his knuckles, satisfied in knowing that Miller's face hurt a hell of a lot more than his fist.

"I'm willing to let her secrets die at the cost of your life," Hayden said bluntly.

"Then get on with it." The valet took a brazen step

forward, letting the tip of Hayden's blade pierce his dirty vest and shirt and press just above his heart. "Go ahead; slide the blade in the rest of the way. It's only a matter of time before Lady Jessica's reputation is well and truly destroyed."

The man had a death wish, but Hayden would not grant him that wish tonight. "Who else has been privy to her secrets?"

"That's for me to know. But it's not me you should fear. She's garnered enemies far and wide. That's what happens when a woman leads a disgraceful life, without thought to her reputation."

All Hayden had to do was buy Jessica a few months by ridding London of the pathetic weasel of a man standing before him. Who else knew about Jessica's situation, aside from him? Hayden needed the valet gone, before he could sell his secrets to the highest bidder. The last thing Hayden wanted to see printed in the gossip columns was Jessica's current predicament.

Wiping his bloodied knuckles on a handkerchief, Hayden reached into his breast pocket to retrieve the papers for the valet's voyage. He watched Miller in case he tried to run again, but there was a defeated look in the man's eyes that hadn't been there the last time he'd taken flight. Had he honestly thought he'd escape Hayden?

The valet snatched the papers from Hayden's grasp. "I wouldn't have minded tossing Her Ladyship down a flight of stairs, you know. It might have done the trick sooner."

Hayden grasped the man's throat tightly. He wanted to squeeze the last breath from his lungs and forever silence him. He watched as Miller struggled to breathe, his face flushing red.

In slow increments Hayden relaxed his grip, though he left the sword's sharp edge resting over the man's heart as he took a step back.

"I'll tell you this once because the repercussions for any disobedience will be the forfeiture of your life."

"I'm a dead man either way," the valet challenged him.

"You'll find no compassion from me," Hayden said. "You're a bigger fool than I imagined if you think I'll end your life swiftly. Board the ship set for Australia. The debt holders after you will be far kinder than me."

The valet pushed himself off the wall to stand on shaky legs; his height was nearly even with Hayden's. Miller really did have a death wish, but Hayden could not fulfill the man's wish to die so easily. In reality—and with no irony lost on him—Hayden had bought the man a second chance at life, since he probably would have been dead inside a week had he stayed in London. But the damage that could be accomplished in even a few days wasn't a chance Hayden was willing to take with Jessica's future.

Hayden motioned his sword in the direction of the ship that was leaving that evening. The valet straightened out his jacket, and held his head high as he stared back at Hayden.

"You haven't gotten the better of me."

"But I have, Miller."

Hayden nodded toward the ship again. He did not want to stand and talk to a man he reviled for threatening the woman he loved. Though he had every intention of waiting here till the ship had truly sailed from the dock.

This man leaving London would be the first right in a long list of wrongs, not wrongs done by him but wrongs committed toward Jessica. Hayden would do everything in his power to ensure her life from here on out started on the right foot.

Miller didn't grumble a moment longer and slowly ambled toward the ship, holding out his papers as he approached. Hayden sheathed his sword inside his cane and leaned on the stylized eagle handle as he waited.

How had everything turned into such a bloody mess?

With a heavy sigh, he left the docks when the ship was but a dot on the dusky horizon.

It was time to pay Jessica a visit and let her know the good news. Though he doubted the valet's removal from London would lighten her spirits; she'd been out of sorts since her husband's death, but Hayden hoped this would cheer her some.

Chapter 2

I would bet my finest pen that you are curious to know what I meant when I said that Mr. W——— might take his seat sooner in the House of Lords. There are few reasons for someone like the Dowager F——— to go into seclusion, so I leave the guessing game with my dear readers as to why she's been absent from society after her boldly inappropriate appearance at her husband's funeral. Or perhaps I should spill every last one of her secrets on these pages and have society wash their hands of her once and for all. In due course, dearest readers. In due course.

Mayfair Chronicles, June 1846

"You'll have a year in your house, Jez, as Fallon's widow. Though I have my doubts that Warren will let you stay that long."

Hayden leaned back in his chair and scrutinized his friend carefully. The bruise on her left cheek had faded to a buttery yellow. The mar on her flesh was a final token of how her husband had treated her, and it had Hayden's jaw clenching in anger to see it still there.

Jez perched forward, her elbows on the edge of his desk as she stared back at him. Her complexion was wan, and her once lustrous red curls looked limp and dull where they were piled atop her head. The constant spark of mischief usually lurking in her light blue eyes had been smothered for too many weeks to count.

"It shouldn't be a surprise that Fallon has reduced me to a pauper. If ever I needed proof that my husband despised me, he's managed to prove so even after his death."

Jez was more candid than usual about her late husband. She never discussed her tumultuous marriage with Hayden, or anyone else for that matter. It was a fine line she wouldn't cross, or she'd have to face too many ugly truths, he suspected. Hayden wished he could have changed the course of her life sooner.

How he would have changed it was anyone's guess. And really, there wasn't much he could have done to help her. When he'd finally discovered just what type of man Fallon was—a mere two years ago compared to the eight years that Jessica had been married—the law, he found, was not in favor of a friend protecting a married woman. They didn't seem to care how barbarous that husband was behind closed doors.

The one occasion that Hayden had witnessed the brute nature of Fallon he'd been escorted to Jessica's drawing room and heard the smashing of glass in the parlor next door. He'd been well and ready to ignore it until Jez's pained voice had begged for mercy.

The scene he'd witnessed upon sliding the door open . . .

Any man would have charged Fallon as he'd done.

After the first fall of his fist to Fallon's face and his attempt to strangle the man, Jez had pulled him off and had refused to budge from the path that blocked her scoundrel husband from further injury. Her dress had been torn at the shoulder; blood had smeared her upper lip where she'd been hit hard across the face. Hayden had never understood why she had dragged him off her husband or why she had protected the bastard all the years they'd been married.

While they'd never mentioned that day again, the knowledge of it had always stood between them. He had never witnessed a repeat of Fallon's high-handed abuse, and while he hoped that Fallon had never raised another hand against his wife after their confrontation, the evidence stared him baldly in the face right now.

He and Jez had known each other for nearly a decade, and looking at her now, he didn't see one ounce of the vibrant woman she once was. What he saw in her gaze was eight years of a miserable marriage weighing down on her soul.

But he knew there was an abundance of liveliness hidden beneath all the sorrow. If he could just find a way to unlock it again . . .

"You have a portion of your dowry that was protected from the estate. That hardly makes you a pauper," he pointed out. "What you do over the next year with that money will be what defines your financial stability in the future. I will make the investments on your behalf."

He was merely repeating the advice given to him by his solicitor. He did not tell her that he'd already allocated some of his money to bonds in her name.

She raised a hand to stall his speech. "Fallon invested a few hundred thousand pounds of my inheritance into the estate and ensured that it was tied firmly into the entailment. Ten thousand pounds is hardly enough to keep me in a decent life for long." She paused for a long moment, tapping her fingers along the arm of the chair. "I'll not leave London behind, Hayden. I can't live anywhere but here. This is my home."

He removed his reading glasses and pinched the bridge of his nose. Now would not be the best of times to tell her that he'd saved well for her future. She'd refuse him. That he knew without doubt.

"And I'll keep reminding you that it's in your best

interest to escape the city for a while"—he held up his hand when she tried to interrupt him—"at least until the gossip settles down about your lack of widow's weeds. We can arrange to have a summer house party at my estate. Or Leo's if you prefer, since his is closer to Town."

Jez shook her head. "And let Warren move in like a hawk on wounded prey? I will not expose my back to that man. He'll turn me out in a fortnight if I give him an open opportunity."

The only reason she had a year was to ensure that the next heir to the house of Fallon wasn't in her womb. While she'd revealed to Hayden that that wasn't a possibility, that didn't mean the rest of the *ton* needed to know that fact.

"Then I'll speak to him, Jez. Make it very clear what his moral obligation is under the law and in the eyes of society."

Jez closed her eyes for a brief moment before pulling herself to her feet to pace the study floor. The room doubled as his library, with heavily lined mahogany bookshelves on three of the walls and paned windows with stained glass decorating the tops on every other wall of the hexagonal room. A burgundy Persian rug covered the center of the room, stopping well before the molding to reveal the zigzag design of the hardwood inlay that bordered the room.

"You'll do no such thing," she said. "I will deal with Warren directly."

"He hasn't listened to your pleas thus far; why do you think he'll listen to you now?"

Her periwinkle silk day dress swished over her legs as she walked to and fro. She wrung her hands together in agitation. "He's my problem."

Hayden didn't agree—and he'd pay the man a visit to let him know that he should leave Jez alone for the foreseeable future.

"I cannot believe my life has been reduced to this," Jez said.

"There are investments you can make. . . ."

"I'll not wager away the last of my money on speculation."

Hayden gave her a droll look. The irony was that the first half of her marriage had been spent in and out of gaming houses. It was baffling that she wouldn't make one small gamble now.

She plopped herself down on the sofa with a heavy sigh, half a room away from him. He pushed his chair out from his desk and walked over to her, his hands in his vest pockets as he studied her.

"It wouldn't be a risk," he assured her.

Jez threw her right arm over her brow dramatically. "I don't want to think about this at the moment."

"This is your reality, Jez." He didn't finish his diatribe, as he didn't want to lecture her any more than she wanted to be lectured. Another time perhaps, but not now. "We'll discuss this when you're in better spirits, then."

She peeked at him from under her arm. "I doubt that'll be any time soon. The only thing I care about right now is what our plans are for this evening."

"Cards. Here, of course."

She needed to stay out of sight for a while, let the gossip surrounding her appearance at her husband's funeral die down; by wearing scarlet to the funeral of her late husband she'd dared society to censure her. Hayden wondered if society would ever look at Jez in a kinder light than the one that currently shone upon her. Only time would tell.

"It's dreadful being a widow. I haven't received one invitation since Fallon kicked the bucket."

"A week is hardly a long time. And just because you don't care for society's rules, you know most others play by the book."

Besides, she didn't look as though she could endure an evening of fanfare despite her insistence. She looked frail, and as the week had progressed she seemed more unlike herself—"distant" and "less vibrant" were the only descriptions he could come up with. He wasn't foolish enough to bring that to her attention, or the fact that she could feel better from a week of self-imposed rest.

It didn't matter what anyone else thought of her; he knew exactly what was going on in that pretty head of hers—she was hiding from the truth of her circumstances. She constantly pushed herself too hard, and while he understood her need to distance herself from reality, it was time to put the reins back on her life and figure out her future.

After living under the reign of her husband for so long, it must be odd to finally be free, to do as she pleased without any repercussions from Fallon.

There were so many things Hayden wanted to show her that would make her smile. He wanted to be the one to give her that second view on life. And he would. But now wasn't quite the time for that.

"What are you thinking so intensely about?" she asked.

He shrugged. "This and that. Nothing of import, unless you want to discuss a few of the ventures I've been lucky to invest in."

"I'd tell you how insufferable you are, but you already know that about yourself."

"Do I?" He smiled a little with her assessment of him.

"Oh, stop being so cavalier. Please sit with me. You're liable to start pacing and I have a megrim coming on. I don't want to grow dizzy watching you think out my problems." She rubbed fitfully at her temple. "I think I should remind you again: my situation is my problem to sort out."

He sat heavily on the sofa and put his feet up on the ottoman next to her ivory-slippered ones.

"What a pair we are," he observed aloud.

He turned his head and stared at her with her arm flung over her eyes. She didn't see him, which he was fine with, since it gave him an opportunity to scrutinize her carefully. The sleeves of her dress were loose around her shoulders and upper arms, her skin had an almost translucent quality, and the light dusting of freckles on her nose and cheeks seemed faded—if such a thing was possible.

"What am I going to do with you?"

She lowered her arm and turned to look at him. "There's nothing to be done, Hayden." She took his hand and gave it a friendly squeeze. The cool press of her fingers could not keep the desires within him banked for long. "Trust that I'll work out my problems on my own. You can't always save the day when one of us makes a mess of our lives."

She referred to their other friends, Leo and Tristan, not just herself. And it was true; he usually had all the answers . . . except, it seemed, when it came to Jez. That didn't mean he wouldn't try to fix what was currently wrong in her life.

"It's something I have to do. I'll always want the best for you."

"I know." She smiled, the contentment reaching her blue eyes this time. "You're the best friend anyone could ever ask for."

And there was the crux of it: in her eyes he would always be just a friend. She really did make him believe that opposites attracted, for there was nothing similar in their characters, yet he wanted her to himself. She'd always been brazen and daring, him steadfast and cautious. Yet he still wanted to protect and cherish her as his own. And he would. There was nothing to stop him now that Fallon was dead.

"Are you sure you're up for a hand of cards tonight?"

he asked cautiously. Jez hated to be told she shouldn't do something.

"I haven't anything better to do, so yes. I'll send Tristan a note to stop at my townhouse; we can walk over together."

"I really think we should escape to the countryside for the remainder of the summer. It'll be too hot to stay in the confines of the city for much longer and I can only bear the smell of the Thames for so long."

"You know I love London too much to move away for any length of time. Besides, I need to work out a few arrangements with Warren tomorrow."

Hayden snapped to attention and sat up straighter on the sofa. "What business does he have with you? You should have told me, Jez."

She sighed more loudly than she needed to. "I knew you would react exactly this way; that's why I didn't tell you."

"What's the purpose of the meeting?" he asked. "Warren treated you with contempt at the reading of the will. There is no reason for you to have to endure his company alone."

"Give me some credit in dealing with him. I can be charming if the occasion warrants it. I want to ask him for the dower house, to live there at least until he's married."

"You know he won't allow it. Hell, I'd be surprised if the man actually took the Ponsley chit as his wife." In fact, Tristan and Leo were both trying to win the favor of the woman set to be engaged to Warren—which had started at Jez's insistence. "Warren is above reproach, and you know that he can't possibly entertain the idea of keeping you on."

"I know I've been a dreadful role model of how a proper lady should act since I married, but it will hurt his reputation to throw me out too soon. Surely there are enough men who hated my husband that they'll side with me in this. I know Warren has it in him to show some compassion."

"This doesn't sound like a good idea to me." In fact, this was an outright bad idea. He didn't want her near another Fallon for the rest of her days. Hayden decided then and there that if Warren so much as raised his hand to her his life would be forfeit. "If you want to negotiate the dower house as part of your marriage settlement, let me do it with my solicitor."

"I wasn't asking for your permission, Hayden."

"If he mistreats you in any way, you're to come to me immediately."

"You sound like an overbearing father."

That was not a character he wanted to be equated to in Jez's life.

"You'll have to live with that," he said, brushing his hand through his hair. Perhaps he should pay a visit to Warren, tell him that should anything happen to Jez then Warren would be held personally responsible.

Even knowing that he was stepping out of bounds by seeing the man behind Jez's back, he resolved to have it done first thing in the morning.

He changed the subject to a more pressing issue. "How have you been feeling?"

"Why do you ask?" she said cautiously.

He raised one eyebrow sardonically. She knew exactly what he meant.

"I'm starting to find the happiness I had before I married."

"Truly?" He had known her long enough to smell a lie when she fed him one. He didn't for one second believe her.

She nodded. "It'll be a long process."

"And what of your health?"

She sat up a little straighter, chin jutted out and full of pride. "Fit as a fiddle."

"Don't lie to me, Jez. I can see the weariness in your face. And it's more than evident that you've shed a good stone in the last couple of weeks."

She slumped back against the couch with a frustrated air. "It's not polite for you to say so. And you know I've been under more pressure than the average person might have to face in all their life. Don't worry about me. I promise I'll fill out my clothes again in no time."

"Consider it my duty to worry about you."

Her smile faded from her lips as she pushed herself off the sofa to stand. "If I'm to be ready for this evening, I should head home."

As Hayden stood he reached for her hand to ask her to stay longer. She shook him off before he even had a chance to touch her.

"I can have a carriage brought around for you," he offered, even though it was only a few blocks to the Fallon residence.

"I think I'll walk since it's such a beautiful day."

He pulled his hat from the hook near the door, intent on walking with her since he wasn't ready to part ways.

Jez placed her hand over his chest to stall him. "I wanted to take in the fresh air and think for a while before I'm home. You needn't walk with me. I'll be fine on my own."

Her head was bowed where she stood, her finger fiddling with a button on his shirt—so he couldn't pull on his jacket, he thought.

"Jez . . ."

When she looked up at him he was struck speechless by the sadness clouding her vision. "I promise you I'll be fine, Hayden. And if I'm not, you've always been my rock when I've needed you, haven't you?"

He gave one succinct nod, but wondered whether she would really come to him if she needed his support. Their friendship seemed strained . . . maybe strained was an incorrect assumption, but she'd certainly been avoiding spending any great length of time with him alone since her husband's funeral—ever since confiding exactly what length her husband had gone to in order to cut her out of the Fallon fortune.

"I know I've been out of sorts from all the changes in my life. I promise you that I'm working on being my old self again."

He didn't say anything, just let Jez take the hat from his hand and put it back on the peg next to the door.

When she stepped away from him, the footman opened the door at his nod. Hayden stood at the threshold, thinking he should follow her home, knowing that would anger her.

He would do it regardless.

A lady on her own was unacceptable to him. Especially when that lady was Jez.

Chapter 3

The estate of the late F—— has been busy with midnight visitors. With all the ins and outs, I can't imagine it to be anything clandestine but more a flurry of activity to cover up something much darker than the simplicity of an affair.

Mayfair Chronicles, June 1846

Lady Jessica Fallon, now fortunately and unfortunately the Dowager Countess of Fallon, opened her parasol even though clouds dotted the sky overhead. She turned to her friend one last time before she left him in his foyer.

His blond hair was a little on the long side—he usually kept it clipped short and pomaded as current fashion demanded. Stubble dotted along his jaw and chin, which was unusual; he was so put together that she often found she wanted to rumple him just to see him loosen up a bit. His dark brown eyes, however, were still the same—deadpan and serious as he watched her step outside without him to escort her.

He seemed eager to walk with her, but she needed to be alone right now. She'd delayed too long at his house and now she would suffer the consequences for not ending their time together much sooner.

"Thank you for everything." She meant it. You could not ask for a truer friend than Hayden and she counted herself lucky to have met and befriended him all those years ago.

"I'd be happier if you'd allow me to escort you." He folded his arms across his wide chest. He was of formidable height and quite fit from riding and regular fencing, two things he managed to find the time to accomplish every day. And as well he should ride daily, since he bred some of the finest Arabian horses in England.

"Don't be a ninny, Hayden. I'm not even a ten-minute walk from here."

His jaw clenched. He clearly didn't like her insistence in this, but it couldn't be helped. She blew him a kiss and walked down the steps of his townhouse. She knew he'd follow, and there was nothing to be done about that.

She needed time to herself. Time to think alone. To be reminded about how much of a pariah she was, no thanks to her late husband—and admittedly because of her own antics since the onset of her dreadful marriage. And while she should rejoice at finally being a widow, she simply couldn't.

With Fallon's death came uncertainty, and a sad end to the life she'd grown to love even with all the pitfalls she'd met over the last eight years.

She pressed her lace-gloved fingers to her temple to try to relieve the tension that had been building behind her eyes since she woke this morning.

She passed Lady Hargrove and her daughter, whose name Jessica could not recall at the moment. She gave them a cordial nod, but the countess ushered her daughter to the other side of the street, not daring to address a woman of Jessica's reputation. Jessica would not dwell on how despicable that made her feel; otherwise, she'd be tempted to just stop and sit on the nearest set of stairs and cry out her frustrations for all to see.

That would be too delicious of fodder for the Mayfair Chronicler not to give their twopenny's worth of thought on.

It was as Hayden suggested; Jessica's lack of widow's

weeds did not help her in the eyes of society, but she refused to don black for Fallon. He was no true man. Real men did not require brute strength to instill their sense of justice and order in a marriage.

Society had welcomed a monster into their homes with open, trusting arms. She was the only person to ever see the ugly side of her husband.

As she approached her townhouse the first twinge of pain she'd been expecting for days stabbed deep inside her womb. She reached out to the railing and dropped her parasol as she tried to remain standing. Why now? Had she not been humiliated enough these past weeks that she now had to lose the babe in front of everyone? In front of Hayden, who trailed not twenty paces behind? This could not happen yet. Odd how the door was so close yet so far all at the same time.

She closed her eyes for a moment and took a deep breath as she weathered the nausea that came with the next wave of cramps. There were too many witnesses to show any weakness now. She needed to remain strong, determined.

She needed to reach the door and find a way into the safety of her home.

She forced a laugh past her lips and took in a deep breath as she picked up her parasol from the stone stairs of her townhouse. With every ounce of strength left in her, she climbed the rest of the way up the stairs without looking back to see whose eyes were upon her, witnessing her shame. Each step was more agonizing than the last as she pulled her weight up the last few steps like an anchor too long at sea and laden with kelp.

If she faltered now, everyone would see and guess at the truth. Not a day had gone by in her marriage when Fallon hadn't humiliated her; she would not be disgraced on the street for her inability to carry the Fallon heir to term.

She would not.

If anyone so much as guessed that the rightful heir to the Fallon title was being ripped slowly from her body, then she might as well admit defeat now and leave this cursed house behind once and for all. But it was hers. And she would hold on to what was left of her life and she wouldn't relinquish one miserable second to Mr. Warren before she had to. He'd have to pry her grip away from this house one stubborn finger at a time.

God, how she wished Hayden were at her side to help her, but she did not want him to see her so weak, so empty of the vivacity she normally prided in herself. This was her humiliation and loss to bear alone. Besides, she'd already told him too much.

On opening the door, the butler looked over her shoulder—probably to see how many enemies were watching her exposed back. She'd never seen a more welcome sight as he discreetly took her by the elbow, helped her over the threshold, and hastily closed the door to the outside world, cloistering them in the darkness of the foyer.

She must appear far worse than she thought, for his concern was etched deep in his old, wrinkled face.

"My lady?"

She patted his weathered cheek affectionately. "I'll be fine, Wilson."

Her teeth clenched tight against the next wave of pain that was far sharper than the last. Her knees buckled and she nearly collapsed before Wilson and a footman caught her around the waist to hold her upright.

And then she felt it. Warmth seeped between her thighs as her body finally let go of the babe it had nourished for nearly five months. She bit her lip hard against the sobs building in her throat.

There was no sense in feigning that everything was all right, not when it so obviously wasn't.

As calmly as she could, she said, "Please take me up to my room."

"Of course, my lady. Shall we send for the doctor?"

She shook her head vehemently. "Have Mrs. Harper come up to my room at once. She is all the assistance I require."

Jessica made it to her private bedchamber with the footman's help. Wilson wasn't far behind, the worry growing in his expression as whimpers of pain passed her lips and a trail of blood trickled across the hardwood flooring, staining her ivory slippers. Once in her room, she crumpled onto her bed as another jolt of stabbing cramps tore through her body. She rolled to her side and pulled her knees up to her chest as she clutched her arms around her legs.

Wilson ran from her room calling out to Mrs. Harper as he took the stairs faster than Jessica had ever seen him move.

Jessica hadn't thought a miscarriage could be so painful. She'd spotted and bled on and off for nearly a week, thinking that had been the extent of the whole ordeal. Even though the midwife she'd seen outside of London had assured her that that would not be the case, the old woman's wise words hadn't stopped Jessica from hoping otherwise.

She heard the jingle of keys before she saw Mrs. Harper, the housekeeper, enter her room.

When Mrs. Harper saw her on the bed, she rushed forward. "Oh, my lady. You're as white as a ghost."

"I'm c-cold." Her teeth chattered together.

"You are shivering something fierce. I'll have a hot bath run for you. That'll be the quickest way to stave off the chill that's taken hold of you."

Jessica could barely nod her thanks at the housekeeper as she went to the bellpull to call up the housemaids.

Jessica forced herself up from the bed and made her way to the washbasin in her room; she lost her breakfast and the little cucumber sandwiches Hayden had plied her with an hour ago. The dizziness was unbearable and she held the stand with both hands and anchored herself as she threw up again. There were hands supporting her as the retching subsided.

Mrs. Harper wiped Jessica's mouth with a handkerchief.

"I need out of this dress."

Mrs. Harper released the buttons at the back of Jessica's dress. Before long the bodice and overskirts were removed, too. Her underclothes were soaked through with blood.

When her corset loosened, Jessica took a deep breath into her lungs, but the smell of lingering sickness had her covering her mouth again. Thankfully, she had nothing left to throw up.

Mrs. Harper assisted her back to her bed and pulled the coverlet down. "I'll remove the bowl—there's nothing worse than a bad smell to put you ill at ease again. I'll give instructions to the maids on my way to the bathing room."

"Thank you."

Jessica hugged her arms tight around her midsection. A feverish chill dampened her skin. She'd thought the damage Fallon had done nearly over. She hadn't expected the miscarriage to be so severe; perhaps it would have been like the rest had she not been as far along in the pregnancy as she was. It was almost like this was a sign that she shouldn't have children.

Hot tears ran down both sides of her face. She didn't bother to wipe them away but instead let them pool beneath her left cheek and dampen her pillow.

When the maid entered Jessica's bedchamber, the young girl rushed forward. "You've fallen ill, my lady."

Only Mrs. Harper and Wilson had known about the

babe; the rest of her staff would soon know the truth Jessica had been desperate to hide since her husband had fallen ill. Thank goodness she had thought ahead and had fired most of the staff who had been loyal only to her husband. She'd given them all a month's worth of wages and letters of recommendation, hoping it would keep them from telling truths Jessica wanted buried.

"I'll need your arm if I'm to make it to the bathing chamber."

"Yes, my lady."

The maid helped Jessica to her feet and wrapped her arm around her waist to keep her from sliding to the floor.

Another wave of nausea had Jessica's head spinning and her stomach in spasms again, so she closed her eyes and worried only about catching a decent breath. She let the maid lead her blindly to the drawn bath.

"Thank you, Claudia. Mrs. Harper can assist me now."

The housekeeper nodded to the young girl as she took her leave, shutting the door softly behind her. "Did the midwife tell you what to expect?"

Jessica nodded. When she'd found out that her husband had been poisoning her so that she would lose the baby, she'd sought the advice of a midwife—the old woman had only confirmed Jessica's worst fears. The life within her was dead. "Only that losing the babe would be no easy task."

And the midwife had known with certainty that the baby in Jessica's womb no longer grew. She'd offered a strong concoction to speed up the process, but Jessica had refused on the off chance that maybe this once the heavens were looking down at her and smiling. Maybe the babe would be spared the violence Jessica had suffered from her husband now that he was well and truly gone.

The heavens had no reason to be kind to her. And she was sure her husband went laughing all the way to his grave and was gloating from his accomplishment from whatever depths of hell he'd landed himself in.

Mrs. Harper helped her undress, piling her soiled clothes into a neat stack before taking her hand to assist her into the hot water. On grasping her arm, her housekeeper looked at her, worry evident in the dark brown depths of her eyes. "I'm of a mind to call the doctor to the house."

Jessica shook her head. There was no way a doctor could come to the house; she'd not risk this secret being found out. "We're in for a long night, and for now the hot bath will have to do."

Mrs. Harper pressed the back of her hand to Jessica's cheek, clucking her tongue in a motherly fashion. "We'll keep adding hot water until your chill breaks."

She nodded, unable to speak through the chattering of her teeth as she sank into the hot water that slowly turned pink as it washed the blood away from her body.

"This is like the influenza that swept through the household six years ago," Jessica said absently.

"Hopefully not so severe as that." Her housekeeper was right in that regard. After half the house had fallen sick, a stable hand and a maid had succumbed to their illnesses, shrouding the house in black for one week—Fallon had refused to let mourning go on longer.

Jessica's limbs started to loosen and the aches and cramps eased somewhat in the soothing water. Enough that she closed her eyes and leaned her head back on the curved lip of the tub.

Mrs. Harper placed a warm cloth over Jessica's forehead. "While the maids prepare your bed for what's to come tonight, I'll have a broth readied for you if you think you can stomach it."

Tears pricked at her eyes. "You're too good to me, Mrs. Harper."

"Now, lass, you've been kind to the staff where your

lord husband was not. And I'll not speak ill of the dead, but I only ever stayed on so I could keep an eye on you. Lord Fallon grew more foul every year past his fiftieth birthday."

Jessica removed the cloth and looked at her housekeeper. "I think his mood had a great deal to do with me. I'm afraid I was not a good wife or, at least, not the kind of wife he'd always envisioned."

"No one in this house would blame you for the actions you were forced to take, my lady. There is a certain amount of self-preservation one must seek in order to bear the brutalities this world sometimes offers us. There is also no denying that Fallon was a wretched man—right up till his end."

A small smile played on Jessica's lips as she reached out to grasp Mrs. Harper's hand to give it a light squeeze. "Broth sounds ideal, though it'll be a miracle if I can stomach even that."

She'd been so hampered by morning sickness at the beginning of her pregnancy. And then there had been the addition of the poison dropped into her morning tea, making her more ill as it worked its way through her body.

Miller, her husband's loyal valet, had been the one watching the food she ate, making sure a few drops of the deadly tincture of blue cohosh and other harmful herbs would do its task over the course of a few weeks. She would never mourn her husband, but she would mourn this unborn child.

What had she done that was so horrible in life that she had faced nothing but ridicule and hardship since marrying Fallon? Was it her youth paired with her much older husband's supposed wealth that made so many dislike her? Little could they know that it was her money that had saved his estate from ruin.

Was it her brazenness that had her husband seeking

her out in the darkest hours of the night to instill his sense of justice for behavior he did not condone?

She would never know the answers to those questions. And though she might not have cared a few months ago why she'd been dealt such a losing hand of cards in the game of life, she cared now because the only decent thing to happen to her was being torn from her body.

Realizing she'd been lost in her thoughts, she looked up at Mrs. Harper and said, "The bath is helping."

"That's good news. I'll leave you to relax for a spell, my lady."

Mrs. Harper placed fresh linens on the bench at the back of the bathtub and left to do her tasks. The sad truth was, Jessica didn't feel any better in the water. She placed her hands over her stomach and closed her eyes. She hummed a lullaby her mother used to sing to her, sobbing softly the whole time.

Chapter 4

*Why steal into the back of the Countess of F——'s
house in the middle of the night? There is something nefarious to uncover, and I promise I'll be
the one to do so. What will become of the dowager
countess now that she no longer has the protection
of the late earl?*

Mayfair Chronicles, June 1846

Hayden had been called from his bedchamber shortly
after midnight. A maid stood twisting her hands together
in the parlor she'd been situated in while he dressed.

"Your business at this hour?" he asked gently. The girl
seemed frightened in his presence, so he invited her to sit
on the settee in his study with a motion of his hands. She
shook her head and stared at him nervously.

"There isn't time, my lord. I'm from the Fallon household.
The Earl of Barrington wanted me to come straight here
and fetch you for my ladyship." She ducked her head as
though fearful of reprimand for disturbing him so late in
the evening.

"Emerson," he called out to his butler, "bring me my hat
and call for a hackney without delay."

A hackney would delay them further, but it was necessary if he was to travel with the maid. Jessica would be in
good hands with Barrington until he arrived.

"Certainly, my lord." His butler bowed and left the room to do as was asked of him.

Hayden glanced at the young woman. "We can't be seen in the street together, as it would draw suspicion."

The maid continued to stare at her feet, nodding her head in agreement.

"Please tell me what's brought you here so late in the evening. Has something happened to Lady Fallon?"

She looked at him with big, round green eyes. "I can't, my lord. I'd never be forgiven for spilling Lady Fallon's secrets. She only kept on a few of us after His Lordship passed on."

"True enough. And think no more of it. I'll see her soon if Emerson can manage to fetch a hackney at this hour."

"I can go on ahead, my lord. The Fallon estate is close enough for me to walk."

"I won't hear of it. It's too late for a woman to be out on the streets."

Hayden took to pacing the small sitting room, agitated that he couldn't act now. There were so many thoughts racing through his head on what might be the issue with Jez. He suspected he was correct earlier; she had looked ill. When Tristan had arrived for cards without her this evening, he should have known something was wrong.

"When did Barrington arrive at your mistress's house?"

"Not a half an hour ago. He called for you straight-away."

He stopped pacing and focused his attention on the maid. "How ill is she?"

She ducked her head again.

"You'll do her no harm in revealing the truth to me. It's a mere matter of minutes before I find out why I've been called to her house past midnight. What ails her?"

he asked, though he had a sneaking suspicion he knew the answer to that.

The maid shook her head before averting her eyes.

The butler came into the room. "Your Grace, the hackney awaits."

Hayden rubbed his hands through his hair, disarraying it further.

When they arrived at Jessica's townhouse, he used the servants' entrance and took the stairs two at a time to the second floor where Jez's room was situated. Leo leaned against the back of a chair, his arms crossed over his broad chest, his dark hair standing every which way. His gaze was worried as he stared at Jez from across the sitting room.

Hayden strode past Leo and toward Jez, who lay on the chaise, head resting on a pillow, her feet curled up. Her eyes were barely open and her skin was covered in a damp sheen of sweat. He didn't say anything to Leo as he ran forward and fell to his knees so he could lean in close to Jez.

"Oh, Jez," he whispered, his heart breaking as she lay prone and almost lifeless before him.

But his beautiful, bold friend was no less strong even in her current situation.

He placed one hand over her shoulder, the other against her forehead to test the severity of her fever. He whispered for her ears alone, "While this is not the time to chastise you, you shouldn't have lied to me, Jez. I would have seen you through this."

"It was my shame to bear alone." Her voice was quiet, as though speaking pained her.

"It will never be yours to bear alone again." Determination laced his words.

She would never have only herself to count on. He would not watch her go through life alone a moment longer. And while nothing could change the deep friendship they'd built over the years, he would always be there to protect her every step of the way. He could not stand passively by waiting for her to notice the man he was, the one who wanted nothing more than to love her as so much more than a friend.

He wanted her to himself. He always had.

Tonight would change everything between them.

Hayden turned enough to see the housekeeper and two maids laying out fresh bed linens. A pile of soiled bedding was rolled up in a basket on the floor. He'd have to remind them to burn the material. There could be no evidence for what went on here tonight; Jez would never forgive him if anyone found out that she'd miscarried the Fallon heir.

Focused back on Jez, he inspected her clothes. Aside from being damp from the fever that had assailed her, it looked as though the maids had already changed her at some point earlier in the evening, for she was in a night rail. Regardless, the maids would have to help her into a dry nightgown, as this one was nearly soaked right through.

He didn't hesitate to lift her up into his arms and take her back to her newly made bed; she would need to rest until her fever broke and he had every intention of staying with her no matter how long it took.

"You needn't be so gallant," she whispered before putting her head to his shoulder as though holding up that weight was too much for her, which only made her argument feeble.

"I'll see you to your bed and make sure you're well enough to avoid seeing a sawbones."

And he would see to Jez's well-being—he'd never seen her so weak and defeated; those were simply two adjectives that did not suit Jez in the least. Leo could wait for him in the sitting room. Hayden kicked the door behind him closed without so much as a word to his friend.

As he placed her on the bed, hoping he didn't hurt her or cause her further discomfort, her arms fell away, limp of life, from his neck. "Go home, Hayden. You can see I'm well looked after by the staff."

"Why should you do this alone, Jez? What Fallon did is indisputably appalling, but that doesn't mean you need to suffer through this by yourself. We've been friends too long for you to fool me with any sort of false bravado."

"There is nothing false about me at the moment. I would prefer to suffer this shame in private."

She pushed herself up on the bed with a hiss of pain as she leaned against a soft stack of white pillows. Her maid mopped her brow with a cool cloth.

"I'm not leaving," he said simply as he turned away from her and gave instructions to the housekeeper. "Mrs. Harper, please have her clothes changed."

"Your Grace, I cannot—"

"Do it. Now."

There was no more argument, not even from Jessica. The rustle of clothes and the trickle of water sounded as the staff sponge-bathed her and redressed her. He did not turn around, wanting to give her some privacy. While the staff was busy with Jez, he removed his jacket and tossed it over a nearby chair.

It would be a long night.

"I'm decently attired," she said.

He turned and looked her over. Her hair had been braided again, the long rope of red curls draped over her left shoulder, falling with a curled tip at her waist. She was tucked under fresh bedding. It was deceiving for a moment how she almost looked better, but sweat beaded at her temples and trailed a slow, wet path from her temple down one cheek.

He came forward, took the damp cloth from the maid

who'd retrieved him at his residence earlier, and sat on the edge of Jessica's bed next to her thigh.

"Shall I call on the expertise of a midwife?" He pressed the fresh cloth to her temples, dabbing away the droplets of sweat.

Jessica shook her head. "That would be far too dangerous. If she were discovered, she'd be questioned about my condition. I do not want anyone to know."

She looked away from him with a frustrated sigh and fell back against the pillows sapped of the little energy she'd displayed for him.

"I understand more than anyone the need for secrecy in this, but you need to see someone that can help you."

Jessica took the cloth from him to place the cool linen over her eyes. "When I first saw the midwife, she told me that losing the babe would be painful. That it would be very near the pain of labor, because I was in the second stage of pregnancy."

"And what precisely does that mean?"

"It means that I'm well enough without the interference of a sawbones or a local midwife. I just need to sleep this off." She waved him away when he dabbed the cloth over her brow again.

"Then I hope you won't be too disappointed when I tell you that I refuse to leave you alone for any length of time while you're in this state."

As he stood from the bed she grabbed the sleeve of his shirt. "Hayden."

"What is it?" He took her hand, squeezing it gently, reassuringly. God, how he wished he could be of better assistance.

"Could you please send Leo away? Ask him to remain silent on all he's seen and learned tonight? I never wanted him to know." Jessica shook her head as she slipped her hand away from his, seemingly disappointed with herself, even though tonight's revelation could not have been helped. "I never wanted any of you to know."

"How can we help you if you can't trust us with your darkest secrets?" He caressed the side of her face.

"I have always been forthcoming. Just don't ask it of me with this. This was private." Tears filled her eyes but did not flow.

"What do you think we'll do with the truth? Jessica, we love you and would kill anyone who dared to hurt you." Which hadn't been entirely true, he realized after the words had passed his lips. There was one person who had hurt her . . .

"There was nothing that you could have done about Fallon. It's only a shame he didn't die sooner," she said without an ounce of remorse.

Hayden hadn't been able to do anything after first discovering her husband's violence and he'd never seen any signs of the earl's heavy hand on Jessica after the day he'd confronted Fallon in the parlor.

"I'll send Leo home and ask for his silence."

"Thank you, Hayden. You've been too kind to me. Everyone's been so kind when I don't deserve it."

"You're wrong, Jez." He'd move mountains for her, and it was in his power to do so now that the impediment of her husband had been removed from the equation.

"Look at me, Hayden. Have you really looked at me?" She raised her hand, encompassing her disheveled state. "I'll be naught but an old widow . . . and a poor one at that once Warren takes the Fallon seat and pushes me out of this house." She yawned and rubbed at her tear-damp eyes. "Right out of my own house."

"You are not without friends."

"Aside from you, Leo, and Tristan, no one else will associate with me. That's a truth I've avoided for too long."

Jessica had surrounded herself with men; Hayden thought she had done it partially to infuriate Fallon and partly because she could find no common ground with other society ladies, aside from Tristan's sister, Bea. That needed to change, since Jessica was no longer able to hide behind the Fallon fortune. It was odd how the one thing that protected you could also be the one thing that hurt you the most.

"You'll have to befriend some of the ladies that hold influence. Most of the *ton* are fascinated enough by the life you've led to take tea with you at the very least."

She raised one eyebrow as she stared back at him. "Do you take me for a circus poodle performing its master's tricks when commanded?"

He frowned as he rolled up his sleeves and took the small towel from the washbasin, wringing it out. "You know I don't believe that for one second. I have always admired your determination and strength."

Not surprisingly, the strength she'd displayed through their conversation suddenly diminished as she slouched back against the pillows.

"Save your flatteries, Hayden."

"They are not said for the purpose of flattery. I mean it, Jez." He turned toward her. "I'm going to remove the sweat from your brow; then I'll leave you to rest."

"There's plenty of time for sleep." Her words were whispered, her eyes drifting shut as she watched him approach the bedside again. It wasn't long before she fell into a deep slumber.

The housekeeper came forward to tuck her mistress properly into the bed, but Hayden held up his hand to stall her. He pulled the coverlet up high enough to cover Jessica to the chin and looked down at her sickly form. After a spell, he folded the damp cloth, placed it over her forehead, sat on the edge of the bed.

He turned to Mrs. Harper. "You only need to stay till I'm back from seeing Lord Barrington off."

"Your Grace." The woman nodded her head in understanding.

"One of the maids can set up the sofa. I plan to stay the evening."

"You understand that I must refuse for the sake of Lady Fallon's reputation," the housekeeper said with a stern look that weighed down her brows.

"There isn't a force strong enough to remove me from this house right now."

The older woman bowed her head, and it was obvious to Hayden that she wanted to deny him even that.

"As you wish, Your Grace. Though I insist you take another room. There is a large guest room only next door."

Hayden crossed his arms over his chest. "I will leave this room once to see Barrington off. When I arrive back upstairs, I will sleep on the sofa so that Your Ladyship may have my assistance if she wakes during the night."

The housekeeper turned to the maid to give her instructions on readying the room. "Do as His Lordship asks. Have bedding brought in and the sofa set up to accommodate his stay." She turned back to him, clearly not happy having to cede to his wishes. "Is there anything else we can get you?"

"I'll need some help keeping vigil through the night, so coffee would be great if it's not too much of a bother for the cook."

There were no further protests, though Hayden could tell by the set of Mrs. Harper's jaw that she was displeased with him.

He went down to the main foyer to see Leo off. He had to reveal why he knew about Jessica's condition, explaining that he'd asked her if there was a possibility she was with child, as it would have kept the Fallon estate in her name. Leo had reluctantly agreed not to reveal Jez's secret to Tristan. What Hayden hadn't told Leo was that he had thought Jez had already miscarried. He'd thought . . .

It didn't matter what he thought. He was here with Jez now, and he'd stay by her side until she was better, and he'd make sure she knew he was a man who would stand by her side, no matter the circumstance.

Hayden climbed the stairs to Jez's private chambers. He dreaded what the long night would bring. All he knew was that he couldn't leave. Because he sure as hell wouldn't abandon her now.

When he checked on her she was sound asleep. He flipped over the towel to the cooler side and watched her till the housekeeper returned, tray in hand, laden with coffee and sandwiches.

"Shall I keep watch first, Your Grace?"

"No, go on up to bed, Mrs. Harper. The staff has worked hard this evening. You'll need your rest for whatever tomorrow brings."

"I don't think I can sleep knowing Her Ladyship is in the state she is in."

"Then feel free to keep me company," he offered, knowing that would put her at ease about him staying the night.

The housekeeper came up next to him and removed the cloth from Jez's forehead and pressed the back of her hand against her to see if she still ran a fever. He knew she did, but it had lessened since his arrival.

"Have you any experience with this?" he asked.

"Once when I started as a ladies' maid . . . though she wasn't as far along as Lady Fallon. It'll be a long night, and we may need to fetch the doctor if the fetus doesn't come out on its own." She leveled him with a stern glare. "It's woman's work you're interfering with here."

"There is nothing you can say and nothing I can witness

that will make me leave this room." He stroked his fingers across Jez's forehead and over her temple. "She's always been so strong."

"She still is, Your Grace. Now if you don't mind the in-
formality of the evening, I'll join you for coffee as we wait
out the night."

He didn't mind in the least, and of course he didn't
expect Jez's trusted housekeeper to leave him alone with
his friend, no matter the outcome of the evening.

"I suppose she'll need undisturbed rest," he finally said,
forcing himself to step away from the bed. "Let us recon-
vene in the private sitting room."

Hayden turned down the gas lamp next to Jez's bed
and tucked the blankets up around her chin again. Whatever the night brought, he promised to be there for her.

The soft snick of the door closing woke him. Wind rattled
against the windowpanes that flanked the sitting room,
indicating an oncoming storm. The housekeeper had taken
the chaise across from him—the very one he'd found Jez
resting on when he'd arrived. She had dozed off sitting up,
but someone had put a blanket over her.

He was on his feet in the next breath, causing the thin
blanket that had been draped over him to pool on the floor.

It felt as though he'd just shut his eyes, so it couldn't be
much later than six in the morning. Hayden glanced back
at Jez's bedroom. The blankets were thrown back to the
foot of the bed, and Jez was gone. The light from the moon
revealed the unmistakable stain of blood discoloring the
ivory sheets where Jez had slept soundly and without incident throughout the night.

Where could she have gone? And why hadn't she wo-
ken him before leaving?

Her dressing robe was tossed over the end of the bed,

so she was wandering around the house in nothing but a thin night rail.

He grabbed his jacket from the end of the sofa and checked the bathing room before heading downstairs. An unbolted door was slamming in the frame at the back of the house, where a small garden was situated. He ran in that direction. He found Jez out of doors and underdressed for the weather. Her slender silhouette stood tall in the summer rainstorm that raged outside.

Her night rail blew this way and that in the strong wind; it flapped around her ankles like the sail on a boat picking up speed. Her hair was loose and whipped around her shoulders and lower back like the wispy branches of a weeping willow caught in the gale of storm. She cradled something swathed in linen in her arms and stared at her rosebushes lining a tall fence that marked the border of her property. There was a beautiful starkness in the way she stood so silent, so still.

He was running toward her as she fell to her knees in the wet grass. He heard her heart-wrenching sobs the closer he got. Wailing, broken sobs as she hummed to the bundle of cloth in her arms.

Hayden swallowed back against the lump of desolation and pain that had built in his throat. By God, he knew what she held. He knew it with every fiber of his being. She needed him in this moment more than she had ever needed him in all her life. And he would not turn his back on her.

She didn't acknowledge him, but she knew he was there. She put the bundle of cloth in her lap, hunched forward, and plowed her hands deep into the damp ground with a growl of frustration. Her fingers came away slimed with mud and grass. She repeated the process until a small hole was dug.

He put his jacket around her shoulders and wrapped her tight in the safety of his arms as he dropped to his knees behind her. She fought him with tears on her face and nothing more than sorrow and sobs in her voice. Her fists pounded at his arms, his hands.

But he didn't let her go.

He *couldn't*.

"Hush. It's all right. I'm here for you." His voice was jagged, raw with emotion.

Fat drops of rain spat down from the heavens as he held her on the ground.

"I'm so sorry, Jessica. I've got you. I've got you." He cradled her head on his shoulder and smoothed her hair away from her face in calming strokes as he rocked her back and forth. "I'm sorry. I'm so sorry that I can't express it deeply enough. Shh . . ."

What did you say to a friend who had lost everything? There were no words that would lessen her sorrow. Her grief. So he did the only thing he could: he held her and didn't let her go until the sobs finally receded. Even then he didn't want to let go, so he held her for a while longer, letting the rain drench them as he vowed never to let this kind of despair strike her down again. He alone would keep her safe. She was his to cherish and protect and he wouldn't let her go.

When she could do no more than stare back at him broken and silent, he found a spade and dug a hole deep under the arbor of roses for Jessica.

Chapter 5

Where does the dowager countess hide? Nary a word has come from her townhouse. One must wonder what society's most daring lady is planning. Considering the state in which she arrived at her husband's funeral, it's doubtful she's donned widow's weeds to properly mourn the late earl.

While it's no secret that I despise the woman, the question is how to properly taint and mar her image for good.

Mayfair Chronicles, July 1846

"Where is my ruby hat pin?" Jessica's palm smacked hard against the white-painted vanity; her voice was shrill even to her own ears. "I can't bloody well find my ruby hat pin, Louise."

Jessica's maid's face was downcast as she knelt to pick up the accoutrements that Jessica had swept to the floor in her rage to find the hat pin her mother had given her.

Jessica slid off her stool to her knees, picked up the tray that held her perfumes, and started placing random items from the floor onto the silver dish.

"I'm sorry." Everything angered her and sent her into silly, stupid, unpredictable rages.

"It's not a worry, my lady."

"Why is everyone being so nice to me?" She felt tears building behind her eyes. She hated uncertainty, especially when it concerned her future. "I don't deserve the kindness you have all been careful to dole out. I've been wretched these past few weeks."

"It's not a bother at all. We understand everything you've gone through, my lady."

She wished more than anything her secret could have remained her secret alone, but it was out in the open and the past couldn't be changed. "Too kind by far. I don't think my late husband would agree with your benevolence."

"He's well and dead now, isn't he?"

The candor in Louise's voice brought a smile to Jessica's lips and a few tears leaked down her cheek.

"He is. And it should be a blessing."

"I can't disagree with you, my lady."

"I'm sorry."

"So you've already said," her maid pointed out.

"What would I do without you, Louise?"

"You needn't think on it. I haven't gone anywhere, nor do I have plans to leave, my lady."

Jessica set the tray back on her vanity and took a deep breath as she looked at her pale complexion in the mirror. She stretched the darkened skin under her eyes, trying to make herself look livelier.

It didn't work. Not really. It was so obvious that she was still on the mend, even though three weeks had passed since the miscarriage.

"I'm afraid you have your work cut out for you. I'm not sure you'll be able to cover the signs of fatigue that have plagued me over the past month."

Jessica pulled at one of the limp red curls hanging about her shoulders. Her hair hadn't been properly set in weeks, either.

Louise placed the items she'd picked up from the floor back atop the vanity and smiled at Jessica in the mirror.

"You'll look just as you did at the viscountess's ball two months past. No one will be the wiser that you've been ill. That I can promise."

"Only because they are none the wiser," Jessica said.

Her maid shrugged and pulled Jessica's hair away from her face so she could put maquillage on to cover the fading signs of fatigue.

It was important that she be perfectly presentable within the hour. Hayden had sent a card—unsure of the state she'd be in, she assumed—insisting that he sit with her over tea today. He'd been specific about the insistence part, underlining it twice. And besides, he never sent a card ahead of his visits.

The first week after the miscarriage he'd come by every day, sitting with her in silence because she couldn't speak, nor did she know what to say. He would occasionally read the paper to her, or sometimes a few verses from her favorite poets. When she'd been able to get out of bed on her own, he walked her around the house and sometimes out to the garden if the weather was decent and they'd sit in the sun and have their morning tea. Finally, when she'd had the strength to do all that on her own, she'd asked him to give her some time alone, to stop calling on her daily or she'd be constantly reminded about just how weak she was. He'd disagreed but ceded the argument in the end.

It seemed his patience had run thin, hence the calling card.

While it had only been a little over a week since she'd seen him last, she knew better than most that she couldn't keep refusing his company. It was time she came out of the doldrums and faced life head-on. She'd handled every situation that way previously, and it was time to get back in the saddle, as the saying went.

Not ten minutes after Hayden's note had arrived, she'd

received another from Mr. Warren—the rapscallion set to inherit everything that should be hers, especially considering it was her money that had put the estate back in order.

Mr. Warren was the last person she wanted to see, and she knew without doubt that he was looking for signs that she might be increasing. He'd find no indication, not that anyone had even known she had been with child—except her husband, of course, for he'd seen fit to end it.

Her pregnancy had been her secret until Hayden had further investigated the will of the estate, at which point she'd been forced to tell him why having the next heir was impossible.

The less Warren knew, the longer she could stay in the house that had been her home these past eight years. The sad truth of the matter was that she had nowhere else to go. Who would take in society's most debauched, reckless countess?

There was only one answer to that.

No one.

In a sense, she had dug her own grave where the *ton* was concerned. No one would allow her entrance into *respectable* society, and though it was good form to not send a widow an invitation for the first six months after her husband's death, Jessica couldn't recall the last time an invite had been directly sent to her and not her husband.

While that had never bothered her before, it bothered her a great deal now.

Hayden's standing in society would only get her so far. She was in every sense of the word a pariah and had been for too many years to count.

She might not have cared before her husband's heart had given out, but without his name behind her she was no one. To her surprise, she now cared a great deal about her standing and reputation. That bastard husband of hers couldn't have held on for a few more months? But what would that have brought her except the humiliation of divorce? He'd threatened to do just that before his sudden death.

Jessica raised her hand to stall Louise and dropped her head heavily against the vanity with a pitiful moan. "I need another day. Another week before I see or entertain anyone."

"You'll always need more time. If you while away your days indoors, you'll waste away to nothing in a matter of months. His Grace is a good, kind friend. You'll be happy enough to see him and wonder what all the fuss was about in avoiding him once you've had tea with him again."

"I don't mind seeing Hayden nearly as much as I mind having to entertain Warren."

"There is no reason you can't find yourself fashionably late and with no time to spare when Mr. Warren comes by the house."

Jessica raised her head and stared at her quick-thinking maid. "You're brilliant, Louise. If I've never said it before, heed it now and gloat if you must. You are brilliant and I wouldn't know what to do without you."

"I wouldn't want to work for anyone else, my lady. You have the kindest soul of any gentlewoman I ever worked for."

Jessica brushed her hair back with her fingers and leaned in closer to the mirror to see how well the maquillage covered her pale complexion. "Now I think you're using flattery instead of telling me the truth."

"I wouldn't dare, my lady. Now sit up so I can properly cover the sorrow that has assailed you these last few weeks."

She did as asked and let Louise work her magic. Jessica closed her eyes as the makeup brush and puff slid over her skin. When Louise was done, Jessica stood from the vanity, catching sight of her mother's hat pin in the stack of items left to be righted from her angry outburst. She pulled it from the tray.

A light rapping came at the door just before Mrs. Harper admitted herself.

The housekeeper dipped her head on entering. "His Grace has arrived, my lady. We've settled him in the morning parlor."

Jessica looked at her reflection in the mirror, assessing the dark lines now covered with concealing powder. She definitely looked better now than she had the last time she'd seen her friend.

Why did Hayden always have to be five minutes early? It wouldn't do to make him wait, either. If she did, he'd just barge into her private chambers and demand an audience; years of letting him do exactly that was at fault here.

"This will do, Louise." She patted her fingers over her skin, smoothing away bits of loose powder.

Louise stood behind her. Her eyes were wide, her expression sincere. "He won't notice anything amiss."

"Yet he will know not all is well."

"Maybe so," the maid said sympathetically. "But he'll know you're on the mend, my lady."

Jessica raised a disbelieving brow. She wasn't so sure of that.

"That's not to say you aren't faring better now than when he saw you last," Mrs. Harper corrected the maid.

"He'll see that I'm the same as before." Jessica stood from the small velvet stool and pressed her hands down the front of her dress. "Nothing fits right."

"It'll take time to heal," Mrs. Harper said. "Marie will be sure to put some weight on you before the fall months arrive."

Marie was the household cook and favored creamy

French foods. Jessica probably would be cursing her weight gain before long.

Jessica smoothed her hands over the few loose hairs at the back of her head. Her appearance would have to do. "I had better make haste. Hayden hates to be kept waiting."

On entering the parlor, Jessica said, "I'm sorry I took so long, darling. I overslept this morning and found myself rushing to throw together an ensemble."

Hayden wasn't sitting patiently; in fact, he looked as though he contemplated heading toward her bedchamber just as she entered the parlor. His hat was tossed carelessly on the sofa and his cane leaned up against a small, round side table. He approached her, his gaze assessing her from head to toe, lingering on her face as he wrapped his hands around her upper arms and held her at arm's length to further inspect her.

"You look well," he said, surprised.

She rolled her eyes, leaned in and kissed his cheek, and pulled away from him to fall gracefully to the sofa. "Of course I'm well. I've done nothing but rest for what feels like forever."

"It was needed. Though I wish you would have let me come by sooner."

"I needed time to myself, to think about my future." *To heal without your ever-watchful eye.* She would much rather have been able to throw herself into the bustle of society and forget everything that had happened. Instead, in her weakened state, she'd been confined to her house.

"Sit with me, Hayden." She indicated the seat available beside her.

He took the chair across from her, perched himself on the edge, and placed his elbows on his knees. He was still assessing her and Jessica had to fight the urge to check that her makeup was still in place.

"I can't stay long," he said. "I just needed to see you, make sure you were well."

"You should have come another time, then." Or better yet, he should have waited until she was ready to see him again. It was difficult to face him after everything she'd been through. After everything he'd *seen* and done for her. They hadn't talked about that night. And she hoped he never mentioned it, for she needed no reminders. But it would always stand between them.

"Jess . . ."

She raised one brow at the shortened form of her true name. He often called her Jess when he was displeased with her. "What could I have possibly done to disappoint you, Hayden?"

"I'm worried, not disappointed."

"I'm feeling much more myself."

"And that's what scares me half to death about you."

She furrowed her brows. "Why should it? Have I always been a great disappointment to you?"

"Stop putting words in my mouth. You know that's not true. We wouldn't be friends if I didn't have the highest regard and respect for you." He sat back in the chair; his dark eyes narrowing. "I should have stopped by sooner."

"And I can't thank you enough for respecting my wishes by not doing so. You're not my keeper, Hayden."

"Someone needs to be."

"Someone like my husband?" she asked, suddenly outraged. "I'm free of the man and it feels like everyone in my life is trying to slip a hood over my face and jesses around my ankles to keep me leashed and away from any potential trouble."

"Jess."

"Stop calling me that," she snapped, smacking her hands against the cushions on either side of her. After taking a calming breath, she placed her hands over her eyes to block out the light around her. She wanted to hood herself and be blind to the outside world for eternity sometimes. "I'm sorry. I find myself overwhelmed at the oddest of times."

The sofa dipped next to her. Hayden pulled her hands away from her face, and his comforting arms wrapped around her. "I can't promise your life will get easier, but you never have to pretend with me, Jess."

"It's been easier to hide from society. I'm never one to be afraid, but when I imagine facing those who have disliked me for so long I'm filled with fear."

"You never cared what they thought before, and I don't think you should start. I won't let you hide away in this smothering household for much longer."

She rested her head on his shoulder, enjoying the closeness and comfort of his embrace. They'd been much more intimate around each other ever since . . .

"It's been difficult to leave. But you'll be happy to know that I'm ready to face the *ton* again." Why she admitted to something she wasn't entirely sure about she couldn't say.

"We don't have to cause any havoc around Town, but you do need to at least show yourself at a few soirees. The gossips are already speculating about your absence."

"I know. I've been reading the papers. The Mayfair Chronicler has been having a heyday with speculations about me, about you . . . us."

His arms fell away, and she wanted them back. She felt safe with them wrapped around her. She didn't say so, though, because it felt inappropriate, considering the topic at hand.

"You've never cared about what they thought before."

"I've barely left the house. Of course I bought into all the hype the Chronicler has built around various tales regarding me."

"If I knew who they were, I'd hang them out to dry."

Jessica placed her hand over his forearm. "You and half the *ton*, I'm sure."

Hayden put his fingers under her chin and turned her head to face him. Sitting so close, he could see the obvious signs of fatigue and her attempt to cover the evidence with maquillage.

He searched her eyes, trying to make out her feelings. He stood from the sofa and gave her his hand. Now that he'd stopped in to see her, he didn't want to leave. The past week away from her had been pure torture.

"My appointment can wait. I think a stroll in the park is in order."

She assessed him before taking his hand. "Warren sent a calling card. I have to meet with him in less than an hour."

Hayden's jaw clenched, his back teeth grinding in irritation. "Why is he even coming here? He has no right to trouble you."

"He has every right. We both know the Fallon seat is his. And it could be sooner if he found out there is no hope of an heir from me." She looked away as though embarrassed. "That is easily confirmed by a doctor."

"And he'll never be given the opportunity to bring a doctor around," Hayden snapped unintentionally. Reining in his frustration, he said, "Warren can be kept waiting."

Jessica's expression looked defeated. "You're right, of course. And I appreciate that you've come to cheer me up, but I won't keep you from your appointments."

"I hate seeing you in this state." Hayden retrieved his hat and cane and pulled Jessica to her feet before she could protest any further. "Let's walk in the park and arrive late for your meeting with Warren. I can't wait to see his face when we stroll in together half an hour late."

Jessica twisted her fingers together in a nervous fashion. Then abruptly she stopped and walked over to a writing desk. "Let me pen a note for him."

"Why does he even deserve that courtesy? He hasn't relented with any of your requests."

"Because he holds my life precariously in his hands, Hayden. Don't be a boor. It'll take me but a moment; then you'll have me all to yourself for the rest of the morning."

He liked the ring of that: *all to himself.* He hoped he had enough time to cajole the old Jez out to play. He should have come by sooner, but she'd asked him to stay away and he could do no more than respect her wishes. They hadn't discussed all that had transpired, nor did he intend to stir painful memories by mentioning it until she was ready to discuss it.

Jez went over to the bellpull and called for the butler to have a maid bring down her hat and shawl. Then she wrote her note to Warren.

"Warren will be livid when he finds that I'm not here and that I'm gallivanting around Town instead."

"We are simply catching a breath of fresh air." Hayden tapped his chin thoughtfully with the eagle tip of his cane. "That's if you can call it fresh air in this heat."

Jessica's maid brought down a light shawl and assisted in tying the satin ribbon of her bonnet beneath her chin. He couldn't believe she was willingly leaving her house. Was she humoring him, or was she happy to leave this godforsaken place for a few hours after weeks of self-imposed solitude?

"Around the Serpentine, darling?" she asked, her mood already lighter.

Hayden's smile was slow and sure.

In the sunshine, Hayden saw the telltale signs that Jez was on the mend. Her hair was shinier, her skin not as wan, and her clothes were marginally tighter on her willowy frame. More important, her disposition was a great deal happier. Perhaps he was worrying too much. It was hard not to do so after everything she'd been through.

He tucked her arm firmly against his side and patted her hand. What he wanted more than anything was to thread his fingers though hers, raise her gloved hand to his mouth, and press his lips to the frilled edge at the back of her wrist.

Dangerous thoughts, those. But hadn't he already determined that she would be his? Yes, soon enough. Right now, though, she needed to heal.

Jessica was taller than most women of his acquaintance, so she easily kept stride with him as they strolled toward the entrance gates of the park.

"So tell me why Warren is visiting."

"He is having an inventory of the house completed. I suppose he'll have to amalgamate both his residences here in Town."

Hayden's hand squeezed hers lightly with the news. "Why does he need to do this right now?"

She looked away from him, focusing on the picnicking families and small gatherings of friends who had found a nice patch of grass to sit on as they fed chunks of bread to the ducks.

"The house will be his in a matter of months, Hayden. Fighting him is nothing more than an exercise in futility. We both know there is nothing I can do to change that outcome."

"He can at least show some decency and wait out the year before he takes charge of your household."

She sighed heavily. "It's not in his nature to wait for anything when it's rightfully his to take."

"And for how long have you known him?"

"Longer than I ever wanted to, I assure you. He is in a difficult position, too, Hayden."

Hayden pulled Jessica to a stop and turned her so he

could look her in the eye. "Why have you given up your fight?"

She shrugged away from his hold. "I don't expect you to understand."

"Help me to comprehend this colossal change in heart, Jessica. It was agreed that you could stay in the house for one year."

She walked on, though he still had a light hold of one of her arms and didn't release her till her fingers slipped completely from his grasp.

"You invited me for a walk." She nodded her head toward their abandoned path. "Don't make me finish on my own."

She didn't glance back at him again, just continued without him. He caught up to her before long, noticing the glances they were receiving from others strolling through the park.

"Explain to me why you think you are leaving sooner than the allotted year."

"Your devotion means the world to me. It also means you keep me out of trouble," she said with a sly wink.

His voice was low as he said, "I'm sorry. I'm the last person in the world who would judge you."

She looked at him sidelong, her gaze disbelieving. "A bald lie coming from you. You're always the first to criticize something you deem inappropriate."

"Only when it's to protect your reputation," he said, tucking her arm against his side again.

Her laugh was throaty and had a few more heads turning in their direction. "You're an ass, Hayden. And it's too late to protect me from the scathing views society holds over me."

Though her words were harsh, they both knew there was some truth in them.

"All the more reason for us to sojourn in the countryside."

That had been his first suggestion with the announcement of Fallon's death. She had refused. Now Hayden wanted her alone and to himself, somewhere he could watch her without having to worry about the trouble she'd find.

"Again with this?" she said.

"Yes, and I'll not let it rest until you are in complete agreement with me on the matter."

"That would feel too much like running away with a tail tucked between my legs. I'll face the *ton* head-on and show them that their hatred for me simply doesn't affect me."

He didn't point out that she was the one lying now; they both knew that she did care about the *ton*'s opinions. Perhaps it was time to face facts: Only Jessica could help herself in this instance. And now that her husband was dead and his fortune no longer accessible to her, she would have to take better care to stop the wagging of gossips' tongues.

But Hayden's name could protect her.

That had the wheels turning in his head. Of course, it was so simple a solution.

"So what will you do now that you are free from the bonds of marriage?" he asked.

"I imagine everyone thinks I'll remarry."

He fell behind a step, the news hitting him like an unblocked punch to the face. What was she saying? Was she open to the idea? "Will you?"

She didn't answer him for a few moments, and he nearly asked her to clarify what she meant, until she said, "I've had nothing but time to think about my circumstance over the past few weeks. Remarrying would probably be for the best. Though I'm not sure I can allow any man to rule my life as Fallon did."

Was she honestly considering marriage? Was that why she wasn't batting a lash at Warren for taking residence sooner than what was agreed upon?

"Not all men are cut from the same cloth." Least of all him.

She rested her head on his shoulder; the action was brief enough to draw speculative looks, but she righted herself with a sigh, ignoring the censure in every direction.

"There aren't a lot of options left open to me. And it doesn't appear that I'll be able to sway Warren to my favor."

Hayden couldn't believe they were discussing this at all. He could barely process the idea of Jez agreeing to remarry. If anyone was going to marry her . . .

It would be him.

He rubbed his hand over his face. She liked to keep him on his toes. You never knew when Jez was going to say "jump," "stop," or "fall."

"Then you should marry me."

She laughed, obviously not taking him seriously. "Don't jest with me, Hayden."

He could only look at her, perplexed. Of course she wouldn't take his offer seriously. He'd gone about asking her all wrong.

Her chin lifted and a mischievous look lit her eyes. "Being out with you, I realize we should really make a night of it like we used to."

"I didn't want to press the matter, but I couldn't agree more. You're sure you are up for it?"

"I've long been ready. I just haven't had any offers." She bumped her shoulder against his arm, hinting that it was he who should have asked her for a night out. "You and Leo are walking on eggshells when you're around me. In all honesty, I'm better than I have ever been."

If she thought herself ready, then Hayden would oblige.

"Perhaps we should have a round of cards tonight? We can go to your favorite gaming hell and cause a stir with your appearance after weeks in seclusion."

"Cards weren't exactly what I had in mind." She smiled at him, the tilt of her hat shading her from any passersby. "Will you be so bold as to allow me to choose the place?"

He raised one eyebrow, intrigued, though the offer shouldn't completely surprise him. "Are you sure you are ready to be up to your old antics?"

Her smile was anything but innocent. "A few new tricks, too, I should think."

"Then it's settled. Should I send a note to Leo and Tristan?"

She tucked a loose curl back up under her bonnet. "No, just the two of us, Hayden. I have something very daring up my sleeve for tonight and the invitation stipulates a plus one."

He gave her a long, assessing look. It was interesting that she'd extended a plus one to him. Well, perhaps not, since she hadn't taken his offer for marriage seriously.

That would change after tonight.

"Consider me more than interested in your offer."

"Perfect." She pulled them to a stop and looked at the mute swans swimming lazily in the water. "We should head back to my townhouse. If Warren is still waiting for me he's liable to be quite angry."

"I'll be sure to see him off if that's the case."

"I have stood him up, so he has every right to be cross with me."

Jessica turned them around and tugged him in the direction of her home.

"I can't say I agree with you on that. I've always disliked the cad."

"Have some faith in me. I can handle Warren."

"I have more faith in you than you can imagine. I know you can handle him, Jez; I just don't like that you have to face him at all."

He let her pull him in the direction of her house, wondering all the while what kind of trouble they'd find themselves in tonight. He was glad to have paid her a visit today; otherwise she might have continued to hide in the Fallon residence.

Chapter 6

*The infamous dowager countess has finally shown
herself to society. It's no surprise she was around
Town with one of her oldest friends. Do you know
what this writer is starting to think where those two
are concerned now that the old earl has kicked the
bucket?*

Mayfair Chronicles, July 1846

What had possessed her to suggest a night out with Hayden?
She must be mad to believe she could hold herself together
for a whole evening. Had it not been for the fact that she
enjoyed Hayden's company as much as she did, she didn't
think she'd have offered more than a walk in the park.
Even after everything that had happened over the past
few weeks, she really was starting to feel like her old self.
And what better way to test her refound bravado than to
get up to some of her old tricks?

Wilson came up to her dressing room to inform her
that Mr. Warren was waiting for her in the drawing room.
He'd come and gone while she was out and Wilson had
told her that he'd conducted an inventory of the household
items in her absence. She hadn't expected Mr. Warren to
come back.

Rouging her cheeks at her vanity—she'd give Warren
no reason to think she had been ill—she left her room
ready to face her current enemy.

"Darling," she said, her voice animated as she brushed into the room with the grace of a dancer and took Mr. Warren's hand. He bowed cordially if a little stiffly.

He was tall, hovering just over six feet. He was lean but fit, someone who spent time in an active life. Perhaps she'd find him handsome with his dark hair and sharp eyes if he weren't usurping her from the life she'd grown used to.

"Good afternoon, Countess. I thought we had an understanding on the hour we would meet?"

Had he come back to chastise her?

She slipped her hand from his and tilted her chin up. "You stated the time you would arrive, inviting yourself into my home without my say-so."

Warren narrowed his gaze on her.

She sat on the sofa, falling back elegantly on the cushions as she invited him to sit. "I *did* leave you a note that I was previously engaged."

"Sending word of your intent to walk with the Duke of Alsborough would not have been a hardship. I shouldn't have to find out you aren't in residence once I've already arrived."

Her husband had expected her to wait in the wings for his every bidding. It seemed that was what Warren wanted, too. She would not make taking the Fallon seat convenient for him. He was, after all, forcing her from her home.

"Have you concluded your business here? I really do have some things to attend to."

"Don't brush me off like one of the bloody sots that follow at your heels."

She stood and stepped close to him. No one had the authority to diminish the position of her dearest friends. "If I had such a power as that, I would not have begged to stay in the dowager house."

And she would never forgive herself for doing so. She'd

humiliated herself deliberately, to a man she loathed. And it had all been for nothing. Never again would she stoop so low as that. Never again.

"You know this is how it has to be."

She looked away, tears threatening her stance in this argument. She refused to cry, because it would only give him more power over her. "And your reasoning is pathetic. I'm glad I never worried so much about what others thought of me throughout my life."

"Your husband is no longer here to protect your standing," he reminded her, though she needed no reminder. "You might find yourself in a position not entirely to your liking if you continue being so narrow-minded."

He wasn't worth the energy that it took to fight, so she glared at him, hoping he felt a modicum of her hatred and disgust toward him. "At least I can say I have lived life. You, Mr. Warren, live life worried about the regard or contempt someone might hold over your actions. That is not the kind of life I would ever envy."

Warren tapped his long, manicured fingers along the sideboard. It seemed her words had finally gotten under his skin, for he was silent for a whole two minutes. That silence was too short-lived for her liking, however.

"Yet, your actions and refusal to live by the rules of society have made you a pariah. I prefer my standing to yours."

He came toward her suddenly, his intent dark and dangerous, though she was not threatened by him; there were so many things worse than him in life and she knew instinctually that he would not raise his hand against a lady.

"You've made yourself an outsider," he said. "An outlander in the society you profess to care for so deeply. That you would beg for salvation from me . . ."

He grasped her wrist tightly in his hand. She didn't flinch; the violence her husband had shown raging at the surface of his control so often was not present in the man before her. Mr. Warren wanted nothing more than to frighten her. Of course, she would never give him that satisfaction.

"And you'll never amount to anything but the weasel you are."

She wrenched her hand away from his and stepped so close to him that he was forced to take a step back. The look in his eyes said he was surprised by the boldness of her action. This would not be the first time a man had judged her wrong.

"Never lay your hands upon me again."

He turned away and strode toward the door. "Don't forget who holds all the cards in this little game, Jessica."

"I'm not likely to lose a battle with you." She tilted her chin up, refusing to cower, even knowing that he could throw her out of her own home today if he so wished it.

Instead of a retort, he gave her a heartless laugh as he picked up his hat from the sideboard. He turned and tipped it in her direction with a sardonic grimace.

"This is still my house and it's ruled by my sole guidance," she said. "I suggest you find the door without delay before I find someone more than happy to assist in your removal."

She stepped toward him, a fury of rage so strong within her that she wanted to lash out as her husband had done far too often with her—Warren standing his ground only infuriated her further. She would never stoop so low as to strike at someone, even someone as deserving as Mr. Warren.

"Your friends cannot assist you as well as mine in our games with society. Ruin me, Warren, and I'll ensure you never so much as marry and propagate, at least not someone worthy of the *ton*."

"You dare threaten me?" He seemed more amused

than angry. "I always did enjoy a good challenge. Consider your time in this house shortened. I want you out by the end of August. I want you well and gone before the little season starts."

"The law is on my side in this instance. I have one year."

His smile sickened her. Then he dared to further challenge her by grasping her arm.

"No, by my discretion and good grace you *had* one year."

"Do your worst," she challenged, yanking out of his hold.

His voice was low, dangerous even. "There will come a time in your lonely life that you will need me."

"Not in this lifetime."

"So be it. But don't say I didn't warn you." He opened the door to leave. "I guess this is adieu . . . until the morrow. I wish to review the ledgers in your care for the household items. I'll need to make offers to the staff and put in some of my own trusted servants."

Her heart fell. She wished it were within her power to take the current staff with her, but that would be impossible considering the size of house she was destined for with her meager annual income. "Are you asking my permission? A lack of it hasn't stopped you from snooping around my home already."

"It's just a courtesy." And with that he left.

Jessica leaned her head back against the paneled door and looked heavenward. She needed to pull herself together, find another husband, one either young and rich—far too hard to come by for her liking—or too old to so much as get out of a chair.

Hayden would be disappointed with her for upsetting Warren enough that he'd shortened the period of time she had in her home. Perhaps she should write an apologetic letter to Warren? He might let her at least stay the remainder of the year if she showed an ounce of contrition. Surely he had enough kindness in him that he wouldn't toss her into the street with no place to go. Damn her quick temper. She'd make do; she always had even in the worst of circumstances.

Tonight would be her first foray into society since the night of the funeral. The invitation had been addressed to her husband and received well before his death. She'd found it in his personal effects and it was too delicious an event to consider ignoring.

She pinched her eyes shut.

It was about time she was more adventurous with her life.

Tomorrow she'd tell Hayden about the outcome of her conversation with Warren. Tonight she'd live wildly and enjoy herself to the fullest.

She opened the parlor door and called for Wilson. "Could you please send up Louise? I need her assistance if I'm to attend a ball tonight."

Wilson gave nothing away in his expression, but she knew she'd surprised him. "Of course, my lady. I'll send Claudia up to prepare your clothes as well."

"Thank you, Wilson. I'll need a hired carriage for nine."

"Consider it done, my lady."

Jessica flicked through the letters stacked neatly on the tall marble-topped table in the foyer and found the invite for the masked ball that she'd tossed there. What would Hayden think if he knew where she planned to take him tonight? Would he convince her to go elsewhere? All the more reason not to tell him. He'd figure out where they were once they arrived.

She smiled to herself as she made her way up to her room. She had time enough for a nap before she readied.

"Louise," she said as her maid came into the room, a curious look on the young woman's face. "I'll be attending a masquerade tonight."

Louise's eyes went wide and her smile beamed so much that her dimples dotted her cheeks. "This is wonderful news, my lady. Which mask shall I unpack?"

"The gold Venetian half mask for me. I will need you and Claudia to pull the men's masks from the attic—some clothes, too, that might fit the duke, since he is in for a surprise when I tell him where we are going tonight."

Louise clapped her hands together excitedly. "We've plenty of time to ready you both."

"Yes. Have Claudia see what she can dig out for me. I'm thinking eighteenth century." Jessica lifted a lock of hair, twisting it around her finger. The red was character defining. "We'll have to powder my hair so I'm not recognizable."

While her maid went off to see to her instructions, Jessica sat at her writing desk. Hayden would have to arrive earlier than she had originally planned if he was to dress here. She felt an excitement bloom deep in her belly as she planned out her evening. It had been so long since she'd been excited to do anything.

Perhaps this was her first step to building a better life for herself. The past would need to stay right where it was; she hoped her secrets stayed buried, too.

She finished her note to Hayden and stuffed it into an ivory-colored envelope. Sometime during her walk with Hayden she'd decided that life was too short not to fully experience all it had to offer. She could make better memories. And who better to create them with than Hayden?

The note Hayden had received was rather curious. He patted his hand over his breast pocket where the parchment was neatly tucked away. It was a marvel that he'd so easily drawn Jez out tonight. Before his hand could reach for the brass knocker, Wilson opened the front door, stepping aside to let Hayden inside.

"Good evening, Wilson. I gather Your Ladyship wants me to wait in the parlor?" He handed the man his cane and hat, which were stowed next to the entrance.

"Not tonight, Your Grace. Lady Fallon has asked that you attend to her in her boudoir."

Hayden barely managed to keep the shock from showing at the request. It had been months since she'd asked anyone into her boudoir. What did she have planned tonight? Certainly it was more elaborate than he originally expected. Was he wrong to assume that a gaming hell and a crashed ball would be enough to amuse his friend?

"Right, good man. I remember the way, so you needn't escort me."

Wilson bowed as Hayden turned toward the stairs. Jez was in a far better mood than he could have guessed. It shouldn't have surprised him after their afternoon walk. Seeing her at the vanity, both her maids readying her for the evening and working on an elaborately powdered style to her hair, was like old times.

Minus the husband.

"I feel underdressed." Hayden motioned toward his clothes, indicating his tails and simpler attire.

She stood from her stool and came toward him. Though he was used to seeing her in a state of dishabille, her corset was nearly indecent the way it cinched in her waist and emphasized the delectable flare of her hips and bosom. Layers of lace covered her beneath and over the corset. The cut was low and pushed her breasts up so high he swore he could see the edges of her areolas.

He swallowed back the rising discomfort that was closing up his throat. Perhaps "discomfort" was the wrong word; what he had was a desire to tear her clothes off and do very wicked things to her. Scandalous things he'd never consider doing with another.

For probably the first time ever, he was struck speechless in her presence. The things he'd give to keep her here tonight. He didn't want any other man seeing what he saw; he didn't want any other man fawning over her.

And tonight he planned on showing her exactly how he felt about her. She'd not brush off his offer of marriage a second time.

"Darling, I'm so happy you arrived early." She took his hands in hers. "I wanted to surprise you, so I had the maids look through the trunks in the attic to see if we could sport matching costumes."

She motioned toward her bed where a hunter-green silk dress was spread out and a black-and-gold cloak with a harlequin laid out beside it.

"Why didn't you tell me we were to attend a masked ball?" He searched her eyes, wondering what mischief she was up to.

Did he know of any masked balls this evening? He could not recall having been invited to one in some time, possibly years.

"I wanted to surprise you."

Her pout was lost under the white powder generously spread to cover her face and chest. What would she do if he reached for the elegant arch of her neck to pull her closer? He wanted to wipe away the white that hid the flush pink of her lips or at least touch her, but instead he balled his fists and shoved them into his pockets. The maids were present. Had they not been . . .

It was becoming harder and harder to resist her. Really, it was only a matter of time before he crossed the line of friendship that had always been between them.

"You're not cross with me, are you?" she asked, with a delectable pout pushing out her lower lip.

"Never. I'm just surprised. Whose ball are we attending?"

She leaned forward and kissed his cheek. He felt the smile on her lips as she pulled away and motioned for the maids to help her dress. "That's also my secret for the time being."

He should not have doubted that the bodice would be as indecently cut as her corset. He could only shake his head at her luscious image and swallowed back the desire clouding his normally sound judgment. He knew his gaze lingered at her bosom; he also knew she noticed where his gaze was focused.

"It's rather daring, don't you think?" she said, drawing his gaze to her eyes. "The perfect attire for husband hunting—all the men will be entranced by my *eyes*."

He'd have laughed if he weren't affected by her lack of clothing. The truth was, men would be clamoring for her attention and he'd call the lot of them out if they dared to make a pass at her.

"Tell me you aren't searching for a husband wearing that?"

"And if I was?" She looked over her shoulder, all innocent.

His eyes widened. "You're not!"

She turned and patted him on the cheek. "You are always looking out for me. No, tonight is not a place I would wish to find a husband. But don't ask me anymore or I'll give away our location. It's to be a surprise, Hayden."

He reached for a powdered curl of her hair. "The forest green would have looked lovely with your true hair color."

"And the red gives me away too easily. Let us be anonymous for one night."

She reached for the lock of hair he'd snagged and pulled it from his fingers. She was smiling, and he'd do anything for her no matter how ludicrous if it kept that smile on her face.

"I wanted you out and about, so you needn't convince me that we'll do exactly as you wish this evening. Now tell me, what moth-ridden costume have your maids dug out of the attic for me?"

"I'll have you know that I had a hand in finding a perfectly respectable frock coat." Her smile widened, and laughter danced in her eyes. "And silk breeches."

Hayden rubbed his hand roughly over his eyes. "Good God, Jez. I'll look like a buffoon."

"Not possible, darling." Her eyes traveled the length of his torso, assessing him. Thank God for jackets that buttoned below the waist; otherwise Jez would have gotten an eyeful. "The ladies will swoon over your well-formed thighs. I won't tell you what they'll admire if you strip down to your shirtsleeves."

He raised a brow without comment. The minx.

"I even managed to find you a harlequin mask that matches mine."

At least no one would recognize him.

She walked over to the wall to pull the servants' bell. Likely calling up someone to dress him. Tonight was turning out to be much more than expected, and that pleasantly surprised him.

"I don't like the look of that grin one bit, Jez."

She turned back to him. "I like hearing you call me Jez again. Does that mean you're no longer angry with me?"

"I could never be angry with you, Jess," he said pointedly. He preferred her true name, but "Jez" had stuck after Tristan had come up with the name when they'd all become fast friends. She was as wicked as a Jezebel, and as shameless—not that Hayden thought she should feel shame for anything she'd done. She might have the reputation of a woman without morals, but he knew otherwise. She was bold and brazen, outspoken and daring. And not one of those traits was bad to have in any woman.

The butler arrived in good order. "My lady," he said with a bow on entering the boudoir.

"Take Hayden to the guest room to be dressed."

"William is out on errands. Shall I act as His Grace's valet?"

"Please do."

Hayden was ushered off to another room he'd never before seen the inside of. It was small and tidy, paned windows on two walls joined, giving a magnificent view of the gaslit street below. The paper on the walls was moss green and the trim painted in gold leaf. The bed was made of blond wood and took up half the room. There was a stand where his jacket hung. It had already been aired and cleaned of lint.

Once dressed, he peered at the image he made in the floor-length mirror. "You're a marvel, Wilson."

"I do my best for Her Ladyship. She's a kind mistress. It's no matter to me what others think."

"She is a good woman. Don't think for one minute that I don't see and cherish exactly who she is."

Hayden was helped into his coat and then directed to the parlor to wait for Jez.

She entered ten minutes later, quite the vision.

Had he not known she would be dressed in disguise, he would not have guessed it to be her at all. Hayden took her black-lace–gloved hand to assist in twirling her about so he could get a good look at her costume.

The half mask fastened around her face—the strings hidden beneath her hair—was a confection of iridescent feathers like those of a blackbird, only they stretched and fanned a foot in the air. The porcelain was painted in golden vines and the shape scooped up over her high cheekbones where dollops of pink blush circled around her cheeks in true Georgian fashion.

"You haven't put your mask on, Hayden."

He let go of her hands to retrieve the gold-and-black mask from the tall side table and handed it to her before turning to give her his back. "I might as well give you the honor of putting it on since it's your night."

"You're teasing me." She pulled the satin ribbons tight and knotted them at the back of his head. The mask rested firmly on the top edge of his nose.

As he turned to her he said, "I live to do so."

She looked him over carefully, her gaze lingering on his silk breeches. He hoped she was admiring his form as much as he'd admired hers earlier.

"I'll have to be watchful of you, won't I?"

"Whatever do you mean?" he said with an air of innocence that sounded believable to his own ears.

"You're more playful than usual, Hayden. Don't try to deny it." Her gaze was distrustful—and he supposed he couldn't blame her. "I can't understand why you aren't lecturing me for not donning widow's weeds and moping about in a dreary state as any good widow should do."

"You're above that type of simpering, Jez."

She rolled her eyes and turned away from him. "Come, I don't want to arrive too late." She took his hand and practically dragged him from the room.

He halted her before she could escape their conversation. "I don't recall my lack of you caring about your late husband bothering you before now. Do you want me to care? Or do you want to move on from the melancholy that's grasped on to your life since his death?"

"People change." She turned to look at him, her eyes not giving away what she was feeling. "*I've* changed," she whispered, and dropped her gaze to the floor.

He didn't know precisely why he pulled back from caressing the edge of her face and chin, but he held his position and gave her a thoughtful look as he crooked out his arm for her to take. She took it.

"Shall we then?" he said, leading them outside.

The sadness that had been awash in her eyes was replaced with renewed amusement.

He lifted her into the carriage, and before long they were on their way to a masked ball.

Chapter 7

The M——s' annual masquerade had no shortage of guests. The rooms were packed so tightly that the invitees were practically crawling over one another. A few newcomers were present, as were a few visitors not easily identified. But their identities were not hidden from me.

Mayfair Chronicles, *July 1846*

As they pulled up to the estate grounds Jessica began to have second thoughts. What had she been thinking in having such an extravagant night out? A simpler affair would have been ideal considering she hadn't attended any functions in weeks.

It was too late to change her mind now that she had Hayden here, and it didn't help that they'd spent the past hour and a half in a carriage to reach their destination. There really was no turning back, now.

It wasn't long before Hayden realized where they were. "The Malverns'? I didn't know you were so well acquainted with them to receive an invite to one of their less than reputable balls."

There was a note of admiration in his tone, which amused her considering Hayden was typically the friend you could count on for being above reproach.

" 'Reputable' hasn't often factored into our affairs in

the past," she whispered teasingly in his ear, feeling a shiver of excitement at sharing tonight with Hayden.

The tips of her fingers slid through his hair as she checked the ties at the back of his mask to make sure it was still tied snugly in place.

"I was merely observing that I was unaware you were acquainted with the Malverns—they don't even invite *me*."

"Ah, but then, I wasn't invited; my husband, on the other hand . . ." The rest didn't need to be said.

It was obvious that while she had caused her fair share of scandals since the first week of her marriage, her husband had been acting just as disreputably—only with company that wasn't as noticed because they preferred their bad behavior to take place behind closed doors.

And while it didn't matter to her, being friends with the Duke of Alsborough had as many advantages and open doors as it did hindrances.

Hayden scrutinized her in his silent way. Was he having second thoughts?

"Live wildly for one night with me, Hayden." When he still didn't respond but gave her his pensive glance of disapproval, she reminded him, "You were the one who insisted I come out of hiding and show the *ton* that the old Jez is still kicking and screaming inside."

He put his hands up as though caught in the act of taking something not his own. "I didn't say we should do otherwise."

"Perfect." She nodded toward the carriage door. "I think it's time we cause some trouble of our own, don't you?"

"We might as well." He exited first and put his hand out to help her down the stairs the driver had unrolled. "Hitch up your skirts, darling; the path is muddy."

"I'm sure this old frock has seen worse. And if I didn't

know any better, I'd say you just want to see a little more than my ankles."

"You have no idea," he responded.

She poked her head out of their hired carriage, giving him a curious look as she did so. She didn't respond to his rib; she knew how much he liked to tease her.

There were at least three dozen carriages lined up along the drive, and she didn't fail to notice that the majority of them happened to be unmarked. The attendees flocked toward the red-painted doors at the entrance of the three-story blond brick house.

Hayden pressed the flat of his hand against the base of her back and led her forward when she all but stalled in moving forward. She swallowed back any trepidation.

"I suppose we could have tried to get closer before leaving the comfort of our carriage," he said, mistaking her hesitancy for discomfort on the walk to the door.

"I thought with it being unmarked, we would draw too much attention to our anonymity."

Hayden's laugh was deep and for her ears alone. "But it seems we'll soon be in a ballroom full of anonymous patrons."

"I underestimated just what a Malvern house party looked like. And while I'm not having second thoughts about attending, I still worry someone will call out my name and our ruse will be done."

"There's no reason we can't simply observe all that is happening."

"When you promised a night out about Town, I thought you meant we should participate to the fullest. I think you should be wicked with me."

"How scandalous did you intend to be tonight?"

She smiled none too innocently at him.

Hayden's hand moved higher under the train of her dress. His warmth and steady presence steeled her waver-

ing resolve. She felt a nervous flutter in her stomach for
attending such a debauched party. Who was her husband
to judge her when he indulged in far worse events than
she would ever dare dream? Sure, she'd been to a number
of gambling hells and kept interesting company over the
years, but not the type of company who skirted the edges
of society.

As she and Hayden approached the door she pulled the
invitation from her reticule and handed it off to a footman
admitting guests. He didn't ask their names, just read the
paper she handed him, then tossed it into a champagne
bucket. She gave Hayden a shocked look. She wondered
if he was as surprised and impressed by the secrecy of
this evening as she.

"I think champagne is in order," Hayden said, leading
her through swaths of guests she did not recognize with
their masks and costumes in place.

The air was thick with the scent of too much perfume
and a haze of cigar smoke. Normally, the conflicting odors
wouldn't bother her, but right now the closeness of the
crowds made her a little light-headed. She held tight to
Hayden's arm as though his presence was the only thing
keeping her on her feet and moving forward when she
wanted nothing more than to retreat.

Large crystal chandeliers hung high above them; hun-
dreds of candles danced above their heads like stars in the
night. The ambient glow aided in keeping the guests name-
less. There was a string quartet playing Mendelssohn in
the background, the cello in the group melodic but com-
pelling the violins' fast pace. The atmosphere was intoxi-
cating.

Everywhere she turned there was a scene of debauchery
unfolding. While many guests in the grand marble room
chatted and giggled behind their fast-fluttering fans,
others could be seen openly kissing. Her breath caught in

her throat and she pulled Hayden to a sudden stop, mesmerized. Some attendees were doing much more than groping . . . they were fornicating where others watched and cajoled.

"My darling Jez," Hayden whispered in her ear, "why have you never invited me out to one of these events before now?" There was a measure of mockery to his question and something else she couldn't identify in his tone.

She stood close enough to him that they looked as though they were having an intimate conversation. "I knew my husband to be depraved. But I did not think a Malvern house party to be quite so . . ."

"Delicious." His finger traced an illicit path over the curve of her plumped-up breasts.

Her eyes snapped to his with the action. He was playing a part, she told herself.

"What shall we do first?" he asked, his finger still intimately pressed against her.

"Indulge," she said, a little breathless. With a dip of her head, she stepped away from his teasing touch and drank the contents in her champagne glass in one swallow.

A footman came by, allowing them to exchange their glasses for fresh ones.

"Let's see who we recognize," she suggested as she tugged him through the swarm of guests. "The scandals happening before our very eyes are too delectable to not investigate further."

She did have an ulterior motive for attending this particular party, and that was to find someone she knew without a doubt would be attending.

"A solid plan," Hayden responded.

Difficult as it was to make out appearances, she did eventually locate some very interesting guests. But not the person she was looking for. It didn't take long for her to start enjoying herself almost as though this were like old times.

"Isn't that . . ." She pointed with the tip of her fan in the direction of the person she referred to as she turned her face toward the curve of Hayden's neck.

It was almost as though she were whispering something naughty in his ear. Perhaps that explained why the heat of his breath fanning over her ear made her shiver in anticipation as she waited for his response.

"Hmm, did you mean to point out that Mrs. Benson is with a man far younger than I remember her husband being?"

"You're a devil to say so aloud. But, yes, that's precisely what I mean. Who do you suppose it is?"

Hayden's hand hadn't moved from beneath the train of Jessica's gown. If anyone recognized them, they might think Hayden was displaying some sort of possessiveness over his friend. While Hayden didn't normally take such liberties with her in a public setting, the closeness didn't disagree with her. But the whisper of his fingers across her breasts . . .

What in the world was wrong with her to be having thoughts like this about Hayden? Perhaps the champagne had gone straight to her head and she was overanalyzing their intimacy.

"I'd put my money on a paramour, the one of questionable lineage that the Mayfair Chronicler wrote of. I believe he's well-spoken—a man of education but without a title," she said.

"So, she's found a young buck to fill her stables when it's well known her husband hasn't been able to play the stud since his duel in '41?" Hayden mused.

"Yes, but where do you suppose she found him?"

"Places like this, darling." Hayden took her empty flute and retrieved another.

She walked around the room. One of Hayden's hands stayed at her back. Looking around her, she understood perfectly well why he was doing it; it let the other men know that she wasn't to be approached.

"Who else do we know?"

"Lord Penworth is with his mistress." Hayden motioned in the direction of the pair with his champagne flute before taking another sip. He turned her so she could see the man they were talking about without it being obvious that they were watching.

She glanced briefly at them before focusing her attention back on her friend. "That's old news. When is he not with her?"

"True enough."

"Do you think anyone recognizes us?" she asked, suddenly worried they were as easy to pick out as the guests they'd figured out.

"To some, maybe, but since we're not regulars at these types of evening affairs we wouldn't be expected. Would it bother you if we were discovered?"

"I prefer to be the one holding all the cards."

"When will you tell me who it is you're searching for?"

It might ruin their evening if she revealed that.

She smiled at him. "I didn't think I'd be able to keep you in the dark for very long."

"That you wanted to keep me in the dark at all . . ."

"I don't, but I thought we were enjoying ourselves. What gave me away?"

"You can't hide anything from me, darling." He leaned in closer, his lips nearly kissing the shell of her ear as he said, "But I do think you'll be thrilled to note that your old *friend* the Countess of Montant currently has a man beneath her skirts. I do wonder who the chap brave enough to do that is."

Jessica spun around, excitement beating in her chest. Hayden's hand landed on her hip, her shoulders bumped back against his chest, and she stared at Lady Montant. She was a vile woman whose sole goal in life was to make other women of equal standing appear inferior. Jessica had tried showing that she was a better woman than her, but it had been at the expense of Jessica looking gauche in front of her husband's closest friends. She would never forget the wrath of her husband the night she had insulted the woman. Lady Montant had always had Jessica's husband's ear.

The countess didn't frighten her now, especially considering that this was the first time she'd seen the woman in nearly a year. This put Jessica at a remarkable advantage.

The woman's skirts bobbed up, revealing her knees, whereupon her paramour took to kissing her calves for all to see.

"Shall we wager on who the kneeling man between her thighs is?"

"We both know it is not her husband," Hayden said. "And that leaves us with two possibilities: Mr. Thickett, her paramour, or, as rumor might suggest, Lord Winston."

Jessica flicked open her fan. "My money is on Mr. Thickett. He's in much finer shape to worship on his knees in tonight's fashion."

When Hayden chuckled, the deep timbre of his voice reverberated through her where they were pressed against each other.

"I love it when you're wicked," he said.

Was it her imagination or did his hand squeeze her hip a little tighter?

"I think that's what drew you to me all those years ago. You're but a moth to the flame, even though you pretend to play by the rule book."

With a laugh at her friend, she turned enough that she could kiss him on the cheek before she parted from his company to trail around the room to see whom else she could identify. Knowing the *ton*'s most dangerous secrets was what had kept her in an elevated position for many years, and it was what would find her in an equally comfortable position as a widow if she didn't manage to find another husband, one who doted upon her this time.

It wasn't long before Hayden caught up to her. His hand snagged hers, bringing her back to his side.

His redheaded minx was leading him on a merry chase this evening. She was one surprise after another from the very moment he'd arrived at her townhouse. Her change of heart and attitude was welcome, and he'd not question his good fortune in having the old Jez on his arm again. It had been far too many weeks since they'd simply enjoyed each other's company. And tonight was no exception.

"So you're looking for fodder," he said, pulling her back to his side. There wasn't a chance in hell he was letting her out of his sight at a ball like this. Her hip brushed against his with every step they took.

"I need it."

"For what reason? You'll not find yourself in the good graces of the *ton* by obtaining everyone's dirty little secrets."

"That's where you are wrong, my friend. I never wanted them to hold me in any regard, good or bad. The only thing I ever wanted from the *ton* was their respect—instead, I was cut from all my husband's circles after a few months of marriage, and treated with contempt."

"You don't like any of the people your husband called friend. And you have plenty of respect where it counts."

She gave him a pitiful look. "Until you've been in my position, you can't truly understand, Hayden. I will always love and remain loyal to my dearest friends." She squeezed his hand. "But I cannot live my life freely if I don't play the highest cards against the *ton*."

"That's a dangerous, reckless game to gamble on, too. Don't walk down this road you're blindly taking."

For a minute, he saw the sadness in her expression that he'd seen the night of her miscarriage—it was gone before his hand caressed her arm above the opera-length lace gloves she wore. "My father had hoped my match with Fallon would be a good one."

Hayden was silent as he searched her expression. "You never talk about your father."

"He adored me. And no matter what he did, I knew his heart was in the right place." Her gaze snapped away from Hayden's to search the room. He swore he saw the beginning of tears, but she held them at bay. "He died a short time after I married."

Hayden stopped them both at the edge of the dance floor and turned her toward him. He caressed the side of her face when she looked up at him with her sorrowful eyes.

"We can't discuss this here, Hayden. I can't . . ." She shook her head and bit her bottom lip.

He couldn't agree more. "Another time. But I want the whole story when you are ready."

She nodded her agreement. "Take another turn around the room with me. Tonight is supposed to be about cheering me up, is it not?"

He handed her a fresh glass of champagne. It was gone before they passed the next footman, and another was in her hand and a smile playing on her lips as they walked around the ballroom.

"So what is tonight about, Jez? Are you intent on getting even with someone from your past?"

"Not quite," she said, suddenly stopping and pulling him up short.

His gaze went around their vicinity, catching sight of someone they both knew well.

He should have known.

Mr. Warren stood with a cigar in one hand, a glass of champagne in the other, as he conversed with three other gentlemen. Hayden only knew one of them, not that it mattered.

Hayden was partly furious and wholly displeased to have not seen this coming. Now he understood his and Jessica's purpose for being here.

Pure madness stole his sanity the moment he realized Jez was here to find Mr. Warren in an unredeemable act, not to spend an evening out with Hayden.

He ushered Jez into a darkened alcove where the shadows further concealed their identities, a place where Mr. Warren wouldn't be able to distinguish their silhouettes from any of the others.

Jez fought him, pushing back with each of his forward steps, but he did not relent. When she looked up at his furious gaze something stilled her.

"Darling," she said in a placating tone. "It's not as though I didn't see him."

"Then you should have asked me to steal you away before you were found out." He tipped her chin up so she had to look him in the eye. "What game are you playing, love?"

"Can't you guess?"

He wasn't buying into the innocent flutter of her lashes.

"Do you honestly expect to find him indulging in amoral behavior?"

"Isn't everyone?"

"We aren't," he pointed out.

"No, we aren't." Her brows furrowed behind her mask as she tried to look around his shoulder with little success.

"Then perhaps we should join the revelry," he suggested.

When she attempted to escape him, he yanked her back to his side. He was so far from done with her, and she would not leave him standing here to watch her chase after trouble.

"I'll be damned if another man so much as considers laying hands upon you. You'll not attempt leaving my side again."

"Hayd—"

He shushed her with the press of his finger over her lips. "If you want to play a role tonight, then you'll play it with me."

She didn't whisper another word as his fingers slipped over the delectable plumpness of her lips, parting them before trailing lower. He caressed the backs of his knuckles over the décolletage she displayed. She hadn't reprimanded him the first time; he didn't think she'd object now. At least he hoped she wouldn't.

He felt her shiver when she inhaled a deep breath. Her eyes slipped shut for the briefest of moments as she visibly swallowed and surrendered to their stolen moment. No regrets. He knew this was his moment. He couldn't walk away from her anymore, couldn't stop the deep desire to have her as his own for another second. It was damn well time he made her aware that she belonged to him.

"We shouldn't be doing this," she said, breathless.

"Give me one reason to stop." His hand spread out, cupping her fragile neck and nape. "You wanted to play at what the other guests are playing tonight. What's stopping you from doing so with me, Jez?"

Her head tilted back and the tip of her tongue dashed out to lick at her powdered lips.

There was some type of madness ensnaring him, one that wouldn't let go until he did what he had always wanted to do to this particular woman. If she wanted to live scandalously, then he'd give her scandal. If she wanted to live on the edge of propriety, he'd throw them both over that line.

There were a million things he could have done in that moment, a hundred things that would preserve their long friendship. He didn't want to play this safe, for there was nothing safe about Jez. There never had been, and that was part of what drew him to her like that hapless moth to the flame she'd likened him to.

He brushed his thumb over her lips again, liking how soft they were beneath his touch.

"What are you doing?" she asked quietly.

"Just this."

His head lowered and his lips feathered across hers. It was the briefest fluttering of lips against lips. Their breaths mingled, and he lingered there, not ready to move away—not now that he'd started this.

Jez froze and grew rigid in his hold. He pulled away slowly and stared down at her confused expression. What had she felt? Was she baffled as to why he'd done it? Had she felt anything close to desire for him with that kiss?

"To hell with it," he muttered.

He kissed her harder the second time, letting their lips meld, letting his tongue sweep out to taste the residue of champagne on her parted lips. She wasn't pushing him away, nor was she kissing him back. Perhaps he'd shocked her and she was still trying to process exactly what had happened to bring on this kiss.

It was long overdue.

Hayden's hand slid over the base of her back again, and in small increments he felt her body loosen and mold to the front of his. Her mouth opened to him and suddenly he didn't care that he was kissing his best friend, nor did he think she minded, either.

He could feel the pounding of her heart where their chests were crushed together. This was how he'd always wanted her: in his arms, desperate to taste something that should be forbidden but needing it all the same.

His free hand shaped to the soft curve of her jaw, working its way higher and threading through the pinned curls at the back of her head where her mask was tied.

She'd been under his skin for so long that her touch was setting him ablaze with need. All the feelings he had for her, buried all those years, were at the forefront. There was nothing to stop him from claiming her as his own now that she was widowed, now that she was in his arms accepting his touch. His kiss.

He wanted her with a ferocity that bordered on madness. He needed her in his life like the very breath that filled his lungs. Now that he'd broken through the thin barrier that had always separated their relationship between friendship and love . . .

There was no going back.

He released her lips, turned his head, and exhaled in a rush. She didn't try to move out of his hold while he reined in his need for more than a simple kiss.

Wrong place, wrong time.

Damn it.

"This is not a good idea," she whispered, her voice husky.

Was she trying to convince herself of that, or him?

He didn't respond, nor did he release her. The best thing for the both of them would be to resume mingling. But there was no denying that for an infinitesimal moment the most monumental, boldest move he could have ever made had changed everything between them.

And he'd be damned if she expected him to forget it.

"Is it really so bad?" he asked.

She nibbled on her bottom lip as she assessed him with renewed interest. "This can't happen between us."

"You felt it, Jess." He released her suddenly, his arms braced on the wall behind her, framing her delicate figure, giving her a chance to take flight if that was what she so desperately wanted. "Don't tell me you didn't feel something more between us."

She cupped the side of his face as she stared at him. "This can never be."

"That's where you're wrong."

She lowered her hand to press her palm against his chest. Could she feel his heart strumming crazily?

"Don't ask this of me," she whispered. "I need you to be my friend."

Didn't she know that there was no way they could go back from this? He'd always be her friend, but everything had changed the first moment his lips had brushed across hers.

Chapter 8

Lady A—— was seen on the arm of Mr. W—— at the annual M——s' masked ball. Their association was so much more friendly than previously noted that this writer predicts Mr. W——'s townhouse for his mistresses shall be set up with a new resident before month's end.

Mayfair Chronicles, July 1846

What in the world had just happened between her and Hayden?

Better yet, how had it happened at all?

Jessica stared up at Hayden, not sure what to do. Did she leave him here and wander around the masked ball to find another bag of trouble or did she stay right where she was in the arms of the man she trusted above all else?

If she stayed would he expect their kissing to resume? She pressed her fingers to her lips. She could still taste and feel him—and admittedly that wasn't a bad thing.

Her thoughts were troubling. She wasn't thinking rationally.

She would not chance ruining one of the most important things in her life. If she lost Hayden . . . there would be nothing left that mattered. When she met his serious gaze, she realized that nothing would be the same between them again.

As though he was reading her thoughts, he assured her, "You'll always have my friendship, Jez."

He squeezed her chin lightly between his forefinger and thumb. "For now, I'll let this go, but we'll discuss this in detail later."

She pulled out of his hold and walked around him. She couldn't be in this place anymore, with people she loathed all around her, with her husband's inner circle of friends whom she despised. She needed to escape the insanity of what her life had become, and tonight's distraction was no longer working. She'd hoped to find Warren in a disparaging position, one she could leverage to her own advantage in negotiating her stay at the Fallon house. Instead, she found him conversing with others, as though debauchery weren't happening everywhere you turned in the room.

And now, with what Hayden was asking of her . . . it was too great a risk. She needed to think this through, weigh the consequences, before she dared to do anything that might ruin one of the most beautiful, reliable, and solid relationships in her life.

Hayden wasn't far behind her and looped her arm through his as he walked beside her

"Are we done here?" he asked.

She felt an edge of anger in his tone. Was it directed at her? She couldn't say, nor did she want to ask him.

"I think it wise we leave." Her voice came off just as cold. None of the warmth was left from their private moment.

"Then we'll call for our carriage."

He led her through the ballroom and toward the foyer, his steps determined. Did he want to be away from her or away from the revelry around them? He gave instruction to the footman to find their carriage, and they waited in silence for it to come around.

"Your Grace," someone bellowed out.

The breath caught in Jessica's throat as she turned slowly to see who had called after Hayden. By the sudden grip on her arm it was obvious he was surprised anyone had figured out his identity. Jessica didn't make eye contact with the gentleman who approached. He was portly, with a dark gray beard and graying hair. He wore a simple mask that matched his head-to-toe ensemble of black. Jessica could not place him, but his voice was somewhat familiar.

Hayden's expression was carefully blank as he turned to face the older man.

"Hilliard," he said simply.

Jessica recalled who the man was now. An old friend of her husband's and not someone she wanted to recognize her. Though the odds were in her favor, being that she'd only ever been introduced to him on two occasions. In all likelihood, he'd not remember her. But who else would anyone assume to be on the arm of the duke?

"I thought that was you, old chap," Hilliard said. "I won't keep you long, as I see your hands are full this evening."

If Jessica hadn't powdered her face to near white, all present would note that it burned hot red the instant he insinuated her being here in a different capacity with Hayden than a friend. Had this man seen them kissing?

She ducked her head. Hayden must have been as uncomfortable at being discovered as she, for his arm came around her shoulder, the position tucking her face down and aiding in the concealment of her identity.

"Should have figured you'd be here," Hayden said with an air of boredom.

Hilliard puffed out his chest, so obviously full of pride by association with those at the house party this evening.

"I've known the Malverns for what feels like forever. Just wanted to catch up with you"—he leaned in closer, lowering his voice—"to see if that matter we discussed had been dealt with."

Hayden cleared his throat, his hand resting over his chest as he answered. "The results are promising."

Was this a political association he had with this man or something more personal in nature? Their conversation was oddly cryptic. Suddenly she felt as though she knew Hayden less than she thought.

Hilliard patted Hayden on the arm and gave an approving nod. "I'll let you get back to the rest of your night. Just wanted to ensure the information I gave you proved to be fruitful."

Thankfully, the other man didn't acknowledge her. As he disappeared around the corner Jessica looked at Hayden. "Whatever in the world was that about?"

"Nothing of importance." He turned them toward the exit once again.

"It sounded like nothing I'd be interested to know until you forced that point."

"Jessica, not now. We have bigger worries."

"Yes, like the fact that you've just been discovered in attendance at a Malvern house party, and by one of the Malverns' oldest friends. There may well be repercussions from our attendance. It won't be long before it's found that I was the lady on your arm all evening."

And their kissing would probably be recalled by half the attendees. She massaged her temples, feeling a headache coming on. Tonight, it seemed, had been more than she was ready to handle.

"No one will ever know it was you, Jess."

She glared at him. Did he honestly think no one would put two and two together? Where Hayden went Jessica was often in attendance, and vice versa. This was turning out to be a nightmare.

"You're mad if you believe that," she said to him.

She walked away from him as their carriage came around the drive. Just as the footman gave her his hand in assistance, Hayden's hands came around her waist possessively and lifted her up the stairs. He didn't say a word as he climbed in after her. Once the carriage was moving away from the Malvern estate, he tore off his mask, crossed his arms over his chest, and stared back at her, silent and brooding.

And why should he be upset with her?

"What is it I've done wrong?" she asked.

"You haven't done anything wrong. Though you could have told me what you planned right from the beginning."

She freed the pins that held the ties of her mask in place. There was no sense remaining in costume now that their night had concluded. "Don't turn this around on me, Hayden. Besides, it seems that I wasn't the only one gathering information of some sort."

Talk about cutting right to the heart of the issue. But it bothered her that Hayden knew one of her husband's friends. That he had dealings with the man.

"Hilliard is well connected, and he had access to information that I needed for some business dealings."

"I think you're omitting information. Why don't you want me to know about your association with Hilliard?"

"Because it was a very brief association, if you want to even call it that."

"What would you call it?"

"He had information I needed. I offered an ear for a proposal he has for a parliamentary matter."

She had a sneaking suspicion that this had everything to do with her. Or her husband. "What kind of information were you seeking?"

"Because you'll not let this rest, I'll tell you. He gave me Miller's location, so I could have a conversation with the man."

Her hairpins fell from her hands, chinking on the wooden floor of the carriage as she stared back at her friend, stunned. His answer was unexpected. "Why would you of all people require Miller's whereabouts?"

"I will always look out for your welfare, Jessica. I wasn't going to let that man roam about London freely with the means to harm your standing and reputation."

Hayden's expression was firm.

She narrowed her gaze. "What did you do?"

"I put him on a ship to Australia."

"Why?"

"We both know it needed to be done."

She swallowed against the lump of nerves suddenly clogging her throat. Did Hayden know the truth? He couldn't. She tried harder to release the stupid ties that held her mask in place. Anything but focusing solely on the man in front of her. "What did Miller tell you?"

"Nothing much. Talking was . . . difficult for him."

"You might think you sent him off for good, but he'll come back." She closed her eyes, thinking of the right questions to ask without revealing too much. "When did this happen?"

"A month ago. He can't hurt you anymore, Jez."

Oh, yes, he could. But she couldn't tell Hayden that without revealing the secrets she wanted to keep buried. She would have to figure out how long it took for a ship to reach Australia and return to London. Miller would not be staying away from England long. And when he returned, he'd have a chip the size of Jez to rub off.

Now that she thought back on it, it was no wonder he hadn't made an appearance in her life these past weeks. Foolishly she'd thought that her purchasing Miller's chits and selling them to a man known for darker dealings in the seedier sections of London had been the reason for his disappearance. How naïve she was.

She tore at the knot keeping her mask in place. It didn't budge.

Seeing her frustration, Hayden said, "Lean forward on the seat."

She did as asked and turned her head to the side so he could see the mess she'd created in her rush to remove the mask. His hands were gentle, his breath moving tendrils of her hair near her ear.

While he worked on untying the mask questions about his action—and hers—hampered her mind heavily. Aside from worrying about Miller again, she had questions about Hayden's actions tonight.

Why after all these years had he kissed her now? What had changed . . .

What a bloody fool she was. Hayden was a man with strong morals; of course he would never have pressed his suit while she was married.

Still, she would have to find some courage before she asked him why he'd done it tonight of all nights. And why he'd never revealed that his feelings for her were not platonic. Not in any sense of the word.

"There," he said, pulling the mask away from her eyes and setting it on the seat next to her.

She rubbed at a tender spot on the bridge of her nose where the mask had dug into her skin.

"Hayden?" She leaned back against her seat, putting distance between them as she searched his eyes for the answers to the questions she didn't want to ask. "About earlier—"

He leaned in close to her and pressed his finger against her lips to silence her questions. When she didn't protest, he caressed his palm over the side of her cheek and jaw with a pensive look.

"There are a lot of things we need to discuss, but right now, we're both tired and angry about the turn of events, so it'll have to wait for a more opportune time." His hand fell away as he sat back in his seat.

She pressed the tips of her fingers against her lips, still feeling a phantom touch of his mouth upon hers. Their relationship had changed the very moment he'd sequestered her in a private corner. Sure, they were still friends, but there would now be a tension between them that hadn't existed previously.

And all for a kiss.

A deliciously dangerous kiss.

"How can you ignore what happened?" she whispered, half-hoping he hadn't heard her query.

"I acted impulsively on something I've long desired to do, so I will not apologize for my actions."

He was watching her actions, his gaze lingering where she touched her lips. She dropped her hand from her mouth and curled her fingers together in her lap. "No good can come of this, Hayden. Don't jeopardize our friendship."

"You've already advised me against that, and I've taken it to heart. Trust me when I say that our friendship has always been too precious to ever dare damage. And I will do everything in my power to protect it."

He brushed one hand through his hair. And while it was normally pomaded to perfection without so much as a stray hair out of place, she noticed it was longer than usual and in disarray. In fact, it had been just so for a number of weeks now.

"You were always daring society to censure you, Jez. I've never seen you care about your reputation as much as you do now."

She swore there was a measure of awe in his voice. She'd have laughed at any other occasion, since he'd been quite reckless and she had been the opposite. But tonight had been too trying on her nerves.

"I can't deny I've lived life the way I wanted. But everything has changed." She looked out the window, unable to face him for what she was about to say. "If anyone assumes that I'm your mistress, I will be locked out of society forever."

He reached for her hands, clasped them, and pulled her over to sit next to him on the bench. "Don't put such a crass word on what we have."

"Whatever this was tonight . . ." She shook her head, unsure she believed the denials any more than he. "We can't."

She wasn't sure if she was trying to convince herself or him that this couldn't happen between them. But she did know she needed to be able to rely on Hayden. But couldn't she?

Now . . .

She was confused. Flustered. She hated this feeling.

"Jessica, if there's one thing I've come to understand with perfect clarity in the near decade we've known each other, it's that your heart is true where our friendship is concerned. I promise you that I will not endanger that for a moment of folly."

What was he even saying? Did he regret his actions earlier? She shook off the momentary disappointment she felt when she realized that was the last thing he was telling her.

"Hayden—"

His hands entwined with hers and he held them up to the light that cascaded through the open blinds of the carriage window. "We'll discuss the recourse of our actions tomorrow, Jess."

A piece of her heart splintered inside her chest. She needed Hayden, of all people, to get her through the months to come. There was no one who knew her as well as he.

But there was no possibility of forgetting what had happened.

Everything had changed, she wanted to scream.

"I just want to forget what happened."

"And I don't wish any such thing." There was something more than disappointment in his voice, and she'd been the one to put it there.

"I believe this might have been a little too much excitement for my first outing."

He didn't release her hand. She didn't have the strength to argue with him further on this, nor did she wish to physically pull away. While they'd always shared a closeness with each other, it felt different now. Not precisely tainted, or wrong. Just different.

She leaned her head back against the headrest and closed her eyes. She'd be home soon enough, and then she'd put the whole day behind her and start fresh tomorrow.

He didn't regret their kiss. Not for one second. Though she might not believe it now, that first kiss had been the inevitable step they needed to take. There was nothing that would change his mind from that fact.

Kissing her had been the right thing to do.

Jez had fallen asleep half an hour ago. She was pressed up against his shoulder, her breaths soft against his neck with each exhalation. When they arrived at her house, he carried her up the stairs. It was late enough that no one would witness their late entry into her townhouse, though he entered through the back entrance where the garden was situated.

On their entering her house, the housekeeper met him in the kitchen. She was a bloody bull whenever he was here. Always had her eye on him. He knew it was because she adored her mistress, so he couldn't blame her.

"Mrs. Harper," he said cordially. "Imagine me finding you up at this hour; it's a perfect opportunity to have you send someone ahead of me to light a fire in Your Ladyship's rooms. The night has a nip of coolness in it, and I wouldn't want Lady Fallon catching cold."

"I can have someone assist, Your Grace." She wasn't referring to the fire he'd suggested. No, she wanted someone else to take Jessica up to her bedchamber. "You shouldn't have to carry her up."

"It's fine that I take her, Mrs. Harper. Just have the fire set up." He walked past her then, uncaring if he was invited or not into the household. Jessica wouldn't refuse him even after everything that had happened between them tonight.

He didn't stop and wait for permission, just carried on through the house and headed in the direction of Jessica's bedchamber. It was still dark when he entered her room, so he'd arrived ahead of the maid. Not that it mattered; all he was doing was putting Jez to bed before he found his own way home and did the same. It had been a long night, with as much time spent in the carriage as at the party.

Jessica stirred as he leaned forward to toss her bedding aside so he could set her on the mattress. "Hayden," she whispered, though he knew she was half-asleep and unaware of her surroundings.

God, how tempting it was to climb into bed with her, hold her tight, and feel her in his arms a while longer.

As much as it pained him to walk away after everything that had happened between them, he had no choice but to do just that when she wasn't fully aware.

Carefully tucking her into bed, he brushed his lips against her forehead and left her just as the maid came in to light a fire. Tomorrow would prove to be another day. Whether he and Jessica started on a tense note or in the same easy fashion they'd always enjoyed depended upon her.

Nothing yet everything had changed. She was still his friend, his Jessica. But now there was more to be discovered between them.

He nodded his farewell to the maid before shutting the bedchamber door behind him.

One thing was certain—he'd see Jessica on the morrow whether she wanted to face him or not. How she would handle it was another matter entirely. While she might find merit in ignoring what they had done, he didn't want to go backward in their relationship. And ignoring that kiss, the start of something more between them, would be doing just that.

Chapter 9

How often can one visit the Zoological Society in a season without drawing suspicion to the possibility of clandestine meetings? I'm beginning to believe that Lady A—— has taken after her mother and is hosting the idea of a paramour. Could someone of revered prestige like Lord G—— fall victim to her youthful charms so easily?

Mayfair Chronicles, July 1846

"Goodness. How much did I drink last night?" Jessica asked herself as she stumbled out of bed, her hand shielding her eyes from the light coming through the sheer curtains.

Her maid came in just as Jessica cinched the ties of her dressing gown around her waist.

"His Grace is here to see you, my lady."

"What hour is it, Louise?"

"Half past eleven." Jessica's maid ducked her head as though embarrassed to admit the time she'd let her mistress sleep to.

Jessica pinched the bridge of her nose and closed her eyes tightly—it didn't alleviate much of the megrim that had her in a full grip of head-pounding agony.

She cracked open her eyes the slightest amount. "Did you try to wake me?"

"We did."

There was still no eye contact from her. Jessica must

have been a boor when the staff had come up to her room earlier in the morning. Not that Jessica could recall any of those instances, though she did remember her maid taking down her hair and helping her dress for bed after she arrived home. She groaned as she took a deep breath and willed her head to stop throbbing.

"Help me ready before the duke barges up here with a mission in mind, one I have no intention of fulfilling today."

"Right away, my lady. Shall I have Cook prepare her special tincture?"

"Yes, that's a fabulous idea. Thank God one of us is thinking straight this morning." Closing her eyes for a moment, she rubbed at her temples.

Her maid left with the speed of a jackrabbit that had caught the smell of a fox. Before the door could close behind Louise, Hayden stepped through the entrance.

"Darling." Evidently, he was far more chipper than she this morning.

She should have known she couldn't keep him waiting downstairs for long. "How much champagne did you let me have last night?"

"A few glasses, can't recall the exact number."

"Must you be so cheerful in the morning?"

He laughed. "Always. I came over thinking you'd like to stretch your legs with a walk in the park."

"You really must give me another hour to ready."

"Afraid I can't do that. I'm meeting with someone this afternoon about acquiring some property in Kent. It's quite a lovely area."

"That's a poor attempt to draw me away from London."

"It's only a day's ride from here."

"I'll have to take your word on that." She sat at her vanity and looked at Hayden's reflection in the mirror as she undid the braid. "You're not here simply for a walk."

She hoped he didn't wish to revisit all that had happened last night. She hadn't sorted through her thoughts and feelings of what had transpired the previous evening, and she wasn't ready to discuss it with Hayden until she figured it out for herself.

"And what's wrong with a jaunt around the park?" he asked.

She motioned to her current state of dishabille. "I'm hardly presentable for an outdoor excursion."

"Then I'll give you ten minutes to make yourself presentable. I have an appointment on Bond Street I'd like you to come to."

"An appointment with regards to . . . ?"

"The estate and some other financial affairs. All dreadfully boring tasks but made exceptionally more fun by your company."

She lightly banged her forehead against the vanity. She had a megrim that bordered on excruciating, and he wanted her to attend appointments with him? "You can't be serious."

"I most certainly am." There was laughter in his voice, no doubt because of her state right now.

"How is it that you drank as much as I did last night and are in a perfectly fine state this morning?" She could not keep the irritation from her voice. She refused to run errands with anyone. And more important, she hated mornings, so, really, why should she have to leave the house before luncheon if it displeased her to be up and about?

"Before you outright refuse me your company," he interjected as though he'd read her thoughts, "there is someone I want you to meet. He can be of great assistance with your finances."

"I have a solicitor," she pointed out.

"I know you are smarter than that, but your head never did fare well with an overabundance of champagne." He placed his hand on her shoulder and squeezed it affectionately. "Put it this way: you have a solicitor, but they hold a personal interest in maintaining the Fallon estate with your entire fortune intact."

Jessica stood from the vanity, walked over to her bed, and flopped face forward onto it with a groan. She really wanted to climb back under the blankets and sleep until her head felt normal.

"We've been over this," she mumbled into the coverlet.

"Give him a chance, Jez."

Hayden still hadn't mentioned last night's activities. Perhaps he was willing to forget everything that had happened and that was why he was here, kind of like a truce, for surely he regretted the actions as much as she. And if that was the case, she was almost willing to see this man of business. Almost.

"I need at least half an hour. I haven't even had my morning tea." She peeked up at him from the bed.

His smile was staggeringly handsome. She frowned at the thought.

Why did his smile affect her now when it never had prior to their kiss? She shrugged, then pushed the image away. She didn't like the direction of her thoughts this morning.

"Half an hour and not a minute less." She pointed a threatening finger at him. "You can wait for me in the parlor. Mrs. Harper will have tea brought down to you."

"Exactly what I wanted to hear." He came forward and brushed his lips across her forehead. It was an action she was used to—or had been used to, but it meant something different now, didn't it?

She banished her wayward thoughts. What had gotten into her head to twist everything around when it had never crossed her mind before? She pressed her fingers to her lips. Hayden looked up at her just as he was about to shut her bedchamber door. She dropped her hand and narrowed her eyes too late. He was smirking, the rascal.

Ringing for her maid, Jessica brushed her hair, which was still damp since washing out the talc last night. Hayden would have to amuse himself for the next hour at the very least. Today was going to be a long day if this ache in her head didn't go away.

Served him right for calling on her at such an ungodly hour and expecting her to run errands with him at the very last minute.

On waking this morning, Hayden had decided it would be best not to mention the intimacies they had shared at the ball. All in good time, he supposed, though he barely had a hold on his patience as it was. Their kiss would definitely be a topic for later, as would the future.

When he'd arrived at Jessica's today, he hadn't expected to find her still abed. And now that he'd seen the state she was in this morning he knew not to expect her for at least an hour. Mrs. Harper had been kind enough to have a sandwich tray prepared for him with tea, so he took the time to read the morning paper while he lunched in the parlor.

Waiting in the first parlor off the foyer, he didn't miss the knock at the front door. Wilson answered, his voice too quiet to hear other than the greetings exchanged. Hayden put down his teacup and narrowed his gaze in the direction of the newcomer. Before the butler could show Mr. Warren to another room, the parlor door slid open, bringing the men face-to-face.

"Your Grace," Warren said, surprised.

Why Warren should be shocked to find him present seemed odd; it was well known that barely a day passed without him, Leo, or Tristan spending time with Jez.

"Wilson," Warren said, "that'll be all. I think I'll keep

company here with Lord Alsborough till Your Ladyship makes an appearance."

The door shut behind the butler, who looked none too happy to be leaving the two men alone.

"I see you've made yourself rather at home," Hayden pointed out.

"It already is my home." Warren tossed his hat on the mantel and unbuttoned his coat before taking a seat on the sofa. "What's your point, Alsborough?"

Hayden took a step toward him, not entirely sure how he should handle the blackguard. He knew secrets about this man that could put him into a boiling tub of water. There was always a time and place to show your cards; that time wasn't quite yet, not without the permission of other parties involved in those damning secrets.

"My point is that you should give Lady Fallon more space. She is still in mourning, and you constantly nipping at her heels makes it difficult for her to move on and adjust to her life as a widow."

"The only thing she's mourning is the life she too freely enjoyed without consequence until now." He folded his hands together and rested them on his knee. "You know as well as anyone that I can end her time in this house without preamble."

"And what of the whispers of cruelty that will befall your name? You wouldn't want to make too many enemies before taking your seat in the House of Lords."

Warren snorted, uncaring. "Politics are not new to me, Alsborough."

Which was true. Warren was a prominent figure in Parliament matters for the House of Commons. But the two circles had very different social obligations—Warren could not easily navigate the *ton* with his *common* friends.

"I'm surprised you would even threaten me when I hold your dear friend's fate in one hand."

"It would be my greatest pleasure to crush you, Warren. Never forget that you are but an interloper in your newfound position."

Warren gave him a sardonic glare. "I'll be sure to remember that when I'm out and about during the evening. Speaking of evenings, yours seemed rather . . . how shall I say this . . . entertaining."

Hayden felt the last reasonable part of him snap. Before he could check himself, he was halfway across the room, with an iron grip around Warren's throat.

"Never for one minute think you can predict the outcome of Jessica's life. It will be your undoing."

And that was how Jessica found them.

She pointedly cleared her throat where she stood in the doorway, dressed in a white-checked day dress, her hair up, curls cascading down at her temples. Her gaze—severe and unimpressed—rested on Hayden, then on Warren. She crossed her arms over her midsection and gave them both a questioning look.

He released Warren just as suddenly as he'd taken hold of him, but he did not take his gaze from the man. Hayden pulled down his vest to neaten his appearance. Though there was no hiding the fact that he'd been about to turn Warren into a punching bag.

How did Warren know anything about last night? They had never made eye contact. Could Hilliard have mentioned his quick meeting with Hayden? Perhaps this had nothing to do with the masked ball.

No, it had everything to do with his attendance at the Malverns' last night. And he would find out exactly what Warren knew before it could be used against Jez. Right now, however, Hayden had a schedule to keep with Jessica.

"We were just catching up," Hayden said to Jez, unable to keep the venom from his voice as he straightened the cuffs on his jacket.

"I'm sure you were." She turned from him to narrow her gaze on their mutually unwanted guest. "Warren, I didn't realize you were coming by today. Do you have your man with you to conclude the inventory?"

"We completed the inventory yesterday for the most part. The upstairs can be done when I take over the house."

"I've made plans this afternoon. Shall I have a plate prepared for you before I leave?"

"Not necessary. I have a lunch engagement." Warren retrieved his hat from the mantel and glared at Hayden before turning back to Jessica. "There were some personal matters we needed to address, but I can come back at a more convenient time."

For some reason, Hayden didn't think Warren was usually so accommodating. If Hayden's presence made him better mannered, he'd make a point of coming over more often, especially when Warren was scheduled to be in the house.

"My day is full and I won't be back till early evening. Would you be kind enough to send a card ahead of you, so I know you plan on visiting?"

Hayden could tell that this was a request she made often. It was just as he thought: Warren was making himself at home and making Jez uncomfortable with the current living arrangement.

Warren did not respond as he put on his hat.

"Hayden, shall we be off?" She put out her arm.

"Indeed, we do have a full day."

"You can show yourself out, Warren," she said.

Hayden shouldered past Warren and took Jez's arm to lead her away from the tension-filled room. Once they left the house, he said, "I'm glad to have intercepted his meeting with you, considering he was not invited."

"About Warren . . ." She fidgeted with a button at the side of her glove.

"What is it?" Hayden prompted.

She looked away from him before she answered. "He's given me till the end of August to wrap up my affairs and find new accommodations."

Hayden halted suddenly and turned to face his friend. "And you didn't think to tell me this before now?" He released her, ready to mete out justice and cause serious injury to Warren.

Jessica grabbed Hayden by the forearm before he could make it any great distance. When she had his attention, she dropped her hands and looked toward the spectators watching them.

She stepped close enough that she could whisper what she wanted to say, close enough that passersby wouldn't hear their discussion. "He knows about the miscarriage."

Hayden stood stunned for a moment, not sure how to respond.

How was that even possible? Hayden had personally watched the last person who knew of Jessica's condition sail away from English shores a month ago. Could the blighter, Miller, have come home after the first docking? If Miller was in London and spilling Jessica's secrets, he'd kill the bastard the first chance he got.

"It's not possible for anyone to know, Jess."

"My husband spoke with Warren after his first collapse. In all probability, there are a great many things that Warren knows that could be used against me. I can't fight him on this. Last night . . ."

Hayden took her arm, realizing that too many eyes were on·them right now. They couldn't risk being heard.

"Let's discuss this later. Did you eat this morning?" he asked.

She shook her head. "Someone didn't give me the opportunity."

"We'll stop at my house," he said. "We can talk without worrying we are being overheard."

"We don't need to discuss this further. I just want this meeting with your man of affairs done and over with."

"I will send a note to request a later time. And I will not allow you to bury this topic so easily, Jessica."

"You're incredibly assertive today."

"Then you've never noticed it before."

"Hayden, really, I'm fine. I've come to terms with my circumstance. I plan to remarry before summer ends."

Had he heard her right? He pulled her to a stop again and studied her. "All I had to do to convince you of that was kiss you?"

His fist clenched at his side and a twitch started in his eye. She wasn't thinking logically, he decided. She'd acted without thought of consequence before, and she was doing it in a dire period of her life. Maybe this was part of her denial that what had happened last night had felt right.

"You've gone from having a year to make arrangements for your future to two months. And you think a husband is going to just happen along?"

"No. But I have no other choice but to move onward." She leaned in close to him, saying softly, "There were things my husband said to me that made me believe he was going to petition for divorce."

"The man would have no grounds." Hayden scoffed at the very idea until he recalled part of his conversation with Miller. "What did Fallon think he had that would grant him that right?"

She ducked her head, the rim of her bonnet covering her eyes. "More than you can imagine."

"We're back to you shutting me out of your life. You need to be honest with me if I'm going to help you, Jess."

She nibbled on her lower lip. "It's no secret that I haven't been cooperative with Warren since my husband's death."

"And you shouldn't have to be."

"I couldn't agree more; Warren on the other hand thinks that I should turn a new leaf and be the paragon of all that is pious and seek redemption for my past sins." She let out a soft snort. "He disapproves of me. And he has no shortage of secrets that could make my life a living misery."

Hayden grew paranoid about being out in the open, so he didn't respond or ask any more questions as they strolled the remainder of the distance to his home in near silence.

Once they walked up the wide stone steps of his townhouse, the door opened and Jessica pulled her ecru lace parasol shut. Hayden took it from her and handed it off to the footman, giving instructions to have finger sandwiches and other refreshments brought into the study. He tossed his hat on his desk and turned to face Jessica once they were alone. She pulled out her hat pin and untied the satin ribbon to remove her hat, too.

She had one eyebrow quirked in question. "Now that it's only the two of us, what did you want to discuss?"

"Miller mentioned the divorce before he boarded his ship."

"And you didn't think that you should have told me this before now?"

"What purpose would it serve? Fallon can't divorce you when he's buried six feet beneath the ground."

Hayden watched, helpless, as tears swam in her eyes. What had he said to upset her?

He stood before her, his hand cupping the side of her face as he searched her eyes. "If I thought that information was vital to you, I would have told you. I wasn't intentionally keeping you in the dark. I would never do that to you, Jess. Never."

"Yet you have been doing just that." She turned away from him and walked over to the window. Her arms crossed over her midsection and her fingers wrapped tightly around her waist. "What else did Miller tell you?" she asked on a shaky breath.

"I'm afraid he was more worried about running than talking."

Hayden went to her, his hands warming her upper arms, trying to soothe her. Her shoulders rose and fell once, a sure sign she was fighting back the tears that had threatened to spill moments ago.

"Did he tell you why?"

"I didn't believe him. I only asked why your husband ended the pregnancy the way he did. I was never given a clear answer."

She nodded her head as a soft sob escaped her. He wanted to pull her into his arms and proclaim that everything would turn out right in the end, but how could he make that promise when not even he was sure how this would end?

To hell with it, he thought, and pressed the front of his body against her back, wrapping both arms around her and tangling their fingers together. She didn't stop him, which he took as a good sign. He was halfway to winning her over, whether she knew it or not.

"You have to let the past go, Jess. There will be children aplenty if that's what you desire."

"So easy for a man to declare." She slid her hands away from his but did not step out of their embrace. "I was married a long time, Hayden. That was my second pregnancy to make it past the third month."

He pressed the side of his face against her temple.

Even though he could guess the answer, he asked after a long pause, "What concluded the first?"

"The main staircase up to the second floor."

Hayden's jaw clenched and cracked.

She turned in his arms, but she didn't look him in the eye. "It was a long time ago."

"That doesn't excuse it, or make it any less tragic."

She leaned forward, her forehead resting against his chin. "What else did Miller tell you?" There was an added firmness in her question. What was she trying to hide from him?

"There wasn't much he could say, as his face was the worse for wear." Hayden looked at her for a long moment, all the while searching her eyes, silently willing her to open up to him. "What other secrets are you trying to hide from me?"

She stepped away from him. It was perfect timing, for a knock sounded as the door opened and trays laden with cucumber sandwiches and pastries were brought in. His staff knew what Jez preferred and always made her favorite dishes when she was here. A glass pitcher brimming with lemonade accompanied the trays.

"If you're planning to ply me with food this afternoon, I may not be able to move from your sofa to see this businessman of yours."

Her good humor, he was sure, was put on for his staff setting out the trays and dishes for them.

"Just an appetizer to prepare you for the day to come."

She turned to him, a sly look in her eyes, and not an ounce of the tears that had been awash there moments ago. How easily she shut herself off from everyone around her—had he ever noticed her do this before? He didn't think so.

"I thought it was going to be an afternoon filled with errands," she said.

"And I thought I might also persuade you to an evening out."

She raised an inquiring brow. "Do tell. It's been an age since we crashed a *decent* party."

"And what of the duchess's ball last month?"

"As I said, it's been an age." She poured out two glasses of lemonade and handed one to him. "Will Tristan and Leo join us tonight?"

"They've both been preoccupied with the task you gave them."

"Yes, I nearly forgot about Ponsley's daughter. She's a conquest neither will easily win." She sipped at her lemonade and then made up a plate for herself.

"Why did you ask them to pursue the young lady?"

"My reason was twofold. First and foremost, I wanted to prove a point to Warren—he gloated about his upcoming nuptials, about filling my childless home with babes, since I wasn't up for the task."

That heartless bastard. Hayden should have taken a swing at him earlier while he'd had the perfect opportunity.

"Jess . . ."

She gave him a sad smile. "When he said that I already knew I was losing the child. I was hurt at the time, even though he couldn't have possibly known that my husband was the reason for the miscarriage. Fallon would never paint himself in so poor a light—the blame would have been put to me. And that brings me to the other reason I asked Leo and Tristan to pursue Lady Charlotte. I wanted neither to take note of my condition. But to do that, I knew their focus needed to be elsewhere."

He set his glass down and sat next to Jessica on the sofa. He caressed her arm. "They wouldn't think less of you for the trial this put you through."

"There are some things that are so private that when

revealed they expose a piece of your soul that should be yours alone to see." Her eyes were awash with unshed tears again. "I wish none of you knew my shame."

"I wouldn't have it any other way, Jess. Some burdens are too great to shoulder yourself."

"So philosophical of you, darling." After flicking her fingers beneath one eye to wipe away a stray tear, she picked up one of the sandwiches and took a small bite.

She leaned back on the sofa with a sigh. "Shouldn't today be filled with fun? I hate rehashing all the ugliness in my life."

He hadn't forgotten that she hadn't revealed what Warren knew that was so damning about her. He'd have to ask another time; he wanted nothing more than for Jessica to be happy.

"And it will be full of fun." He gave her a warm smile before chomping down on one of the sandwiches.

"I don't know why your cook's cucumber sandwiches are as divine as melted chocolate, but I wish I could steal her to my household to make these for me every day."

"You're always welcome here."

She smiled, though the gesture didn't touch her eyes. "So when will we see this man of yours?"

"Anxious, are you?"

"Curious."

Chapter 10

*Can you believe that the Duke of A—— would con-
duct himself with such impropriety in public? He
was seen about Town, purchasing fripperies and
sharing ices with a certain dowager countess. I'm
beginning to wonder if there is more than meets the
eye where those two are concerned. Considering
their recent appearance at a disreputable house
party, one can only assume what is becoming more
and more obvious to this chronicler.*

Mayfair Chronicles, July 1846

What mattered most was that Hayden didn't know the full
truth. Jessica wouldn't have been able to face him had
Miller revealed the reason her husband was petitioning for
divorce. Though she was left wondering why Miller hadn't
spilled that particular secret long ago.

She wasn't naïve enough to think her secrets safe indefinitely; it wouldn't be long before Miller ran out of
money and started selling the gossip he had on various
members of the *ton*, including her.

When Hayden had introduced her to a man of business,
she'd been pleasantly surprised by his suggestions—all
sound investments with minimal money to start. Hayden
explained her finances to him, since he had thoroughly re-
viewed the will and estate, searching for a loophole that
would grant her fortune back to her; that loophole did not

exist. To no surprise to her, Hayden had it in his mind precisely how she should allocate what was left of her inheritance, too. He had wanted her to meet with this man, so she humored Hayden in allowing him to speak on her behalf. She'd mull over her choices when she had a moment alone.

What was left of her dowry protected from the entailment was enough to live off indefinitely—so long as she lived modestly—but that was not the type of life she could see herself living easily. More than ever, Jessica realized that it was imperative she marry into a new fortune. This was a difficult predicament to be in, especially considering most potential husbands wouldn't marry a woman in her first year of mourning.

She returned her focus to her friend. *Except perhaps Hayden.*

Could she ask that of him, knowing he harbored feelings for her? Knowing he'd never refuse her request on the basis of their friendship? But what did she want? The one thing she'd not allowed herself to focus on was their kiss. What was she so afraid of in accepting that there was something more between them?

Hayden could do so much better than her, though. While he might not agree with that, it was the truth. She was damaged goods. Ruined by her past. Her secrets would bring too much shame to his name, and that was not something she could live with. So she had to turn his thoughts away from something more with her.

"There are few options left to me. I'm going to have to marry again, and soon, Hayden." She hated saying it. Hated it with every fiber of her being. It felt wrong to entertain the thought of marrying someone other than . . .

No, her thoughts had to stop right there. She could not start seeing Hayden in that light.

"I'm not inclined to agree with that sentiment, Jess. The solution is obvious to me."

Releasing the curtain on the carriage window and slicing out the sunlight from the turquoise velvet interior, she pouted out her bottom lip as she looked at him. "Don't be such a spoilsport. I need you and Tristan to help me find a husband at tonight's ball."

"You needn't rush a decision like this."

There was an edge of anger in his statement. She chose to ignore it for now. Perhaps this had something to do with their kiss last night. Which, to her surprise, they had yet to discuss—she was positive that discussion would be high on Hayden's agenda today.

"Of course it'll be harder to marry now that my fortune is entailed and my value near worthless."

Hayden reached for her hand and squeezed it sympathetically. "You are far from worthless, love. And stop with this talk of finding a husband. The solution should be obvious to you." He looked at her a long moment. She knew he expected her to suggest they consider that option, but she looked away from him instead.

"I think we should turn this afternoon into a shopping excursion."

She rolled her eyes and pulled open the curtain to watch the passing streets. "That is exactly the kind of thing I should not indulge in."

"Then let me treat you," he offered.

She looked at him sidelong, considering the idea. It wasn't unusual for Hayden to purchase baubles for her or to spend an afternoon shopping at all her favorite stores. But it felt different now.

How had she been so blind for so long? How had he never acted on his desires before the masked ball? While she was desperate to ask him those questions, she couldn't.

Instead, she relented. "Only on the condition that we go for ices afterward."

He nodded his agreement.

Their first stop was her favorite millinery shop. The proprietor gave Hayden a chair while she tried on various hats. None of them interested her, nor did the gloves and shawls she tried on.

Hayden must have noted she wasn't enjoying herself to the fullest; how could she when so many things were clouding her mind? He suggested, "What about trying on some dresses for this evening?"

She nearly laughed at the stunned look on the girl's face behind the counter, who was fixing the hem of a pink silk gown. "They won't have anything on short notice."

"Then maybe some jewelry?"

Jessica trailed her finger over the shawls that hung around the shop, not meeting Hayden's gaze.

Where was he going with this? It was one thing to purchase baubles for her, another thing entirely to gift her with jewels.

"I haven't decided what I'll wear tonight. So I couldn't possibly select jewelry ahead of time."

"Who says it has to be for tonight?"

He stood from his chair, his expression devilish as he held his hand out for her to take. She hesitated for only a moment. Before she could ask where they were going, he whisked her out of the store and into one of the larger jewelry shops on Bond Street.

The thought of Jez remarrying infuriated him so profoundly it left him speechless. Speechless only because anything that might come out of his mouth would need to be censored from the general public surrounding them. Censored even from Jessica's ears.

Why did she refuse to see what was right in front of her? In all likelihood, their friendship probably made it difficult to think beyond committing to something more intimate.

If she insisted upon marriage, he would be the only candidate for husband. Who better to marry her than someone who respected and adored her completely?

After their kiss last night she must see that he harbored a desire to have her as his own. That desire ran so deep that he would most likely call out any man who so much as thought to court her. Was she perhaps afraid of the feelings developing between them?

First thing first, he would have to obtain a special license. Not only was Jez a woman of sudden decision making, but he'd damn well better be ready to hie off in the middle of the night, if necessary, to marry the moment he knew she was ready to accept him as her partner in life.

When their carriage pulled up to the front of the jewelry store, he rolled out the stairs and took her hand to assist her down. He tossed a coin up to the driver and dipped his head in thanks.

When he opened the door to the shop for Jessica, a brass bell jingled above their heads. The shop was brimming with customers.

"What shall we look at first?" he asked.

"Hairpins, of course."

He gave a succinct nod and motioned toward the cases that flanked the large room.

"Can I persuade you to try on some of the necklaces?" This was one of the nicer jewelry shops for such things.

She leaned closer to him, whispering, "The other patrons might mistake me for your mistress should we be so familiar and dare look at the jewelry."

"Do you honestly care?"

She thought on that a moment, her smile secretive. "You know, I don't think I do, even though I should."

Jez found a gold hairpin with a pearl on the end that she adored and had to have—he bought it for her, even though she insisted the simple piece was well within her budget.

They drew a lot of stares as Jessica tried on a multitude of necklaces with Hayden's assistance. Today was no different from any other day they'd shopped together, but for some reason there seemed to be more whispering behind gloved hands than usual. He did his best to tune it out, but Jessica's gaze was drawn to the unwanted attention all too frequently and he could see that she was growing uncomfortable, despite her insistence that she didn't care what anyone thought.

After purchasing a few items, Hayden took her for ices at Gunter's.

"Do you suppose everyone hates me, now" she asked as they sat on the lawn across from the ice shop.

Her frankness took him by surprise, but he didn't miss a beat in answering. "I think they are surprised to see you out when you've hidden away in your house for the better part of a month."

"I haven't hidden away. I was forced into solitude because of my health."

"You know what I meant, Jez."

She twirled her spoon around in her ice. Why would the *ton*'s reaction bother her now when it had never fazed her before?

"You want to know what I think?" he asked. "They're all jealous. You are the only lady I ever have on my arm."

She took a spoonful of ice, sucking it into her mouth in such a fashion that he had to adjust his position on the lawn. He was starting to believe her teasing was done intentionally.

"I never took you to be conceited," she said.

He winked as he scooped a thin layer of her pistachio ice with his spoon and offered up his glass for her to try his lime-flavored one. She shook her head and leaned back against the tree they'd had the good fortune to procure a seat beneath.

"Have my actions been irredeemable? So much so that half the patrons here have turned their backs to me?"

There were plenty of acquaintances but no one present whom he and Jessica would invite to sit with them. "Since when"—he motioned toward the patrons sitting on the lawn—"did you let them start bothering you? You've never cared about their opinions before."

"It'll be difficult to find a husband when so many women dislike me." She looked away from him.

"I don't think it's the ladies you have to worry about liking you. You have made many a friend in the card and game rooms over the years."

"I wouldn't wish to marry any of them, though."

He wanted to discuss the matter further, but this was a private conversation to be had where no one could overhear them. "We can talk about this tonight, Jez. Just try to enjoy the afternoon. I'm starting to think I'm a terrible friend for not keeping you carefree and happy today. And for failing to keep your mind on us instead of the multitude of suitors you want calling on you."

She reached for his arm, squeezing it for all present to see. And he realized that was part of the problem—though he didn't see it that way in the least. They'd always been familiar with each other and intimacy of this nature might be normal between them, but looking at the faces around them he knew it was not acceptable, especially now that Jez was widowed. Even though it had a visible effect on her reputation, he'd never ask her to consider monitoring her actions when they were together. Not when he intended for her to be his bride.

"Do you suppose Warren attended the ball last night with his mistress?"

"From what little information I gathered, he doesn't currently have one. I looked into it after you came to m[e] about the will," Hayden said.

"I guess that's unsurprising, since he probably doesn't want to muddy his name with the announcement of his engagement not far off." Jez tapped the spoon against her lips. "What other reason do you suppose he would attend a ball of that caliber, then?"

"Hilliard is part of his inner circle of friends, so it's possible they were discussing nothing more than politics."

Jez put a small spoonful of her ice in her mouth, the utensil lingering between her lips as she sucked it clean. Hayden swallowed. Why did the act have to look erotic? Better yet, it had his imagination traversing waters better left for the bedroom.

He took a bite of his own ice and looked out over the lawn. "When were you planning on telling me that you needed new lodgings?"

"It was decided only yesterday. I didn't have an earlier opportunity."

"What did you say for Warren to take such measures?"

"I may have pointed out a few of his flaws."

"May have?"

"All right, I did. But it was a truth he needed to hear. You needn't worry; I think this will be for the best. And it made me realize that I wasn't taking an active part in creating a better future for myself."

His gaze met hers. "So that was when you came up with the idea to remarry."

She nodded. "When Fallon died, I couldn't see myself ever marrying again. But I see now that there are more good men than there are inherently evil ones."

"You know three of the best," he teased, and was rewarded with a smile and a slight blush to her cheeks.

That blush told him everything he needed to know about how she felt. She didn't blush for Leo or Tristan. No, Jez was thinking about him as the flush colored her face and stole any further words she had. Hayden leaned back against the tree, the side of his body lining the length of hers from shoulder to hip as they finished their ices, intermittently commenting on and gossiping about the other patrons nearby.

Chapter 11

*A perfectly respectable lady has caught Mr. W——'s
eye this season. Though it is my opinion that she
has no interest in him. Has the coldest of men's
hearts finally melted or has circumstance and an
impending acquisition of a title spurred a marriage
for convenience's sake?*

Mayfair Chronicles, July 1846

Hayden took the stairs to Jez's townhouse two at a time
on his arrival. He didn't care who saw him, but he was
running late this evening and he wanted to discuss the
night with Jez before they left.

She was in her room still readying, but he was led upstairs to sit with her while her maid did some finishing
touches on Jez's ensemble. She stood at his entrance but
turned to face the mirror to adjust the curls at her crown.

Her dress was a rich, deep emerald with ruching at the
hips, and layers of silk, satin, and delicate lace layering
the train. He well imagined she'd make many women envious with the radiance of her beauty. She had spared no
expense on her wardrobe when her husband was alive and
it seemed she had a few dresses left to parade about in. She
was by far the most handsome sight he'd ever laid eyes
upon.

Her hair was twisted back in an elaborate bun with
curls cascading around her temples. A simple tortoiseshell

hair comb was tucked deep into the base of the bun at the front, small white flowers were woven into the twists, and a bronze silk ribbon wrapped around it all and tied in a bow at the back.

"You're not wearing any jewelry tonight?"

Subconsciously her hand went to her bare neck as her gaze met his in the mirror. "The first thing Mr. Warren took an inventory of was the family jewels." She gave a nervous laugh. "I suppose he thought I'd try to take them with me or, worse, sell them."

"The bloody blighter." Hayden motioned toward the maid. "Can you give us a few minutes alone?"

The young woman curtsied. "Your Grace. My lady."

Jez turned away from her mirror to face him. "What was that about?"

He walked over to her, pulling his hand from his pocket where he'd placed the necklace he'd purchased. "I required privacy for this."

He looped the diamond and pearl necklace around her neck and fastened the clasp at the back of her neck.

Round pearls surrounded with diamonds were strung together with two looping rows of gold-backed diamonds in between. Larger diamonds and teardrop pearls hung from each clustered piece at the neck. The necklace was fit for a princess.

Or better yet . . . the one woman who would be his duchess.

She trailed her fingers over the necklace as she turned to face the mirror again. "Hayden, you know I can't accept this."

He shrugged and tucked his hands behind his back to keep from touching her. It was becoming more and more difficult to not take her in his arms. And he only stopped himself because he hadn't properly proposed to her yet.

"When I saw it, I thought of you."

"It's so beautiful. But it's far too much." Tears filled her eyes but did not fall.

"I knew it would suit you perfectly when I found it. Accept it as a token of our long friendship." And our impending marriage, he wanted to add, but held off.

She looked as though she'd argue further, but instead she ran her fingers over the piece again as she stared at her reflection in the mirror before meeting his gaze.

She cleared her throat and stood, breaking their connection.

Her hands pressed over the bodice and skirts of her dress. "Am I presentable for our outing, or will I need to change?"

"You always look ravishing."

She smiled at his compliment. "You sounded like Tristan for a moment. Speaking of . . . when will he join us?"

Hayden's smile widened. "We'll be stopping at his place first."

"Is our destination to remain a surprise?"

She slid on bronze-colored gloves that matched the ribbon tied around her hair.

"It's only fair, considering your secrecy last night."

"At least tell me if we're staying in London."

She took his arm and led him out of her boudoir and down to the foyer. Wilson helped her with a silk short jacket that matched her dress.

"I know your preference for remaining in Town. I also recall you saying something about the lack of balls this past month, and it just so happens that this will be your last chance to attend one till the little season starts up."

"Who would host a ball at this time of year?" When he only raised one brow in response, she demanded, "Give me at least one clue!"

"I've already confirmed that Tristan will join us. If I told you any more, it wouldn't be a surprise."

"What if I'm not dressed for the occasion? You know how important it is to me to make a good impression."

"Yes, to find this new husband of yours," he said drolly. She would know soon enough that he had designs on her and that he'd be her only suitor.

She bumped her shoulder against his arm. Unable to keep his hands to himself a moment longer, he wrapped them around her small waist and lifted her into the waiting carriage.

He nearly took the seat across from her but stopped himself and squished in next to her. Tristan's townhouse was close, so they made it there quickly. Their friend was waiting for them outside.

Tristan kissed Jez's cheeks, then sat on the seat across from them. "I hear we're to cause a stir tonight."

"And apparently find Jez a husband," Hayden added, only because it would keep Tristan occupied in finding eligible suitors while Hayden asked for her hand in marriage.

Tristan looked at Jez, one brow cocked. "This should make for an incredibly interesting evening."

It was just like Tristan not to question Jez's motives. She was always the exception to the rule for them all. They did not cosset or shield her from any truths, and why should they? They let her do as she pleased. How could they not when she was one of them? An equal in every sense of the word.

"Will it be the card room or the ballroom first?" Tristan asked.

"The company is always more interesting in the card room," Jez said.

"And most of the men there are likely married," Hayden pointed out.

Jez pouted. "I despise dancing with gentlemen who have two left feet. Lessons seem to be a thing of the past."

"I'm more than happy to lead you out in your first dance of the evening," Tristan offered. "I'll show the young bucks how it's done."

Jez cheered up immediately and gave them both a winning, yet mischievous, smile. "Now that is a perfect plan. And so long as we don't run into Torrance, we'll have a fabulous evening. That man was such a boor to me when last we met."

She referred to the last "decent" ball they had all attended. Torrance had dared to insult Jez for her presence on the day of her husband's funeral. Hayden had of course defended her and had the incident under control—but Jez wouldn't let the situation rest and had outright insulted Torrance's very manhood. It wasn't as though Torrance could call out a woman for the insult, either. They'd left the ball shortly after that incident, but Hayden had been ready to deck Torrance right between the eyes for his insolence. Yes, they could do without running into that particular cad.

The carriage rolled to a stop in front of a large four-story brick house on the edge of Berkeley Square.

Jez nibbled at her lower lip. "I didn't know you were so well acquainted with the Glenmoores." Awe filled her voice. "Then again, who wouldn't invite the Duke of Alsborough to every event running in Town? Any smart mother would want to snag a duke for their marriageable daughter."

"We're both full of surprises these days." Hayden placed his hand at the base of her back possessively as he helped her from her seat.

"What have I missed?" Tristan asked, taking Jessica's hand as she stepped down from the carriage.

"We attended a Malvern masquerade," Jez said.

Tristan's mouth dropped open before he could compose his surprise. It took him a few tries before he could mutter anything coherent. "And how did *you* procure an invite?"

"I didn't," Jez clarified. "As it turns out Fallon is good for something now that he's dead."

"I'm impressed, though disappointed you didn't invite me." Tristan took her arm as they ascended the stairs at the entrance of the house.

"It was a plus one, darling."

"And you choose that lout." Tristan motioned toward Hayden with a sour expression.

Jez only smiled. Hayden realized—when he should have clued into the fact before—that she tended to acted riskier when she was with Tristan. Tristan always encouraged the worst behavior in everyone. Now that Hayden thought about it, it was interesting that she'd chosen him even knowing his proclivity for tamer social gatherings. Looking at the other side of the coin, she had attended in the hopes that she'd find Warren in a disparaging, unredeemable situation.

"Well, if another invitation finds its way to your household, do call on me. I'm a lot more fun than this stick-in-the-mud you insist on dragging about to our social gatherings."

"I'm far better company than you'll ever be, dear friend," Hayden argued.

"You're both wonderful. And while I enjoy being fought over by you both, you're bound to frighten away any suitors tonight, so be quiet on the topic now that we've arrived."

"You're not honestly going through with another marriage, are you, Jez?" Tristan asked, suddenly somber.

"If I had a choice I wouldn't even consider it. But choices are for widows left rich by their doting husbands. We all know how much Fallon reviled our union."

Put that way, neither of them disagreed with her—not

while they were in public. People like Fallon had reservations in the worst kind of hell for their misdeeds. Even if half the people Fallon dealt with on a daily basis were blind to how sinister a man he was, he was paying for his sins now.

As they entered the foyer Hayden turned to Jessica. "Will we separate here to let you go to the meeting area for the women? Or shall we cause a stir and skip that particular formality?"

There was no hesitation in Jessica's decision. "Let's skip right to the dancing part."

Hayden was happy to oblige. Tristan took her short jacket and passed it to a footman to deal with before they headed into the marble-columned ballroom that would make any Greek historian salivate at the architecture.

Jessica didn't fail to notice the way other guests looked at her. It was more difficult to ignore them then it had ever been in the past. She would have to pretend it didn't bother her—even though it did hurt her more than she cared to admit.

She pasted on her brightest smile as she walked forward on Hayden's arm. Perhaps the other women in attendance were jealous. Telling herself that small lie gave her the added confidence she needed to stare everyone in the eye when they glanced her way.

She was here for one purpose, and that was not to impress the women who so loathed her. They didn't matter, she kept telling herself. But their hate for her still hurt.

She had to find a husband or risk falling for Hayden with every sweeping gesture he'd made toward her. She touched the pearl and diamond strands at her throat. His actions were less and less platonic. Had that been recent? Had she ignored it before? She thought maybe she had and felt like all kinds of fool for not noticing.

Oh, Hayden, why did you keep it a secret for so long? she wondered.

She had to stop thinking about him, so she thought about the fact that she was at her first "decent" ball in a month and it felt good to be back in the game, to leave behind all the sorrow and anger from her ordeal since Fallon's death. There also happened to be plenty of bachelors to choose from at tonight's party and none of these men could be as cruel as Fallon. That just wasn't a possibility.

Tristan offered his hand to her for the first dance. She smiled, thankful for his good humor even though it was obvious that she was not a welcome guest—if a scathing, reproving look could kill, she'd be dead on the ground from the glares she was receiving.

Hayden cut in before they could make it onto the dance floor. "Sorry, old chap," Hayden teased, as that moniker was something Tristan often used for Hayden. "Her first dance should be with a man worthy of her hand."

Jessica blushed as she recalled their previous evening with perfect clarity. While she made others flush with her brand of bluntness, she never found herself in a position to do the same.

"Hayden," she admonished, because she couldn't seem to articulate anything coherent beyond that.

"You know I'm a better dance partner than Tristan."

She smiled and shook her head, but she did give Hayden her hand. He was a very good dance partner. Probably the best she'd have tonight, not that she would tell Tristan any such thing.

"Don't worry," Tristan said. "I can find my own amusement while the two of you take a turn around the floor."

Hayden pulled her away with a sly grin.

Jessica gave him a questioning look. "Are we not waiting for the next set?"

"You're never one to shy away from living life to the fullest," Hayden said, leading her toward the other dancers. "And there is no time like the present, when they are playing a redowa."

She looked up at him. "You're right, as always." She narrowed her gaze. "It's rather annoying, you know."

He smiled in response as he pulled her into a closed position, her hand on his shoulder, his at the middle of her back, and their free hands clasped tightly together. The waltz-like dance had them spinning every few steps in time with the orchestra. It felt as though he held her closer than he needed to, and while other paired dancers talked, they only stared at each other.

It was far too intimate and reminiscent of everything that had happened the night before. Jessica knew she needed to break the silence between them even if it had to be done with mundane conversation.

"And who will you dance with next?" she asked. Most of the young ladies present would clamor for a chance to be on a duke's arm, especially Hayden's. She tried not to let that fact bother her, but sometimes she relished having him all to herself.

"Depends on the dance. The first real waltz will be yours."

"You cannot monopolize my time, or my dance card, this evening."

He raised an eyebrow. "I most certainly can. Besides, you aren't wearing a dance card."

She couldn't help but laugh at the obvious as they took another turn around the room. Before the song had a proper chance of finishing, Tristan stole her from Hayden for a quadrille.

"You'll both tire me out before the hour is done at this rate." She was breathless and she'd only had three dances so far. Though all were fast paced.

"Is such a thing possible?"

A month ago, perhaps not. Since she'd been ill and on the mend, yes, anything was possible. She'd never say so, since Tristan was the only friend to not know about her condition.

"Some might consider me an old crone now that I'm widowed. Ten years of marriage is a long time."

"It happens often enough—an old goat marrying someone too junior to complement his age, and then when he's had his fill and finally croaks he knows he's leaving his merry young wife to find someone more to her choosing."

"I certainly hope you're right that I'll find my match. But I don't think Fallon ever wanted me happy." They broke apart to partner off with other guests.

When Tristan took her hand again, he asked, "Must you marry at all?"

"Fallon made sure my misery would never end by cutting me entirely out of the estate. He knew how much I hated the institution of marriage, and he knew I'd have no choice but to marry again. So, yes, I unfortunately must."

Tristan tapped her chin, forcing her to meet his gaze before her thoughts wandered too far in the direction of Hayden. She caught glimpses of him on every rotation and almost wished he were still dancing with her so she wasn't having a conversation with Tristan about whom she should marry when it no longer seemed like an ideal solution. She wasn't sure when she'd decided that, but the thought of conversing with anyone other than Tristan or Hayden tonight made her nervous and uneasy.

"Cheer up, dearest. We'll find the perfect husband for you."

Tristan was always looking on the brighter side of things. That was one of the reasons she adored him as much as she did. Forever an optimist. How she wished she could be more like him in that regard.

"I'd offer," he said, "but we'd make each other miserable, since we're more like brother and sister than we could
ever play the role of lovers."

Her face soured up. She didn't like that idea any
more than he. And she ignored the niggling voice reminding her of another friendship that did not feel like
a sibling relationship. "Well, who are my potential suitors then?"

Jessica made a point of looking around the ballroom—
all the most revered members of the *ton* were present.
And scandal was never afoot at a Glenmoore ball, though
with her presence that might change after tonight. Even if
she was on her best behavior.

There were a number of eligible gentlemen, a few out
to please their mamas, but they did not interest her. A few
of the married gentlemen danced with the wallflowers
present, making them feel less like outsiders.

"What of Longsmere?" Tristan nodded toward a lanky
gentleman directly across from them.

"There are rumors he's in love with a married woman."
Jessica did not want to be a second thought or a burden
when she married again.

"Balderdash, Jez." Tristan shook his head. "I've known
the man for fifteen years."

"Just because you went to school together does not
mean you really know the type of man he is."

And men changed behind closed doors. She had first-
hand experience with that.

"You're right. Which reminds me that he's far too boring to have caught the attention of a married woman."

"Not if she's lonely," Jessica said. "When marriage is
made for the sake of convenience, it is often an unhappy
arrangement for both partners."

"I think most couples make do over time, and learn to
appreciate each other in the run of their marriage. Fallon

was an arse, and would have never been happy, no matter whom he married."

"Well, if you think Longsmere's a match, ask him if he'll dance with me."

Tristan smiled down at her. "I definitely will," he said before passing her off to the partner next to her.

She ended up in the arms of Lord Crosthwait. A middle-aged man who was generally quiet and let his wife do most of the talking. But he had a kind disposition from what Jessica remembered from their few interactions.

"Good evening, my lord," she said with a sweet smile.

His lips flapped, but nothing came out other than a startled gasp.

"I know I'm not generally found at these types of affairs, but it's a pleasure to dance with you. I don't think I've had this honor until now."

When she gave him a friendly smile, he seemed to put more distance between them, his hands barely touching her.

When he passed her back to Tristan, she swore she heard a sigh of relief.

"I can't be that terrible a dance partner. I didn't step on his toes once; how could I when he tried to put three feet between us?"

"Ignore the lout. Though I thought he was going to have a fit of apoplexy dancing with the most beautiful woman present."

When she looked toward Lord Crosthwait, he was wiping his brow with an already damp handkerchief. The poor man didn't know what to make of his fleeting encounter with her. But it didn't appear that she was the first to flounder him this evening. That made her feel marginally better.

"Do you think most of the attendees dislike me?" she asked in a small voice.

"Never, dearest. You are far too stunning a creature for the awkward men in the room—which there are many—to ever have the gumption to start a decent conversation with. Freethinking women scare them and they are precisely the sort of men you need to avoid at all costs."

"You're just saying that to be nice." And it was working, because she was smiling and in higher spirits.

"I wouldn't dream of lying about this. Besides, you're liable to shove me out a moving carriage if I ever dared lie to you."

"I might," she agreed with a small laugh.

Tristan eventually twirled them right off the dance floor and toward the punch table.

Hayden was waiting with champagne for her. "I know this is your favorite."

"The new Perrier-Jouët?" she asked as she reached for the fizzing flute.

Tristan took a sip before her. "Indeed," he said. "The Glenmoores have spared no expense for the final ball of the season. That is probably the only way to have such a showing with the stench of London during this heat. I'm off to snag you a few dance partners. I'm sorry to leave you in the clutches of Hayden. I promise not to be long."

Hayden glared at Tristan as he weaved his way through the guests, and muttered, "Cad," affectionately.

Jessica took a sip of her drink. She couldn't believe she was at a respectable ball, with respectable company. It was probably best she didn't join the gentlemen in the games room, even if she could trounce the lot of them at most card games.

Hayden turned to talk to someone next to him while Jessica focused on those mingling nearby. No one approached her, which she had expected. And with Tristan's good mood having rubbed off on her, she wasn't as bothered by their cutting glares.

"Can you believe she invited herself here?" Jessica heard women talking behind her. She turned slightly to see if she could identify them, but they were hidden behind a series of potted green leafy tropical trees that created a wall, likely dividing the ballroom from some sort of parlor.

"She arrived with the duke and the marquess," a high-pitched voice said.

"The duke and marquess would have had an invite."

"Alsborough most certainly," came the nasal voice again. The woman sounded as though she was eighty. Who in the world could it be? Jessica stepped away from Hayden, hoping to catch a clear glimpse of the women through a break in the tree wall. She had no such luck.

"Perhaps she plays mistress to them both."

The stem of Jessica's champagne flute snapped between her fingers and the remainder of her champagne spilled over on her gloves. Shushing whispers were all she could hear through the buzzing anger in her head, and then the women behind the trees dispersed. A flush washed over her as she tried to sort out the voices in her head. One might very well have been Lady Hargrove, but she couldn't be sure. *Damn it. Why did they have to go and ruin a perfectly good evening?*

A footman was suddenly in front of her, his tray raised to take her glass. Jessica placed the broken fine crystal on the tray and wiped her soiled gloves off on the towel hanging over his forearm. She took it and nodded her thank-you.

Once she handed it back to him, she realized that the guests closest were gawking at her as though she were a circus animal. Some of the more prudish members of society turned away from her, their husbands following suit. Jessica pinched her lips but held her head high as she met the eyes of the others, who were probably curious to how she'd react. They seemed mesmerized and unable to turn away from the spectacle she had made.

Stepping back toward Hayden, she bumped lightly into his arm, hoping to draw him away from the gentleman he was currently engaged with. She got Hayden's attention.

"Shall we take a turn around the room?" He leaned in close to her ear, his voice darkening as he gave her his arm. "You'll want to seek out that potential husband you're determined to find."

She didn't bother to tell him that it was unlikely given the way she'd just conducted herself and the censorious glares she was receiving from the majority of women present.

"If I didn't know you better"—she laughed nervously, hoping those closest weren't listening to her and Hayden's private conversation—"I would say you almost sound jealous."

"Maybe I am. I don't want anyone to stand between our friendship again."

She looked at him, confused. "I never allowed Fallon to stand in the way of my friendships."

"I know." Hayden ran the back of his free hand over her exposed arm. "And that was probably part of the reason he resented you so much."

She shrugged, feeling uncomfortable with their conversation, especially after the things she'd overheard. Was it any wonder she resorted to recklessness? She'd never been well loved—Fallon had seen to that once he knew her ugly truth.

Would Hayden despise her if he ever knew she was the illegitimate daughter of Lord Henry Heyer? That her mother was a whore who lived in sin daily with Jessica's father and his wife? Tristan, she thought, might be the most accepting, considering the questionable parentage of his children. Leo wasn't inclined to care a great deal, either. But how would Hayden judge her? The respectable and ever-proper Hayden?

The room felt like it was closing in around her. Her head felt light and her stomach queasy. Fresh air would help to clear her mind and temper her thoughts. "Let's take a turn outside," she suggested.

He directed them back to the open French doors they'd just passed. Her hand went to her throat, where the necklace Hayden had given her was looped around her neck like a weighted collar.

What was wrong with her? Was she not ready for social functions? She felt like a wild bird stuck in captivity and under the scrutiny of too many eyes.

"I'm sorry to have brought up Fallon," Hayden said remorsefully as soon as they were under the star-dotted sky.

"Don't apologize. I don't know what came over me." She closed her eyes and inhaled deeply. It was a cooler night than it had been in a long while, so instead of the pungent smell of the Thames she was surround by the fresh scent of full-bloomed flowers in the garden below. It was uplifting, and the vise that had taken hold of her slowly loosened.

Hayden stepped close to her, blocking her view of the small garden tucked at the back of the property. "We're here for you to enjoy yourself, Jez."

His hands cupped her arms. It must be obvious that she was distressed; she'd not explain why, because Hayden always played the hero and he'd search out the gossips whispering about her.

"I know. And I haven't had this much fun in a long time." She looked into his dark eyes, almost black in the cover of night. "I'll forever be grateful to you and Tristan."

"Because we are *friends*." There was sarcasm, or something much darker she couldn't place, in Hayden's words. Had she upset him?

She tilted her head to the side. "Of course; how else would I mean it?"

"You could forget this foolish nonsense of finding a husband."

He seemed almost angry. Most wouldn't recognize the shift in his stance or the hard glint in his eye to indicate it, but she knew him well enough to see that something was wrong.

"If I could forget about marriage altogether, Hayden, don't you think I would after all I went through?"

The one thing about their friendship was that they were always honest with each other. Well, some secrets needed to remain private.

Surely he knew that marriage was the last thing she wanted with any of the men here. Though she knew in time that if it came down to a choice between marrying and living a life too close to poverty for her liking she would without second thought choose the first.

"Would it be a hardship if you married me?" he asked.

The idea was absurd coming on the heels of her and Tristan's discussion, but she also knew Hayden would inevitably ask.

"Be serious, Hayden." She shrugged out of his hold, needing space.

"Would you like me to get down on bended knee to prove how serious I am?"

While part of her wanted to say yes, she knew she could never bind him to her in that way for eternity.

When she turned back to him he started to lower to the ground. She caught him around the arms and pulled him back to his feet, shaking her head as she did so.

"Please don't do this," she pleaded.

"Why not, Jez? I'll not stand by as you find another man to fill the shoes of what you envision the perfect husband for your circumstance."

"You're being cruel." She released him, tucking her hands behind her back, and looked to her slippers where they peeked out from beneath her skirts. "You're my dearest friend."

"And apparently that's all I will ever amount to."

She looked at him, alarmed by the bitterness coating his comment. How would she convince him that this was his worst idea ever without giving away her feelings or the secrets only she knew?

"Have—have I ever given you a reason to think we were otherwise?"

He stepped toward her, forcing her back against the balcony wall till they were hidden in the darkened cove awash in thick vines of ivy. The leafy greens tickled the sides of her neck and upper arms.

"Have you forgotten last night so easily?" he countered.

His breath fanned over her cheek; hers hitched in her lungs when the moon reflected off the determined glare in his eyes.

"We both know last night should never have happened. Neither of us were thinking clearly," she couldn't stop from babbling. "The champagne didn't help matters any."

"Is that what you need to tell yourself to pretend you didn't feel the pull between us?" His hand was as light and fleeting as a feather brushing over her cheek. "That you didn't enjoy it every bit as much as I did?"

She pushed lightly against his chest, hoping he'd step back and give her space to breathe, to think of another reason this couldn't be. He didn't.

"Why are you doing this to me?" she whispered, her voice breaking at the end of the question. She felt as though she'd cry, but she fought against the tears.

"I will never put last night behind us, Jez. I know you felt something for me, fleeting as it was in our stolen moment. You'll only hurt us both if you keep lying to yourself."

Was there truth in his words? She thought there might be, and that scared her a great deal. She needed to escape Hayden. She couldn't think straight with him hovering over her, demanding answers she didn't have.

She ducked her whole body and slipped to the side . . . putting very necessary distance between them. He didn't let her escape far, so she stood for his perusal. He didn't touch her, but she could feel heat radiating off him as though she were standing too close to burning coals in a brazier. Would she burn herself if she brushed up against him? That was a thought better left alone. But still . . . she had to wonder. She took a step toward him without really meaning to.

"What do you want from me, Hayden?"

"I just want you."

She stared back at him, speechless. What if their kiss had been about more and the best thing she could do for her future was explore what was between and beyond their friendship?

What if, what if, what if.

Her knuckles brushed against his chest. How had she ended up in touching distance of him again?

As she went up on the tips of her toes, her breasts brushed against him ever so slightly and her mouth closed in on his.

"There you are." Tristan's voice boomed into the silence.

She fell to her feet, her breath frozen in her lungs.

What had she been about to commit to?

"Tristan," she acknowledged as she dropped her hand and stepped away from Hayden. How much had Tristan seen?

When she turned to look at Tristan, he stood at the doors off the ballroom, his gaze betraying nothing.

"I found you a dancing partner, so come inside before Longsmere is cornered by another young lady looking for a husband. There seems to be a great deal of them on the marriage market this evening—hadn't realized that when we arrived."

Now he sounded worried for himself. Jessica would have laughed at the observation, but she couldn't stop thinking about what she and Hayden had nearly done. She looked at Hayden once more before taking Tristan's arm.

Hayden's expression was dark and unreadable; his jaw clenched tight against whatever he'd been about to say.

Distance for the evening would put him in a better mood. And give them both some time to think of the folly she'd just about committed. Or so she hoped. The problem was, she didn't think he'd see their actions as a mistake any more than she did.

Chapter 12

After what started as an unpromising night for the Duke of A—— his eyes thankfully landed on better company than whom he'd arrived with. He danced with a woman proven to be a veritable diamond in a sack full of coal this season. And the duke did not dance with her once, but twice. Will the duke finally take a bride? One would hope that at his age he'd at least consider settling into married life. So who will the lucky lady be?

Mayfair Chronicles, July 1846

"I've taken all the dancing I can take tonight." Hayden brushed his hands roughly through his hair. "The Duchess of Glenmoore had me dance with every wallflower and every debutante present. I say we head back to my house and open a bottle of champagne to unwind from a very full evening."

"Sounds delightful." Jez's cheeks were flushed. She, too, had been dancing all evening.

Once Longsmere had danced with her, other gentlemen had followed suit. Every one of them was undeserving of her attention.

All Hayden could be thankful for was that Jessica hadn't been interested in any of the gentlemen she'd taken a turn around the room with. And despite the fact that he wished she wouldn't dance with anyone but him, she seemed to

have forgotten their earlier disagreement on the verandah. Damn Tristan for interrupting them.

For the most part, Hayden had spent the night staring
after Jessica. It didn't matter whether he was on the out-
skirts of the ballroom, dancing with his many partners,
or conversing with a few of the guests. He'd watched her,
and he didn't give a damn that he couldn't stop himself
from doing so. The best thing to come out of tonight was
that Jessica was smiling and laughing and had enjoyed
the evening to the fullest.

"I have an early-morning outing, but a glass or two can
be accomplished before I head home," Tristan responded
when Jessica's thoughts had wandered from the topic at
hand.

"Too bad Leo is preoccupied," Jessica said. "We could
have played a hand of cards. Though I suppose we could
make a trip to our favorite gaming hell before we head to
your house, Hayden."

"Out of the question." Tristan caught Jez's arm before
she tripped up the stairs of the carriage.

Perhaps champagne was a bad idea. But Hayden wasn't
ready to say good night to Jessica when he had every intention of finishing their earlier conversation once Tristan
called it an evening.

Hayden stepped in when his two friends could do no
more than clasp each other and laugh at their clumsiness.
Grabbing Jez around the waist, Hayden hauled her up
into the carriage and followed in behind. She giggled.
She never giggled.

"What am I going to do with you two?" he asked in
exasperation.

Tristan sat across from him and Jez. "A midnight
snack will be in order if we're to make it through another
bottle of champagne."

"We may want to call it a night."

Jez pouted and pinched his cheek like one might do chiding a child. "Poor Hayden, always trying to do the right thing. What happened to living dangerously?"

"A late meal it is, then," Hayden said as he clasped Jessica's hand before recalling his friend sat across from them. He released her with great reluctance. While he was more than ready for any show of affection, he knew Jessica was not.

"And I'm perfectly well; I just can't recall the last time I had so much fun."

"It's about damn time, too," Tristan said. "We should get out more often."

"I'll choose better dancing partners next time. Poor Mr. Hemsworth gaped at me like a fish with a hook caught in its mouth. I don't think he managed one coherent sentence."

"I daresay, Longsmere warmed up to you," Tristan said.

"None of the men you danced with were worth your time." Hayden crossed his arms over his chest. He did not want to hear what Jez thought of every man on her arm or how those men might measure up as husband material.

"Don't think I didn't notice that you glared at all the gentlemen on my arm," Jez shot back.

"Poor old chap," Tristan said. "You're just disappointed to have been appointed most eligible bachelor tonight. Had you not had to dance with every debutante and wallflower, you might be in a better mood."

"You needn't remind me."

Jez and Tristan laughed. Hayden supposed it was a damn sight funnier to them than it was to him.

By the time they reached Hayden's house Tristan was yawning. Jez seemed wide-awake and ready to continue their party into the wee hours of the morning. Hayden was happy to oblige.

"I'm parched from all the dancing. And worse, I don't think I can remember all the gentlemen's names, either."

"All that matters is that they know you are back on the market for marriage," Tristan said.

Jez leaned back on the sofa, toed her slippers off, and put her feet up.

And all Hayden could think was that if one of those men dared to leave a calling card at her house tomorrow he'd call the blighter out and beat him to a bloody pulp for any attempt to court her. Jez was his. Perhaps Hayden had always been waiting for her husband to kick the bucket so he could make his intentions clear. No other man would come between them now.

True to his word, Tristan left after only one glass of champagne. Hayden offered Jez a game of cribbage to keep her for a while longer, which she accepted.

"About earlier . . ."

His gaze snapped up to hers, surprised that she would bring it up first.

"I know I was out of line." Though he didn't think he'd stop himself from doing it again.

She looked at him with narrowed eyes. "Do you really mean that?"

"What do you think?"

"I know when you're lying, Hayden." She moved her peg on the board when she hit thirty-one.

He folded his cards together and set them facedown on the table; she was winning the game and he hadn't a chance in hell of catching up to the points she'd racked against him. "My offer still stands, Jessica."

"Because of a kiss, you would risk our friendship?"

"It wasn't *just* a kiss." He shook his head. "You are trying to mitigate a risk that doesn't exist."

"We were both caught up in the moment." She looked back down to her cards, avoiding his gaze.

"Isn't that exactly the point?"

She sighed and set her cards down, too. "And what happens to our friendship when we realize that we've made a mistake in wanting more?"

"How can you predict the outcome?" he countered.

If she wanted to have this conversation, he'd give her every reason he could think to give them a modicum of a chance.

"Why did you come back here?" he asked. "Considering what happened earlier?"

"Because if we didn't talk now, you would have barged into my home demanding answers tomorrow morning. And I hate mornings."

He couldn't argue with her on that because that was exactly what he would have done.

"So you're simply humoring me?"

"Not precisely."

He looked at her for a long moment. They needed to come to an agreement on how to carry his plan forward, because, by God, he would not let her turn him off this idea.

"I can't stand by and watch as you court and marry another man. In fact, I refuse to do any such thing."

She reached for one of his hands across the table and squeezed it. "You are my best friend. You've stuck by my side when half the *ton* was divided on whether or not they should welcome me with open arms or shun me for something they deemed inappropriate. If we were to marry, everything that we have built over the last eight years could very well crumble around us."

"You only assume our relationship will change because you lived through a horrendous marriage." He clasped both her hands in his, needing to touch her, never wanting to let go of her. "Trust me when I say it won't be like that for us."

"Men change when they can no longer cat about Town, bedding whom they wish whenever they wish. You'll eventually find a young wife that can give you everything you need. But if you ask me to play the role of wife . . ." She shook her head and slid her hands from his. "I don't want to be responsible for changing the man you are. I would never forgive myself."

It was unbelievable that she was arguing this point with him. "Do you even recall my last mistress?"

"The redheaded one?" Should it surprise him that she did remember? "I saw her onstage recently, but for the life of me, I cannot recall her name."

Hayden grasped both of Jez's arms and lifted her from her chair till they were face-to-face over the table. "Are you so blind, Jez?"

She blinked at him, confused.

His *mistress* had filled a void more than a year ago. It had been an on-again, off-again relationship for years, but it didn't take long for that particular woman to realize she was filling the role for the woman he could not have. When they'd split off once and for all, he'd not found anyone else. He hadn't wanted anyone else. None of them were Jez. No one could even come close to comparing.

Instead of explaining himself, he planted his lips against Jez's. If she wouldn't listen to reason, perhaps she would listen to action. She did soften in his hold, going so far as to lean in close enough that the upper halves of their bodies came together over the small table dividing them.

But his victory was fleeting, and before long she pulled out of his hold and walked over to the window to look out onto the darkened street.

"I'm sorry." He'd acted too soon.

"Stop saying that when we both know you're not sorry in the least."

"Believe me, Jez, if I could act rationally around you, I would."

He came up behind her, standing close enough that the heat of their bodies mingled as he rested his chin atop her head.

"Can you not consider the idea that we might be right for each other?"

"And what if I lose you in the process?"

His arms went around her waist. She didn't fight his touch this time, allowing him the small liberty.

"Have you ever asked yourself why you've always been cautious with me? Could it be that I'm more set in my ways than Leo and Tristan? And I'm always the sound of reason when reason seems far from everyone else's thoughts. But think about it, Jez; where they might be brothers to you, I've never played that role.

"Leap with me this once. Trust me. You've never known me to lose a challenge. You've never known me to act rashly. I assure you I've had plenty of time to think this through and I know in my heart that we are right for each other."

He coaxed her to turn in his arms; she complied. Once she faced him, her head tilted back, her eyes searched his, searching for answers and the truth of his words, he thought. How he wanted to ask her what she really saw.

"It's not in my nature to trust a man with something like this."

"You know I'm nothing like Fallon."

"Do I? Because aside from our friendship, I certainly do not know what kind of man you are with your paramours or lovers."

He brushed his thumb over her lips, wanting to dip his head and taste her mouth again. "You know me better than you think, Jez. I wouldn't dare hurt you."

Patience was the name of this game. He'd not frighten her off now that she was willingly in his arms discussing the possibility of a future that involved *them*.

"It's the best solution to your current circumstance."

"How romantic." She rolled her eyes and glanced away from him.

"And finding rich gentlemen on your evenings out is any more so?" He couldn't keep bitter sarcasm from tainting his voice.

When she didn't answer him he lifted her chin, forcing her to face him again.

To hell with it, he thought. Why wait when he needed her just as much as she needed him?—even if she wasn't ready to admit that.

He lowered his mouth in slow increments, giving her plenty of opportunity to pull away, to stop him in any fashion she might deem appropriate in her moment of vulnerability.

Their lips melded, his lips parted and tasted hers. Their kiss was like fresh honey drizzled over warm bread. And the bear he was, he couldn't pull away now that he was tasting the sweetest nectar life had ever offered him. When she relaxed into the kiss, he delicately traced her lips with his tongue.

Any fight left in her dissipated as she stood on her toes to better reach his mouth. The press of her soft breasts met his chest as the palms of her hands rested over his shoulders. Incrementally, she pressed her body tighter against his. With his arms wrapped around her small waist he held her with a reverence that belied the desperation clawing at him to claim her as his own.

In returning his kiss she proved that she wanted more between them. He would not let her insecurities or her stubbornness stand in the way of their future.

She would be his bride.

Releasing his hold at her waist, now that he knew she wouldn't flee, he placed the palms of his hands on either side of her face. Her skin was as soft as the silk that made up a butterfly's wings. And while she was not so delicate as that, he wanted to show her a gentleness she'd never been shown before.

Their kiss deepened, their tongues danced lazily as they explored this unfamiliar side of each other.

As she lowered her feet back to the carpeted floor they both opened their eyes and stared at each other without words. Was there anything they could say? There was no denying that this was the right thing for them.

That kiss could never be called a mistake.

"Hayd——"

His finger pressed against her parted lips. "Unless you agree to marry me, I think we should part on the highlight of the evening without further questions, assumptions, or denials."

She did not argue. "You're right. I should go home."

Even though he wanted her to stay the night so he could take his time exploring every facet of her, he nodded his agreement. When she thought through their night would she try to convince herself that what they had was still wrong? He didn't think so.

"I'll walk you home."

They gathered her jacket and his hat and cane at the door. Taking her arm, he strolled through the clear night with her. It wasn't overly late by any means; it was only an hour past midnight, in fact, and the streets seemed bustling.

"What are your plans for tomorrow?" he asked.

"You know I have nothing planned for the foreseeable future. And we'll have to wait till September to enjoy any more balls, since the season is officially done."

"I'll call around eleven. We can take a turn around the park."

"That sounds lovely."

Looking around them, he didn't recognize anyone who would note his late-night stroll with Jessica, so he pulled her to a stop and turned her around to face him. He would see her expression as he told her this was only the beginning for them.

"There is nothing you can say to stop me from pursuing this."

"My mind cannot be made up overnight."

He smiled. How could he not when she was admitting there was more than friendship and all she was asking for was time to adjust to the idea? He'd give her some time, but he would not wait overly long.

"You can't string me along like you have so many gentlemen in the *ton*." He ran his forefinger down the side of her jaw, before pulling away and turning them to walk again. Lingering was dangerous, because he wanted to sweep her up in his arms and do things no gentleman should do in public. "I'll not be led on a merry chase, Jez."

"And the more you push this when I'm not ready the more I'll resist. That's simply my nature," she responded.

And didn't he know that to be the truth.

With her hand on his arm, she pulled him to a stop and looked around his shoulder to the darkened streets surrounding them.

"What is it?" he asked as he glanced from face to face that passed them.

She shook her head and walked with him at a hurried pace. "I thought I saw someone."

"Who?" He searched the area but saw no one he knew. There were few people of note out at this hour, only a few familiar faces stumbling home from gaming hells and other less-reputable places. And most were too far into their cups to take note of him and Jez.

Her gaze didn't stop searching their general vicinity, so he kept his eyes to the shadows, looking for what she might have seen.

It was easy to disappear in the night when only gas lamps and the stars illuminated the street. "I thought someone was following us. I was mistaken."

"Who did you think it was?"

"No one. My imagination is playing tricks on my tired mind."

He let her drop the topic for the time being.

"I expect to see you bright and early in the morning, Jez. Your days of hiding yourself from society are long gone."

She gave him a small smile as he walked her up the front stairs of her townhouse.

"Until tomorrow," she said, looking at him expectantly.

Though most of those around on the street weren't worthy of their notice, there were still too many eyes to dare kiss her good night. Instead of leaning forward like he wanted to do, he brought her hands to his mouth and kissed the inside of one of her wrists. Her mouth parted, tempting him to lean in closer and take more than that small liberty. Not tonight. He released her instead of indulging further.

As he strolled toward home he was diligent in watching those around him. Perhaps it was Jez's overactive imagination earlier. But one could never be too safe.

Jessica wasn't sure why she'd indulged his request, but now that she had, she had so many questions she needed answered. And the only way to get the answers she needed was to continue in the game of hearts she was playing with Hayden.

Marrying someone for his fortune was one thing, taking that step with her dearest friend . . . ?

It seemed ludicrous, frightening, but oddly like this was the right direction she'd always been headed in—she just hadn't realized it before now.

She pressed her back against the entrance door and closed her eyes. Fingers curled around the necklace he'd given her, she exhaled a long breath she hadn't realized she'd been holding since she'd closed the door behind her.

What was she doing? What would she ruin in the process of pursuing her feelings . . . her desires?

She turned and pressed her forehead against the cool surface of the door. There was a soft knock on the other side. Her breath caught. Could it be Hayden? Dare she open the door without really knowing? What if she hadn't been mistaken earlier and she had seen Miller? Really, it could have been no more than a passing face on the dark streets of London. But it had struck a familiar chord in her and had drawn her attention so completely that she wanted to trust her instincts.

She waited for another knock at the door. None came. Shaking her head at her own folly, she turned toward the stairs and headed to her bedchamber.

Once she'd removed her dress and the last of her hairpins, she turned down the bedding. When her chamber door pushed open she turned to give Louise instructions for tomorrow. Jessica came to a halt on seeing Hayden standing in the threshold, removing his tall hat and staring at her as if she were the last image he'd behold.

Her voice chose that moment to abandon her. Words weren't needed when he came into her room, tossed his hat to the chaise, and let the snick of the door closing fill the silence.

It was obvious neither knew what to expect of the other, for Hayden stood just inside the door while she stared at him in a kind of wonderment and expectation.

Who should make the next move? What did each expect of the other?

Would they regret any of their actions come morning? She most definitely would, but that didn't stop her from taking a few tentative steps toward him.

She hadn't asked him to leave for one reason alone: they both wanted to know the answer to one conundrum:

What if?

What if this was the right thing for them? On the other hand, they might very well be a terrible fit and the marriage proposal nothing more than a passing joke they could laugh about in their old age.

There were far too many questions she wanted answers to. So many questions neither of them could ask when it seemed they were both beyond speech.

Reaching for his shoulders, she pushed his jacket off. Hayden assisted when the material caught at his elbows. Jacket removed, he caressed his hand down the side of her face before tugging on one of the curls at her temple.

Doubt filled her when she realized that she hadn't a clue what he expected of her tonight. Fallon had simply taken whatever he wanted whether she wanted the same or not. Her expression must have given light to her sudden discomfort, because Hayden's hand dropped away.

Though she missed his touch immediately, she didn't voice her dissatisfaction. She didn't want to ruin the moment.

"I won't ask for more than you are willing to give. Tell me to stay the night, Jess."

"You wouldn't want to—" She couldn't finish her question, but she couldn't help but glance toward the bed.

He moved closer, his body pressed lightly against hers. "I don't want this night to end." His hand was caressing the side of her face again. "Just let me hold you."

She could do no more than surrender to the moment, allowing her desires to supersede everything her mind was telling her not to do because this—whatever *this* was—felt right.

Closing her eyes, she nuzzled the side of her face into his open palm. The warmth surrounded her, dissipating the nerves and reservations she'd felt moments ago.

He bent at the knees and lifted her, carrying her toward the bed. Her arms were around his shoulders, their eyes locked together.

He sat her on the edge of the bed and went about removing his shoes so he could join her. When he faced her again she inched backward on the soft covers, moving toward the mountain of pillows stacked at the headboard. He followed on his knees; each move that brought him closer she countered, until they could go no farther.

"What do you want from me, Hayden?"

"Nothing," he whispered. "Everything. You make me question my every action and my every move. What I do know is that I want you and only you. I've always felt this way."

He covered her lips with his but made no move to claim her in any other way. In fact, their bodies weren't even touching.

As she leaned back, Jessica's weight was perched on her hands enough that she couldn't wrap them around his neck and pull him closer. His kisses were fleeting, gentle. Was he afraid he'd hurt her? Frighten her off now that she'd invited him into her room . . . into her bed?

While she loved the lightness of his touch, she wanted to feel the solid weight of his body crushed against hers. Eventually, his lips parted hers and they tasted each other. This was not simply discovering each other on a new level but devouring something long denied between them.

She nearly laughed with that realization. When her lips tilted, Hayden pulled away. They both opened their eyes.

"And what have I done to make you laugh?"

Her grin turned into a full smile. She couldn't help herself.

Shaking her head, she felt silly telling him but felt she owed him the honesty of her self-revelations. "I realized that I've wanted this for some time."

One eyebrow cocked, Hayden assessed her. "Honestly?"

"Don't ruin a perfect moment by doubting me now."

"I could never doubt you."

"Why did you come back tonight?"

"Need you ask?" His hands clasped one of hers. He massaged her fingertips before exposing the inside of her wrist and pressing his lips there. The feel of his touch, his mouth, had her eyes slipping closed for the briefest moment.

"Hayden . . ." She meant to ask him what he planned, but his name sounded more like a seductive sigh instead.

"Don't say anything. Just let us have tonight without questions or worries of what tomorrow will bring."

And that was exactly what she wanted. Regrets would have to wait for another day. Right now there was only one thing she wanted, and that was Hayden in her bed next to her.

"If I still can't agree to marriage, what will be between us?"

"We'll cross that bridge when we come to it." He tucked her curl behind her ear. "But I believe that if you follow your heart that's not what will happen."

"You're asking for a great deal. Maybe too much if I had enough of my wits about me to snap out of the daze you've put me in."

"I'm asking for your trust, Jessica. I want to stay the night. I want the feel of you in my arms. I don't care about the rest right now."

That was exactly what she wanted, too, so why did she continue to question him? She had accepted him into her private chambers. Into her bed. And at no point did she think she should refuse his company, since that was the last thing she wanted to do.

"I don't want you to leave. My feelings and desires are all jumbled together right now and I confess that it's confusing me."

"Once the heart is involved, I fear there's little sense to be had."

His observation made her smile. Reservations set aside, she took his hand, guiding him up the bed so he could lie behind her. She lay with her back to his chest, her head resting on his curled arm. His free hand found its way to the flat of her stomach and it stirred nervous butterflies and caused a shudder of excitement to course through her veins. She had forgotten that she'd removed her corset and the only material she wore to separate them was a light cambric chemise.

Hayden on the other hand was fully clothed. It was too late to worry about her lack of dress when she lay half-naked and more than willing in his arms to explore something more.

Slowly, she relaxed in his hold. As their breaths evened out she felt herself nodding off into a slumber she wanted no part of. It had been an incredibly long day, and having Hayden here like this, she felt safe and cherished for the first time in a very long time.

Hayden knew the precise moment she fell asleep. He brushed her hair away from her temple and lightly pressed his lips there.

Why he came back to her house had been twofold. He'd worried about who precisely had caught her attention as they'd strolled the streets of London. And then there was the more obvious reason: he couldn't leave her alone tonight when he needed to hold her in his arms. Did she realize that by allowing him to stay she was admitting that there was so much more than friendship between them? She'd admitted as much.

"I love you, Jessica Heyer. I'll not walk away from you, either," he whispered next to her ear, even though she was deep in sleep.

Tomorrow would reveal a host of new realities in their relationship. For the moment, she was wholly his. And he'd be damned if he ever let her go.

After tucking her body tightly against his, he finally fell asleep.

Chapter 13

How ever did the Duke of A—— find himself in-
volved with a certain sect of immoral pleasure
seekers? Considering his standing, and his father
before him, and his father before even him, one
must assume he is hiding something of an illicit
nature.

Dear readers, don't fret over any disparaging
words I may pen of your fair duke; I'm merely spec-
ulating aloud considering the inordinate amount of
time he's spent with a certain dowager countess.

Mayfair Chronicles, July 1846

As Jessica awoke, it was as though hot coals lined her
back. She nearly jumped out of bed before remembering
how her night had ended . . . with Hayden. He'd not only
stayed the night; he also hadn't left before she'd awak-
ened.

While technically nothing untoward had happened, she
was now questioning her judgment. There was a man,
whom she was not married to, in her bed.

The first thing she took note of was that the sun hadn't
yet kissed the horizon, but the sky was lightening outside
and creeping through the windows with dim amber tendrils. She had no way of telling how late or early it was, but
the fact that she was still exhausted told her she couldn't
have slept for more than a few hours.

Needing to relieve the heat at her back, she turned carefully in Hayden's arms so as not to wake him. His hand slid from her stomach to her back as she faced him, the deadweight comforting even though it wasn't easy to maneuver. His eyes were closed, his breathing still deep, so she hadn't disturbed his sleep.

She took the opportunity to study his familiar features in the semi-darkened room. It was like relearning someone you'd always known theoretically but unexpectedly saw in a new light.

His lashes were a few shades darker than his ash-blond hair and were thick enough to make many a woman envious. His brows were heavy and light brown in color, their emphasis on his face adding to his strong character. His hair wasn't coiffed and pomaded as usual, but it was thick and she couldn't stop herself from running her fingers through the disarrayed strands, brushing them back from his chiseled cheekbones.

He'd removed his cravat at some point in the night, and she trailed her eyes down to the deep vee of his shirt. A speckling of hair lay at the center, and she barely caught herself from touching the exposed skin there.

Last night had been no more than an escape from the harsh reality of her world. A beginning for new things. But in her moment of weakness when he'd appeared in her bedchamber she'd been selfish to want him as her own.

It dawned on her in the reality of the morning that she could not ruin his future associations by agreeing to his offer of marriage. She couldn't trap him in an arrangement that had more disadvantages than benefits to him.

While he'd been sincere and she did not doubt his feelings nearly as much as she doubted her own, she would never give cause or reason for him to regret his decision later. Their friendship was and always had been very precious to her. She cherished it above all things. There were too many secrets and lies about her past that once exposed could ruin even that.

He was the bloody Duke of Alsborough. Rightfully, he should be untouchable by the likes of her.

So lost in thought, she hadn't noticed that her explorations had stirred his awareness.

"Is it morning already?" he asked on a whisper.

"Still quite early, I should think."

She focused on his dark eyes. Though she could see the tiredness clouding his gaze, there was something else present that she did not recognize. Or maybe she did. . . .

"About this—" She started to pull away, sliding her hands to her side of the bed, putting necessary distance between them now that she had her wits mostly about her.

He halted her, tightening his hold on her hip so she couldn't escape far. "Don't say anything, Jess. The night is still ours."

"It won't be for much longer. What did you say to Wilson when you came back to the house?"

"Just that we had something left to discuss."

She pressed her forehead to his chest for a moment. She would miss the feeling of being in his arms. But all good things had to come to an end eventually. "You have to leave before my maid arrives."

"If that's what you want."

Releasing her hip, he moved to trace the side of her face. As his thumb parted her lips her eyes slipped shut. She wanted to kiss his hands, his mouth, every part of him, but daren't or else risk doing so much more she might regret. So much more that would make him angry with her when she refused his proposal once again, because she knew she had no choice but to do so. She might not be able to save her reputation, but she'd not drag him down in the process.

"Don't deny that you want more, Jess."

"What I want and what has to be are two very opposing things." It surprised her that she admitted that much. She hated to appear vulnerable to any man, but this was Hayden.

Both his hands cupped her face as he pressed his lips to hers. She was helpless to push him away when that was the last thing she wanted. Instead, she accepted his touch, their tongues searching each other's mouths as though they had all the time in the world.

Hayden's knee rode up between her legs, holding her captive where she lay. She welcomed the press of his body and the feel of his hands on her as he cupped one of her breasts while his other hand tangled deep in her hair.

She'd never been so attuned to anyone in all her life as she was in this moment. She wanted to do the wickedest of things. How far would be too far, though?

Hayden pulled away from their kiss, though he didn't relieve his weight from her. "I can hear you thinking."

How well he knew her. "It's what I do."

"Stop for a moment and just surrender to your desires this once."

His gaze trailed to where his hand held her breast. When his fingers brushed lightly over the distended tip the most delicious sensation fluttered deep in her stomach.

"No thoughts left," she whispered, breathless from the sensual feelings bombarding her as he gently rolled her nipple with exploring fingers. He did it over and over till her breath hitched in her lungs and she was biting her lip to keep from making a sound that might indicate she'd lost control of the situation.

"If you want me to go, you'll have to tell me to stop."

She shook her head, unable to voice her thoughts, especially considering he hadn't ceased with his wicked ministrations. She'd never felt anything so beautiful in all her life. Her body nearly hummed with the excitement, his touch only further setting her body ablaze with a need so deep she was helpless to fight it.

"Tell me to stop," he said again, only much more quietly.

She shook her head. Words were truly lost to her. Instead, she pulled his head closer so she could kiss him deeply.

Why was it that the things you knew were wrong always felt so right? Whatever the reason, she'd have to think on it later, because reason was flooded out by his sure actions.

Braced on one arm, Hayden pushed her knee out and wedged himself in the cradle of her spread thighs. The sure thickness of his desire confined by his trousers rocked against her core.

While they weren't together flesh to flesh, this was certainly the most erotic thing she'd ever done. She should be embarrassed for acting like an untamed wanton . . . so like her namesake—a complete Jezebel.

While one arm kept his weight from crushing her his other hand lowered to her waist, her hip . . . and kept moving lower. Grasping the bottom edge of her chemise, he yanked it higher. The fabric gave as his hand skimmed determinedly over her knee, then her thigh, as he pushed her leg out farther, never stopping the easy rhythm of their bodies rocking together.

His hand caressed her leg, squeezing it at intervals that matched the easy thrust of their bodies coming together over and over again. He pulled the material of her underclothes hard enough that it slit right up to her bare buttocks.

Jessica pulled his shirt free from his trousers, settling her hands on his lower back, feeling the latent strength beneath her fingers as their pelvises continued to grind together, never losing momentum as she brushed her hands lightly over his sides, learning his shape and every dip and contour of his muscled body.

He stilled for a moment, pulled away so far that she nearly voiced a protest, but he only shucked his shirt before returning to her. Holding himself above her on both fists, he gave her time to explore him more intimately. She traced every lean line, running her fingers through the coarse hair that trailed down to where their bodies joined. The leg he'd worked free of her chemise she hitched over his hip and she used it to keep him pressed tightly to her. She didn't want him escaping again.

He lowered his head to her material-clad breasts and pulled gently at one peak with his mouth. The tug of his lips and teeth had her arching off the bed in a silent plea for more.

Could she forget herself for one day and just *be* with Hayden like they were? She didn't want to stop what they were doing; she didn't want him to leave.

"Can we lock ourselves in here all day?" she asked even though it was her house and her rules.

His mouth trailed upward, nibbling a hot path along her neck and biting at her rapidly beating pulse before his lips were tugging lightly at her earlobe, sucking it into his mouth and releasing it. A cool kiss of air brushed over her dampened breast, causing her to shiver with the sudden absence of his ministrations.

"Yes," was his response.

"I want this and nothing else." She ran her hands over his broad shoulders and arms, loving the strength and hardness of his body. No one could ever steal this memory from her.

"I gave you the night. Who's to stop us from taking the day?" He held himself above her and looked into her eyes. He wanted this as much as she wanted him. The intensity of his desire was clear in his gaze, as though it echoed exactly what was in her heart.

She trailed her finger over the side of his face and his hair-roughened jaw. "Make me forget everything except us."

"Your wish is my command."

The promise in his words was emphasized with a thrust of his hardness against her core. Her breath caught in her lungs as he swept his tongue into her mouth and kissed her deeper than he'd ever kissed her before. It was as though she'd broken through the levee that had stopped him from tipping over the edge all this time.

"Are you sure you want to commit to this?"

"Don't ask a question like that at a moment like this."

"I have to," Hayden said.

She pulled him back down to her mouth, unwilling to relinquish him and not willing to hash over the consequences that would be born of their actions.

He was determined to get his way, for he pulled back from the kiss yet again, his smoldering gaze dead serious.

"I need your answer to us, Jessica."

She shook her head and placed her hands on either side of his face.

"I can't answer you right now. I'm sorry."

"Not as sorry as I am." He was off her before she had enough sense to pull him back.

She sat up, pushing her chemise down to cover her exposed knees. "You're angry."

"It doesn't take much to deduce that." He retrieved his shirt from the floor, pulled it over his head, and draped his untied cravat around his neck.

She slid her feet under her, feeling suddenly exposed as she wrapped her arms around her breasts and waist. "I'm sorry."

"You're willing to test our friendship by laying with me, yet you worry about what marrying will do to our friendship?"

"One is permanent and cannot be changed," she argued.

"I love you, Jessica. I have always appreciated and admired every facet of your character. But I never thought you could act so foolish as this."

She stood from the bed, reached for her dressing gown, and slid into the soft silk while he sat on her vanity stool and pulled on his shoes.

"Don't be angry with me."

He looked up at her in the midst of sliding on his second shoe. "I'm not angry; I'm disappointed. You want the impossible from me, Jess, and this time you can't have it. How long am I supposed to wait for you? Surely you know that even I cannot wait forever."

He stood and placed both of his hands on her arms. She knew that he couldn't wait for her forever, but having just heard those words from his mouth left her in such a panic she could do no more than throw her arms around his shoulders and bury her face in his neck. She inhaled the familiar and comforting scent of his cologne as she waited for him to embrace her in return.

His arms eventually came around her, his hands resting at the small of her back. She took comfort in the embrace.

She looked up at him then and found that his expression was torn. He wasn't angry, she realized. That look was all disappointment.

"So much in my life has changed these past few weeks that I can't make a life-changing decision at the drop of a hat."

He pressed his forehead against hers, his thumbs tracing her cheekbones. "I'm done waiting for you when I've waited as long as I have."

"I need time enough to put my affairs in order. To sort out the final details with the estate."

"All excuses." He pulled away from her and slid the back of his hand over her cheek as he looked at her once more. "I'll call on you in a few days. If you don't—"

She pressed her finger to his lips. She didn't want to hear an ultimatum pass his lips; it would ruin their night and what little they had of the morning.

Chapter 14

There comes a time in every writer's life when they feel as though they've found that golden pot at the end of a rainbow. A reliable source has given me some very delicious news. What I'm about to reveal will ruin one person so thoroughly that their subsequent banishment from society is delightfully expected—which we all know has been a personal goal of mine for some years while penning this column. Your fingers must be tingling where you grip the edges of the paper. . . .

Dear readers, what I say here must be spread far and wide, for the Dowager Countess F—— was never who you thought. Perhaps the tension visible in her marriage provides timber to the flames I am about to burn bright enough to shun her from society once and for all. The woman who has been a blight for too many years to count is in fact of questionable parentage.

"Where's the proof?" you say? I'll give you that and so much more. I'll tell you a little story about how she fooled everyone for so long. I warn you, this story is reserved for the mature mind, for the scandalous nature in which the Dowager Countess F—— lived during her most formative years would make even the grand Duchess Georgiana of Devonshire turn in her grave. . . .

Mayfair Chronicles, August 1846

Hayden met Tristan at their club, slapping his paper down on the table in front of his friend as he sat across from him. Tristan sipped his coffee and glanced down at the well-known rag detailing the more scandalous events of the *ton*. Tristan slid it closer to read the headings.

"Bea showed this drivel to me this morning." Tristan pushed the paper away as Hayden rubbed his hand over his face.

"I understand the columnist's desire to exploit your friendship for something it is not."

Hayden didn't bother to correct his friend in that regard, because he wasn't ready to discuss the particulars of his relationship with Jessica with anyone other than Jessica herself.

But he did say, "I wouldn't precisely say that. We've been out every night for the past two weeks. It makes assumptions inevitable. That, however, is not what worries me."

Hayden stirred lemon into his tea. He wasn't thirsty for tea but for revenge. Tea kept his hands busy when all he wanted was to find the persons responsible for the gossip circulating and wring his hands around their necks good and tight.

"The rest, then. What interested me is where they would have come by that information. Jez's father is long dead, as are any other living relatives she had."

"That's all you have to say? You're not even questioning the validity of this information?"

Tristan took a sip of his coffee. "What makes you think I would judge her for her parentage, or lack of? Have you forgotten what my children are in the eyes of the *ton*?"

Hayden gave his friend a scathing look. He'd always been accepting of Tristan's children. Always, and without question. "The Mayfair Chronicler has been writing about us for the better part of a decade. I wouldn't put much stock into what they say, though I'd like to hang them out to dry in front of all those they've exploited for the sake of their column."

"Come now," Tristan drawled. "This writer has been far kinder to us than some of the other more sanctimonious members of society; while some of them have been slaughtered and raked through the coals time and time again, we've practically been lauded."

Hayden drummed his fingers along the table, irritated by his inability to act on this, since he had no one to blame. And Tristan was right for the most part.

"Except for Jez."

"Which makes me think the Chronicler is a woman," Tristan said.

That was something worth investigating further, just as soon as Hayden figured out how to deal with the fallout sure to come from the recent scandal tied to Jessica's name.

"You understand that everyone will turn their backs on Jez permanently for the nonsense printed in the paper. How can you sit across from me as if none of this matters?"

Tristan set his cup down with a clank, the contents spilling over the side and onto the saucer it was set upon. "How little you know me. I've already been to see Jez this morning and we had this very conversation. I've offered any support she needs, Hayden. Now get off your high horse for a moment and think about remedying this instead of worrying about it. You're the one who usually finds a solution in these situations. So I recommend you find one."

Tristan was right; Hayden did need to come up with a plan. The only problem with his idea for salvaging Jessica's reputation was that she didn't seem to want to discuss his offer of marriage.

"Jez has to stop avoiding what's right in front of her," he said.

"We both know that's simply her nature."

His friend couldn't possibly understand what Hayden was referring to, so he drank down his last bit of tea and stood from the table. He needed to see Jessica before this went any further.

"You want to know how we solve this problem? What it all comes down to?"

Tristan looked amused as he leaned back in his chair, elbow hooked over the high back. "And what is your plan?"

"It's bloody well time I took a wife."

Hayden tipped his hat toward his friend, who seemed stunned and confused by the suggestion, for he said nothing—his mouth merely flapped open and closed before settling into a grim line. Hayden spared his friend no further thoughts as he turned and left the club.

There was no better time to confront Jessica than now. The iron was hot, so to speak. They'd be married before the day was through if he could convince her that she had no other choice. Really, she didn't have a choice in the matter. Everything seemed to have gone to hell in a handbasket quite literally overnight.

Jessica had been sitting in the morning parlor for the better part of an hour, too stunned to dress herself, too shocked to even begin her day. She fingered the paper Tristan had brought over earlier in the morning.

The woman who has been a blight for too many years to count is in fact of questionable parentage.

"Shun" was too gentle a word for what was about to happen to her. She'd become the lowest form of human being in everyone's eyes. She would always be unworthy of their notice . . . beneath their notice.

She could say good-bye to the balls and soirees, good-bye to befriending the society ladies to try to make amends with what little of her reputation remained. Now she had *no* reputation, which was far worse. She pressed back into the chair, pulling a blanket around her shoulders, unable to even cry about her predicament. Maybe tears would flow once the shock of the situation wore off.

Most of all, she could say good-bye to this house she wanted nothing more than to stay in, despite its awful, unforgiving memories. How long would it be before Warren came barging in and tossed her and her possessions out into the street? He'd want her out immediately, of course. Could she blame him?

Someone knocked at the front door. The hour was far too early for it to be someone of decency. She cinched the tie at the waist of her scarlet Chinese robe and made her way toward the entrance. She would not allow Warren to evict her from her home before the time they had agreed upon. Well, she hadn't agreed upon any length of time, he'd given her a date, and she'd not let him renege.

Her anger was so palpable that she didn't bother to check her words before shouting, "If that is Mr. Warren, tell him I'll have someone tie his balls off before he can so much as scream for his mother."

Once the door opened, she came to a halt, shocked to find a woman about her age standing on the other side, twisting her fingers together nervously.

Jez knew she looked a dreadful mess; her hair hung in a loose braid that had suffered a fitful night of sleeplessness. She wasn't dressed decently and had planned on greeting Warren in her current state to scare him off until a more respectable hour, which would give her enough time to pull her thoughts together and think of a reason for him not to throw her out. Her world had already crumbled down around her when she had lost the baby; it was unfair of the universe to press its weight upon her as though she were an annoying bug. She would not be so easily squashed.

"And who are you?" Jessica asked.

The woman gave a slight dip of her head and fidgeted nervously with her hands, as though she never imagined she'd be standing on a pariah's front porch.

"Miss Camden, my lady."

Jessica narrowed her eyes, wondering if she was having difficulty placing someone she ought to know. She didn't think they'd met before, but Jessica often overlooked society's belles—though this one looked more like a poor relation in her demure navy-colored dress that covered her from neck to toe.

"Do I know you?" Jessica asked.

"No, you don't. But I know a great deal about you. If you would." The woman motioned with her hand, silently requesting admittance. "I have a private matter to discuss with you."

Intrigued by her boldness, Jessica peered over the woman's shoulder to see if she could identify her by the carriage she arrived in. No such luck there, it was unmarked. Convenient, considering.

"Who sent you?" It felt as though there was some sort of trickery at play.

"I came on my own after learning of your scheme to ruin my cousin's engagement to Mr. Warren."

Jessica unceremoniously yanked the woman through the door, slamming it behind them both as she assessed the woman with a clearer understanding.

"Let's not announce our misdeeds to the world, Miss Camden."

"They were not my misdeeds," she had the audacity to point out.

"Where did you come by this information?"

"Barrington told me what you planned."

"Leo? Why would . . ." It dawned on her then.

Leo, that rascal!

"Come, we'll take this to the parlor."

She led the lady to the comfort of her morning parlor. Most of the curtains were drawn against the morning light—Jessica had felt the need to block out the world after Tristan had left her to her own devices.

"Please excuse the state of the house. I go from loving and hating it alternately. When I hate it, things are broken, so we've left the windows dark today."

When the young woman didn't respond, Jessica motioned with her hand toward the settee. "Sit, please. We may be here awhile." She perched on the very edge, looking uncomfortable as Jez relaxed into the chaise, putting her feet up.

"I only came to ask that you leave my cousin alone."

First Tristan had come by an hour ago to inform Jessica of her secrets being revealed in the *Mayfair Chronicles* and now this woman was here begging a favor. What an odd day Jessica had ahead of her if this was how it was to start, and all before a decent hour.

"She'd be better off without Mr. Warren, you know."

"Whom my cousin should marry is not your decision to make."

She couldn't argue with that, considering she hadn't really elongated her stay in the Fallon household meddling with his impending engagement.

"I'll be saving her from a long life filled with nothing but misery."

"Do we even know the same man who is courting my cousin?" Miss Camden frowned. "He's been nothing but kind."

Did this woman truly have no idea what kind of man

Warren was? Jessica picked her fan up from the table and flicked it open. "They always are in the beginning. It's how they lure in young, biddable brides."

"So it's your cynical nature that led you to the simple decision to change the course of my cousin's life."

"Not precisely, but I'm bored with this conversation." She sat up and leaned closer to her guest. "Now tell me what Leo told you."

"Why should I? Is it not enough that he's told me everything? Shouldn't you feel some sort of regret for your part in this?"

"I feel nothing actually." Which wasn't a lie. She'd felt rather numb since Tristan's visit. She dreaded Hayden's commentary on the whole debacle of her life. Now that her secret was out, Hayden would want her to clarify the dirty details and it bothered her that she would no longer be able to keep the truth from him.

Miss Camden seemed aghast. "Why did you do it?"

"You don't know me, Miss Camden. Why would you care what my reasons are?"

"I suppose I don't need to hear your reasoning. I came because I want reassurance that you'll leave my cousin alone."

Jessica perched her elbows on her knees. While she might not know the woman before her and that she'd befriended Leo sometime in the past few months, Jessica knew Tristan quite well. And Tristan was smitten with someone, and she had a very good idea who that young lady might be.

"I have a suspicion that Lady Charlotte won't need me to persuade her to not marry Mr. Warren." The orange juice mixed with champagne Jessica had had made not ten minutes before Miss Camden's arrival was too tempting not to pick up and drink. Today required getting lost in her cups. "Not only is Mr. Warren a complete bore; he's an imbecile."

Not a lie. How fascinating that she was being so truthful to this woman she didn't really know. When the woman stood, Jessica lowered her fan. Would Miss Camden leave her? Jessica didn't want to be alone, she realized. Alone meant Hayden would be by to press his suit for marriage, which she still wasn't ready for. Or, worse, Warren would visit her and ask her to leave without delay.

"Have I already frightened you off?" Her voice sounded small even to her. Would Miss Camden find her desperate?

"It does me no good to talk to a brick wall."

Hand clutched to her chest, Jessica laughed for some time before finally catching her breath. "Calculating, frosty, degenerate, harlot, charlatan, and player. Those are the typical choice words society showers down on me." She shrugged. "I don't think I've ever been likened to a brick wall."

Miss Camden was making her escape, walking toward the exit. "If you'll excuse me, I have somewhere else to be."

"Don't let me frighten you off," Jessica said, her voice cracking. She hoped her desperation was only noticeable to her. And then she remembered who the woman was. "You are the chaperone Hayden mentioned, so I imagine you are needed back at your duties."

Miss Camden stood proudly tall. "*Was* . . . I *was* the chaperone."

"Oh, my wicked ears hear a story in the making. What has changed your circumstance?"

"Lord Barrington."

Now wasn't this interesting. In all the years Jessica had known Leo, he'd never dared to ruin a lady's reputation.

"So that is what has occupied my friend's attention this past month."

"A ruse, I assure you. One that finally played out in his favor."

"You have nowhere to go, do you?"

"Does it matter?" The woman was suddenly defensive.

"Perhaps I'm offering a bone." Setting her drink on the table, she stood. "Don't you think you should consider nibbling if only to humor me?"

"No." With a stubborn clasp of her hands, the woman stared steadily at Jessica. "I think it most unwise. I only came—"

"To persuade me onto the righteous, more acceptable, and sanctified path I should be following?"

"No. I only wanted you to leave Charlotte alone. She is my closest family—"

"And yet you've been locked out of her life and labeled a harlot."

"I am no harlot." The woman took offense. "And I see my time here is wasted."

She turned on her heel to leave. Jessica couldn't allow that; she was sure Leo would have her head, and when a woman was in similar need to her she felt an empathy that was completely unlike her. She blocked the woman's exit.

"Where will you go?" she asked, studying the woman's tired deep brown eyes.

"Your moral obligation to me is nonexistent. Please, let me by."

Oh, but Jessica didn't want to do that, not at all. "Is it hard to believe that I might have changed my ways?"

"I can't see why." She recognized a kindred spirit in the way the woman crossed her arms, defiant. "Shouldn't you be gloating at your achievement?"

"To do so would mean I indulge in life freely. Sad to say, nothing comes free in life. Especially mine."

"You don't enjoy a certain amount of freedom then?"

Freedom, she nearly scoffed at the idea. "You should

stay. I have so many empty rooms that it would be a shame to not use them before I'm kicked out of my own house."

She thought Miss Camden would turn her down. And she didn't know what to say to sway her decision should their meeting end as abruptly as it had begun.

"Are you feeling remorse for putting me into a destitute situation similar to what you find yourself in?" Miss Camden asked.

"Not at all." Jessica couldn't hold this woman here against her own free will for long, so she stepped aside. "But I'd like the company and I imagine Leo will come looking for you. And if you are not in my possession, I'll not know how to locate you."

"Why should you care?"

"Because Leo is my friend."

And her friends mattered to her a great deal.

There came a time in everyone's life when they only had their friends to lean on. It didn't matter that that had been how most of Jessica's life had played out. What mattered was that she'd found the best of friends to lean on and she'd support them with the same compassion they'd always shown her.

"And he has remained a devoted friend despite what the rags have printed about me."

So had Tristan. She was surprised that she hadn't heard from Hayden yet. Would he believe what was written? Certainly it would dawn on him that Fallon sought divorce on the grounds that she was an imposter. Would Hayden avoid her? More than anything, she had dreaded this secret getting out. How had it gotten out? There were so many questions flying through her head, none of which could be answered.

"Leo's no better than you." The woman was speaking in anger, Jessica knew.

"Prejudice is but one form of ignorance, Miss Camden."
She tapped her fingers along her folded arm impatiently.
"Now, breakfast is being served in one hour. Shall I ask
the cook to prepare two dishes?"

Jessica knew she'd won this woman over when she
placed her reticule on a chair.

"There is a carriage outside waiting for my direction. I
need to tell him that I've found temporary accommodations."

Jessica motioned toward the door. The woman wouldn't
leave her reticule if she didn't plan to stay for breakfast at
the very least.

Releasing the tie that bound her hair, she shook out the
loose braid, hoping she looked more presentable. Though
she supposed she should change. No, she would not dress;
Warren would not stay long when he saw the state she was
in—and that would give her a fighting chance for at least
another day.

Miss Camden might prove useful, too, in keeping Warren from being a complete arse. Warren was unlikely to
keep a civil tongue, even if he knew the former chaperone.
He would no more approve of her guest than of Jessica now
that the scandal rags had muddied both their names. Maybe
if Miss Camden stayed with her it would delay Warren
from removing her from the townhouse for a couple of
days. It was a possibility, and one that she was more than
willing to test.

It was settled. She had a friend to make of this woman
who on first appearance seemed to despise her. Jessica
knew she could win her over.

Chapter 15

*The duke and the dowager countess? Never could I
dream up a more unlikely pair. Or maybe we have
all imagined it and it's always been right before
our eyes, but we've refused to see anything beyond
friendship. All men must be forgiven for their trans-
gressions, for they simply cannot refuse the plump
fruit placed directly in their path without first sam-
pling the fare.*

Mayfair Chronicles, August 1846

"Wilson." Hayden greeted the butler with a nod. "I would
assume your mistress is in."

"She is, Your Grace. Let me show you to the study."

"The study?" Hayden paused to look at the butler.

"Lady Fallon already entertains in the parlor." The man
motioned toward the study.

If Warren had beaten Hayden here, he couldn't allow
the man to stay long.

"Excuse me, Wilson, but I need to see Your Ladyship
immediately. The matter is urgent."

He walked ahead of the butler before any disagreement
could pass the older man's lips and stormed through the
parlor door with the grace of a bull in a museum of artifacts.

"Jez, I thought we could—" He halted mid-step upon
entering the room. "And here I thought Mr. Warren was
paying you a visit."

"Hayden." Jessica came forward, hands out in greeting, which he didn't hesitate to take. "I wasn't expecting you for a few hours—for our walk." She didn't sound convinced that he'd planned to show up at all. "What a delightful surprise to have you here now. Let me introduce you to Miss Camden."

So this was the woman Leo had been spending an inordinate amount of time with. Hayden tipped his hat as the lady stood from the settee. "It's a pleasure to make your acquaintance," he said. "I must apologize for barging in as I did."

"Miss Camden," Jessica said, "this is my dearest friend, the Duke of Alsborough."

"It's a pleasure to make your acquaintance, too," the young woman said with a curtsy. Her eyes were a deep brown, which matched the color of her hair, and her smile was quite charming.

"Where, might I ask, is Leo?"

Miss Camden's brow wrinkled as she took her seat again. "I haven't heard from him since he left the Carletons'." She looked up at Hayden, and the flicker of anger and sadness was nearly enough to floor him. "Please don't tell him I'm here. I'm not ready to see him. And it's only fair for him to suffer a while longer for what he's done."

"You should join us, Hayden," Jessica cut in, pulling him farther into the room. "I might as well explain Miss Camden's presence."

"I didn't intend to intrude," he said, wondering if his and Jessica's conversation would have to wait till Miss Camden left.

Jessica motioned toward the settee with a smile. "Please, I insist you stay for tea."

He didn't argue and took a seat near Miss Camden wondering what trouble the women were brewing.

"I've invited Miss Camden to live here for a while. At

least until Warren decides to exercise his right as the new earl and remove me from my home once and for all."

He raised his brow at Jessica, unsure what he could say in front of this woman and not wanting to give away too many of Jessica's secrets. "About Warren and your time here . . ."

"Tristan came by this morning. I already know." She poured out his tea, sliced a thin piece of lemon, and put it in before handing him the cup. "Miss Camden and I have discussed our strategy going forward. We've both been shunned, you see, and have decided that misery does love company, especially when we seem to get on so well since our initial introduction."

"Warren is likely to shorten the time frame in which you reside here," Hayden felt compelled to remind Jessica. Surely she knew that.

Miss Camden spoke. "We think my presence will keep him from throwing us both out."

He looked between the two ladies; they were unlikely accomplices: Jessica with her verve for life and scandal, Miss Camden with her past as a respectable chaperone. "Mr. Warren will only be kept from this house for a few days, Miss Camden. He's rather like a bear with his scent caught on a beehive full of honey when he wants something."

"While I won't pretend I've not compromised my standing in society, I did always have an amicable relationship with Mr. Warren. I very highly doubt he'll be able to toss us out without feeling great remorse, especially considering he's always been kind to me in the past."

Her attitude toward a man Hayden loathed was somewhat surprising to him. "You think rather highly of him."

"As I said, we had no reason to be on disagreeing terms before now."

Hayden crossed his ankle over his knee and looked

back and forth between Jessica and Miss Camden. He addressed them both. "Your confidence is inspiring."

What he did not like was that having Miss Camden around put a dent in his plans for marriage.

"I've already made arrangements to visit some houses around Town this week. I would love it if you could join us, Hayden," Jessica said confidently.

This was not how he envisioned today unfolding.

"Of course, darling."

"Perfect." Jessica sipped her tea. "Shall we go for our walk?"

He nodded and stood. "It was a pleasure meeting you, Miss Camden. I'm sure we'll see each other again in the coming days."

While Jessica gathered up her shawl he put on his hat. They exited the parlor arm in arm. He was thankful to have her alone for a short while, as there was much to discuss about their future.

"I've always known you were crafty, but this takes on a whole new level of deviousness," he said as they left the house.

"You've known me long enough that this shouldn't surprise you."

"Have you thought about my proposal, Jess?"

"In all honesty, I haven't had time to put much thought into it."

Hayden clenched his jaw. "Are you intentionally insulting me?"

She glanced at him from beneath her hat. "Hayden, you know how much I value our friendship."

He set his mouth to a grim line. "And what of the latest on-dit to hit the paper?"

"It was inevitable," she said unapologetically.

"So you aren't even going to refute it or try to explain how something of this nature found its way into the paper?"

"We both know exactly how this information was leaked. I didn't want to believe it possible, but I did see Miller that night you walked me home. The night . . ."

The night he'd slept over. It was odd, but he had the impression that she was trying to push him away now that the truth was out. Did she think that he could turn his back on her? There wasn't a force in all of nature that could keep him from her side.

She pulled him to a stop before they entered the park and searched his eyes with worry evident in her gaze. "Does the truth bother you?"

"I've seen you in your darkest moment and didn't for one second think I should run from it. There is nothing in this world that could change how I feel about you."

Jessica nibbled on her lip, as she was wont to do.

"I had Miller dispatched from London," Hayden continued, "and you failed to tell me the most important piece of information he held against you. You should have told me before now; I'd never have judged you for it."

"It's not as though I'm going to shout from the rafters of the theater that I'm the product of my father's indiscretion. In fact, it's a very long, convoluted story I'll share with you one day, because it's possible those details will also slip into the rags for further consumption. I'm to be made a laughingstock, it seems."

Hayden clasped one of her hands between his. "You could have been honest with me. You're the one so focused on our friendship, and you couldn't tell me this one piece of information? Just think for a moment about how I felt having to read it in the paper."

"What would you have done with the information, Hayden? Stopped the Mayfair Chronicler? Pressed your suit for marriage?" She pulled her hand from his. "It was my secret, and I would have taken this one to my grave, had I been given the opportunity. But apparently,

I'm not given my fair say in anything that is personal in my life."

Hayden looked around them. Unwanted glances swung their way. This conversation was far too animated and intense to be having outdoors. He'd have had this conversation in her parlor had Miss Camden not been present, but it looked as though the woman was going to be a constant companion to Jessica now. He wasn't sure how he felt about having someone wedged between them. Perhaps that was another reason Jessica had asked the woman to live with her, no matter how temporary the situation might prove to be: not only would they keep Warren at arm's length but him, too.

He'd given her too much space. He should have hied her off to the church and had them married instead of giving her time to think through the changes in their relationship.

"Why are you avoiding answering me?" he asked.

"I can't be occupied with thoughts of fancy, Hayden. You should understand better than everyone that I have to focus on fixing the damage that's been done. I refuse to let society run over me with any additional ammunition."

"You are treating this as a game."

"It *is* a game, Hayden." Her gaze was deadpan serious and brooked no argument. "But they forget that I hold far more secrets than the Mayfair Chronicler."

"You'll lose fighting the battle out with society that way."

There was a flash of defeat in her eyes, and he didn't think he was the one to put it there. And then he realized she just wasn't ready to admit that defeat.

"If there was something I could do to change this, I would." Hayden rubbed his hand along his jaw.

She shook her head as she grabbed his arm so they could continue walking through the park. "Our focus should be on Miss Camden, not us; she's in a far worse situation than me."

"And what are your plans for the young woman?"

"I haven't any plans for her. While she may yet prove to be a buffer to stop Warren from removing me from my house, she'll also play my companion until Leo comes looking for her. It appears they've formed an attachment that could be . . . life lasting."

"Leo mentioned her to me some time ago."

Jessica looked at him with so many questions in her expression. "Why didn't you tell me?"

"It wasn't my place to tell his secrets."

"Point taken," she said, though the tone of her voice indicated that she wasn't happy to be left in the dark on this tidbit of knowledge. "I can't imagine she'll be here more than a week. In fact, Leo is bound to be searching for her as we speak."

A deadline. It might not be Hayden's, but he'd use it to his advantage.

"Then that's all the time I'm giving you, Jess. Once Miss Camden is on her way to wedded bliss with our friend, I'll come for you and I won't take no for an answer. You're not fool enough to choose social ruin over marriage to me."

Jessica merely sighed and took a seat next to him on a bench that faced the Serpentine. She leaned in to say something to him. "When the time comes, we'll discuss my options in greater detail. But I will not muddy your name with the scandal that has flooded into my life. You might think you're invincible now, but once doors start shutting you out . . . I could never forgive myself for putting you in that situation."

He pressed his back against the bench and turned to watch a flock of geese land in the water. "That you even think you have more than one option is laughable at this stage in the game."

"I'm not fooling myself in anything, Hayden. Let me come to terms with this on my own."

He leaned forward with his elbows on his knees and stared out over the water. "Let me ask you this: will you deny all the accusations printed in the *Chronicles*?"

"That you would even ask me that . . ."

"Just answer the question."

"True or not, it cannot be proved."

"How do you know?"

"My parents and Fallon are dead. Warren may have heard it from Fallon's lips, but what proof does the Chronicler have? Miller? His word is hardly credible, considering his gambling debts."

Hayden had every intention of finding Miller and ensuring the weasel of a man said no more. The valet's life, as Hayden had previously promised, was forfeit the moment Miller stepped on English soil.

"How did Fallon ever learn the truth?" Hayden asked.

"My father was easily trusting and too kind for his own good. At least he wasn't stupid enough to commit those truths in writing." She closed her parasol and leaned it against the bench next to her knee. "Thinking Fallon decent, my father told him the truth shortly after we were married. He thought Fallon should know that I was the only child he could beget from his mistress because his wife was barren. My father had hoped our union to be fruitfully blessed with swarms of children to keep me occupied, unlike my other mother. . . ."

Other mother? She must mean stepmother.

"So why did Fallon not petition for divorce years ago?" Something wasn't adding up here.

"I don't know. Maybe he liked tormenting and punishing me for my lies."

"So you always knew who your mother was?"

"I always knew my father loved his mistress as much as he loved his wife. I don't wish to discuss this right now."

"But your father's wife, how did she treat you?"

"She was kind to me, but so often sad. I remember her crying all the time. She truly did think herself barren. And then, when I was around eight, she grew fat with child. I can't recall a time she was happier than in those months."

"But you have no siblings."

Jessica looked away from him and stared after the ducks waddling along the bank at the edge of the water. "No, I haven't. Both she and the babe died after four days of labor."

He took her hand, not caring that they were being watched. "It's a tragedy that your life wasn't happier."

"I had plenty of happy times. My father adored me. His wife was never unkind, though I think she might have resented me at times because she couldn't have children of her own. The only fault my father had was his trusting nature—especially with Fallon."

"I'll not argue that he was a fool in that regard."

"Fallon couldn't divorce me then, because my fortune was doled out annually from a trust my father set up. My father hoped that I could persuade Fallon over time that I could be the perfect wife when really the only thing he cared about was the money going into his entailment."

"Fallon was despicable on so many levels. I wish I could have done more to free you from that marriage."

"There was nothing you could have done, Hayden." She squeezed his hand in return.

"You should have been spared the life you had with Fallon."

"I've never been one to dwell too long on the past."

There was no arguing that Jess was a fighter. That she trudged ahead no matter how dour her situation.

Their time alone was too short for Hayden's liking, but it would be the height of rudeness to leave Miss Camden alone for much longer.

"I have a small dinner party to attend this evening, and would be honored if you joined me."

"And who is hosting this dinner party?"

"The Duke and Duchess of Randall."

Her gaze snapped up and held to his. He could see her working out the particulars of how she could attend one of *their* dinner parties. "They despise me, Hayden. It would be bad form to show up at one of their hosted events, considering how my visit to their ball ended. And especially considering the rumors printed about me."

"There will be a select few attending tonight." He wasn't listening to her protests. "I've already responded that you will be attending with me."

"You make it nigh impossible to say no." Her response was sarcastic, of course.

"I'm glad you think so. I'll be by with the carriage at eight this evening."

She stammered for an excuse, to argue, he wasn't sure which, for she pinched her lips shut for a moment before settling on, "I haven't said yes."

"The Randalls are exactly the types of friends you need. I've known them my whole life, Jess. I wouldn't lead you wrong in this. Besides, I think you'll be pleasantly surprised by how understanding they can be about your situation."

"You think one night of good behavior will convince them of my worth?"

"You are charming when you choose to be."

"Charming?" Jess laughed softly.

He patted her hand. "Choose to be so tonight and you'll win over not only the Randalls but all their guests, too."

Jessica paused a minute on the stairs of her townhouse,

turned around on the spot to take in the sights around them. She let out a heavy sigh as her gaze lingered on the park across the bustling road they'd just crossed and the passersby who didn't acknowledge either of them.

He didn't need to ask why she stalled to take in the scene around them. He knew perfectly well she would miss living here. Even though it had few good memories for her while her husband was alive. Now was not the time to mention that she'd live only just down the street once they married.

"Why are you grinning?" she asked.

He hadn't realized he was doing any such thing. "Was I?"

She took his hand with a shake of her head and pulled him toward the door. "Come in for luncheon before you leave. You'll find Miss Camden as lovely as I do."

He couldn't refuse.

She had him wait in her drawing room while she changed out of her walking dress. Miss Camden joined him before long. The lavender-striped dress she wore was recognizable as something Jessica had once worn.

"You look lovely, Miss Camden."

Miss Camden's gaze dropped and she ran her hand over both sides of her skirts. "Lady Fallon had her maid dress me."

Which told Hayden Miss Camden had few clothes with her and Jess wanted the other woman properly attired—probably in the event that Mr. Warren stopped by.

"She's only magnified your beauty."

Miss Camden poured Hayden a glass of lemonade and gave him a winning smile when she handed it to him.

"I hope you are getting on well," Hayden said.

"I am, thank you." She sat across from him on the yellow brocade settee, her hand resting on the arm as she looked over the grand parlor. "I didn't ever imagine myself in a position quite like this."

"And what position would that be?"

Her gaze slammed into his.

"Shunned," was her blunt answer. "Though I suppose that predicament is my own fault."

"Have you had a chance to speak with Leo since you arrived?"

She nibbled on her lower lip. "I haven't. We did not part on good terms."

"Does Leo know that you're here?"

"This is the last place he would expect to find me. So no, my whereabouts are unknown to him. And I would appreciate it if he didn't know just yet. Being here gives me time to think about everything that's happened over the past few months. Reevaluate things . . ."

Women. It was in their nature to lead men around at their every whim. Wasn't Miss Camden putting Leo in the same position Jessica had put him in delaying an answer on his proposal?

"I never expected to like her, you know?" Miss Camden said.

He could attest to that sentiment. Once you really got to know Jessica, you wondered why you hadn't struck up a friendship earlier. There was a magnetic quality about her personality. While she might seem enigmatic, she was very open and loving with her closest friends.

"I imagine it was a shock. How did you find yourself here of all places, if I might ask?"

"Leo told me what she had planned for my cousin. Once I left the Carletons' I knew I had to confront her."

He raised an eyebrow, interested. "And one goes from confronting Jez to moving in with her, how?"

"That was a funny story. Needless to say, I had little choice on where to go once I had said my piece. She was gracious enough to invite me to stay, since her own situation seems similar to mine."

"You make it sound so dire."

She narrowed her eyes, scrutinizing him. "It most definitely is for a woman."

"There are many things that can change your fate . . . for instance, if you were to send a note to Leo of your whereabouts your situation could change in the blink of an eye."

There was no doubt in Hayden's mind that Leo was probably looking for her right now, but he would not betray Miss Camden's trust, since she was safe staying with Jess at least for the time being.

Miss Camden's chin rose marginally. Her expression said she would not be told otherwise. "I'll face Leo when the time comes, and not a moment sooner."

"I see." Hayden couldn't help but smile. "You wish to make him suffer a little, before you reconcile."

"I do. It's fair punishment for lying to me in the first place."

"I like how you think, Miss Camden. Your nature is as fierce as Jez's. And it doesn't surprise me that you've struck up an easy friendship."

"It has been enlightening."

"I can imagine." He laughed. "I look forward to spending time with you again in the coming days."

Chapter 16

It baffles me that the duke would continue to consort with that woman after all that has been revealed about her origins. Does he have no class? Is he not the man I always thought? Are my readers as disappointed as I am over his friendship with a woman who should be shut out of every home in England?

Mayfair Chronicles, August 1846

Hayden stood on Jez's entrance into the parlor only hours after spending time with her over an extended luncheon. He'd spent the last half hour with Miss Camden discussing the most prominent gossip over the past few weeks and how it had shaped her and Jessica's lives.

When Jessica entered the parlor, she stole his breath away. He stood there speechless at the breathtaking image she made.

Her dress was a deep scarlet satin, not the same one she had worn to her husband's funeral but just as beautiful and bold—so much like her personality. The sleeves barely hugged her shoulders, making the dress drape around her as though it would fall off at any moment. The scooped style highlighted the diamond necklace he'd bought for her. She noticed his gaze was affixed there and her hand touched her throat.

"I hope you don't mind. I still had it in my jewelry box

and thought I might as well wear it. It's the most beautiful thing in my possession right now."

"You look lovelier than ever," he said, completely forgetting that he and Jessica were not alone.

Jessica gave him a shy, if not a little nervous, smile. But when was Jez ever shy about anything?

The bodice of the dress was layered with a fine black lace and delicate beadwork; the skirts were heavily layered, too, and pulled back at the hips so the material draped around her becomingly. Black lace gloves sheathed her arms up above her elbows, and a diamond and pearl bracelet adorned her wrist.

Her hair was up, with a waterfall of curls cascading down the back and skimming the delicate spot between her shoulder blades. Two onyx hairpins crossed at the back. If he pulled them out, would her hair fall around her shoulders?

He put out his arm and had to clear his throat. "Shall we?"

"There's no time like the present."

She didn't sound convinced that this was the best path after today's revelation to the rest of the *ton*. Or at least that was his impression. Her mind, he knew, would be changed before long.

"At least pretend you want to attend this dinner party," he teased.

She raised one eyebrow as she addressed him. "If only I could have better prepared myself for the onslaught to come. I hate to be in a position I can't wiggle myself out of."

Hayden smiled, then turned toward Miss Camden. "It was delightful talking with you. I'm sure we'll see each other on the morrow if Leo hasn't found you and stolen you away by then."

"It was a great pleasure, Your Grace. I look forward to

your company again. Countess, I hope your evening proves fulfilling."

With that he whisked Jessica out of the house.

Once in the carriage, Jez scrutinized him from her leather seat. "What did you discuss with Miss Camden? And why would this evening be *fulfilling*?"

"She told me how exactly she ended up staying with you. And about the various scandals that took place over the past few weeks that had led up to her seeking you out. We also discussed the fact that we were attending the Randalls' dinner soiree. You will soon find out what she meant by *'fulfilling.'*"

"She's very lovely, don't you think?"

"Yes, though I do think someone should tell Leo that she's residing with you."

"Let him sweat it out. I'm surprised he waited as long as he did to tell her his part in the charade with her cousin. One would think that once you were involved with someone so completely as he was you would divulge your secrets far sooner."

"Do you think?" Hayden said drolly. And what of the secrets she'd kept from him? he wanted to ask. "Leo loves you, as well, and to disclose your part in his charade would have felt like a betrayal."

"I'm not so sure about that. It would have been harder, I think, not to tell Miss Camden what he'd agreed to accomplish because I'd asked it of him. He'd been spending so much time with her that I was probably the last thing on his mind. And this coming from the man who refused to participate in said charade."

"You know why I didn't. What's odd is that all your closest friends are willing to do whatever you ask of them, yet they know little of your secrets," he pointed out.

Instead of responding she changed the topic to something more neutral. "Do you know who else will be attending tonight?"

He didn't fail to notice that Jessica was twisting her bracelet around her wrist in a nervous fashion.

"Less than fifteen. A few of the Randalls' closest friends and family members."

"So I don't have to worry about spending the evening with any of Fallon's old friends."

"I wouldn't have accepted the invitation if I thought any of them would be present."

He reached for her and stilled her hand by twining their fingers together in her lap. She stared down where their hands were woven together, flexing her fingers but not pushing him away.

"I don't know what I've done to earn your unerring trust, Hayden." She looked back up to him, her expression sincere. "But thank you for always being here for me."

"I know the real you; that should suffice for an answer." There wasn't much he wouldn't do for her. Surely she knew that.

He scooted over to the bench seat next to her and caressed the backs of his knuckles along her jaw. "Chin up, dearest, you are about to be the most adored guest this evening. This will be the first step in mending your tattered reputation. That I can promise."

"I still don't see how that is possible." She gave him a sad smile. While she might be of the opinion that the Randalls' home was the last place on earth for her, she'd soon wonder why she hadn't gotten to know them better before now. "I hope I don't disappoint you."

"That's simply not possible."

Had they had more time, he'd have taken her in his arms to show her how much she did not disappoint him, but how much he worshiped the very ground she walked upon. But they pulled up to the front of the house and the window coverings were drawn, inviting anyone nearby to spy on them.

Once inside the grand house, they were led to separate rooms to divest themselves of their shawl, hats, and coats. When Jessica entered the ladies' retiring room a hush fell over the guests before Lady Randall came forward to greet her.

Lady Randall took Jessica's hand as one might do with an old friend and faced her toward the room. "The evening is complete with the attendance of the Dowager Countess of Fallon." She leaned in close to Jessica's ear. "I will introduce you to everyone in my small gathering. All the dearest of friends."

And all over the age of fifty, Jessica noted, except for Lady Randall's oldest daughter, who was heavily rounded with child and sitting with her feet up in the middle of the room.

How had Hayden orchestrated this? There was one commonality with the women present: They all had pristine reputations. And sway.

Jessica had only had brief encounters with most of them in the past and introductions weren't necessary, but she knew this was the hostess's way of letting the others know that Jessica was invited into their fold, despite the gossip that had so recently leaked out marring the last shreds of her reputation.

Thanks must be given to Hayden the moment she saw him. Whatever tale he'd spun for Lady Randall to invite Jessica into her small sect of influential friends, this was one blessing she needed more than anything right now. While the older women seemed to have never approved of Jessica and had made no secret of that disapproval, tonight felt different. The proverbial weight lifted from her chest and she breathed easier for it.

Jessica inhaled deeply and offered a genuine smile as she was reintroduced to Lady Chestney, a woman with hair as white as snow, eyes as deep as pitch, and a smile that was more welcoming than anything Jessica had seen on another woman in more years than she cared to count. Women as a general rule had always disliked her. Jessica thought it had more to do with jealousy for the life she led—the way she wanted it, not the way her husband thought it ought to be—than any true animosity against her as a person.

Jessica took the dowager's satin-gloved hand in hers and bowed slightly. "It's a pleasure to see you this evening."

Lady Chestney pulled her hand away and made a clucking noise with her tongue.

"I hadn't realized that you were so shy in public, dearest. Where's that fiery nature of yours when you're facing down us lot of old crones?" was how Lady Chestney greeted Jessica. "Show some brass, lovey. You're young yet, full of verve; don't look and act so downtrodden or your enemies will strike you down while your back is exposed."

Lady Randall cut in, "You'll have to ignore any advice coming from her; her husband went to the grave twenty years ago when he lost a duel to her paramour, then she tossed the love of her life aside to be a spinster."

"Old business that, Penny. Besides, the worst is out. Lady Fallon might as well own up to it and let the catty members of society dither when she goes on as she always has." This was from Lady Pembers; her kind blue eyes were focused on Jessica as she came forward and bowed her head slightly in greeting.

Not knowing what to say, she didn't even try to formulate a coherent response. Who knew that these women were as forward as they were or that they had shunned society at one time—or at least that was the impression Jessica had.

"Say something, dear," said Lady Pembers. "It's nice to meet in an official capacity. We've only had chance encounters previously."

"Say what you're thinking, not what you think ought to be said." This came from Lady Arndell.

"My first thought is that the Duke of Alsborough begged you all of a favor and that is why we find ourselves in one another's company."

Lady Randall laughed low in her belly. "Hayden did no such thing. I've known that man since he was a child and not more than two feet high. It didn't need to be stated why he was bringing you to this particular dinner party, I understood what he needed, and I had promised his mother that I would always be there for him when he needed me."

Jessica narrowed her eyes, her heart suddenly thumping heavily in her chest. Had Hayden mentioned his intentions?

"Please forgive me for not understanding why you said yes. You've always been distant with me in the past."

Lady Chestney patted her on the shoulder. "I knew you had some sass in you left. You can only be kicked down from the good graces of society so many times before you stop caring what any of the simpering prudes think."

"I said yes because Hayden's mother was a childhood friend and when she passed away I knew I had to look out for her only boy. I don't approve of anyone he pines after," Lady Randall said, her eyebrows raised in suspicion. "Especially when the woman in question is married."

If they were able to go back one month, Jessica would deny that charge. But what could she say now when Hayden was constantly pressing his suit for marriage? How many years had he "pined" after her?

She was embarrassed to have not realized it sooner, but Hayden had always been the perfect gentleman, the perfect friend. And had certainly never committed anything untoward. He'd just always been there for her whenever she needed him.

"Don't tell me you didn't realize that man's been trailing you like a mongrel waiting for a scrap to fall behind all these years," Lady Randall's daughter said from where she rested on the sofa.

Jessica's focus was drawn to the younger woman. She was one of those lucky women who glowed and looked radiantly youthful and beautiful with pregnancy. Jessica wondered briefly if she would have ever been so fortunate. Probably not.

"This is my eldest daughter, Lady Miranda Locksley."

Lady Locksley's blonde hair was pinned up in the latest fashion; her face was a little flushed and rounder than what Jessica remembered. The cut of Lady Locksley's gown was in the old Regency style, with an empire waist that accommodated the girth of her belly. "I'd get up, but my ankles are swollen this late in the evening. The only thing that can motivate me to move is the ring of the dinner bell." She lifted up the bottom hem of her cerulean-blue dress, revealing her swollen ankles, feet absent of slippers.

Jessica walked toward Lady Locksley. Something very close to envy snaked through her before she squashed it. She chalked it up to the fact that she'd had very few dealings with other women and couldn't recall a single acquaintance of hers being fat with child in all her life. Aside from her father's wife, that is. And Jessica certainly couldn't recall being around any children besides Tristan's.

"When is the baby due?" She should have bitten her tongue but was still mesmerized by the perfect roundness of Lady Locksley's belly.

"Two more weeks. I've had enough already, so I'd be happy to have the baby sooner."

Lady Randall sat beside her daughter, hand caressing the baby bump. "It'll be any day now. The baby has been very active. A sure sign they are settling in and getting ready to greet the world."

Lady Randall grabbed Jessica's hand and placed it next to hers. Jessica nearly jumped when the heel—or maybe even the elbow—of the baby rocked against her hand. Tears of joy pricked at her eyes, but she blinked them away and her vision focused again on where her hand rested.

So this was what it was like to carry to term. Would she ever do so? Was it even possible? Her heart pounded heavily in her chest as questions she had no answers to flooded her mind.

"I didn't know you had a fondness for babies," Lady Randall said.

Jessica removed her hand and took a step back from Lady Locksley. "Tristan's children call me Aunt. I've known Ronnie—the girl—since she was toddling around and could first cause mischief. Rowan I've known since the day he was born."

"Ah, yes," Lady Pembers said, taking a seat in the circle of chairs. "How could I ever forget those rapscallions? They've all inherited the beautiful Bradley blue eyes."

"That girl of his is growing into a great beauty like her mother."

Jessica whipped her head around to stare at Lady Mallory, the last guest and the only woman to not have said anything to Jessica yet. The woman had aged so flawlessly that it was impossible to tell exactly how old she was. Her husband, the Earl of Mallory, on the other hand, looked to be in his sixth decade—not that a disparate age gap between husband and wife weren't common among the peerage. Regardless, Jessica had never had many dealings with any of the women present and was pleasantly surprised by their welcome. Now Miss Camden's and Hayden's cryptic comments made sense.

"Is this an annual gathering you've invited Alsborough and me to?"

"Alsborough has been attending as far back as I can remember. He used to attend with his mother, before she took ill."

Jessica remembered the duchess. She'd died two years after Jessica had met Hayden. And she'd been one of the most kindhearted and levelheaded people Jessica had ever met. Two traits at the forefront of Hayden's defining character attributes.

"Thank you for including me. It means a great deal to me to be invited anywhere considering . . ."

She didn't need to finish her sentence. Every one of them would have read the rags by now.

"There's no need for thanks," Lady Pembers said. "We were anxious to meet the latest victim of the Mayfair Chronicler. She has had something against you since you arrived in Town, married to Fallon. Though I wouldn't envy any woman married to that lout."

Jessica opened her mouth to ask why they cared, but closed it again, realizing in the nick of time how rude that would be after they'd extended the olive branch, so to speak. "Do you keep track of all those butchered by that writer?"

"Only those that affect the people we love most," Lady Randall said.

"I ignore the Chronicler most of the time." Jessica shrugged her shoulders. "My friends tell me anything interesting, or anything I need to know—and that's good enough for me, because I don't care overly for the gossip of others. Their business is their own." She knew she sounded defensive. So she asked in a calmer tone, "How do you know it's a woman who writes the *Chronicles*?"

"There was so much fun to be had in figuring out who

is behind it all, and how precisely they obtained their information," Lady Locksley piped in.

"Of course we have a good idea of who it might be. We'll not give away her identity any more than that. But you should know, she'll regret her choice in exploiting those around her one day," Lady Randall said.

"Now I'm intrigued," Jessica said. "I don't know how it's possible to attend every event across the country and write about it simultaneously. That means it's more than one person."

"It's one person with a lot of friends to provide her with the details she needs to pen her chronicles," Lady Locksley said with a spark of mischief in her eyes. "As my mother said, it'll work out poorly for her in the end now that she's made more enemies than she has friends to protect her. Especially of late."

"That's most interesting."

Lady Randall stood suddenly and clapped her hands. "It's high time we made our way into the parlor to mingle with the gentlemen."

There were murmurs of agreement as everyone got to their feet. Jessica helped Lady Locksley. "I'll take your arm if you don't mind waddling behind the rest of the company with me."

"It would be my pleasure," Jessica said.

While she walked down the corridor with her newfound friends, Jessica's mind was spinning over any tiny facts she might have about the Chronicler. If these women had figured out who the mysterious person plaguing society for over a decade was, then she, too, could uncover the identity of the person who had been smothering Jessica's name for far too many years.

When the ladies joined the gentlemen in the parlor, everyone stood. Hayden made his way to Jessica's side, bowing to Lady Locksley. "You're looking lovelier each time I see you, Miranda."

Miranda fluttered her fan over her flushed cheeks. "You're saying that to be kind. I know I'm as big as a horse and as chubby as a newborn babe myself."

Hayden smiled and took both ladies' arms to lead them farther into the room. "Miranda here," he said to Jessica, "used to chase me around the garden in the summer when we were no more than three or four."

"You never told me you were so close," Jessica said under her breath. He heard the jealousy tainting her voice.

"We have an annual visit nowadays," Lady Locksley said, obviously sensing she'd ruffled Jessica's feathers.

Hayden smiled, more to himself than his companions. For as long as he'd known Jessica she'd never admitted any jealousy over another woman in his life.

"Miranda married six years ago, and spends most of her time in Scotland with her adoring husband, the Earl of Locksley."

"You're just envious of my castle," Miranda said.

"Drafty old places give me no pleasure. I prefer my modern amenities."

Their banter had Jessica chuckling before long. "You sound like brother and sister."

Hayden and Miranda looked between each other. "I suppose that's the truth," Hayden said with a shrug. "Can I steal Lady Fallon for a moment?"

"Absolutely. My husband is looking anxious to be at my side again. I think sometimes being with child has been harder on him than on me. You'd think I was the most fragile of things, considering how he's gone about."

Despite the girth of her belly and her swollen state, Miranda made it to her husband's side gliding delicately as a horse in dressage.

"You don't talk about her often, you know."

Hayden looked at Jessica. "I hadn't realized that. I suppose now that she's moved so far from London, and rarely comes home now that she's busy making a family of her own, she's just not on my mind as often as she used to be."

"Did you ever harbor feelings for her?"

"Is that more jealousy speaking for you? Twice in one night, Jessica. I don't know if I should be flattered that you're worried about Lady Locksley or annoyed that you might possibly treat every woman in my life like a potential lover or some rot."

"I didn't say that. You were just on such friendly terms that it's hard not to imagine. She's quite beautiful."

"When you've slept in the same bed with someone whose bladder has yet to fully form, romantic attachment is the furthest thing from either person's mind. In a sense, she's more like a sister to me. Does that appease your curiosity about our past?"

Jessica shrugged and looked away. "Maybe."

Hayden only shook his head. "It's the height of rudeness for us to monopolize each other's time."

"I know, but I don't want you to leave me just yet. I wanted to ask you something important."

She looked up at him, her gaze so trusting, so full of life, that the hardest thing for him right now was stopping himself from leaning forward to plant a kiss on her tempting mouth.

"What exactly did you say to Lady Randall to have her invite me to this soiree that is reserved—from all I've witnessed in interaction alone—strictly for her closest friends?"

"You are my closest friend, Jess; why shouldn't you be invited?"

He didn't point out that it was only a matter of time before they wed and then she'd attend these dinners on an annual basis regardless.

She gave him a look that said she didn't believe him. He couldn't tell Jessica what he'd told Lady Randall when he'd called on her this morning.

"Tell me you didn't mention our personal affairs."

He swallowed. *Damn.* She could always read him so well.

"Hayden, tell me you didn't mention the one thing I still haven't decided on."

Who was she kidding? She'd decided; she just hadn't admitted that truth to herself because she was hung up on the fact that they had been friends for so long.

"Are you sure you haven't decided?" was his quick retort. This denial had to stop. And after her display of jealousy, why was she still trying to convince herself that this wasn't the right path for them? "It's inevitable at this stage."

Her gaze narrowed and she slid her arm away from his without drawing notice from those around them. "Is that how you see this playing out?"

"I don't see this playing out any way other than your way. You've always been headstrong and have done exactly what everyone suggested you not do."

Her eyes widened, and he was sure had they not been in a room full of people she was barely acquainted with she'd have crossed her arms over her breasts and given him a glare that could turn a man to ice.

"Headstrong?" was her only response.

He took a deep breath and calmed the ire slowly rising in him. "Can we discuss this later?"

"I don't know. Are you going to tell me what you told Lady Randall to get her to extend an invite to me?"

Hayden looked around them, smiling toward those who glanced their way, all the while looking for an escape. This conversation required privacy. Partition doors across the room were ajar, leading to an adjoining parlor that opened up wide if the party was large enough. He placed his hand at the base of her back and guided her toward that part of the house.

Thankfully, she didn't argue or pull away from him. He'd expected both of the above considering she'd taken insult to his character description of her.

When they were safely on the other side of the room he slid the door shut. Ensconced privately, she crossed her arms over her breasts, just as he'd guessed she'd do earlier, and tapped her foot as she waited for an explanation. She was not going to be happy with his answer.

"The Randalls are influential."

"You don't need to rehash any of the facts I already know. There's something you aren't telling me. How did you secure my invite?"

His gaze narrowed. "Did anyone treat you with contempt? With unkindness?"

"No. They've been remarkably kind considering the fresh rumors surrounding me. Why are you evading my question?"

"Lady Randall was my mother's closest friend. By 'closest' I mean they grew up together, went to school together, married, and lived next door to each other all their lives." Hayden leaned against the back of a tall cushioned chair. "She treats me like one of her children; my mother did the same with Lady Randall's children."

"Is this where you tell me it's all right to divulge our secrets because she's an old family friend?"

"It's nothing like that. I asked her about the article written about you, and how much damage she thought it would do to your reputation."

"Why would you do that, Hayden? My personal affairs are not to be discussed with anyone."

He grabbed her arm to keep her close when she looked liable to storm off back to the party. If she wanted this conversation now, she'd get it. He was so sick of letting her call all the shots. When she said "jump," he always did. When she said "stop," he always waited for her to tell him to go again. He was done playing nice.

"What you don't know about Lady Randall is that she can put word out into society that is false or true—whichever she wishes—and it will come back to the Chronicler as truth and be printed."

"So you're saying not all the gossip is true that is printed?"

"Most of it is. But there are a few people that have enough sway to make the Chronicler retract some of their damning words."

"And you discussed this with Lady Randall why?" Jessica's color was high, her lips pinched in anger. He'd really angered her by discussing her personal affairs with someone who, for all intents and purposes, had always disliked Jessica. He understood that, but dire situations meant drastic actions needed to be taken to correct potential future problems.

And as his wife Jessica would never be shut out of society.

There was probably no way to win this argument. Not that it was about winning.

"I told her that I loved you, Jess. And that I had every intention of marrying you even if you haven't agreed to be my wife yet."

"How dare you discuss our personal affairs with anyone."

He was sick to death of her denial, her bullheadedness.

He grabbed both of her arms with his hands and held her still in front of him. "I tell you I love you and that is your only response?"

She threw her hands in the air, made a noise of frustration, and stormed past him to rejoin the guests in the

other room. Hayden stood there a moment, stunned that
he'd lost the upper hand in this particular argument. Had
he just lost that fight? He smoothed his hand over his vest
and took a few deep breaths to regain his equilibrium.

He hadn't lost that argument, he decided. They'd only
touched the surface of what needed to be put on the table
and examined closer.

Hand brushing through his hair with a heavy sigh, he
shook his head as he, too, joined the rest of the company.

Chapter 17

Lady R—— and the Dowager Countess F—— under the same roof for a social function—never did I think such a thing possible when the animosity between the two parties has always been so clear to this writer.

In more interesting news: Lady A—— was strolling through Hyde Park alone today. I did spy her sitting briefly with a gentleman not unknown to this writer, but certainly too staid to be caught in a muddle with someone of her reputation.

Mayfair Chronicles, August 1846

The last thing Jessica would admit to Hayden was just how much she'd enjoyed the dinner party. What right did he think he had to confirm her secrets, to reveal things about herself and her private affairs to people she didn't know?

It was easy to say no when Hayden asked if they could go to his house for a game of crib, so the carriage continued along the road toward her townhouse.

"You're still angry with me, aren't you?" he asked.

"Disappointed," she corrected. "Considering how long we've known each other, I assumed you would never brandish my secrets about to gain a reputation more desirable to you. Are you trying to change how society views me for your own purposes?"

"Don't be ridiculous, Jess. I'm merely trying to preserve your reputation so that you needn't worry about being shunned by every household. I know that it would kill a small part of you to have every door shut against you."

"Is that because as your wife you'll never want me on the wrong side of society's good graces?"

"No, because no one will ever humiliate or turn their backs on my closest friends. I'll not stand for it as your friend, nor will I stand for it as your husband."

The carriage rocked over the bumpy road and came to a halt in front of her townhouse. She knew Hayden was waiting for an invite, but she had a guest to think about, too. What would Miss Camden think of his joining her so late in the evening?

Jessica nearly snorted to herself. Miss Camden was no innocent flower. There was no danger in Hayden staying for a glass of wine so they could finish their conversation.

"It bothers you that this is one of the few things to ever truly be out of your control, doesn't it?"

He looked at her for a spell before answering. "If I can control the situation, you know I will."

"Is that what you would do with a disobedient wife? Control her to a more desirable state of what you consider acceptable?"

"That you would even ask me that—let alone consider it—is appalling on so many levels."

She opened the door in a huff and looked over her shoulder at Hayden as she descended. "Are you joining me, then?"

"And what of your guest?"

"It's past midnight. Miss Camden will be fast asleep. Besides, it's only for a drink so we can finish this discussion."

Hayden didn't hesitate to follow. Wilson opened the

door with a bow. "Good evening, my lady. Your Grace. Shall I have the kitchen prepare a tray?"

"Don't bother, Wilson. We'll only share a bottle of wine. Send everyone to bed for the evening; you needn't wait up for us."

Wilson bowed again. "Then I bid you a good night, my lady. Your Grace."

Jessica grabbed Hayden's hand and pulled him toward the study. The room was very masculine, with dark wood lining the walls, rich burgundy Turkish rugs covering the hardwood floors, and furniture that was overly large, ostentatious in its display of power.

The room overlooked the street and the exterior gas-lights illuminated it enough to see the large green velvet sofa and leather chairs that could seat two that filled the center of the room. It had been her husband's favorite room. And while she'd always hated coming in here when he was alive, it just so happened to be the only room fully stocked with an array of spirits and half a dozen selections of wine. Retiring to the study meant she didn't have to disturb the staff. The darkness faded to an amber glow as she turned on a gas lamp and lit a few candles on the sideboard that held various decanters.

"I understand your desire to continue our discussion, but I'll not be lectured on my actions earlier this evening."

She handed a wineglass to Hayden and settled into the corner of the sofa. She kicked off her slippers and tucked her feet under her with a heavy sigh.

"It was too damp and cool to sit out in the carriage for any length of time." As if to demonstrate that the chill had really set in under her skin, she rubbed at the goose bumps that rose on her arms beneath the scalloped sleeves of her dress. "While I'm disappointed that you discussed very private matters with the duchess, I understand why you did it. I think it was important for you to know that.

But this does not give you the right to brandish my secrets where you see fit in the future."

"You would have done the same if our positions were reversed."

"There's the difference between you and I. I've been taken advantage of enough that I prefer to play dirty when my enemies try to maim those I love. If it was you, I would have stopped at nothing but social ruin for the other person, and believe you me, I have every intention of sorting out who the Chronicler is. The column will soon be a thing of the past."

Hayden hitched up his trousers at the knees and sat next to her on the sofa. She dipped toward him. He clinked their glasses together. "The only person I've ever played dirty for is you, Jess. We're more alike than you realize."

She took a sip at the same time as him. She licked the residue from her lips and stared at her friend. Could she really marry him? Be his wife? He was a duke, he would need children, and the likelihood of her being able to provide them was grim. She and Hayden would be a good match in some ways, terrible in others.

The smashing of glass had both their heads snapping toward the entrance of the room.

"The servants?" Hayden asked quietly.

Jessica pushed herself up from the sofa without answering. Setting her glass quietly on the side table, she slid her feet back into her slippers and headed toward the door.

Hayden halted her. "Let me investigate the source of the noise."

"As you indicated it's probably just one of my servants."

He held both of her arms as he faced her, crouching to her level so they were face-to-face. "You sent them to bed. So that's not a chance I'm willing to take. Stay here, Jess."

The firmness of his voice brooked no argument. She pinched her lips shut, knowing that it was futile to argue.

She never took orders well. Her husband had thrived on control and then became enraged every time he realized he could never rule her every action. No man would cow her again. No man would tell her what was best for her, how she should act, and what she should do with her life. Not even Hayden. And it was better for him to learn that now.

She let him leave the room in search of the broken glass and followed not two minutes later. She knew the lay of the house better than he did and could navigate it flawlessly in the dark of night.

Gracefully, and on tiptoes, she headed in the direction of the main parlor. Wherever the sound had come from, it was close, so she checked the immediate rooms first.

If the noise were caused from one of the servants, there would be a light on somewhere close by. Everything was just as dark as when she'd entered the house. She walked around the room to check the windows to make sure they were locked.

There was nothing out of order.

A stumble and grunt in the direction of the stairs drew her gaze toward the open door. Could that be Hayden? She walked over to the door to peer down the dark hall. There was no one nearby, but the soft shush of someone walking above her head could be heard through the floorboards. She'd only been home a short while, so the servants could be shutting up the house before they headed for their own beds.

She chose to turn toward the smaller green parlor, her heart racing now that her imagination had run wild with possibilities of where the sound had come from.

As she walked the perimeter of the room her foot crunched on the result of the broken glass. She lifted her foot away from the shards and focused on the broken window banging in the breeze.

The sheer curtains billowed out ominously, tauntingly, as she realized the worst of her imagination was indeed the truth. Someone who didn't belong here was prowling around her house. She clicked the window shut and turned over the latch to lock it again. The window would have to be boarded for the night and fixed first thing in the morning.

Where in the world was Hayden? She couldn't hear any walking above her now. The only sounds to be heard were of the wind whistling through the broken windowpane and a clock ticking the seconds out in the hallway.

As she walked past the fireplace she picked up the iron poker; the slide of the metal across the marble was an eerily sharp slice of sound in the almost silent house. Jessica held her breath as she tiptoed more carefully from the room, poker raised and ready to strike if someone popped out into her path. She held it aloft, not pointed, so that anyone she crossed would meet the hard side of the iron instrument, not the deadly poker end.

When she was in the hallway and mounting the bottom of the stairs a thud rang in her ears from one of the bedrooms. It sounded as though a shelf had fallen . . . or a person. She swallowed against the nervousness building inside her. Her right arm shook from holding the weight of the poker. Well, maybe not from the weight but from fear.

But she'd not admit to the latter when she might need to face her intruder head-on.

Closer to the top of the landing, there were more crashes of furniture, heavy objects hitting the floor and walls—or people tumbling into heavy objects—all coming from within her husband's old room.

"My lady." Miss Camden came rushing out of her room and toward her; she wore her dressing robe. Her hair was covered under a mobcap. When she reached for Jessica's arms she said, "I thought at first the noise was my imagination, but it's only intensified. I was frightened to come out of my room, but I saw you come up the stairs."

"Go back to bed. Hayden is in there, and has everything under control," she lied. She didn't know if Hayden fared well or not. Oh, God, she hoped he did. She couldn't bear the thought of something terrible happening to him.

"I couldn't possibly leave you here."

Jessica grasped Miss Camden's sleeve, ready to plead and beg for her to let well enough alone. At least until Jessica knew who had come into her house and for what reason. "Everything will be fine. Please, go back to bed. I'll find you later."

Miss Camden very reluctantly left Jessica standing outside her husband's bedchamber door. She looked at Jessica for a spell from across the upper-floor landing before shutting her door.

It was a miracle that the servants hadn't heard the commotion and come running upstairs.

No candles or lights had been lit upstairs, so it was quite dark when Jessica stepped away from the stairs and closer to the thumps and heavy groans as the fight ensued beyond the double doors. She had avoided crossing them while her husband was alive and even now that he was dead. She hated that room; it had been certain torture to enter it under any circumstance in the past. And so she never willingly crossed that threshold.

Putting her shoulders back, she pressed forward with the poker still in her right hand as she turned up the latch of the door. She heard a great roar as the door slammed open and she entered the scene of a fight unlike any she'd ever witnessed before. Though it was dark, she could see a smear of blood across Hayden's forehead. The man he had by the throat seemed limp and lifeless in Hayden's hold.

The clang of the iron poker hitting the floor rang through the room like a church bell brought up short as she ran forward to pry Hayden's hands loose from the intruder.

She shouldn't have run forward with Hayden's angry state, as he was liable to strike out unintentionally, but when she realized that he held Miller in a death grip she snapped to attention and acted before thinking. She could not stand idly by and watch Hayden kill another man in cold blood. No matter that the man deserved death and by her own hand if she could accomplish it—not that she would.

"Hayden. Don't do this," she begged of him as her fingers curled around his wrists and yanked until her nails cut half-moons into his skin.

He finally looked at her with his dangerous gaze and dropped Miller so suddenly that she stumbled back. Hayden caught her before she tumbled to the floor and crushed her body along the length of his. Finger tracing featherlight along her temple, he brushed away the curls that had fallen from her chignon.

"I didn't mean to frighten you."

"You didn't."

She brushed her hand over his forehead where a smear of blood had dried from a knock he'd taken to the head. He hissed in a breath when her fingers brushed against the goose egg hidden in his hairline just above his temple. It looked like it hurt a great deal and she'd have to take care of it right away.

She pressed the balls of her feet to the floor as she gained her balance, which was difficult to do in his iron grip. "You could never scare me when I know you'll never hurt me."

There was a moment when she didn't want to let him go. She'd give in to any of his demands so long as he never left her and always made her feel safe. She shook away her silly, sentimental thoughts.

Had she not invited him in . . .

Who knew what could have happened? Who knew what Miller's purpose was?

A groan emitted from the victim of Hayden's fury behind Jessica. She flinched in Hayden's arms. She couldn't help her revulsion at Miller's presence. She daren't turn around just yet or she might commit to some unspeakable act she might later regret, whether or not he was deserving of her wrath.

"I can't face that man right now." Her voice was small. Frightened.

"You don't have to."

"I don't think it's a good idea to leave you with him, either, but I want to know why he's snooping around my home." She gazed around the darkened room, feeling bile rise in her throat even knowing her husband wouldn't come in at any moment. "I want to know what he was looking for in here."

"I already planned on getting that out of him."

Hand once more brushing her hair back from her forehead, Hayden let her go completely and kissed her on the cheek. "He's waking. Go before he's aware of his surroundings."

She nodded, trusting Hayden to deal with Miller when she could barely look at him without wanting to lose her dinner. He reminded her so completely of her husband, the vileness swept right off him and wrapped around her throat, choking away her desire to fight for what she believed was right. How could such a slimy, lowly man ever make her feel so worthless?

He should be nothing to her.

Yet.

Yet . . .

He *was* something. Something vile. Like a snake slithering and flicking out its tongue evilly, he made her skin crawl whenever he was near. Maybe it was the poison he'd fed her in the end that had enlightened her to his true nature as a human being. Maybe it was the way he watched her with a cruelness in his eyes just as her husband had done. Whatever instinct was telling her that this man was to be avoided at all costs, she trusted it without question.

She backed away from Hayden and edged toward the door, never letting her eyes leave Hayden's.

Once in the hallway, she pressed her back against the paneled wall and took a steadying breath. Her hand covered her mouth when she felt she'd be ill, but the sensation passed. She closed her eyes and focused on the moment and not on everything that Miller represented and the violation she felt on him stealing into the house. She breathed steadily through her desires to run and managed to stay right where she was, knowing she needed to hear what Miller had to say.

She flinched as Hayden's hand smacked the perpetrator, the sound of flesh on flesh raising bile in her throat again. She slid down the wall, holding her hand over her mouth, the other clutched against her stomach.

"Wake up, man. I've a few questions for you before you're thrown out in the gutter for the trash you are. Before your debtors happen upon you." Another slap of Hayden's hand against wet—bloody, she imagined—skin.

She bit the insides of her cheeks hard, hating the violence she allowed to rise in Hayden. Hating herself more for thinking herself safe from Miller and living so complacently, vulnerably, when she'd vowed never to do so again.

"Speak, man."

A mumble of incoherent sentences was all that followed, then the disgusting sound of Miller spitting on the floor before he laughed, the sound broken and garbled as he wheezed in a lungful of air. Had Hayden broken the man's ribs? Why did violence have to follow her everywhere? Was there something about her that incited anger in men?

She pinched her eyes shut tighter, hoping it would get the image of the valet bloody and beaten out of her head. It helped long enough for her to hear Hayden smack him hard across the face again and demand, "Answer me," in a much firmer, more dangerous voice than previously.

"I'm fetching my master's things."

"There is nothing left of your master. Personal effects were cleaned out after his funeral."

The man coughed and hacked up something from his throat before he spat again. Jessica swallowed back her disgust, unable to move, not wanting to listen, yet needing to know everything said between the two.

Hayden had told her about his run-in with Miller before, and while she didn't know exactly what was said then, she knew she could never leave him alone with Miller in fear he'd have another man's blood on his hands. And all because of her.

This wasn't right, but she didn't have the strength to stand up, to stop it; she didn't have the might to move from where she crouched against the wall like some defenseless victim.

"What were you hoping to find?" Hayden asked in a voice that tolerated no argument. She was sure Hayden would hit Miller again if he didn't answer this time.

"Nothing is ever truly lost forever," Miller responded, cryptic as usual.

She grasped on to that thread of familiar that made her hate this man so much and steeled her nerves bit by bit.

"You had a chance to start new, and you pissed it away the moment you stepped off that boat."

"It doesn't matter. I'm doing as my master wishes. Nothing more, nothing less. I made a promise, Duke, but of course you're too good to understand exactly what that means for a man like me."

When Hayden chuckled the sound slithered uncomfortably down Jessica's spine. She took full responsibility for turning him into the man she suddenly didn't recognize. Would he have ever acted so lowly, gotten his hands so dirty, if not for her?

She had to stop running away from this. What choice did she have but to face her fears once and for all?

She took her first calming breath since the whole ordeal with Miller had started, and pushed herself higher on the wall. Almost to her feet, she took another steadying breath and braced her stomach for the sight she was about to witness. She would face whatever came tonight. She was done shying away from the violence that had made up her marriage. Miller could not hurt her. He was helpless, really, without Fallon's backing.

She turned away from the wall and toward the entrance of the room. Hayden looked up. She could tell he was surprised to see her, but he did not ask her to leave again. Perhaps he knew she needed to see this with her own eyes, witness his truth with her own ears.

Hayden grasped the lapels of Miller's jacket and nearly lifted the man from the floor, since he was limp in Hayden's arms and by all appearances too weak to stand on his own.

"What did you hope to find?" Hayden asked.

"What right have you to it? His Lordship always thought your friendship resembling that of a consort to the slut that was supposed to be his wife. Was it your bastard in her womb? Did you fuck the wench the nights you took her from this house?"

Hayden shook Miller once. Twice. The valet only cackled before coughing up another mouthful of blood and spat that on the floor next to Hayden's boot. "Guard your tongue, man, or I'll cut it out and damn your reasons for stealing into the house like a thief."

Jessica walked farther into the room. Her fear receded with every step as she neared her foe. She felt no desire to act out against him; she just wanted to know his reasons for coming into her home.

What did he think to find?

"Why are you here, Miller?" Her voice was strong, not feeble and weak as she feared it might be.

"The bitch comes to your side quickly, Duke. You should be proud to have tamed the redheaded witch. She's fierce but tamable with the right amount of force, my lordship always said. He brought her to heel in a fashion."

"I'll not warn you again about guarding your tongue."

There must have been something in her look that stalled Hayden, for he raised his hand to strike the man again but dropped his fist as she approached and knelt next to Miller, where he hung precariously from Hayden's grip.

She was unafraid for the first time in so many years that tears pricked at her eyes. Miller wasn't deserving of them, though, and she shed none as they first blurred her vision before drying.

"Let him go."

"Jess."

She pressed her hand to Hayden's strong jaw. "Trust me."

Before long, Hayden released him. Miller thumped to the floor with a heavy thud.

"Does it bother you that I'm not afraid of you, Miller?" she asked, her voice calm and even.

"Don't matter much to me. I'm not here for you, now, am I?"

"What good can you do for Fallon when he's cold and lonely in his grave?"

"It's his lasting wish that I destroy your life."

The energy such hatred must take. That was probably what had killed her husband in the end. The poison he spewed out finally ate him up from the inside out.

"And how do you think to accomplish that? You've already ensured that I'm a laughingstock, the brunt of all jokes among the peerage. You've stolen the child from my womb in fear that it was not Fallon's." It surprised her how level her voice was when she'd avoided this man like the plague all the years he'd been in her husband's service. "Look at you, Miller. You're no better kept than a street urchin; you smell like one, too. Do you believe Fallon wanted you to live your life as a wastrel, running from those you are indebted to?"

"It never mattered what I wanted. I promised to bring you down so far that you were forced into a poorhouse."

"What a fool you are." She was proud that the disdain was sharp in her comment. Superior and without remorse, which was good for what she was about to tell him.

"Do you want to know one of my secrets, Miller?"

He looked at her with suspicion. Rightfully, he should. For he would not be long for this world if he didn't run fast and far away from London.

"You don't have any secrets. His Lordship told me everything." He brought his hand up to his mouth and wiped the sleeve of his stained coat across his mouth.

"Oh, but I do have secrets. Many that you wouldn't have been privy to once I tossed you out of this house."

His hatred was so palpable that it should have caused her resolve and determination to falter. But it didn't. Once the truth had been revealed about Miller and her husband's involvement to destroy the baby in her womb, she'd had one important task to complete before the estate funds were completely out of her control.

"I purchased your gambling debts, you see."

Hayden stepped closer, his legs brushing the bottom of her skirts.

"I used the money that would have been your annual wage toward your chits. I paid top dollar for some of them, and do you know what I did once I held them all in my hands? I gave them all away. Do you want to know who I gave them to?"

She didn't think it possible for his color to fade to a wan, deathly yellow, but it did just that.

"Mr. Enders was ever thankful." She paused, letting the name linger in the air between them. That had been the one thing she had control over once she'd learned the full depth of Miller's betrayal and contribution in poisoning her. "You do know a Mr. Enders, do you not?"

She leaned in close to Miller's ear to whisper what Mr. Enders had told her when she'd given him the chits with one request, one favor. Miller's smell was fetid—as though he'd forgotten to bathe after sleeping in a gutter. It was as though death already clung to him.

While she'd been frightened of this man for so long, he no longer had any power to hurt her. His time was limited, and she'd not feel sorry about it when all she had to do was look outside to the roses in the garden to be reminded of what he'd done to her.

"He said to tell you . . . he's coming for you and will catch you the moment he has word that you've crossed over into London. What he'll do to you will make anything we can do amateurish. I suggest you run."

She stood away from Miller and smoothed out the front of her dress. It was a nervous habit of hers, but she deserved the solace it brought for finally standing up to this man.

She placed her hand on Hayden's arm when he made a move to grab the worthless man by his dirty cravat again. "Let him leave on his own."

Hayden looked at her, eyes narrowed. It was obvious he didn't trust her judgment in this. She wasn't sure she trusted her own judgment right now.

On unsteady legs Miller stumbled toward the door. Not only did he look and smell like hell; it also appeared like he hadn't eaten well since he'd been discharged from his position, for his clothes hung on his skeletal form like secondhand rags.

Jessica didn't want to be anywhere near the culprit, so she stepped closer to Hayden. Despite her bravado, she wished his protective arms were wrapped around her. Hayden must have sensed her unease, for he stepped between her and Miller. The anxiety she felt was almost overwhelming.

Once Miller left the room, she'd breathed a sigh of relief.

Hayden turned, his expression questioning, worried, as he pulled her into his arms and hugged her close. She pressed her cheek to his chest and listened to the steady, soothing rhythm of his heart.

"Don't move from here," he said, releasing her. "I'm going to make sure he leaves and that he doesn't have a way back into the house."

She numbly nodded and hugged her arms around herself. Was it really over? Would she see Miller again after tonight? There were so many questions flitting across her mind. First she must assure Miss Camden that all was restored to normal order. What would Miss Camden think if she saw Hayden's bleeding head? Jessica resolved to visit her guest as she waited for Hayden to rid the house of the abomination who was Miller.

Chapter 18

Oh, the things I dig up with regularity are sometimes alarming. What does that say about the depravity of society? The things I'm about to reveal this time are about a certain Lady H——. The most revered Lady H——. She has been caught in so compromising a position that word has washed the streets of London that her husband up and left her on her return from her country stay. I always knew she'd be caught in the act, as it were, before long. Her young Mr. T—— will probably go on to boast about his conquest, though I don't see the attraction. . . .

Mayfair Chronicles, August 1846

When Hayden came back into the house, Jessica was waiting for him on the stairs that led to the second floor. He stretched out his hand to brush his knuckles down the side of her face. She did the same, hating the evidence of his injury.

"Let's get this cleaned up." She couldn't express how sorry she was for the cut on his head.

"The blood will wash away. I'm fine, Jess. Tell me you're well, too."

She nodded her head as she hugged him close. "I was so worried you'd be hurt. And then, when I couldn't face Miller a moment longer . . ."

"Never feel bad about that. I had the situation under

control, and I wouldn't dare chance letting that man any-where near you."

"Thank you. For everything."

"Come, we should adjourn to a more comfortable set-ting."

He tried to lead her to the parlor on the main floor, but she needed to go up to her husband's room. There was something there she needed to find. And aside from that, there was a bathing chamber where she could clean the blood from Hayden's brow.

"There's something I overlooked." She took his hand in hers and pulled him up the rest of the stairs and back into Fallon's private chambers.

She left Hayden standing in the spacious sitting area so she could wet some linen towels to wash away the blood smeared across his head. When she came out of the bath-ing chamber Hayden was sitting on the edge of a chair. He sat forward with his elbows on his knees and his head resting in his hands as though he held up the whole weight of the world. In some aspects he did hold up parts of her world.

She stood in front of him and dabbed away the blood. For such a small wound, it had bled a great deal. Once the evidence of the cut was washed away, she brushed her fingers through his hair and pulled him gently against her belly.

"Why did you let him leave?" Hayden asked.

"Because he had made his point in breaking into my home. What was I going to do, Hayden?" She searched his eyes, feeling great remorse for everything that had hap-pened. Her hand reached out to touch the laceration high on his head. "I couldn't watch you beat him to a pulp. I would rather have his blood on my hands, not yours."

He captured her hands and pulled her down to sit across his lap. "We could have called the bobbies. They'd have at least put him somewhere secure for the evening. I can't have you living here, fearing for your life, having to check every sound that's out of order."

"Believe it or not, I can take care of myself, Hayden."

"I never thought you couldn't." His hands brushed over her back, catching on the beaded buttons of her gown. "And I would rather Miller's death was on my hands than yours, Jess. Why didn't you tell me you purchased up his chits?"

"I needed leverage in the event that he tried to expose any of my other secrets." She closed her eyes and snuggled closer to Hayden. The comfort she took in his presence was astounding.

Worried. Defenseless. Agitated. Angry. Those were par for the course for her life with Fallon. But Fallon was no more. He couldn't hurt her and he certainly couldn't lay another finger on her for the rest of her life. She wrapped her arms tighter around Hayden's waist, not ready to give up the sensation of perfect peace she felt in his embrace.

As soon as she let go would he barrage her with more questions about Miller, about marriage, about her future? She just wanted to tune it all out and think only of herself for a moment.

"I'll always be worried about your welfare, Jess. I swear I lay awake at night wondering what trouble you've found yourself in when you're not with me and how I can dig you out. That's my constant state of mind where you're concerned."

She pulled away from their hug and met his steady gaze. "I haven't caused any lasting trouble for years. So your worry is for naught."

"Had Fallon not been the man he was, you'd have continued to swindle away his false fortune in gambling hells and God knows where else. You caused quite the stir in the first few years as the Countess of Fallon. Do you blame me for worrying?"

"How many years ago was it that I last stepped into a gaming hell?" She smiled, finding amusement in his worry.

"Not long enough."

"Dare I remind you?"

"Not right now. I'm just glad I found Miller tonight before you did."

She was, too, but didn't say so. What would have happened had she happened upon Miller first? He could have treated her like he'd witnessed her husband treating her far too many times to count. He might have raised a hand against her. He could have hurt her and done far worse a crime than he'd already committed.

Her fingers curled tighter around Hayden's arms. None of it deserved thought. She had to put it behind her. What she should be worried about was that she'd placed a death sentence on Miller's head. It wouldn't be long before his seedy *friends* caught up with him.

Hayden's hand never stopped stroking the length of her back. The soothing sensation put her in a trance-like state.

She pulled away from him even though it was the last thing she wanted to do. The night had been trying and her emotions were all over the place. She had tears so close to falling that even her voice wavered as she tried to say something.

"Jess."

When he reached for her she shook her head, evading his touch. One comforting embrace was all it would take to have those tears let loose.

She shook her head and put her hand between them to stall his forward momentum. The press of him against her nearly melted her back into his arms, but she resisted the temptation.

"Will you help me find what Miller was looking for? There has to be something here. Letters, a journal, some indication he was sharing personal information with someone outside of this household. It would have to be small enough that I overlooked it." She bit her lip as she glanced around the room looking for anything that might not belong. "This is probably the only time in my life I'll ever admit to wanting to know my husband better. But there you have it."

Hayden walked over to a candelabrum and lit the wicks with a match from the box atop the fireplace. "Do you recall him keeping a book close at hand?"

"No. I avoided him at all costs. I can honestly say I know little about Fallon other than the fact that he hated me with a conviction so pure I screamed inside whenever he was near. Surely a form of self-preservation for the punishments he doled out."

Hayden handed her a candle, caressing her arm as he did so. "Jess . . ."

She held up her free hand to stall his commentary. "Don't say anything. I'm out of sorts tonight from all that has happened. I just want to find what Miller was looking for and destroy it if it's something he was going to hand over to the highest bidder for gossip fodder."

When Hayden carried on to search the small desk near the window she asked herself where she would hide something of value. Her journals, while plentiful, were full of drivel for the most part but encapsulated the odd thought on her feelings, her situation, her most personal of theories about the life she lived.

Those she kept in plain view. They were safer there, when others thought you had nothing to hide.

In plain view.

She stood up tall, turned slowly to look around the room.

It made sense.

There was a built-in shelf that housed a number of books. She walked toward it, pulling down titles that seemed typical Fallon reading, and tossed them aside. Book upon book hit the floor. All the titles were for learning matters. Agriculture, mathematics, economics, there were even a few books written in Greek. She shook her head at that. As a good Eton student he'd learned the languages men learn, as though he'd ever have use for them. Her search grew more frantic as she hit the third shelf, not finding anything out of the ordinary.

Hayden was by her side, assisting in her hunt as she threw more and more books to the floor. Though he didn't know what she was looking for, he caught what she tossed aside and gave it a second look-through.

"There was nothing in the desk, not even a blank sheet of paper," he informed her, looking at the titles before them, reading each inscription with the tip of his finger as though he'd find something out of place where she hadn't. Or perhaps he had trouble focusing on what was written without his reading glasses.

"This room was cleaned of personal effects right after his death. I didn't sack Miller for two days. Any number of things could have been removed. But if there was something important, or damning against me, Miller should have had ample time to collect it before he was forced from the house."

Nothing was ever out of place with her husband. He had a method that was too careful to find idiosyncrasies.

"There has to be something here, Hayden. I know it with every fiber of my being." She pulled the last book from the lower shelf and looked at the mess she'd created around them. The books lay open and bent at odd angles, a macabre scene if you were the type to preserve books as though all were precious.

Jessica walked around the room. Looking in every
nook and cranny, even sliding her hands beneath the mattress to see if something was tucked away out of sight. If
Miller hadn't found it when he'd abetted her husband's
cruelness for more than twenty years how did she expect
to find it? Perhaps if there was something written about
her he kept it in another room.

"Here, hold this a moment." She pressed the candle-
stick in Hayden's hand.

Fingers pressed to her temples, she closed her eyes and
thought for a moment about exactly what she should be
looking for. Her mind kept coming back to letters or a
journal. What else could her husband possibly have that
would be damning against her? Now she wasn't so sure
that her father hadn't written to the earl at some point to
confess all.

Fallon spent a great deal of time in his study. But he
also used the small sitting room on the main level whenever his friends called at the house. She picked up her
skirts as she charged out of the room, descending the stairs
at a dangerous speed, nearly flying off the bottom landing
before reeling around and dashing down the long corridor
to the room at the back of the house.

There was a small desk in her husband's favorite parlor
that he often sat at. He never sat on the settee across from
his guests; he felt less important if he treated someone as
an equal.

Hayden tore into the room seconds after her, the flame
on the candle swaying as he came to a sudden halt. "What
is it?" he asked, urgency coloring his voice, as she stood in
the middle of the semi-dark room looking around her—
trying to recall a moment in time so long ago. There was
something here. Something in plain view that had always
been here.

She raised one finger to shush her friend before he

could ask any questions. The information she sought was on the tip of her memory.

"I recalled a time when I came in here when Fallon was entertaining Lady Montant." Jessica perched herself on the edge of the cushioned chair behind the desk. "He sat right here."

"Was he doing something out of the ordinary?"

"Not precisely. They hushed their conversation the moment I entered the room." She closed her eyes and thought back to that day. What vital piece of information was she missing? What had she forgotten?

Then she knew. Laugher tainted with bitterness bubbled out of her. How had she been so blind? So stupid?

It was Lady Montant all this time.

And in plain view all these years. Lady Montant had been the very source of Jessica's misery when she'd first moved to London.

"Miller didn't know what he was looking for; he only knew that there had to be letters."

She pulled the drawers open on the desk. There was nothing out of the ordinary, ink and nibs for pens, paper. She slipped her fingers toward the back to see if anything was hidden.

"How is that possible? The only person aside from Fallon that knew your true parentage was your father. And he's been dead for a long time."

She shook her head, still amazed that she hadn't put two and two together.

"It's not impossible. Fallon was always so close to Lady Montant. It comes back to his connection with the Malverns. Their friendship goes back a great many years before I ever stepped into the picture."

"What information do you think Lady Montant was privy to?"

"I think she knew everything about my past all along.

There is no doubt in my mind that there were letters that revealed my secrets to the Mayfair Chronicler. Notes that my husband would have provided directly as he slowly built a reputation against me. He wasn't going to go to the grave softly. In fact, Fallon wouldn't have taken chances with me living life as I saw fit once he was gone. He'd have wanted to ensure that I would be shunned. That everyone would ostracize me. It all makes perfect sense now."

Her finger found a hidden lip at the back of the drawer. She tried to pull it forward, but the drawer was jammed half-shut with a piece of wood on the side.

"I should have put two and two together." She tapped her lip in thought. "I don't believe there was intimacy between them. But there was always an exchange of letters. I remember a few occasions when I happened upon them in this room and Lady Montant had folded letters tied together in neat little stacks."

She wiggled the drawer, but it didn't pull any farther out.

Hayden stepped behind her, set the candle on the table, and grasped the knob on the drawer tight before yanking it hard, snapping the wood holding it place. The back end of the drawer fell into her lap, laden with folded papers.

Her breath caught in her lungs as she ran her hand over the dried lavender tucked beneath the twine tying the stack of letters together.

"Well, I'll be damned," Hayden said.

It amazed her that Miller hadn't known what he was looking for. One would think that her husband's right-hand man would know every intimate detail, including the fact that Fallon took tea with Lady Montant every other week on Tuesday afternoons to discuss matters that remained a mystery to Jessica. Or perhaps Miller knew what he was looking for but hadn't known where to find it.

It was obvious to her now that the Malvern parties were just one of the places her husband could gather information with Lady Montant about the *ton's* deviants. But to what end?

"What do you suppose is written in them?" she asked as she leaned against the back of the chair and tilted her head up to look at Hayden.

He put his hand on her shoulder and squeezed it.

"There is only one way to find out."

There were six stacks. She placed them on top of the desk and tossed the drawer to the floor. Pulling the twine free on one set of letters, she opened the first envelope. It was addressed on the outside to her husband; the date on the top right corner was "December the seventh, eighteen hundred and forty."

Darling,

Of all days, why did you choose my birthday to bring that whore of yours to the Capris'? The sight of her sets my teeth on edge, for I know we'll have little time to talk alone with her nearby. I had news to give you yesterday, but since you neglected my company I'll have to explain my newest conquest within these pages. The bloody deviant Hallsburg has finally been won over. You said I couldn't do it, for he hadn't the disposition or inclination to look to the fairer sex. I won't tell you how I won his affections; you'd be disgusted, and then I'd also have to relive the depravity I've stooped to for the information we so sought.

Jessica couldn't read much further than that, for she knew what would be contained in the lengthy letter she held in her hands. She handed the letter to Hayden; he could read it if he wished, but she didn't think he'd care for the gossip contained within, either. It appeared Lady Montant was sleeping with the enemy, or with many of them—anyone who could give her information. Did that mean Jessica's husband had done the same? She covered her mouth with a shaky hand. She thought she might be sick.

"What are we supposed to do with this information?" she asked not of Hayden but of herself. She wanted to burn the letters, but in all likelihood the pages contained everything that Lady Montant knew of her.

She could only imagine the worst of what was detailed in the letters. The people this woman had been responsible for ruining. Lady Montant had to be exposed for who she was, but how?

"Your friend the duchess knows who the Chronicler is." Jessica pushed away from the desk, needing to be away from the deceit, the wrongness, of what was contained in the pages set before her. "She said as much earlier this evening."

Hayden tossed the parchment onto the desk without a second thought. He didn't seem any more impressed than she by the contents.

"Is there anything else I should know about the dinner party?"

She waved his concern away with a shake of her head. "You know everything. I think I need to pay a visit to Lady Montant tomorrow."

"I don't think that wise, Jess. What can you possibly say to her that won't backfire? She'll resort to lies if you push her too far. She's always been a difficult woman. It's no wonder her husband never comes to London; he wants to avoid her at all costs, for she's nothing but poisonous."

"It's possible I can use these"—Jessica waved her hand in the direction of the evidence—"against her."

"That's a dangerous game to be playing. You could set yourself up for a bigger fall."

"She can't continue to do this, Hayden. I can't allow it now that I know what she's done, and what my husband did to so many people that were undeserving of their trust."

"I'll only agree to you confronting her if you let me go with you."

She gave Hayden a hard, thoughtful look. "I doubt she'll be reasonable if I show up with the Duke of Alsborough on my arm. No, this is something I have to do myself."

He pulled her into his arms, giving her the kind of comfort she was growing to crave. "What about Lady Randall? She has enough clout to protect you should things not turn out the way you hope."

Jessica was exhausted by the turn of events tonight. "It's been a long night. We can discuss this in the morning."

"I don't want to leave you alone."

"I'd feel safer and sleep better if you took a guest room."

He pulled her into his arms and hugged her so tightly that a rush of air left her lungs. "You don't even have to ask. I'll stay as long as you need me to."

She pressed her cheek to his chest and closed her eyes as tiredness swept her over the edge. "Thank you." She turned them toward the stairs. "The guest room is always made up, so we won't have to wake anyone."

"I can stay with you in your room."

She thought about it, but Hayden would only provide a distraction to her thoughts. She needed to plan the coming days carefully, so she gave him her full honesty. "Not tonight. I have so much information rolling around in my head that I need to sort through it on my own. I won't be able to do that if you're there with me."

"I don't know if I should take that as a compliment or not."

She looked up at him. "It's a great compliment to your ability to distract me." She motioned toward the room he was to occupy, the very same room he'd dressed for the masked ball in.

Hayden kissed her forehead as he left her at her bedchamber door. "I'll see you first thing in the morning."

Chapter 19

I cannot believe that Lord B—— has stooped as low as he has to find a bride. It is one thing to find solace in the arms of another to keep you warm on a cold winter night, and quite another to publicly ruin her and then make a mockery of your name while you pursue the object of your desire without remorse for your actions. What storm has taken the ton's most eligible bachelors and made them into lovesick fools this season?

Mayfair Chronicles, August 1846

How much longer would Jessica attempt to lead him on a merry chase for her hand in marriage? Hayden hitched up his trousers at the knees before taking a seat in Jessica's private sitting room in her boudoir.

While the events with Miller had happened three days past, Hayden had not been far from Jessica's company. They hadn't discussed how she would confront Lady Montant, but his patience was wearing thin for her hand in marriage.

Jessica's maid was putting in some final touches with her hair, pinning the curls at the perfect angle.

Hayden looked around at the cozy setting of furniture in her boudoir. "Did you ever wonder what your husband thought of you entertaining in here?"

"You're forgetting that he was ancient, and used to an

older set of rules than what we grew up with." She was looking at Hayden's image in the mirror. "His mother would have entertained her guests in here, men and women."

Hayden shrugged as he leaned back into the cushioned seating, pulled his reading glasses from his pocket, and opened up the paper. The housekeeper had brought up a tea service for him while he read the morning's news.

Yes, definitely the usual routine before Jessica's husband had died. Was she up to something? Was she avoiding everything that had happened of late? He'd always been a patient man and pushing Jessica was like pushing a cart without a horse. Besides, he took a certain amount of enjoyment that oftentimes it frustrated her when he waited for her to come around. It was like a battle of the wits.

He turned the page in the paper, perhaps with a little more gusto than usual.

Jessica inviting him up here upon his arrival meant she was far from ready to do anything; she was not a morning person and their morning stroll was often after eleven—or what Jessica referred to as a decent hour. It amazed and irritated him that they could so easily fall into their old routine when all he wanted was answers to the questions about Lady Montant and, more important, his and Jessica's future.

"It still surprises me he didn't have us tossed out," Hayden said.

"He wouldn't dare toss a duke out of his house." She spritzed some perfume at the vee of her neck. Whatever was in her perfume, there was an underscore so subtle, yet so desirable, it reminded him of lilacs blooming in May. He turned another page in the paper, not really reading anything, as his thoughts were focused on Jessica.

"I was young when I took my father's place, hardly the man I've grown into. I'm sure Fallon thought little of me."

Hayden's mother, bless her sweet soul, had made sure

he turned into a man worthy of a dukedom. While his father had played a pivotal role in raising him, it was his mother who understood him completely, had smoothed Hayden's feathers when a spat brewed between him and his father because of their so often differing opinions. Looking back, Hayden knew there was really no substance to their arguments. He would be mindful of that when he had children.

Hayden gazed at Jessica from above the rim of his glasses. She spun around from the mirror to face him.

"But always so respectable." She scrutinized him with narrowed eyes. "I'm not sure how we even ended up friends."

He smiled and didn't respond. It was no surprise to him that they'd ended up exactly as they were. Maybe he'd fallen in love with her the first time they'd met. He'd have been too young to know what had hit him even if it had the subtlety of a sack full of bricks hitting him in the head back then, but he knew it well now.

"It's perfect, Louise," Jessica said to her maid, touching the curls pinned neatly in place at the back of her head. "Leave us a moment, please."

The maid paused, as did Hayden with one brow quirked.

The maid didn't argue, but she didn't look happy to be leaving them alone, either.

Once she left, Hayden asked, "Is there any particular reason you wanted a word in private?"

He removed his glasses, folded them, and tucked them in his pocket. When Jessica sat next to him on the settee, he noticed her eyes were rimmed subtly with red, as though she hadn't slept well the previous night. He was not so crass as to mention it, but he noted it. And then he wondered how many nights she hadn't slept.

"I wanted to discuss the night—the night we . . ." She nibbled at her lip, looking for the right words.

It was endearing that she couldn't finish her sentence, if it was the night he was thinking of and not the night Miller had ruined. . . .

"Since when have you ever been nervous around me?" he asked.

"Since you started kissing me," she snapped, her back ramrod straight in defense.

He put his paper down so he could cup her chin between his finger and thumb. He leaned in close, their breaths dancing and swirling together. The only thing that mattered was that she didn't pull away. Or at least that was what he told himself.

Had he finally won her over? Would she agree to marriage? Would she agree to him dealing with Miller once and for all? God, how he regretted not dealing with that man months ago.

"Is that why you wanted me alone? To kiss you some more? To prove that there is something deeper that needs to be explored more thoroughly between us?"

There was no one to interrupt them in her room, not even Mr. Warren, should he stop by the house. Hayden was more than happy to pick up where they'd left off, so long as she had the answer he wanted to hear.

"Even you can't expect me to jump at my first offer of marriage."

She pulled away from him.

That was not the answer he wanted to hear.

"Stop playing with me, Jess. It's one thing to lead the men of the *ton* on in one of your games. You're walking between the fine threads of our friendship as though snapping a strand wouldn't hurt either of us."

"I wouldn't dare, Hayden. How little you know me to say something so harsh. I merely wanted to tell you that I'm still thinking of your proposition."

He turned to her and momentarily stopped pacing the

small room. " 'Proposition' sounds so dirty. Call it what it is."

"Fine. I am thinking on your *proposal*. I needed time and space away from you to sort out my feelings."

He came toward her, pulled her to her feet and flush along the front of his body in a crushing embrace. "Time for what? To find excuses? To deny what we are together? Or do you want time alone to deal with Lady Montant on your own?"

He kissed her hard, demanding more than she was willing to give. Waiting for her to surrender if even for one single, fleeting moment.

He didn't want to hear her arguments; he was sick to death of them. Maybe that was selfish, but he wanted her to himself once and for all.

And by God, he'd have her in the end so long as she stopped wavering with her answer.

While her lips did not part for his immediately, her body did yield. The soft, supple feel of her had him hardening beneath his trousers in less time than he could catch his breath. And he wasn't feeling polite enough to hide exactly what she did to him. If that made him a cad, then so be it.

"I'm sick to death of denying this. Us," he said.

Grip tightening on her arms, he kissed her again. He wanted her to forget herself. To completely let go and trust him to catch her before she ever fell. While she might trust him implicitly with some things, he knew there were still parts of her that she kept hidden even from him.

When their kiss ended, she tucked her head against his heart and wrapped her arms around his waist. Her breaths came at an even and steady pace.

"You confuse me."

"I'm still the man you have been friends with all these years. Still the man you have always confided in."

She pulled away hesitantly, as though she couldn't bear to release him. "I have a number of errands I need to run today. Alone."

"After the night Miller was here—"

She pressed her finger against his lips, stalling his words. "Don't speak of it," she whispered.

He wanted to nip the tip of her finger, but it felt inappropriate considering the direction of their conversation.

He did so anyway. She laughed before pulling her hand away, shaking her head all the while.

"What is it you have to do that's so important you are putting us off? I should accompany you everywhere; at least until Miller washes up."

"I will not be cosseted." She walked over to her vanity and riffled through a small box of hairpins until she found what she searched for.

Hayden came up behind her, took the dainty silver piece from her fingers, and buried it in the twisted braid at the back of her head. She made eye contact with him in the mirror. He rubbed his hands over the length of her arms.

"What are we doing?"

He shrugged, never breaking eye contact with her as he pushed the edge of her dress away from her shoulder so he could plant delicate kisses over the freckles there. Eyes half-closed, she leaned back against him as he showered more kisses along her nape, not stopping till he was at her ear.

He pulled away to whisper, "Do you want me to stop?"

When she didn't respond, he slid one hand around to her midriff, his hand flat over her abdomen as he pulled her fully along the length of his body.

His eyes closed for the briefest moment, and when he opened them again Jessica's head was thrown back on his shoulder with a look of pure ecstasy shaping her expression. If a simple touch and a few light kisses had the ability to put that expression on her face, how would she view him in the throes of passion?

Soon, he told himself. Soon she'd be his fully, because there was no way in hell after all that had happened between them that he'd let her slip through his fingers. She was already his. She could deny their mutual attraction all she wanted, but in the end she'd come to the realization that she was fighting him for no good reason. It was a losing battle, that.

Placing his hands on both of her thighs, he gathered up her heavy skirts. She didn't protest. In fact, her look grew darker with need as he revealed her underthings inch by agonizing inch.

"We shouldn't be doing this." Her lips were damp from nibbling on them, and tinged red like the skin of an apple.

He held the material with one hand and snaked his finger around her upper thigh until his hand cupped her womanhood through the cambric and lace drawers she wore. "Then tell me to stop."

Her lips parted revealing the neat rows of teeth top and bottom. He rubbed her cloth-clad mons, hard and slow.

"I can't," she said breathlessly.

"Then I won't stop till you come apart in my arms. Till you lose control of yourself for me to see."

Placing her hand atop his, she pressed him harder into her core, stopping his motions. Her eyes closed, as though she warred with her decision to let him continue or to pull him away and stop their intimacy altogether.

Her breath was jagged as she inhaled, causing her breasts to quiver where they were plumped up at the front of her dress. Pulling his other hand away from where it held up her dress, he slid it over her bodice so he could cup her breast. He squeezed it, wishing she were naked so he could feel her in his hands.

It appeared that her desires had won over her better judgment. Her gaze broke away from his as she turned her head to the side to catch his lips with hers. He kissed her deeply as his hand found the slit in her drawers so he could touch that sensitive part of her without impediment. Her tongue rolled around his, tasting and searching his mouth with an intensity that had them both panting.

His fingers slid through the moisture of her desire, making him groan into her mouth. He had a sudden urge to taste her there but didn't want to stop the sweet friction of rubbing her, making her wetter as his forefinger found its way into her sheath while the palm of his hand rubbed her clitoris.

As he yanked the front of her dress down on one side the top part of her breast plumped out and the very edge of her pink areola was revealed. He shoved his hand under the delicate material, tearing it at the side. He needed to touch her; that was all there was to it. He needed to taste her. Fuck her. God, he had never wanted her more than he did now. But he knew if he did more, broke away from their kiss, removed his hand, reality would flow back in and she'd stop his exploration.

This was no different from the night he'd slept in her bed, only this time he was willing to take her without the piece of paper saying she was pledged solely to him. No, he'd bind her another way if he must, because it was about bloody time the Duke of Alsborough took a bride.

"God, I need you," he said just before twining his tongue around hers once again.

Jessica turned slightly in his arms, his hand losing hold on her breast as she faced him.

Lips swollen, breasts rising fast and furious in her heightened state of pleasure, she pressed one hand against the vanity behind her and used the other to pull up the material of her dress where it had fallen back down around her thighs.

That was all the invitation Hayden needed to reach for the bodice of her dress and tear down the front enough that he could free her breasts. He sucked the tip of her right nipple into his mouth, bringing it to a firm peak, then released it with a sucking pop before tasting the other.

When he reached for her center this time, he thrust two fingers into her core so hard and fast with the aid of her juices that she made a sound between a moan and a cry that had his cock throbbing in his trousers.

"I want you."

Rear end precariously balanced on the edge of her vanity, Jessica's hands tangled in his hair and she pulled him away from her breasts so that she could look him in the eye.

Her gaze was fierce with lust and desire. Determined.

He knew then that she wanted this as badly as he needed her. What kind of man would that make him, taking her before they were properly wed? Did that matter? He would make her his bride in the end no matter the outcome of today.

If he could think rationally he would definitely pull away—as that would be the right thing to do. But his ardor was high, his need overbearing, and he'd wanted her for more years than he could count at the moment.

He lowered his head enough that he could lick the tips of her breasts and tongue the tight peaks.

"I want to tell you to stop, but I can't," she said breathlessly.

"Then don't. Tell me you need this as much as I." She released her hold on his hair so he could kiss and suck at her other breast. "Tell me to take you once and for all."

Instead of answering him, she lowered her hands between them and pulled at the buttons of his trousers. Her hand easily found its way inside and slid along the smooth length of his cock. He nearly fell over from the pleasure her touch gave him. Her hand curled around the base and slid over the length. Hayden had to grip the edges of her vanity to hold still.

"Make me yours, Hayden." Her voice was just above a whisper and hoarse with desire.

He needed no more urging than that. "Wrap your legs around my hips." She did so, poising his cock at the right spot to enter her. He felt compelled to remind her, "We can't go back from this."

"Just show me how good this can feel. I need you, Hayden."

The head of his cock brushed against her damp center, ready, so ready to claim her as his own once and for all. He took his time, sliding the head around the opening, slickening her entrance, and drawing little whimpers from her lips as he did so.

Jessica locked her ankles around the base of his back and pulled him in close enough to lodge the head of his penis inside her. He groaned and held still, wanting to call the shots in this. He'd waited nearly ten years for this moment; Jessica could wait a few minutes as he indulged in the very feel of her hot, wet sheath clasping his cock. He pressed his forehead to hers. "You feel so damn good."

"Then take me."

"Only if you beg." He wasn't sure why he'd asked her to do that, but it might stem from the fact that she'd done nothing but deny her attraction to him since he'd confessed his true feelings. He did want her to beg.

The tips of her fingers combed through his hair. Her touch was firm but gentle, needy but reserved. "I want to feel you all the way inside me."

And then she gave him what he wanted, her little moans and whimpers enough to propel him forward and finally take her. Her thighs were tight around his hips as her arms wrapped around his shoulders and held him tight against her body.

The rhythm of their pelvises joining was steady, hard. He rubbed the bud of her desire and swallowed her pleasure noises with hard kisses. Her sheath clenched around his cock, pulling him so close to the edge that he rubbed her clitoris harder, faster, till she came undone in his arms, nearly screaming out her pleasure as he pumped harder into her, finding his own end.

They stayed that way for some time, her legs wrapped around his hips, his legs growing shaky holding her against the vanity as his manhood throbbed inside of her, not nearly sated enough. Could he ever get enough of Jessica? He doubted it. He still couldn't believe this had happened.

He pulled slowly out of her; otherwise he'd want to go again. And again, until he was truly sated. That could keep them in here a week at the very least.

"The next time we do this, I'm undressing you to the buff."

Jessica blushed. "We should get dressed. Louise could come back at any moment."

"She won't. You sent her away and she'll not be back until you ring for her."

He lifted her from the vanity and pushed her skirts down. Her breasts were pink from his ministrations, the nipples still firm and jutting above the edge of the dress. And just with that view alone, he knew he needed her again. She didn't hide her knowledge of that, either, for her gaze dropped to his groin area and when she looked at him one eyebrow was raised. She halfheartedly fixed her dress, pulling the material up as much as she could. Her areolas still kissed the air, begging for his touch.

"I'll have to assist you in donning another dress." He brushed his finger over that tempting pink flesh revealed by her décolletage. "We'll have a hard time explaining the tatters of this dress to your maid."

"I don't for one second believe they thought we were innocently conducting ourselves in here."

"Think about what this means, Jess."

She spun around, giving him her back. "Release the buttons. And I know what I've done. Give me some time to sort through this, Hayden. Good God, I barely know what to say to you and I feel like a stammering fool."

He turned her about, hands cupping her arms with a firm grip so she couldn't look away. He'd make her face this head-on and he would no longer allow her to hide from him. "You've never been a stammering fool. Look at me, Jess. I'm the same person you've always known. And while this changes things between us, changes how we move forward, you weren't denying the desire between us any more than I was."

"I believe any normal woman would hide her face in shame for what we've just done outside the sanctity of marriage."

"You're the most brilliant, adoring, kind, and annoyingly perfect woman I've ever known. And there's no shame in what happened between us. It was inevitable after that first kiss. Surely you see that for the truth."

"I do." Her gaze dropped and she spun around again. "Please undo the buttons. I want to find something else to wear before anyone chances upon us."

He didn't argue again that no one would dare interrupt them. Instead he assisted her in removing the bodice and skirts. She kept all her underclothes on, which was fine, considering he hadn't damaged them, just the stitching on her outer clothes. And this was the perfect way to show her what he'd brought along.

* * *

After he helped with the buttons on the new dress Hayden reached into his breast pocket and pulled free a folded piece of paper and handed it over to her.

"What is it?" she asked, genuinely curious.

"Open it."

She did just that. The parchment detailed both their names delicately scrolled one atop the other.

What could she say to such an offer? The only thing she could do was walk away. She set the paper on her vanity in front of her and ran her fingers over their names inked on the paper. She'd never imagined what their names would look like side by side. Never imagined herself as the Duchess of Alsborough . . . but here it was, written out in bald evidence of what could and should be.

"When did you do this?"

"After I spent the night," was his easy answer.

Had he really known they were meant to marry after one night in each other's arms?

"But I haven't given you my answer yet."

"It doesn't change the facts, Jess. I know how I feel about you. About us. Marriage would work between us."

Up till now her back had been to him. When she faced him after a long silence she still couldn't find the words she needed to express how this made her feel. Her thoughts had been scattered the last few days as she sent letters back and forth with the Duchess of Randall on how precisely they would deal with the Mayfair Chronicler. The only thing Jessica had told the older woman was that she knew who the Chronicler was and wanted to find a way to stop the *Chronicles* from being printed going forward. She'd not once mentioned the damning letters she had in her possession written in Lady Montant's hand and addressed to Jessica's late husband.

Now Hayden was here with a special license for them to marry in the midst of everything.

She searched his eyes. What other reason did she have for denying him this? "Did you know I'd eventually say yes? Or were you hopeful I would come around to your way of thinking?"

When his hand cupped the side of her face and his other rested lightly upon her hip as he searched her gaze . . . it was as though he willed her to see just how he'd always seen her. Just how he'd always felt about her, yet she'd been too blind to truly see.

"Why did you wait so long to tell me anything?" she asked.

"What purpose would it have served when you never saw me in the same light?"

"Was our friendship a lie?"

"Never think that. Your friendship has been the one I value above all others, Jess. We were and will remain friends first. And we'll be partners in marriage."

"I don't understand why I didn't see it before."

"Take a leap of faith with me in this."

There was shouting coming from the main level of the house that drew both their attention to her bedchamber door where a knock reverberated.

"Come," she called.

Wilson came through the door, short of breath, hand extended with an envelope between his fingers.

"This came urgently for His Grace."

Jessica raised one eyebrow inquisitively as she plucked the parchment from her butler's hand and gave it over to Hayden without a word.

An urgent post arriving at Jessica's was definitely not out of the ordinary. But one arriving for him was odd.

"Is a response required?" Hayden asked Wilson.

"Yes, Your Grace."

Hayden flipped over the envelope, seeing Tristan's seal. "Give us a moment, please."

He knew Tristan was at his country estate until news of his hasty marriage had a chance to settle down and become old news. Jessica came forward and saw the seal but didn't say a word or ask if Hayden knew what was urgent. Sliding his finger beneath the flap, he tore the parchment open and read it with a curse falling from his lips.

Hayden,

I call on our friendship in a moment of great need. Ponsley has seen it to have my head on a platter for stealing away his only daughter and has called for seconds. I need your level head and negotiating powers. Come north without delay, for this is a summons I cannot ignore for long.

With gratitude,
Tristan

"What does it say?" Jessica asked.

Hayden handed her the letter—better that she read the news for herself.

She skimmed over the contents and looked up at him with narrowed eyes. "He can't seriously entertain this idea."

"It's not so easy to ignore Ponsley, Jess. Tristan will have to respond to the challenge or be ridiculed and accused of having no honor—something neither he nor his new wife can afford considering the scandal their marriage has caused."

Jessica handed the letter back to him and sat on the bench at the end of her bed, hand pressed to her mouth.

"It's sickening that any man would resort to this type of violence."

"Sometimes it's necessary. Especially when one must consider their honor."

"I couldn't agree less." It was useless debating this point, since she could well guess how Hayden had *persuaded* Miller to leave London. Perhaps he preferred to use force if his silver tongue couldn't get him what he wanted. "What will you do?"

"I hate to leave you here with Warren now that Miss Camden has left."

"I was surprised Miss Camden was able to persuade Warren to my favor while she stayed on. But there's nothing that can be done about her absence now. I've always known that it was only a matter of time before Warren asked me to leave once and for all."

He pulled her to her feet and into his arms as he planted his lips against hers. She clasped his arms as though to hold him close to her indefinitely. She couldn't bear the thought of him leaving, no matter the circumstances. It was a selfish notion.

"Our walk will have to be postponed, for I'll have to be off before the lunch hour." He brushed his hand over her cheek. "Come with me. Miller is still wandering the city and Lady Montant can do a great deal of damage to your reputation if she continues to hold whatever vendetta it is she has against you."

"Miller has either left London or he's dead. I'm not worried about him."

"Assumptions can be dangerous in this instance."

"He'd have come back by now. I'm not worried about Miller. As for Lady Montant, she hasn't the slightest inkling that I know her secret. The time will present itself eventually."

He took her hands in his. "I'll ask again, not as your friend but as your suitor, come with me."

She could. But what would that mean with Lady Montant? While Jessica might be in no hurry to reveal Montant for the charlatan she was, she needed to deal with her sooner rather than later. Preferably before she ruined someone else's name.

"I should stay, Hayden. I only have a few weeks left here. I want to pack up my things. Say my good-byes before I am introduced as your fiancée." She looked around her sunny room, unable to meet his gaze. He hadn't proposed again, though he'd shown her the license.

He gathered her in his arms and kissed the top of her head. "I'll worry about you if you don't come."

"I've taken care of myself this long." When his eyes narrowed she added, "I'll be fine until your return."

"There's so much we need to discuss." He looked pointedly toward her vanity where the special license was laid out. "I won't leave without making a proper fiancée of you."

Hayden knelt in front of her, clasped her hands with his, and asked, "Would you make an honest of man of me and be my wife?"

Why hadn't she said yes when he'd gone down on bended knee in the garden-surrounded verandah all those weeks ago? How stupid and stubborn of her to refuse this man. She could never refuse him again. Tears pricked her eyes as she nodded.

"Don't cry, darling." He used his thumb to brush away the tears that welled over. "You should be happy."

"I am. I just . . . I will never be deserving of you."

"Come to Tristan's with me. I can't bear the thought of leaving you here with Warren."

She shook her head. While she agreed to marriage, she

still had things to take care of in Town. "A few days apart, even a week, won't hurt. When you come back we can sort out the details for the wedding, but Tristan needs you right now."

She could tell Hayden was torn. Between two friends. Between the woman he loved and the man he considered a brother. But Hayden's brother was in much greater need of his company than she was. Besides, it wouldn't be for more than a week. Just enough time for her to pack up her home and leave behind the part of her life that was the Countess of Fallon.

"I'll be back in London before you know it," he promised.

She curled her fingers around his.

"Will you take the train out?"

"It's quickest that way. I can have a horse readied in Birmingham this evening and be at Hailey Court tomorrow morning."

"It makes sense. Will you do the same coming home?"

"Yes, the faster I'm home to you the better." He pressed his palm against her cheek. "I'll miss you while I'm gone."

She closed her eyes as she stood from the bench so she could kiss him lightly on the mouth. "Godspeed. And keep Tristan safe; he never was one for weaponry."

"That I can promise."

His head leaned in, his forehead pressed to hers so fleetingly before he stepped away from her. He looked reluctant to leave, and she could tell that he wanted to ask her to go with him.

"The moment I'm back, we'll fix everything. Us, your reputation, your living situation."

The promise in his voice brought fresh tears to her eyes. This man turned her into a watering pot. The tears were not derived from sadness but from her stupidity at being so blind to the man before her . . . all these years.

Not that either of them could have acted sooner. She'd not have cuckolded her husband, despite her hate toward him.

Could they ever fix the damage that had been done to her reputation? She didn't think so but didn't want to sour his good mood before he left, so she said nothing.

Hayden planted one last kiss on her mouth before departing.

Chapter 20

Jilted before making it to the altar. Can you fathom such a thing? Lord P——'s daughter has created quite the stir hieing off and marrying the Marquess of C——. One must wonder what wickedness the man committed to make off with the daughter of someone who's always loathed him. Though I do believe the feelings are mutual between the men. All that remains to be seen is what type of retribution will be sought.

Mayfair Chronicles, August 1846

The moment Hayden left, Jessica immediately regretted not going with him. Sitting at her vanity, she pulled a sheaf of paper out of the drawer and picked up her pen. Hayden was right: she could escape the city, leave it all behind, and build the kind of life that made her a hell of a lot more content than her current circumstances allowed for.

Jessica penned the first note to Warren, explaining only that she had been called away from London and that she'd taken a maid for a companion on her travels. She did not commit to pen and paper the fact that she didn't plan on coming back to this house—she'd let him stew on that and wonder if she would return. She did technically have two weeks left.

She penned a second note to Leo and Genny, the woman

who had captured Jessica's friend's heart. She would require his attendance for what she had planned. It was amazing that once she made up her mind on something she tended to charge forward without thought to anything else.

Jessica rang the servants' bell to call up her maid. She had a long list of things that needed to be taken care of before she left. Because she knew that once she left she'd never be able to come back. And if she didn't act now . . . she would regret not spending the coming days with Hayden. She couldn't put him off a moment longer; she wanted to be by his side, as his partner. As his equal. The thought made her smile. She'd never stood on even footing with her late husband. Fallon saw her as inferior. Hayden would never think of her that way.

"My lady," Louise said on entering the bedchamber.

"We are preparing for a trip north to the Marquess of Castleigh's estate. I will go ahead on train, but I need a number of things from you before you follow behind me."

"My lady?"

"I'm not asking you to leave the house permanently."

"I wouldn't mind, my lady. You've been good to us here."

"Thank you, Louise." Her words brought Jessica comfort. "I'll notify Mr. Warren of my whereabouts. While I have no intention of coming back, I can't possibly remove all my personal belongings in two hours' time. I'll need everyone's assistance to get this done in my absence."

"I'll have everything arranged with Mrs. Harper. Nothing that is yours will remain, unless there is anything you wish to leave behind."

"I'll leave no reminders of me behind. I'll need you to pack three of my favorite dresses, my diaries, and what remains of my jewels straightaway for the trip north."

She looked around her private chamber, the place she'd called home for nearly nine years. For the first time, she felt the coldness seeping around the room and through her. How had she ever loved this oppressive place? "I suppose none of the rest truly matters."

"You've built your home here, my lady. No one would fault or judge you for your disappointment in leaving. Memories have a way of forming you, be they good or bad."

Jessica turned and looked at Louise. While Jessica's maid—and all the staff, really—knew exactly the type of justice her husband had doled out, they never discussed what was in the past.

The past was where it needed to be. Over with and done. She needed to move forward. Dwelling on the bad things had a way of leaving you haunted and unable to grow. She'd not fall victim to her husband's many abuses. She was stronger than that.

"I would not be the woman I am today without having endured marriage to Fallon." She wrapped her favorite lace shawl around her shoulders. "Reminiscing does little good. Come, Louise, we have to get ready for the trip ahead."

Jessica was really going to leave it all behind. It was amazing that she could think of the future without palpitations and anxiety bombarding her.

When Hayden had left he hadn't retrieved the special marriage license, she assumed so she could keep it in her safe possession. She walked over to her nightstand, pulled out her journal, and tucked the parchment into the folds for safekeeping with a smile on her face.

"Before you go about your tasks, Louise, will you pack a valise with my riding gear?" She was sure that Hayden would procure a horse for her, since his stables were close to Birmingham at his private estate.

"I'll be quick, my lady; you'll have to be off long before lunch."

Jessica retrieved the letters from Lady Montant to her husband that she'd had the good sense to pack away in the bottom of her wardrobe with her unmentionables. They'd have to go with her, for they were too valuable to leave behind.

After she readied for her trip, she made her way below stairs to say her good-byes to the staff. She could not part without hugging Mrs. Harper, whispering how much she adored her and appreciated her guidance as a matronly figure over the years she'd lived in this house. Holding Cook's hand for longer than she needed, wishing her a grand future in the household, for her dishes were sure to please everyone. Embracing Claudia and telling the young woman that she would make a perfect ladies' maid for the next mistress of the house. And then there was Wilson. Reliable old Wilson.

"You've been more kind than I deserved over the years."

"You daren't be so harsh. You're the finest mistress I've ever served in all my days."

"And you're too kind to say so."

"It's the God's honest truth, my lady. I've enjoyed your beautiful compassion, your tender heart, and, most of all, the fiery nature that is all you. I could die a happy man knowing I had the utmost pleasure serving you."

Tears came to her eyes and trailed slow paths down her cheeks. She wiped them away with the back of her gloved hand.

"Now, my lady, I didn't mean to turn you into a watering pot."

She shook her head. "You haven't, Wilson." She accepted his proffered handkerchief. "I will hold our memories together close to my heart."

"You do me a great kindness."

"Not nearly enough to repay you for your presence and sympathies when I most needed it." She hugged him tight, burying her head between his shoulder and neck. "Thank you, Wilson. For everything."

She probably frightened poor Wilson by showing so much affection, for his hand swept over her back lightly in a mutual embrace before it was gone as though he would never dare touch her.

"There's one last thing I need to do." She tried to hand his handkerchief back, but he motioned for her to keep it. "I'll be in the garden for a moment."

None of the staff said a word. They knew where she was going. They'd been instrumental in pulling her from the pit of despair that had engulfed her after the last miscarriage. No one questioned her or offered to accompany her. What she needed to do needed to be done alone.

Tying her bonnet under her chin, she made her way down to the garden. For all she knew, she'd never be able to sit in her little arbor of roses again and this little place would be forgotten when she moved on with Hayden. This had always been the one spot on the property she enjoyed in complete solitude. This was also the one place she allowed herself to let go and cry when she needed to.

Taking a strip of linen, she placed it on the ground in front of her roses. Hitching up her skirts so they wouldn't muddy, she knelt on the linen. The roses were thick along the fence, the thorny briar near impossible to see beyond even in the dead of winter. You could only see the marker if you pressed your cheek to the grass, and then only barely. She'd hidden it well, needing the grave to remain undisturbed when she could no longer protect this place that she'd made sacred.

She cut two fat pink roses from the bush and trimmed the thorns off. Taking the first one, she cut the stem down to no more than an inch long and pressed it in her journal. The second she took in her hand and laid flat out on the grass so she could see the painted marker pressed against the wooden fence. It was no more than a simple cross. She'd carved only a short good-bye into the wood: *You will always have a piece of my heart with you. Soar to the highest heavens and be free, little one.*

She traced the rough wording, tears slipping from her eyes as she did so. "This is officially our good-bye. I'm sorry we couldn't have met, sweet darling."

Leaving had been bittersweet, but the moment Hayden had left the house she suddenly knew exactly what she had to do. This was the start of her future with a man she not only respected a great deal but loved. While their love was rooted in friendship, she didn't think that made it any less significant than falling in love with someone you just met and connected with.

The hackney she hired pulled around Fenchurch Street Railway a half an hour before the trains were set to leave for Birmingham. She wondered if he would already be here. Would he arrive just before he was ready to set off? So many thoughts bombarded her. She realized she needed to buy a ticket for herself.

Before she made it up to the ticket booth, Hayden stepped out of a hired carriage. Just as he put his tall hat on he caught her eye and paused at the bottom of the stairs.

He handed a few coins to the driver. A boy hopped down from the back, bringing Hayden his case for the trip. He'd packed light, too, but she supposed that made sense since he'd be visiting his estate. A smile tilted his lips upward as he walked toward her. She was far too nervous to reciprocate the action, so instead ducked her head enough that the dip of her hat hid her expression from everyone around her, including Hayden.

Polished boots came into her line of vision first, then his dark trousers.

"I'd ask if you're here to see me off, but I know that's not the case when I can see your valise tucked behind your skirts."

She looked at him with a teasing smile. "I couldn't let you go alone. Tristan is my friend, too, and we both know Ponsley is a sure shot if he's to choose the weapon."

That was not the answer Hayden had expected. He narrowed his gaze at her before leaning over not to press a kiss to her cheek but to gather up her bag for her.

When he stood he held a bag in each hand. "Are you sure you want this? There is no turning back once you board that train with me."

She opened her mouth, but what should she say? So many things needed to be said, but not in the open where anyone could overhear them.

"Even I need coaxing once in a while and maybe a little wooing," she said.

"Comfort is the last thing I had in mind for this trip."

"There is nothing you can throw my way to dissuade me from joining you. My maid will travel on the morning train with the rest of my trunks. For surely we'll be staying on more than a day or two."

"Jess, I need you to be absolutely sure about this." What he was really asking was whether or not she was sure about them.

"Even I know when I'm playing a losing game of cards. Warren has beaten me. There is nothing I can do to salvage my reputation and even less I can do to convince Warren to let me stay. I have to move on and I wouldn't want to do so with anyone else at my side but you."

Hayden turned and put out his elbow so she could thread her arm through his. After purchasing their tickets, Hayden hired someone to take their luggage for them and they boarded the train. They'd thought ahead and taken a private car, which meant they could talk in private about their future.

"What will we do for the next five hours?" she asked.

"We'll eat at the dinner hour. I've made all the reservations for the dining car. But that's three hours off."

"There are a few things we need to discuss before our plans for the future are set in stone." He must know everything about her past.

"I hope you didn't join me on this trip because you've changed your mind and you want to convince me we shouldn't marry."

"Not at all." She drew the blinds on the window that faced the main corridor inside the train and sat next to him as she untied the ribbon of her bonnet to remove it.

Hayden took her chin between his thumb and fingers. "I've known you a long time, Jess. There is nothing you can say or do that would shock me."

She looked away from him as she gathered her courage to tell Hayden something she'd never told another soul. "And what if my secrets hurt your standing in society?"

"I doubt anything can be so bad."

"Then I may just surprise you yet."

"Look at me, Jess."

She did. And while the compassion he'd always had for her was visible in the dark depths of his eyes, she still feared he'd turn his back on her once the whole truth was out. What would he think of the life she'd lived? Of the life her parents had exposed her to so they could live like hedonists.

She took a deep breath. "You once said that my husband would have had no grounds on which to petition for divorce, but now know otherwise. And I did read through all the letters that were in Fallon's desk and it appears that he knew more of my secrets than I imagined, which brings me to believe that Lady Montant knows my full history as well."

When she paused, he took her lace-gloved hands in his and said, "Go on."

"My father was a good man." Tears filled her eyes. "The best man I've ever known. And he doted upon me." She pulled one hand free of Hayden's hold and used the handkerchief Wilson had given her to blot away the tears building in the corners of her eyes.

"This is difficult for me to talk about when I've not shared this part of my life with anyone."

"I'll never judge you for the actions of others."

"My father loved two women all his life. And while this is not unusual, considering most men's proclivity to keep on a mistress, it was unusual that both women lived under one roof.

"I had two mothers growing up. Anna was my father's wife. My birth mother, Jane, was his mistress. Anna was barren, so when it came to light that Jane was pregnant both women underwent confinement until I was born."

Hayden remained silent as she dabbed away more tears.

"Say something," she whispered.

"I'm not sure there is anything to say. You said yourself your father loved you, as did the women who raised you. Was it unconventional? Absolutely. Would I judge you for something out of your control? Definitely not."

"It's not whether your opinion will change, but the *ton*'s, should my secrets ever be revealed." She took a deep breath that did nothing to calm her nerves. "On the grounds of illegitimacy, Fallon would have been able to petition and would have succeeded in divorcing me."

"How long did he know the full of it?"

"Father liked nothing more than to tell his life story when he was in his cups. So Fallon knew the story early on in our marriage."

"When did your inheritance stop paying into the entailment on his estate?"

She had to think on that a moment. "I believe the

funds were released over five years. I can't say for sure since I wasn't involved with the finances that directly affected the estate."

"So why did he wait an additional three years before threatening divorce?"

"I don't think he hated anyone so much as he did me."

"And that's always baffled me."

She looked away, but a small smile tilted up her lips. "When it became apparent that I could not have children, and after his first palpitation episode with his heart, he made it very clear that he wanted to seek out a new bride before he was on his deathbed. I think he thought himself invincible before his health problems started. But in order to take a new bride, there was one problem. . . ."

It pained her a great deal to recall that conversation with her husband. The cruelness of his words, his hate more evident than it had ever been prior to that outburst. Hayden didn't prompt her to continue but let her take her time. The words were hard to find for what she was about to admit.

". . . It became apparent that I was increasing further then I ever had before."

"If he was willing to have a child—and desired to have the next Fallon heir, which you carried—why would he go so far as to poison you?"

"I think he had a change of heart after the first fall. And he knew he could not successfully divorce me if I was increasing. And while this is entirely my opinion, I think he felt he had no choice at that point. He was so fixated on the fact that I was a whore's daughter—his choice of words, not mine—that he thought I sullied the Fallon title and any children I had would do the same."

Jessica pulled her shawl tighter around her shoulders even though it wasn't cold.

Hayden rubbed his hands over her arms in an attempt to stave off the chill that overtook her. After wiping away the last of her tears, she sat up and looked at Hayden.

Though she expected to see something akin to disgust—toward Fallon, never her—she only saw compassion. There wasn't an ounce of pity in his expression, either, which she respected and appreciated a great deal more than she wanted to admit.

"What do we do now, Hayden?"

"I wish I would have killed Miller before I let the bastard ship off to Australia."

"Then you would have had to live with blood on your hands. I would never want that, especially in the name of our friendship."

"I should have at least gotten the full truth, so I could have acted on this sooner."

Hayden kissed her forehead, then each of her tear-dampened cheeks. "If I could erase the pain he caused you, I would."

"That pain made me the woman I am today. I wouldn't change the memories of his treatment toward me. You know it's unlikely I can bear children, considering my past."

Hayden pressed his thumb against her chin and shook his head. "I haven't changed my mind."

She smiled in return. "If we are going to go through with marriage, I want it done properly. Banns need to be read. I'll not go into our marriage as though I've been compromised. I don't want to play to the tune of the *ton* anymore. Though I despise them, I don't want to be the brunt of all their jokes, and the example of what young ladies should never strive to be."

She waited for him to think that through. What it would mean for them.

"And here I thought starting off in scandal would be your preference."

She shoved playfully at his shoulder. "Don't make jokes at a time like this."

"I've been waiting for this for a long time, Jess." He cupped her face with both his hands.

"Under normal circumstances, it might be different; we could run away, escape to Scotland, and be married before the week is out. But that's not what I want. Not with my secrets hanging over our heads. I'll deal with Lady Montant in good time, but right now, I just want something normal, something I can count on going right."

"While I prefer to claim you as my wife, now, as I've longed to for so long, this is one wish I will grant you. Though I can't promise I won't try to persuade you otherwise when this whole business with Tristan is looked after."

Jessica placed her hand atop his and nuzzled into his arms, closing her eyes. "That's all I want." She pressed a light kiss to his hand.

Hayden pulled her onto his lap and set to kissing her full on the mouth. They explored each other for some time. The dinner trolley rolled past their car and they couldn't ignore the smell of food for long. Hayden helped straighten out her dress so they were presentable before entering the dining car.

"All this time together and I've been talking about myself," she said. "What do you think will happen with Ponsley?"

"Ponsley is a man of honor above all things. I think he only needs to prove a point to save face with Warren. He can't just let his daughter be stolen away in the same week his chaperone was found to be having an affair with Leo."

"Warren . . ." It suddenly dawned on her that he might not be in London any longer. "Do you expect he'll be at the challenge?"

"Couldn't say." Hayden shrugged as he curled a loose strand of hair behind her ear. "But we'll find out soon enough."

Chapter 21

Word of a duel between two prominent houses has come my way. Will it be Montague or Capulet who wins this time? Or will the old man step in to divert disaster among the young lovers vying for one lady's heart? Who knew she was worth the trouble they've gotten themselves into? Perhaps her dowry is cushioned far more than I previously imagined, not that either gentleman needs the treasures attached to Lady C——'s name.

Mayfair Chronicles, August 1846

The sky had darkened significantly with the threat of an oncoming rainstorm by the time their train pulled into Birmingham Station. While the hour was still too early for bed, they couldn't risk riding out to Hayden's estate in the dark, so they sought lodgings at a reputable inn instead.

Hayden stepped up to the reservation counter. "Two rooms, adjoining doors, if you have them."

"We have no adjoining rooms available. The storm brewing outside has brought in stragglers that might not otherwise worry about lodgings." The woman looked down at her ledger, her mobcap the only thing Jessica and Hayden saw for some minutes before she looked at them with her wrinkled face and gray eyes. "And we certainly don't have any rooms grand enough for your wife—"

"One room will be fine," Jessica said, stepping forward.

Hayden turned to Jessica, his look full of astonishment, but she only shrugged in response. There was no reason they couldn't share a room. Even though they'd shared a bed before, this felt . . . *different*.

"We'll make do, Hayden." She smiled innocently.

When Hayden turned back to the proprietor the woman asked, "Your name for the books, fine sir?"

He hesitated only a brief moment. "Lord and Lady Duchene of Lancashire."

Since Jessica wanted a proper engagement, it did make perfect sense to make up a married name for them. Especially since they had already shared a room prior to marriage. While they'd been intimate already, he didn't assume they would be again this evening.

He rubbed a hand over his eyes. It could prove to be a very long night.

"Would you like a tray brought up, my lord?"

"Yes," he said, threading Jessica's arm through his. "Can you have someone carry up our cases, too?"

The woman snapped her fingers and a young man came forward and led them to their suite for the evening. He opened the door for them and brought their bags in behind.

"What's your latest post out in the evening?" Hayden asked.

"Monday through Thursdays by five. If it's for London it should be there in two days' time. Otherwise it depends."

"And what about special posts?"

"We've a rider for local deliveries, my lord."

Hayden gave him a few coins for his services. "The maid can collect the letter with the food tray. I'll need the letter to arrive before midnight, and it won't take your rider far from Birmingham, maybe two hours each way if he makes it ahead of the rain and rides swiftly."

"Of course, my lord." The young man bowed, then shut the door on his way out.

"Where do you need to post a letter to? Surely Tristan knows you are on your way?" Jessica asked.

"I need to get a letter to my estate. They'll bring horses down for us to ride the rest of the way."

"I don't know that I should go with you to Tristan's just yet. We've a few days before the duel actually happens."

"Did you want to stay on at my estate alone?"

"I think that's best. I don't want to distract Tristan with our news when he needs all his focus for Ponsley."

"And you don't think his new wife is distracting enough?" he asked, one eyebrow quirked.

Jessica tossed her shawl at him playfully. "I suppose it shouldn't surprise me that your mind is focused there, when we happen to be sharing a room."

"I make no presumptions, Jess. Besides, the sofa looks comfortable enough." He glanced over at the short settee, which lacked pillows. It didn't look the least bit suitable to sit on, let alone sleep on, but if need be he could make it work.

She reached for his hand and threaded her fingers through his. "It's not as though we haven't shared a bed before."

He brought her knuckles up to his lips and kissed them. "And look at where that led us."

Hayden pulled her slowly into his arms. His timing couldn't have been worse. A knock sounded at the door. He released her reluctantly to answer it.

A young kitchen maid carried a silver tray laden with soup dishes and sandwiches. He motioned for her to come in, and she placed the service on the table in front of the sofa.

"If you'll wait a minute, I have a letter I'd like to write for delivery this evening," he said.

The girl curtsied. "Yes, my lord. Will you require a response?"

"That won't be necessary." Walking over to the desk in the room, he took the hotel stationery and wrote a note for his butler—instructions for his needs. He handed it to the maid along with some coins. "Thank you for taking care of this so promptly."

"It's not a bother," she replied before she closed the door behind her, leaving him and Jess alone again.

What did you say to the woman who was to be your wife? Not only did they know everything there was to know about each other, they'd also been more intimate than most couples ever had the opportunity to be before their wedding day, yet he didn't know quite how to approach sharing a room and possibly a bed with his wife-to-be.

Jessica sat on the settee in front of the service of food that had been placed on the table. She lifted the first lid and leaned over the steaming broth to smell the contents and sighed. "A most delightful-smelling vegetable broth." She turned to him, a spoon in hand. "Would you like to join me? There are ham sandwiches, too. Though I think I'll stick to the soup after the dinner we indulged in on the train."

"Enjoy the soup. I'm not hungry." Not for food, anyway.

While she delicately sipped at her soup he unpacked his bag, hanging up his clothes for the morning ride to his estate and washing his face with a damp cloth from the basin.

Jessica watched him as he walked around the room readying for the night ahead.

"I do hope you know I'll need your assistance?" She reached the spot between her shoulder blades, where a delicate row of buttons lined up like little soldiers guarding what lay beneath.

He sucked in a breath.

"Why are you staring at me with that expression?"

"What expression?"

She put down her spoon and joined him in the middle of the room. Only a handspan separated them. "As though you're starved for something other than food."

"Perhaps I am." He grabbed her, pulling the lower half of her body against his hardness, and he kissed her.

She pulled her head slightly away, her lips damp. "I have a question for you before this carries on any further."

He was tempted to lean into her neck and inhale the soft scent of her floral perfume that always got his blood pumping and his body needing more. "Your question, my dearest lady."

"The time you slept in my bed, you pulled away from me before we could . . ." She filled the sudden silence with her hands. As though that explained what was in her head. She cleared her throat in a very dainty, ladylike fashion. "Before we finished what was started. You could have taken full advantage of the situation to the point you could have pressed your suit for marriage then and there. Instead you stopped."

"Yet we've been intimate since then," he pointed out.

She blushed a deep scarlet. "Our passions were high and we acted in the moment without thought to the consequences."

He took a deep breath. There hadn't been much thought in pulling away from her, other than preserving the last shred of his decency. When they'd been in bed together, so close to consummating something he'd wanted to do for nearly a decade, he had realized he couldn't fulfill that desire unless Jessica was fully cognizant of what she was allowing and what their joining would mean. And though he knew she'd eventually come around, he would never have forced her into marriage before her realization that they were the perfect match.

"You weren't willing to accept the consequences of a union between us. And there was no sense in rushing things along when you knew deep down that I'd already won you over."

She took another step toward him and grasped the lapels of his jacket. "And what about earlier today? You didn't press your suit when things got carried away with our actions."

He rubbed the back of his hand down the side of her face. "I've known you long enough to know that you won't do something until you're damn well ready to do it. I will not be the hand that forces you to do anything you are unsure of."

Jessica slid her hands over his strong shoulders and tangled her hands in his hair to hold him still as she looked him in the eye. "You're right in that regard. I'll never go back on my decision now. I feel like a fool, not having realized sooner how well suited we are."

"When I've wanted something, I've always taken it. You know this about me, Jess. But with you . . . it's been different."

"Why?"

"Because I love you." He paused, letting those words sink in. "Not merely as a friend and as your confidant all these years, but because I have always wanted you to be mine and mine alone."

His arm slid around her lower back, holding her close.

"You hid your feelings so well, Hayden. I should have known sooner how you felt, but I was blind for so long when married to Fallon."

He pressed his forehead against hers. "Put the past out

of that pretty head of yours. You see me now, Jess, and that's all that matters."

"I wouldn't want anyone else in my life but you, Hayden. I want you to be with me tonight." He took a few steps away from her, closer to the bed. So much for sleeping on the sofa as a gentleman would do. But then again, wouldn't a gentleman argue for separate rooms? Something inside of him had rejoiced at her insistence on one room.

He sat on the edge of the mattress, pulling Jessica down to straddle his hips in such a provocative fashion that he groaned and thrust his pelvis up into hers.

"There's no going back from this. If we continue in this fashion, we may not be able to wait for the banns." His hands grasped her hips, holding her still, and then skimmed higher to hold her around her small, cinched waist.

"I wouldn't dare dream of stopping this. So long as I have you by my side, I can face anything, Hayden, even censure from the *ton*."

He rolled them so their positions were reversed, she on the bottom, he on the top, with his hands free to start removing her many layers. He took his time revealing the underclothes beneath her day dress while she traced invisible lines over his sleeve.

Hayden kissed her neck and nibbled delicately at her chin before claiming her mouth with another deep kiss.

"Stand up for a moment." He pulled her to her feet and shed each of her outer layers, tossing them on the floor, slowly revealing the delicate linens that she wore closest to her bare skin.

She yanked his shirt free from his trousers and over his head before pressing a kiss above his heart. The material slipped from her hands and fell at their feet with the rest of her clothes.

Threading his fingers through her pinned hair, he turned her head enough that her cheek was pressed to his chest and embraced her tightly in his arms. Soon her arms wrapped around his waist, her hands tracing over the muscles in his back. The pins were easily pulled from her hair, and he dropped them to the floor around them.

When her hair fell in loose curls around her shoulders she gazed up at him with an unreadable expression. She stretched her hands tentatively toward his face, her finger tracing his lips.

"The whole night is ours. Make love to me, Hayden."

Lowering his head, he kissed her gently as he reached around her back to loosen the strings cinching her waist. The corset eased open and the weight of the whalebone contraption sagged enough that she could release the hooks on the busk. Jessica took the heavy material off, folded it, and placed it at the foot edge of the bed.

With her back to him, Hayden wrapped his arms around her. Her head turned enough that he could claim her lips with his own.

His free hand brushed over her breast, skimming the distended tip of her nipple. "I could live like this forever."

There was a perfect harmony about them embracing intimately. There wasn't a day that had gone by that he didn't want her, and now that he had her he didn't ever want to let her go.

"Will it always be like it was earlier with us? It felt right. Perfect. I know it was fleeting last time because we were both afraid of being caught."

Hayden turned her around so they were chest to breast. "I should be embarrassed by my earlier display of need."

She reached for him, her fingers grasping his face as she stepped up on the tips of her toes to kiss him again. "I liked every stolen moment."

"I can show you so much more, give you so much more."

They fell back on the bed, him atop her, her legs spreading to accommodate the fit of his body against her. He was careful not to crush her but allowed enough of his weight to press his hardness firmly against her core.

He pulled away from their kiss so he could look her in the eye. "If we start this now, promise me you'll kick me out of bed in the morning to fulfill my obligations with Tristan. Otherwise I may never leave your side again."

"You can't be serious."

"Completely."

She nibbled her bottom lip in contemplation. "I will personally kick you out of our shared bed should you find it difficult to stop yourself from laying in all morning." She laughed her sultry laugh, and it had him hardening further in the already tight confines of his trousers. "Though I don't understand how you could stay here all morning once you've fulfilled yourself."

"You'll not want to leave this bed in the morning, either. That much I can promise." Once could never be enough with Jessica. Forever and always was more likely.

Her look was skeptical.

She reached down between them and ran the palm of her hand over his cock.

He had to close his eyes and swallow against the desire to claim her properly.

The worst thing he could do was rush this. He left his trousers on, knowing that was the only deterrent he had from finishing this off as quickly as he had this morning. Pulling her chemise up to her waist, Hayden found the ties keeping her pantalettes in place. They were delicate satin ribbons and he pulled the dangling string with his teeth, licking at the flesh he revealed bit by bit at her waist.

When he ran out of string and new skin to bite and

nibble at he pulled up to say, "Sit on the edge of the bed, so I can remove these."

He skimmed his hands over the bare skin of her hips, pushing the material down over her buttocks and halfway down her thighs by the time she did his bidding. Hayden knelt on the carpeted floor in front of her and slowly stripped her of the first layer of her underclothes. Placing his head in her lap, he inhaled deeply. For how long had he wanted her? For how long had he dreamed of doing just this?

"Jessica," he whispered, kissing first her knees and then her thighs as he pushed the chemise higher and higher, revealing every sweet inch of pale, porcelain skin.

The higher he kissed, the more she edged forward on the mattress, closer to him, until finally she slid off the bed and onto his lap.

"We've come this far, Hayden. Don't tease me. There's time for exploration later."

He clasped her head in his hands and rubbed the tips of their noses together. "There is no such thing as taking this too slow, Jess. I've wanted you for as long as I've known you. This time we'll cherish and remember every moment of tonight and not our bumbling first attempt that we'll laugh about later."

She bit his bottom lip, sucking it into her mouth before tracing it with her tongue. "I didn't find it laugh worthy."

"Just let me love you my way." He shut her up with a kiss that locked their tongues together.

When he broke away she was panting a little as her eyes sparked with mischief.

He held either cheek of her buttocks in his hands and lifted them both from the floor. He tossed her gently on the bed and followed her down. Jessica leaned back on her arms with her hair tumbling around her shoulders provocatively.

"You're a minx. My mischievous, teasing minx. I'll teach you a few new uses for that smart mouth of yours."

She swallowed visibly, but her smile turned to something more alluring and sultry as she slid her legs open for his perusal. "I think I can teach you a few uses for both of our mouths."

"Is that a dare?"

"It might be."

He sat on his knees beside her and pulled her chemise right over her head, tossing it to the end of the bed with the rest of their clothes.

Naked and set out before him like a feast for the taking, she was the most beautiful sight he'd ever beheld. Her breasts were full, the areolas the lightest of pinks, the nipples red. He took a moment to appreciate the perfectness of her form, tracing the back of his hand over the plumpness of her breasts, along her delicate rib cage and waist, and ending at her hip, squeezing it lightly. He leaned over her, forcing her to relax against the small stack of feather pillows.

As he kissed her full on the mouth their tongues tangled and her hands explored his arms and his shoulders. She rubbed her hands over the stubble covering his jaw as their kiss gentled.

Kneeing her thighs apart, he situated himself between her legs, letting her feel just how hard he was for her by pressing himself against her core, rocking into her as their passions increased and they were both panting for more.

They were in a position they'd been in before; only this time there wasn't a force in all of nature that could make him pull away. Did she truly understand the depth of his

feelings for her? The intensity of his desire that out-
weighed reason itself? That would be the one thing he'd
show her before he left her at his estate tomorrow. God,
that was the last thing he wanted to do. At least they had
the night.

Had she ever truly understood just how fulfilling it was to
be in Hayden's arms she'd have encouraged and begged her
husband to petition for divorce long ago. She'd never expected to desire any man as deeply as she did Hayden. He
made her forget every harsh word used toward her, every
hand raised against her, every violence brought upon her,
by the weak man who had been married to her.

Her only crime in marriage had been that she would
not be stifled by a man filled with so much hatred.

There was no hate in Hayden.

There was only love.

There was unending kindness toward her when half
the time she didn't believe she deserved it.

She asked herself again how she could have been so
blind as to not see what had always been right in front of
her. There could be no regrets, though, of not knowing
this truth sooner, because they belonged to each other
now.

What mattered was that she now knew what it was like
to share the hopes of a better future with Hayden. She
knew what it was like to be in his arms in the moment.
And she wouldn't trade this feeling for all the sorrow or
misery she had suffered previously if it meant losing this
precious, beautiful moment.

Jessica wrapped her arms tight around Hayden's shoulders, tracing the sinew of his back as he moved above her.
His arms braced on either side of her to keep his weight
from crushing her into the mattress.

She wanted his clothes gone, so they were finally

naked—with nothing left to hide from each other. She reached down between them and found the buttons fastening his trousers.

She broke away from their kiss to whisper, "Take them off. I want to know what it feels like when we are flesh against flesh."

He nibbled at her bottom lip and with a groan tore away from her so he could shuck the last of his clothes. Standing from the bed, he released the ties she'd missed on his trousers and pushed the material below his hips. His cock sprang out, demanding her full attention.

On seeing him bare, less debonair and all masculine with the absence of clothes, she had a sudden desire to learn his body much more intimately.

She pressed one hand to her chest, finding it suddenly hard to breathe at the sight of him. His manhood was a great deal larger than what she'd seen on any man before: real, statue, or etched. She knew it fit perfectly well, so she wasn't sure why the size was so shocking.

There were butterflies in her stomach and her nerves were on edge. She was afraid to even speak as she traced every muscled line and protrusion of his body with hungry eyes. Taking in her fill, she crawled toward him, where he stood next to the bed, and perused his form more closely. She wanted to touch him, but she hesitated.

Throat dry, she attempted to swallow, but all the saliva from her mouth was nonexistent. Nerves, this was all nerves. She didn't know the first thing about seducing a man in the flesh. With words, yes, but she lacked for words at the moment.

Fists clenching and unclenching at his sides, he stared back at her with a hooded gaze, his breathing ragged, his cock flexing in need in the triangle of dark blond hair at its root. The image he presented was so animalistic, so raw, that her body clenched in response. She did not think she'd get enough of this new side she was seeing of him in one evening. Maybe not ever.

She reached for his arm, a neutral spot that wasn't so new to her. The muscles flexed along his forearm as she slid her hand lower and grabbed his hand and led him back onto the bed with her.

"I'm trying hard to take this slow when what I want most is to throw you on the bed and take you hard and fast." His voice was hoarse, his body tense, as though he was holding himself back from doing just that.

"Maybe I don't want slow." She rolled her hips suggestively where she knelt. Cool air touched the wetness that slicked her core. "The night is ours, and it's without the chance of interruption."

When he joined her on the bed the tips of her breasts brushed over his chest so lightly that her nipples hardened further with the sensation of his heated touch. His chest surged against hers on a deep inhalation and his arms came around her waist to pull her right along the length of his torso and thighs.

His cock pressed demandingly against her belly as he slid his arms up her back and beneath her hair to hold her head in his big hands as he devoured her mouth with renewed fervor now that he had ahold of her and they were flesh against flesh.

Jessica didn't remain idle. Her hands traced, molded, and squeezed parts of him she'd never dared dream of touching until now. He was solid muscle everywhere she explored. Lean lines of sinew formed and moved on his back; his buttocks were just as solid as his thighs when she skimmed over the backs of them before trailing her hands higher once again.

Hayden lowered his hands and gave her the same treatment she'd given him. Only when he reached one cheek of her buttocks he slid his hand down and forward enough that the slickness at her center coated his fingers and made him groan in her mouth where their tongues were entwined.

He hitched up her thigh as he tipped her back on the bed. Her hair fanned out around her shoulders. One knee bent, her legs spread around his, Hayden pulled away from their kiss to look down at the image she must make. She was sure she blushed in places she'd never blushed before, but she couldn't blame him for taking his time. She'd studied him in much the same manner.

Manhood trailing over her belly and the thatch of hair at her center, Hayden kissed his way down her body. His lips pressed lightly over her neck, breasts, and rib cage— and bypassed the most sensitive part at the tips of her breasts. She tangled her hands in his hair, grasped tightly, and pulled him up enough that she could see the smile playing on his lips.

He knew perfectly well what she wanted, and he was going to make her beg for it. She was tempted to give in but stopped herself and released her hold on his hair so she could push him off her instead.

She'd not remain still for his ministrations; she wanted the same opportunity to explore him as he had with her.

"I don't think that's fair," she said, finger pushing at the center of his chest as she drove him off her and knelt once again on her knees to face him. "I want to play, too." She pouted out her bottom lip, trailing her finger down his sternum, between the strong cords of his abdominal muscles, until finally she reached his jutting manhood.

She didn't cup it, just rubbed her hand back and forth over the formidable length. She saw that Hayden had to restrain himself from tossing her back on the bed and finishing this once and for all. With his fists clenching at his sides again, she watched his jaw grind as she increased her tempo and pressure to the sensitive underside.

"What do you want, Hayden?" Her question came out a seductive purr.

She waited for him to tell her to suck him, because she wanted to and would without hesitation if that was what he wanted. Instead of saying anything, the tic in his jaw grew more prominent the longer he stared at her.

As she grazed her finger over and around the tip of his cock a bead of fluid emitted from the tip. She rubbed her finger over it, swirled it around the head of his sex, testing his restraint. She wanted to be the one person who could push him past the last threads of his control. . . .

It didn't take too much to accomplish just that. When Hayden reached for her this time his hold was strong, determined. She couldn't tease him a moment longer. She knew he wanted her to submit. It was evident in the way he stared at her, a hungry man who wanted nothing more than her surrender. And she could give him nothing less than what he desired.

This time, when he laid her back on the bed she went eagerly. He pushed out her thighs with his, settling his body between her spread legs.

Her breath hitched in her lungs as he grasped her by the hips and lifted her lower body completely off the bed so that he could tongue at her core.

Deep, needy moans slipped past her throat with the ministrations of his tongue against those sensitive parts. It was almost too much to bear. But bear it she did, for she wasn't sure she ever wanted the delicious assault to end.

His tongue swept around the folds of her sex, intermittently thrusting hard into her sheath. And all she could do was hold herself up on her elbows as he ate at her like a man starved of the one thing he'd always been denied.

Her eyes slipped closed as she absorbed every sensation, every feel of his tongue. She wanted to hold him in her arms, wrap her body around him till there was no knowing where she started and he ended. His tongue flicked around the little bud of her sex, over and over again, relentlessly, deliciously. She ached so deep inside that something foreign unfurled as he continued to suck and tease at the most private part of her body.

"Hayden," she said, her voice husky. Needy.

Falling back on her shoulders, she grasped his forearms and held on for dear life. "Oh, God, I can't." She shook her head, her breathing beyond ragged. "Oh, God. Oh, God. Hayden."

That elusive *something more* was at the precipice and ready to fly free. Her nails dug into his arms. She wasn't sure if she wanted him to stop or to continue, to suck and lick harder or gentle his touch. A tempest of emotions and unfamiliar feelings ran rampant in her head and her body until the dam finally broke and she cried out his name again and again, coming completely undone in his arms.

He lowered her hips gently to the bed, came over her, clasping her head with his hands, and kissed her deeply. She could taste herself on his tongue, and while she should be embarrassed by the intimate act, she could do no more than squeeze her thighs around his hips and tangle her hands through his hair, sucking his tongue deep into her mouth as he finally entered her body in one hard thrust.

Her breath caught in her throat and his body stilled, but he continued kissing her. She explored and stroked his shoulders, arms, and back, this time with less tentative touches. Her body flexed around his and finally . . . finally he moved deep inside her at a steady, breathtaking pace.

He broke their kiss so that he could gaze into her eyes as he made love to her as though they had all the time in the world. He didn't say anything, just traced the side of her face with his thumbs, the motion rhythmic, and matched the timing of his body moving inside her.

That fluttering sensation deep in her womb, her body, radiated out again, and she felt herself close to tipping over that edge into a complete free fall of sensation once again.

"I never want it to stop," she said.

A boyish grin tilted Hayden's lips before he kissed her again, his pace increasing. Before she could comprehend what was happening he reversed their positions, propping himself up on the pillows as she sat astride his thighs, unsure what exactly she should do.

While she was no shy virgin, she had only known intercourse one way.

"Ride me, Jess." His demand was guttural, raw.

How could she deny him anything when he was showing her a gambit of feelings in his expression she'd never seen before? She lifted herself up slowly, liking the way he felt inside her when she was on top.

His hands grabbed her hips and guided the slide of her body atop his. The bounce of her breasts proved too much for him to look at and he sat up and sucked one deep into his mouth, biting playfully and licking the nipple and undersides in tandem. The thrust of her pelvis increased with the encouragement of his hands, and he started to plunge up into her as she rode him harder and harder till their bodies were slick with sweat and sliding over each other.

Waves of pleasure continued to bombard and fill her until she felt herself letting go again. Hayden stole her screams this time with a kiss and let her ream out every bit of pleasure she could, before he flipped her around on hands and knees and took her hard from behind.

Her arms stretched out in front of her as he wrung out even more pleasure from her. She was panting hard, unable to form one tangible word. Not that she cared to say anything.

Hands firmly holding her hips, Hayden kept her close as their bodies slapped together in some primal dance she wished she'd experienced sooner. The pace picked up and then Hayden was pulling out of her with a curse. His arms were shaking where he knelt on the bed, his fist pumping his cock as his semen spilled out between the tight grasp of his fingers. The sight was new to her and so erotic that she felt her sheath clench tight inside, her body missing the pulse of his cock pumping hard inside her.

She rolled to her side and stared up at him with sleepy eyes. That had taken the last bit of life out of her today, though her body wasn't ready for rest just yet.

"Why did you pull out?"

He leaned forward, kissed her brow, and stood from the bed. "Do you want me to ring for a bath?"

"You're not even going to answer my question?" Why it bothered her she couldn't say. But it did. Especially considering he hadn't done so earlier in the day.

"Jess, we're not married. We can't take a chance like that and risk censure should you find yourself pregnant and having that baby before we've been married a year. I will not have society thinking either of us cuckolded Fallon."

While his reasoning was sound, it still upset her more than she wanted to admit.

"What about this morning, then?" she reminded him.

"That was the last thing I expected to happen, and should my actions have consequences . . . We'll have to worry about it then."

He headed toward the washbasin.

His backside was just as impressive as his front, and Jessica enjoyed the view of his bare buttocks as he stood with his back to her. As his hands moved so did the muscles in his shoulders and arms. She wanted to feel those lines moving under her tongue. Her heart beat heavily in her chest, and her breaths came faster. He'd made a wanton of her and she doubted she'd ever get enough of him now that she'd tasted of the forbidden fruit, so to speak.

As he wiped his hands off on a fresh towel he turned to her with an amused expression. Had he noticed her riveted gaze? She was sure she was blushing, which was nothing new; she'd been doing that a lot lately.

"I'm exhausted, which I think has something to do with you. It's been a long day and I've never traveled well." She stretched out her arms like a lazy cat sunbathing. "Come to bed. Sleep awhile with me, though I'm not sure we'll sleep much."

Hayden wrung out the towel without answering and brought it over to the bed. "We do have an early start."

When he leaned over the bed and pushed her knee out she tried to take the towel from him. He pulled it away from her with a "tsk" and one cocked eyebrow that dared her to argue.

The cool cloth brushed over her womanhood. Jessica closed her eyes, feeling suddenly shy about their intimacies, embarrassed that she was without a stitch of clothing to hide behind as he stared at very private areas of her for reasons other than intercourse.

Warmth brushed over her lips a second before he kissed her long and deep. Her arms snaked around his shoulders as the wet slap of the cloth met the floor. Hayden came over her again, their mouths never breaking. One big hand cupped her hip as he lay down on his side, turning her so they faced each other on the bed.

She kissed him back but had to pull away to ask, "Don't you think we should at least get under the covers?"

With a quick exhale, Hayden lifted her up, practically tossing her to the middle of the bed, and yanked the bedding down. Then he climbed into the bed with her and pulled the covers up, him between her spread thighs. "Is that better?"

She narrowed her eyes. "Yes, but you really must stop tossing me about as though I were no more than a rag doll." She laughed, making the request less serious than she'd meant.

"Can't promise that."

"And why is that?"

"If I told you, you'd box my ears."

"You can't possibly know that unless you tell me your reasoning," she countered.

"You always have the last word, Jess." Which was very true and would probably never change. "I'll always have strength over you, but I'll never hurt you."

She pulled away from him, turning to give him her back as she sat on the edge of the bed. She wished then that she'd brought a robe that she could slip into and escape him for a short while. Why had he brought *that* up?

His legs came around her hips, his manhood semi-hard and pressed along her spine. Hayden pushed her hair over one shoulder and kissed her exposed nape. "I don't think I relayed that quite how I was thinking it in my head."

"You have to understand that I will never allow another man to use force on me again. Men may often be stronger than women, but we don't need to be reminded of that fact."

"You're everything to me, Jess. You always have been. And I'd never hurt you."

"Yet you just let me know that you have the strength to overpower me if you so wish it."

His hand brushed over her arm as he continued to plant kisses over her nape and her shoulder. Moments ago, before his admission, she'd have melted into the intimacy. Now she couldn't. Not till he took back his words and admitted the stupidity of them.

"I would never raise a hand or fist in anger against you, Jess. Has our friendship not taught you that? Do you not feel as if you know the *real* me after nearly ten years of friendship? I have strength; you have a will stronger than anyone I know. I have to bring something to the table in our marriage."

She turned enough that she could look at him over her shoulder. "Promise me you'll never remind me of our differences in strength again. We will be partners, Hayden, not just man and wife."

"I promise wholeheartedly that I wouldn't dare hurt you. I never meant to make you uncomfortable. Believe me, that's the last thing I ever want to do. I love you too much to betray the trust you have for me. And I've always said that we would be partners. Do you believe that?"

There was no denying that his words were sincere.

She leaned back against him; the hair speckled on his chest tickled her between her shoulder blades. He snaked his arms around her waist, sliding his hands over her stomach and giving rise to butterflies and a host of renewed desires.

"This is so new to me, Hayden. I think I've forgotten what it is to have dreams of a happier life, one that I have the ability to control. My freedom will take getting used to. Your constant kindness will take getting used to—my married life never offered that security."

"The one thing I hope is that you can forget what it was like to be married to a cruel man. Just trust me to keep you safe."

"I do."

The now familiar sensation and tingling his touch caused swirled deep inside her. She turned enough that she could kiss his lips. Their tongues rolled around lazily, indulgently, as though they had all the time in the world. Though she supposed they did have forever ahead of them, they needed to be in bed and rested up for their early-morning ride to his estate.

Hayden's hand slid higher to cup her breast and pluck gently at her nipple.

It was going to be a long night, one that wasn't going to involve sleep of any kind.

Chapter 22

*My younger, more impressionable readers will be
disappointed in what I have to report today. The
Duke of A—— has eloped. Eloped. And with that
woman if you can believe it. At least that is what I
assume when they boarded a train heading north
yesterday afternoon. Another title to die out over
time; as her first marriage wasn't fruitful I assume
much the same for this one.*

*My dear readers, what has society come to when
three bachelors and society snubbers have taken to
matrimony as a result of scandal?*

Mayfair Chronicles, August 1846

She noticed Hayden's surprised expression the moment
she approached him in the courtyard of the inn. She had
donned her riding gear, something less ladylike that she
could ride in with ease. They needed speed this morning,
and skirts would be a bother riding over rough terrain
while the sun had yet to rise. At least the rain had passed
through Birmingham overnight and that wouldn't be an
impediment for them.

"I'm surprised you travel so light, Jez." His voice was
hoarse. The ensemble definitely had an effect on him if
the trail of his gaze lingering at her breasts and hips was
any indication of where his thoughts were. He turned

away from her to address the boy who was suiting up the horses. "We'll need another saddle."

"You seem to have forgotten that I am a country girl at heart. I was born and raised in Yorkshire." And her father had insisted that skirts hindered a woman riding. At least her trousers still fit from her younger years.

She turned in a circle for him to see just how well trousers molded her curves. It was a miracle she'd been able to shove the two dresses she'd brought along into the satchel Hayden had given her this morning.

"I'll never forget that fact." He pulled her into his arms, lifted her off the ground, crushing their bodies tightly together, and kissed her hard on the mouth. There was no one other than the stable boy to see them this early in the day, not that she'd protest anyway. "I've always found it odd that you wouldn't leave Town once in a while to enjoy the country air you are so used to. London is absolutely putrid in the summer months."

When he set her down she walked over to the mare she was to ride.

"I never wanted to return after my father's death." She put her hand out to the horse, introducing herself to the animal as the stable boy changed out her saddle.

"I'm sorry. It was unkind of me to mention it," Hayden said.

"There's nothing to be sorry about. It was long ago. The past doesn't haunt me." She stroked the horse's muzzle. "And what is your name, my fine white beauty?" While her coat was white, the horse's rump and face were ticked gray. Her coal-black gaze focused curiously on Jessica, and the mare's ears pricked forward as she sniffed at Jessica with interest.

"I call her Bandit."

"Without a marking to indicate such," she mused with a laugh. "Dare I ask why?"

"You'll find out soon enough on the trip. She's a fine horse to ride. Perfectly spirited to suit you."

"And yours?"

"This is Gusto." Hayden ran his hands over the hindquarters of his solid black gelding. This one was a good deal larger than Jessica's horse—not an Arabian, like hers—and his long mane was braided to one side.

"Help me up, Hayden. I'm anxious to try such a gorgeous horse. Wherever did you procure her from?"

"She's one of mine."

"I feel privileged to be riding one of your famous breeders, then."

"They'll be yours soon enough." Hayden grasped her by the waist and lifted her enough that she could stick her foot in the stirrup and settle herself astride in the saddle. He followed suit, only he leaned forward to rub the gelding's neck affectionately. The horse tossed his head back with a playful neigh.

"What type of horse is he? He's a full three hands taller than Bandit."

"One of the prized Andalusians my grandfather acquired from the Spaniards." Hayden clucked his tongue, turning his horse around. "Let's go so we have enough time for breakfast on the open road before I head out to Tristan's estate."

They both peeled out of the courtyard. She didn't know the area, so she stayed behind Hayden, though her mare was champing at her bit to lead the race. The wind against Jessica's face felt good as they rode out of town and onto a dirt road. Despite her having grown up with horses, it had been a long time since she'd been on one not hitched to a carriage of some sort. Her legs would feel this later, she was sure, but she enjoyed every moment sitting astride her mare.

Their pace slowed once they turned off the road to

transverse tall, grassy fields. They rode abreast, though her mare was trying to pull forward. Feisty indeed.

"The sun is rising, so we've missed any potential rain." Hayden tightened his grip on the reins, slowing his horse. "I had breakfast sandwiches packed, if you'd like to stop here for a while."

"I'm famished after last night." She smiled innocently as she brought her horse around to face his. "Do you have a blanket we can picnic on? I'm anxious to be off my horse, since I can barely feel my legs and I don't think I have had any feeling in my thighs for the past half hour."

Dismounting, Hayden opened up one of the satchels and pulled out a small blanket. "I think this will serve our purposes." He fanned it out on the ground, then fetched the sandwiches that were neatly wrapped in thin pieces of white linen.

Jessica slid down the side of her horse. Her legs were a bit wobbly and her inner thighs sore, which was no surprise. She brushed her hands over the insides of her thighs. "It's been so long since I've been on a horse. Perhaps too long."

She walked over to Hayden, stretching her arms above her head, which tightened her shirt around her breasts. Hayden's gaze was fixed on the tight fit of her clothes.

"I can think of a few things to help you practice riding."

She pushed his arm away when he tried to grab her. She swiped one of the sandwiches from his hold and sat on the small blanket he'd put out on the grass. Biting into the thick slabs of bread with wedges of cheddar and ham made her groan in contentment. Apparently she was starved from their morning exercise.

"Should the horses be tied?" she asked after swallowing the first bite.

Hayden shook his head. "Bandit won't wander far, and she comes when you whistle for her."

Jessica raised a disbelieving eyebrow. To prove his

words, he let out two high-pitched whistles in quick succession. Bandit threw her head with a neigh and turned, head bobbing as she walked toward Hayden and nuzzled his shoulder.

Impressed by the horse's obedience, Jessica laughed and clapped her hands together.

"I've never seen the likes of that in all my life, Hayden. How did you ever teach her that? And why would you?"

He rubbed his hand over Bandit's neck, praising her obedience. "She comes from a long line of horses that were all highly trainable. Her blood has been in our breeding line since the eighteenth century, so we've kept the best generation after generation, culling out those that had less desirable traits. Horses serve many purposes, but they are also companions when you are with them day in and day out."

He gave Bandit a carrot from his satchel and called his other horse over by name, giving him a tasty treat in reward.

"I spent most of my days in the company of horses, since it was part of the family legacy I would take over from my father."

She patted the blanket beside her when he faced her once again, hoping he'd join her for more than a bite to eat. "And Gusto? He's a different breed. Is he as intelligent?"

"He is. Don't worry"—Hayden grinned—"we won't find ourselves horseless after an afternoon interlude in the woods."

Hayden bit into his sandwich as he sat next to her. She did the same, truly famished, since they hadn't had time for a bite to eat before they'd left the inn that morning.

He dusted the crumbs off his hands and took her half-finished sandwich and set it aside before leaning into her and pressing their foreheads together as he pulled the tie loose at the top of her shirt.

"What if someone should happen upon us?" Not that she expected any such thing to happen. It was just fun to tease Hayden. "It's not as simple as tossing my skirts aside," she said, nudging his shoulder.

"We've already hit the outer reaches of my land." He bit playfully at her cambric-covered shoulder. "There's no one for miles to interrupt us."

He grabbed her around the waist and hauled her beneath him. They lay that way for a spell, staring into each other's eyes. She traced her finger over his jaw, liking the feel of the rough stubble. He hadn't shaved this morning, since they'd been preoccupied in bed well past the time they should have been breaking their fast. She suddenly imagined him rubbing his face along the sensitive parts of her inner thighs, wondering what precisely it would feel like.

"How long before we reach your estate?" she asked absently. She didn't want today to end. It almost felt as though they were already married and had all the time in the world to lie idly about in each other's arms. Was this what she could look forward to, marrying Hayden? Goodness, it was heavenly and she had to wonder why she hadn't jumped at the opportunity the moment Hayden had asked for her hand in marriage.

"An hour at the most. Though I can still make Tristan's by the afternoon if we find ourselves delayed."

"I wish we had another day to ourselves."

"You can still come with me."

"No, I'll come when it's done. Tristan needs to be focused on the duel, not on us or anyone else."

Hayden parted her lips with his thumb. "I'll miss you while I'm away. I've wanted you for so long that I didn't actually plan to spend any time away from you once you agreed to my mad plan."

His comment had her grinning.

She pressed a light kiss against his mouth. "And I

know I'll be lost without you. But we've spent time apart before."

"That was long before we had a taste for each other's flesh." Hayden hiked the shirt from her trousers and kissed her corset-bound breasts.

"If we start this, we'll never leave this lea."

He pulled her shirt down and reluctantly rolled over onto his back. She could see that his passions were fired and that he needed her. The evidence was pressed against the front of his trousers. She wanted to stay with him for the remainder of the day, but Tristan was in greater need of Hayden's time than she. She tucked her shirt back in, picked up the remainder of her sandwich, and grasped Hayden's hand to tug him to his feet. "I can eat the rest of this on our ride to your estate."

His look was stern, as if he couldn't decide whether they should stay on here or spend a few hours alone at his estate. "We'll have some time to ourselves once there." There was no mistaking the meaning behind his words.

After kissing him lightly on the mouth she smiled up at him. "Perfect."

Hayden called the horses over without another word. After lifting her up onto her horse, he mounted his and they rode in what she assumed was the direction of his estate. The grounds were vast and well maintained. There was an old wood that stretched from his lands and flanked the borders of the surrounding estates and towns. Small gardens sprouted up the closer they drew to the main house. There was a grand fountain fed by a large pond in the valley before the house. Once they'd arrived, the sight nearly took her breath away. Sheer size alone made Hayden's townhouse seem modest.

"How many rooms does it have?" she asked.

"Sixty." He laughed a little. "My father came from a

family of twelve children. You can imagine how full the house would have been fifty years ago."

The thought had the reality of her inability to stay pregnant overwhelming her so suddenly she found it difficult to breathe properly and tears filled her eyes.

"Hayden—"

He cut her off on seeing her expression. "Don't say it, Jess. We have plenty of time for children. And if we aren't so blessed, I have a plentitude of uncles and cousins that I respect a great deal. Any one of them could assume the title with my blessing."

Her tears fell, and more replaced them till her vision was blurred. "You can't throw that away for me."

Hayden drew his horse close enough that one of Jessica's thighs rubbed along his. Feebly she wiped away at her tears. It wasn't till she used the back of her jacket to rid herself of them that Hayden came into view.

"I can and I will if it's necessary, Jessica. But I think the fault was with Fallon, not you. Time will tell." He took her hand and pressed a kiss against the backs of her knuckles, his eyes never leaving hers, as though that alone would make his point stick. "We have a lot of time on our hands."

Her smile was smaller this time, but he had at least coaxed one out of her. She really ought to stop feeling sorry for herself. It would amount to nothing but wasted moments in the end.

"Feeling better?" he asked when she sniffled and wiped away the last of her tears.

She nodded.

"Good," he said, dismounting from his horse.

This time Hayden helped her down from her horse. It had to be around eight in the morning by the time they'd arrived at his estate. Feeling slightly more normal, she inhaled deeply and set her shoulders back with newfound determination. There wasn't time to be nervous, as she was about to meet the staff who kept the house running. Hayden didn't hesitate to introduce her as his fiancée and the future mistress of the household to the long line of servants on the drive. She hadn't expected that for some reason. And now she almost had second thoughts about wearing trousers for the sake of ease in her and Hayden's ride. Almost.

Though she did wonder what the staff would think of her traveling without her maid and the lack of clothes she had brought along with her.

Not one of their expressions showed an ounce of disdain with Hayden's announcement that she'd soon be their mistress. Keeping her disposition sunny, as though she'd not felt like a failure of a woman only moments before, she was determined to win every single servant over. If she could win Fallon's servants over, she could do the same here, she thought as she smiled and greeted each member of Hayden's household.

Once they completed introductions, Hayden took her hand in his and led her up the front stairs so fast they were nearly running. Once inside, he picked her up, spun her around, and crushed their bodies together so he could kiss her good and hard.

"I should have carried you over the threshold," he said with a frown.

She shook her head. "It's too soon for that."

"It's never too soon for anything. But now that we are here, what should we do before I clean up and head out to Tristan's?"

"I can think of a few things to occupy ourselves." She looked up at the high ceilings all around her, recalling how he'd teased Lady Locksley about her old drafty castle. Hayden's house stretched a good quarter mile in both directions. "How am I ever going to find my way around here?"

"You'll have time to explore all the rooms in my absence."

"I don't think that'll be enough time." She laughed and focused back on Hayden, her hands resting on either side of his face as he set her down on her feet again. His gaze was dark, the brown of his eyes eaten up by the black of his pupils. There was no doubt in her mind that he wanted her again. She stepped up onto the tips of her toes so she could nibble at his lower lip.

"You're insatiable," she whispered.

"That, Jess, is all your fault."

Then he pinched her bottom.

Her mouth dropped open in surprise as she pulled away from him in shock. "I cannot believe you just did that."

His look was devilish. "I can do it again so it's more believable."

She shook her head, backing away from his outstretched hands.

"I think that's something you should be saving for behind closed doors, Hayden."

"I can't say I agree to those terms."

The look in his eyes told her he had every intention of doing it again, so she did what any intelligent woman would do and hoped she didn't get lost as she ran up the stairs to the second floor, Hayden hot at her heels.

He caught her at the farthest end of the long corridor. She turned and pressed her back against the dark wood of the doors, which she thought might be the master bedroom, since these were the only double doors on the second floor.

"Good guess," he said, then he tumbled them both into the room and toward the bed.

The room was the size of a ballroom, with high arched

ceilings painted with a fresco of angels. The walls were painted a sky blue, enhancing the brightness from a wall of windows that faced south. The sitting area was large enough for three sofas and too many chairs to count. The bed was a four-poster monstrosity of blond wood and flanked between bay windows so tall she could imagine the room turned into a sunroom by midday.

When they tumbled onto the bed she felt his hardness against her thigh. "Don't you have to be rushing out of here to see Tristan?"

"I need another reminder"—he released the buttons on her trousers and yanked them below her hips, which she aided by lifting her rear off the bed—"of exactly what I'll be missing."

She threw her head back and surrendered to the intimacy they had been flirting toward since the moment they were awake for the day.

"I'll miss you just as much." There was no telling if he'd be gone a few days or for a whole week. "I suggest you make love to me without delay, because I'll need a reminder, too."

Hayden didn't disappoint, and they did spend a number of hours locked up in the master bedroom together.

When Jessica awoke late in the afternoon, Hayden was already gone. She stretched out on the bed, her hand hitting a folded piece of paper as she loudly yawned her greeting to midday.

Darling,

   I had your dress pressed and hung in the dressing room, which is to the right of the master bedroom. The house is yours to explore, and the staff will help you with anything you are in need of.

    I hope this task doesn't take me away for too long. I will miss you. And I cannot wait till we are wedded so I can call you wife.

With all my love,
Hayden

    Jessica found her dress precisely where he said it was and resolved to learn as much about the house today as she could. She'd need something to keep her mind off Hayden. She thought perhaps she should pen him a note and send it to Hailey Court—and discarded the idea just as quickly. No, that would leave Tristan wondering why she was writing to Hayden at all. She could wait a few days to see Hayden again, and then they would both give their friends the news of their engagement.

Chapter 23

Our fair marquess has been maimed by his challenger. Can you believe such a thing in this day and age? Though it's still a mystery as to who precisely pulled the trigger, and it's unknown how serious the marquess's injuries are.

Mayfair Chronicles, August 1846

Jessica's maid arrived on the second day, with a carriage full of trunks and the last of her possessions. She'd amused herself during that morning by unpacking, even at Louise's insistence she take to the garden with tea instead. She needed to keep busy, to keep her mind from worrying over Tristan and Hayden. It was tempting to have someone give her directions to Tristan's estate, but she held herself back from doing that. Hayden would ensure nothing untoward happened. She trusted him implicitly to take care of Tristan.

"Did you have a chance to read the rags before you left London? I'm desperate to know if word got out about the duel."

"I didn't, my lady. It's better you don't fret."

"I'm merely worried about the well-being of my friend and was curious what was being said."

"Let the men take care of their business like the fools they are. Who would dare duel in this day and age?"

"I couldn't agree with you more, but you'll recall that it

wasn't Tristan demanding retribution. He'd gladly continue to thumb his nose at Ponsley for the rest of his days."

"All we can hope is that His Grace can sort out the issues before it comes to a duel. He has a way with words that makes you want to agree to something you might not necessarily agree to."

That comment had Jessica smiling to herself. He might have the ability over most, but not her; otherwise she'd have agreed to marry him a lot sooner. Her heart ached for him, though. She'd missed him terribly over the past two days, partly because there was little to amuse her time in the country, aside from her thoughts. And her thoughts had only been focused on three things: marriage, Hayden, and the duel. She closed her eyes and inhaled deeply, trying to catch the scent of his cologne in the master bedroom, but it had long since dissipated.

When Louise cleared her throat, Jessica's eyes snapped back open. "Warren didn't stop by the house in my absence?"

"Not once. I'd have told you sooner if he'd picked up the note you left for him."

And then it dawned on her why that might be. "He must be Ponsley's second. I can't think why else he'd not have stopped by, now that Miss Camden has left and can't act as a buffer between us."

"That would make sense. You said he was set to marry Lord Ponsley's daughter, didn't you?"

"He was."

She suddenly wondered if Hayden would take his anger out on Warren while she wasn't around to step in the way, and she realized she didn't care. Hayden had every right to defend her.

"I just hope Hayden is back soon. I wanted to post the banns this Sunday, but I won't if he's not back." Besides, she wasn't so sure she wanted to wait another month to be married. She'd discuss that with Hayden upon his return, which she hoped was sooner rather than later; otherwise, she would search him out at Tristan's estate.

❧

My darling,

Proceedings and negotiations on the precise weapon for the dueling field have finally come to a conclusion. By the time you receive this letter, it will be two days' time before the duel comes to pass. I long to have you at my side, and I urge you to join me once again. If you still feel you'll be a distraction to Tristan, know that you are a more than welcome distraction to me. I will see you in three days should everything wrap up quickly on this end.

I miss you more than words can express.

All my love,
Hayden

Jessica folded the letter and placed it under her pillow, fingering the edge as she closed her eyes. Under different circumstances she'd respond. She could wait a few more days to see him. Though even one more day felt like forever. She missed him more than words could express, too.

Hayden looked at his watch once again. It was half past four in the morning, and he felt as though he hadn't slept a wink as he'd strategized with Tristan on what was to be done should he be shot by Ponsley. The likelihood of that happening depended on two varying factors. First, it mattered whether Ponsley wanted to make a widow of his

daughter after only a couple of weeks of marriage—
Hayden and Tristan hoped that not to be the case. The
second factor was just how angry Ponsley was with Tristan
for stealing away his only daughter before he could benefit
from a political alliance with Warren. Warren did have
significant sway over the House of Commons and Warren
would use that influence to Ponsley's benefit when he sat
on the side of the Lords after officially taking the seat as
the Earl of Fallon.

It was hard to say how this morning would play out,
hence the reason Hayden had demanded his own physician attend the duel. Dr. Leonard stood next to the folding
table that held the pistols to be used in the duel. He was
tall and slight and easily in his mid-fifties. But he was the
most capable and trustworthy physician Hayden knew.

The only difficulty Hayden had in the proceedings was
facing Warren without physically striking out at him for
the undue cruelness he had levied on Jessica. Lashing out
as Hayden wished would serve no greater purpose for
Tristan, so he stood his ground, considering his friend had
a greater dislike of Warren, and for good reason.

While the fog had yet to dissipate and Hayden couldn't
see well beyond thirty paces, Warren seemed in a hurry
to finish with the proceedings.

"The rules, gentlemen, are simple." Warren's voice cut
through the still morning like thunder as he turned in
Tristan's direction. "The field of honor was given to you,
Castleigh. Ponsley will choose his pistol first."

"Let's be sure there is no funny business." Hayden
stepped forward, determined to have his say in this. "The
pistols came with you, so Castleigh has every right to
choose his firearm first."

"Do you have a preference?" Warren asked of Ponsley,
as though seeking permission to change this one rule.

"Let him have his pick." Ponsley crossed his arms over

his midsection, puffing out his chest like a cock strutting around as if he owned the world. "Castleigh, you've been a thorn in my side since your father died. It's about time I plucked that nuisance free."

Once Tristan picked his pistol Hayden loaded the little round ball that he knew would be lost in the field behind them. Tristan insisted on leaving his wife's father unharmed. Though he could not be sure the old man would have the same reticence toward Tristan.

"We've agreed on first blood, not death," Hayden reminded everyone present.

All nodded, including Warren, which seemed to catch Tristan's attention. "Why are you even here, Warren? You don't honestly expect me to believe you of all people have been wronged where Ponsley's daughter is concerned."

"My business is my own." Warren seemed unimpressed by the whole situation.

"If it's your own, then why do you stand here for his honor?" Hayden knew Tristan was only talking because he was stalling.

"She was to be *my* wife," Warren said firmly.

"You don't deserve her."

When Warren stepped forward as though he'd charge toward Tristan, Hayden moved closer, grabbing his arm and wishing he could do more harm, like plant his fist in Warren's face. "Stand aside and mete this out as was predetermined."

Warren relented; pulling away from Hayden, he walked back to Ponsley's side. To Hayden's surprise, Warren's gaze was on Tristan, not Hayden, as he handed the loaded pistol over to Ponsley.

"This is a bloody joke," Tristan whispered for Hayden alone.

"Just see it to the end and all will be fine." Hayden

prayed again that Ponsley was only here to save face and honor, not to do lasting damage to Tristan. How Hayden would hold back if the latter came true was anyone's guess.

"Let's finish this, then. I can't stand the buildup," said Tristan.

Hayden looked at Ponsley. "Are you ready?"

Ponsley nodded.

Both gentlemen put their backs together. They were discussing something, but Hayden couldn't hear their words, so he assumed Tristan was doing whatever he could to delay what was about to happen. They eventually took their steps to distance themselves evenly apart.

Tristan turned to Hayden before he faced the dueling field to ask, "First blood. So if he hits me we're done here?"

Hayden nodded. "But you will have to take aim and shoot at the same time."

"Bloody hell," Tristan said as he turned with the pistol held out. Ponsley was in much the same position, only his hand was a lot steadier.

"Hayden, if I should perhaps be maimed beyond saving . . ."

"Don't even think it," Hayden said, looking past the field and toward the shifting fog around them. "I hear riders; this needs to be finished or we'll be discovered."

"We're on my land."

"The women?" Hayden asked.

"Shit," Tristan cursed before calling out to his opponent, "Are you ready, Ponsley?"

"As ready as I'll ever be."

Hayden stepped away from Tristan and took up his post next to the doctor. Whoever the riders were, and Hayden assumed them to be two very angry women, they were fast approaching. The reports of the pistols were deafening when the shots finally rang out. Hayden watched his friend fall to a kneeling position on the ground.

"Damn that bastard," Tristan muttered, dropping the pistol before slumping further.

As Hayden moved into action with the doctor one step behind, everything became a flurry of activity: Lady Castleigh came into the clearing, jumping from her still-moving horse to hurry to her husband's side, Bea not far behind. Warren stepped forward to assist Tristan or pull the women back—Hayden couldn't tell which.

Please, God, let him not be seriously injured.

As he approached his friend he heard him muttering something. Tristan was talking as he caressed his wife's face just before he collapsed, taking them both right down to the ground.

"Tristan!" Her shout was hysterical as she tried to shake her husband back to wakefulness. When that didn't work she tried to pull at his clothes, looking for the wound that had struck him down. She was talking to Tristan, but he did not respond. Turning to Hayden, tears awash in her eyes and running down her face, she said hoarsely, "Help me!"

Bea knelt beside them. "Here, let me help." Yanking the frock coat from her brother, she freed his arms. When they saw no wound there, Bea turned to Hayden. "Can you see where he's injured?"

Hayden's worst suspicion came true when a stain of red grew alarmingly fast over Tristan's side. Charlotte ripped his shirt open to spread the material. That was when the doctor stepped in, pressing a white towel hard against Tristan's side to sop up the blood before pulling it away to prod at the raw wound to see how deep the bullet went.

"It's no more than a grazing," the doctor announced to everyone's relief. "Bullet only skidded across his ribs."

The doctor continued to press the cloth to Tristan's side, giving Lady Castleigh direction to hold it there as he opened his case.

"Why isn't he awake?" Charlotte asked.

"Could be the shock," the doctor said, taking out long strips of linen to tie around Tristan and hold the cloth in place to staunch the flow of blood.

"The blood," Bea said, pulling Charlotte to her feet to give the doctor room to work on Tristan. "Let the doctor look him over. We'll be back at the house soon enough—you can fuss over him there."

Hayden turned to the doctor to ask if he needed his assistance, but the doctor had it under control as he placed a wooden stethoscope against Tristan's heart and stuck his ear on the other end.

"I'll leave you with Castleigh while I send off the opponents." The doctor nodded.

Approaching Warren and Ponsley, Hayden said, "You're not invited on this land a moment longer. I expect you'll be on your way now."

Warren's expression of concern looked as though it weighed his brow down. "He'll fare well?"

Was that actual concern Hayden heard in Warren's voice? "He'll be better off if he doesn't see you when he's conscious again."

"I'd like to talk to the doctor to ensure he's fit as a fiddle before we are off." Warren stood taller, trying to intimidate Hayden, but that would not work.

"Leave, Warren. You're nothing but an outsider here." He hoped the words wounded the man deeply, for Hayden knew he was speaking on behalf of Bea, too, who had a long history with the weasel standing before him.

Before he could insist again, Lady Castleigh charged right past him and toward her father like a raging bull.

"What did you think to accomplish?" Hayden cringed at the harshness of her tone.

"You don't belong on the field of a duel," Warren responded.

Charlotte turned on Warren, finger pointed threateningly at him. "You will never tell me what to do. Your worth as a decent man was called into question with this little charade."

Warren didn't seem bothered by the insult, as he crossed his arms over his chest and said, "I was not the one to call out your *husband*."

"She's right, Adrian." Bea came forward, her anger just as palatable as Charlotte's. "You have no honor, so you could never have called a challenge to begin with. Yet, here you stand as though to prove something."

"I ought to put you in your place, Beatrice." Warren's focus was solely on Bea. "You've no right to talk to me as you are. There are things I know."

"And you've no right to step foot on my property without a proper invite. You can hurl as many insults my way as you wish. They no longer have the gravity they once did, because I know you. I know the *real* you. And you'd do well to hide yourself away from the truth of your vile nature, lest the world find out what sort of man you really are. Leave," Bea's demand brooked no argument and Warren backed off, hands in the air, in surrender to her wishes.

Charlotte reached for Hayden's arm. "Your Grace, will you help my husband into the carriage?"

"Of course." Hayden left Lady Castleigh to discuss private matters with her father. Tristan was bandaged up enough for the ride back to the house. Hayden lifted his friend's limp arm over his shoulders and pulled him to his feet. Tristan wasn't quite lucid, and his head bobbed to the side as he tried to walk where Hayden took him. They eventually made it to the carriage. The doctor rode back to Hailey Court with Lady Castleigh in the carriage. Hayden rode back to the house with Bea in near silence the majority of the way. They had each tied off extra horses to their saddles.

"How did you know we had left so early this morning?" He had to know how they'd even been found.

Bea gave him an all-knowing look. "I like to think I know my brother better than everyone else. He was acting oddly last night at dinner. So I knew something would come of today."

"You'll never cease to amaze me, Bea. I'm sorry you had to bear witness to what transpired at all."

"The only thing you should be sorry for is not telling us when you'd duel. And seriously, why would you let my brother choose pistols? He's got the worst aim of any gentleman I know."

"Because he refused to have any advantage over Ponsley."

"Bloody honor and men," Bea muttered.

"He'll be fine, Bea. I trust the doctor to make your brother as good as new."

"He had better, or I'll have his head right after I take yours for sheer stupidity." Bea clucked her tongue to spur her horse to a trot, leaving him behind and to his own thoughts.

After Tristan was settled and he knew his friend was on the mend, he had every intention of riding back out to his estate and, more important, to Jessica. She'd insist on seeing Tristan straightaway, and he had no intention of keeping her in the dark on his condition. While the bullet had only grazed him, Tristan still faced the risk of infection from the wound. He clucked his tongue to encourage his horse to a faster pace. Gusto complied and trotted on the heels of Bea's horse the rest of the way to Hailey Court. Hayden was desperate to see his friend well and in good hands so he could head back to Jessica.

Chapter 24

On second thought, could it be that the duke has taken the dowager countess to his estate so as to not tie himself to a woman of her reputation indefinitely? Perhaps his purpose is merely to make a mistress of her. A justifiable ending to her reign in society if I do say so myself.

Mayfair Chronicles, September 1846

Jessica awoke with Hayden's warmth sliding into bed next to her. With one arm wrapped around her waist, he pulled her close. She stretched her arms out, her back arching as she yawned sleepily. Missing him desperately, she'd dreamed of him every night pulling her into his arms for almost a week, just as he was doing now.

"I missed you," she said, her voice still groggy.

He nibbled at her neck, her chin, and finally kissed her mouth. "And I missed you more than you can imagine."

She cracked her eyes open. It was still dark outside, which meant they didn't have to get out of bed any time soon. "This has to be the most pleasant way to wake up."

"It's too late in the evening to even consider wakefulness." He kissed her eyelids and the tip of her nose before pressing his mouth to hers.

"Yes, but that means you've been up all day and riding late into the night. Why would you take that chance? I'd have been beside myself had anything happened to you."

"I missed you dearly." He rubbed his nose against hers. "And when I can think of nothing but you and us together again it makes me act irrationally."

Her room was too dark to really see Hayden. She'd found this room connected to the master bedchamber, and while she'd snuck into his room the first few nights so she could smell the scent of him as she fell asleep, she'd finally resolved to sleep in this bed so the servants didn't question whether she was the new mistress of the house or Hayden's mistress of the night.

"What time is it?"

"One in the morning."

She pushed him up, trying to sit, worried suddenly what the outcome of the duel might be. "Has something happened to Tristan to bring you home at this hour of the night?"

"I like it when you call it home." His tone grew somber. "The doctor assured me Tristan would be fine. They will need to watch for infection, ensure that there's no poisoning from the bullet that grazed his side."

Eyes wide, her hands shot up to cover her sound of shock. She kicked the blankets down to slide out of the bed and light a candle on the bedside table. She couldn't remain idle when her friend had been injured. "We need to be there for him."

Hayden pulled her back down next to him. "His wife is all a-tither. And they don't want the children to know what happened, so he will remain in bed until we've un-missed each other."

She nibbled at her lower lip. "Ronnie will know something isn't right." Tristan's daughter was a bright girl, and she'd know the moment she saw her father that something was amiss. There was no doubt in Jessica's mind about that.

Hayden had been prepared for the direction of her

thoughts, for he replied, "The children think he took a fall from his horse on an early-morning exercise. A fallen log mixed with too much fog was the reasoning we came up with, since he knows his lands blindfolded."

Her hands curled into fists. "I am going to kill Ponsley myself."

"You'll do no such thing. Their issues are resolved—for the time being. I'm sure it'll be a long road before he and his daughter sort out their differences."

"Well, I can't sit here knowing Tristan is injured. I need to see how he fares with my own eyes."

"We can head out to his estate first thing in the morning if that gets you back in this bed."

"What if he has blood poisoning by then?"

Hayden tried to grab her arm, but she evaded him. He let out a frustrated growl as he reached for her again, this time catching his mark.

"Trust his wife to look after him. They are happy to spend this time together without anyone intruding."

"Tristan needs his friends, too."

Hayden sighed as he pulled her back onto the bed. "I'll agree on going under the condition that you give me the morning . . . though I'd like some of the afternoon, too. I was gone longer than I anticipated and I've longed to be in bed next to you since our first night apart. Let me hold you in my arms for a while."

She sat next to him on the bed. "Our friend has been shot and you expect me to wait it out?"

He rolled to his side and gathered Jessica close so she couldn't escape a second time. That was exactly what he expected. If he thought Tristan's situation dire, he'd have wakened her and a team of riders to head back to Tristan's estate. But that was not the case.

To her, he said, "That is exactly what I expect from you right now. Tristan came out to enjoy some solitude in the country as he acquainted himself with his new wife. A woman who probably knows the full depth of your machinations for her ruin."

She huffed out an annoyed breath. "I have to disagree with you on this. I heard that she went so far as to seek her ruin to avoid marrying Warren. I was simply assisting her in the end."

"And where did you hear that rumor?"

She shrugged. "I didn't quite *hear* it. I came to that conclusion on my own when Tristan came to see me before leaving for the countryside."

"Interesting, but that still doesn't negate the fact that they are honeymooning and we'll give them the space they've requested. Besides, there are things we can do to amuse ourselves for the next few days once you turn off those worrying thoughts of yours." He traced the outline of her breast before drawing her closer and kissing her shoulder.

Jessica didn't fight him; how could she when she had missed him as much as she had? It wasn't as though they'd never spent time apart before. In fact, they'd gone weeks without seeing each other when Hayden had to focus on his estate and his horses.

It was different now for so many reasons. First, she was staying in his home alone. The only things to pass the time had been long walks and rides over the vast lands surrounding the ducal home. Her maid had arrived only two days after her, which had been a blessing, for she didn't feel comfortable befriending Hayden's servants without him here.

She guessed that Hayden wouldn't mind hiring on Louise, so she'd asked the young woman what her preference would be. Louise wanted to stay and had accompanied Jessica daily as she learned the house, the lands, and something of the people in the scattered villages.

Jessica brushed her hands through his hair and pulled him in for a kiss. "I'll agree to the day, but after you're rested I want to ride out to see our friend."

"And what of us? Our marriage? The first banns were not read this past Sunday, and I can't apologize enough for that."

"Our marriage will happen soon enough." She pressed her lips to his again. "And I don't care about the banns. I've missed you so much this week that I realized we shouldn't waste time in finalizing the paper portion of our future. Let us marry by special license."

He smiled against her lips and rolled her over onto her back. "We can be married in the morning."

She traced the lines of his face, staring into his dark gaze. It was a tempting offer but not precisely what she had planned over the past few days. "I want our friends present to witness our union."

"Then it can be done before the week is through. We'll send a fast post to Leo tomorrow. He can be here in a few days with his new bride. We'll have to marry at Tristan's, as I doubt he'll be up and about before the week finishes."

She smiled. "I very much like that plan."

"Good, because that's all I've got," he said as he bit gently down on her lip and stole many more kisses.

When he broke away she rolled on top of him. "There's something I've been meaning to tell you."

His hands skimmed over her hips and grasped her waist. His thumbs pressed against the undersides of her breasts. "What's that?"

She leaned over him and nibbled at his earlobe before whispering, "I meant to say this before, but it hadn't occurred to me that I hadn't said it until you'd left. I love you, Hayden. I've always loved you as my friend, but now it's grown into something so much more than that."

His expression was carefully neutral as he thumbed

her bottom lip. "I'm glad to hear it. I've longed to hear those words pass your lips."

"That's not the response I was expecting when I just confessed my true feelings to you."

His smile was slow. Seductive in a sense.

"Don't you recall me saying something similar?" he asked.

She narrowed her eyes. "I was in a state of shock by the confession."

"It was no confession. It was right there for you to see all along."

"I see it now."

"Good, because I love you more than life itself, Jessica, and to have you as my wife will make me the happiest man alive."

"And to have you as my husband will make me complete." She kissed him full on the mouth, this time slipping her tongue erotically past his lips and tangling with his tongue before pulling away to demand, "Now make love to me."

Hayden reversed their positions before she could demand anything else, his hardness pressing into her core and sending lightning bolts of pleasure through her body.

"Your wish is my command."

He kissed her hard on the mouth, stealing her breath away. Her legs fell open around his hips, welcoming him closer to her body. She'd craved him so deeply that having him here finally in her arms again set her body instantly ablaze with desire.

With a deftness that shouldn't surprise her, he reached between their bodies and pressed his thumb against her clitoris. She moaned into the next kiss, losing control of her body as she allowed Hayden to pleasure her. Though she didn't remain idle for long, for she was desperate to have his body naked against hers, so she helped him remove his shirt and released the ties at the center of her night rail.

The motion of his hand never ceased, and before she could comprehend everything that had happened in so short a time he'd shucked his trousers, taken himself in hand, and thrust deep inside her.

"Hayden—" Her voice came out panting, needy.

He didn't stop, only kissed her deeper, the plunge of his tongue matching the thrust of his body. She bit his lip to stall him as she felt the first wave of her orgasm hit.

Her body quivered as Hayden moved slowly inside her, licking gently at her arched neck as he cupped her breast lightly through the material stopping them from being completely flesh to flesh. She tried to prolong the finale, but her body had a mind of its own and flew right over the edge of sanity as her whole body trembled in pure pleasure. Hayden joined her in flying off the edge; this time, though, he didn't pull out of her as he met his end.

Jessica held him tightly in her arms, never wanting to let go of him. As her body relaxed in his, drifting back to reality, she ran her hands through his sweat-damp hair and stared into his eyes.

"I think you missed me a great deal," he said, his tone teasing as he pulled playfully at her lips with his own.

"I did. But you should be saying the same about yourself. You weren't far behind me."

"No, I wasn't, was I?"

He rolled off her, putting his front to her back. She tucked her buttocks tight against his pelvis, an area that showed no sign of being finished with her just yet.

"I think we need to undress you before we settle down into bed."

"I couldn't agree more." She turned and looked at him over her shoulder, shimmying her body to lift the night rail above her thighs.

"Minx," he said.

She smiled and gave him a sly wink as he helped her remove her nightclothes completely. They didn't do all that much sleeping for the remainder of the night.

If there was one thing that Hayden could do, it was keep his word. They left his estate after luncheon to ride over to Hailey Court to see their friend. When they arrived, Tristan was sitting up in his bed, his wife next to him, with a chessboard between them on a small folding table.

When Tristan looked up there was a twinkle of amusement in his eyes and then surprise. "Jez, Hayden. What are you doing here?"

"How could we not come? Once Hayden told me what happened, I had to see you were well with my own eyes," Jessica said as she stepped over the threshold into the bedroom, a smile on her face.

Lady Castleigh stood from her chair, a welcoming smile on her own lips. "I didn't know we would have guests. I'll just slip out and have the kitchen prepare a light meal and tea. I insist you stay for dinner, since you've come all this way." With that Lady Castleigh left.

Jessica sat on the edge of Tristan's bed and took his hands. "You scared me half to death. When Hayden told me you were shot, I nearly lost all sense of reason and wanted to rush out here immediately." She looked at Hayden, a mischievous gleam in her eyes. "But he talked some sense into me, insisting that your wife was a darling woman who would take good care of you and I could see you with my own eyes after giving you a day of rest to heal up."

"You needn't have traveled all this way, Jez. I'll be up and about by tomorrow at the latest. Charlotte keeps plying me with soup, insisting it will cure anything that might ail me."

"I think I like her before even getting to know her."

"And you should. She's a darling. I believe I fell in love the moment you sent me in her direction." Tristan smiled brightly at them both. Hayden sat in the chair Lady Castleigh had occupied before leaving them alone with their friend.

"It's good to know my tricks can lead you down the right path every so often," Jez said.

Tristan quirked one side of his mouth up in a grin. "If all it took to get you to join us in the country was me getting shot, perhaps I should have stepped out on the dueling field much earlier."

"Don't tease about something so dreadful. I was worried sick from the moment Hayden told me you were called out by that worm Ponsley. And besides, you'll love the story I'm about to tell. I have no doubt it'll cheer you instantly."

Hayden cut in, "Did you want to tell him? Or did you want me to?"

Jessica smiled brightly at Hayden, ducking her head the moment her cheeks blushed. "*I* have this, Hayden. Besides, I've been dying to tell someone all week when you left me to fend for myself at your estate."

That caught Tristan's attention, for his brow furrowed as he asked, "You've been here a week already? Hayden, why didn't you say anything?"

Hayden put up his hands. "Only at Jessica's insistence."

Hayden calling her by her true Christian name was Tristan's first clue that not everything was as it always was between them, for he stared back and forth between the two of them.

"We're to be married," Jessica said before her friend could puzzle out the mystery himself. Not that he'd ever guess that outcome.

His mouth fell open for a brief moment before he composed himself. "I thought you were acting oddly at the last ball we attended."

Jessica could only smile at the reminder of that night.

"We want you to bear witness with Leo as we take our vows," Hayden said. "I've already procured a special license so the local vicar can marry us."

"Have you already told Leo?"

Jessica reached out to take Hayden's hand, looking at him as she spoke. "We haven't had the opportunity. But he should have received my note that you were to duel Ponsley, so I imagine he'll arrive in mere days, as he was honeymooning in Scotland."

"We've always done everything together," Hayden said. "It should be no surprise to anyone that we've all married in the roots of scandal."

Jessica looked at him and squeezed his hand. "It'll be something to tell our children."

Tristan laughed uproariously just as Lady Castleigh joined them again in his room. "Whatever have I missed?" When Tristan coughed from all the laughter and hunched forward with a groan of pain, his wife ran forward. "Tristan, you're not to make any sudden movements, or you'll tear the lovely doctor's stitching."

"But the moment calls for celebration. Bring us the decanter of brandy and we'll all toast to the road ahead of us."

Jessica stood from the bed and took Lady Castleigh's arm. "I'll explain everything if you'll let me assist you in gathering the tumblers."

The young woman was too baffled by the situation to argue, so she let Jessica lead her out of the room as the men continued with their laughter. It was good to hear Tristan's laughter. Jessica had been terrified wondering what state she might find him in once they arrived. But he was indeed on the mend.

"I think it's going to be a long night of celebration, Lady Castleigh."

"So it seems," she responded.

"I hope you have an iron stomach; you'll need it to keep up with them."

"I'm well versed in sipping spirits."

Jessica patted the younger woman's hand. "I think you'll do just fine, Lady Castleigh."

Epilogue

Jessica turned over the letter sent to her at Tristan's house. With the griffin seal on the back of the envelope it could only be from one person: the Duchess of Randall, the very woman who had befriended Jessica after Hayden had introduced them, even when every other door had closed from the vicious revelation of Jessica's past the Mayfair Chronicler had published.

Slicing the letter open, Jessica pulled out the parchment and read the contents over quickly. It was a veritable novel, and it detailed all the events she'd missed while away from London these past three weeks.

She read through the contents of the letter quickly, not sure if she could believe all that had happened while she prepared for her wedding and her new life with Hayden, happily removed from the vile rumors that were always circulating about Town.

"Is it bad news?" Genny asked as she took the letter opener from Jessica's lax fingers and placed it on the vanity.

Genny and Leo had married two weeks ago in a very private ceremony at his estate in Hertfordshire before taking a train north to Scotland. Once word had reached them of Tristan's brush with death they'd headed immediately to Birmingham.

Jessica shook her head, nearly speechless by the contents of the letter. "Quite the opposite."

Charlotte stepped down from the stool where she was adjusting the tiara set atop Jessica's veil and Bea came forward with Jessica's shoes still in hand, since they were being buffed out.

The four women had become fast friends over the past two weeks. There were no hard feelings against any of them for Jessica's past actions against the young woman who had won Tristan's heart. Jessica was happy to see both of her friends happily married.

"The expression on your face tells me it is bad news."

Jessica handed the letter over to Tristan's sister, Bea. "Read the first page. You'll understand my utter shock."

Dearest Lady Jessica,

I hope this letter finds you happily married to Hayden once it's reached you. I have the best of news to impart. It was a bit of a challenge to find out where you were staying, but news of your elopement seems to have reached every corner of England and someone had finally heard or seen someone that knew of your exact whereabouts.

That is all here and there, however.

The biggest news I have is that our friend Lady Montant has found herself in the midst of the greatest scandal in England's history. Can you imagine that? It's rumored she's slept with half the ton's married men. Word is everywhere that she's been in every bed to gather information on our peers so they could keep her column going indefinitely. I think one of her lovers took offense to the rumors of

her sleeping with other men and spread the word
about the true identity of the Mayfair Chronicler.
You can well imagine she wouldn't be invited into
any house after the truth finally came out.

The city is abuzz with confusion and speculation
of the news she's printed over the years. Just think of
the reputations she's lauded or ruined with the stroke
of her pen!

The last I heard was that she was setting off for
the Continent. Good riddance is my only thought. . . .

Genny's mouth fell open as she looked back at Jessica.
"Did you know that Lady Montant was the Chronicler?"

Jessica smiled. "It was easily deduced, but it was not I
who exposed her."

Charlotte sat heavily on the stool she'd used to fix the
tiara in Jessica's hair. "I'm almost embarrassed to say that
I was one of the readers who couldn't wait for the latest
gossip to be spilled in those pages, no matter how scandalous and damning. But I stopped reading them when
the Chronicler took it upon herself to ruin my best friend,
Ariel."

Jessica gave Charlotte's shoulder a comforting rub.
"Your friend's brush with scandal will be forgotten in
time. It was her mother who misstepped, not her."

Charlotte smiled at the confidence in Jessica's voice. "I
do hope you're right. I've lost too many people in my life
lately. Ariel won't even see me; she's worried to taint my
new marriage. Let's not even discuss my father, who's
sent a post my way every day since the day he left."

"You'll have to forgive him at some point."

"I know, but he should suffer a while longer. Had he
aimed just a small step to the left, I'd be a widow."

Bea hugged Charlotte. "Your father knew what he was

doing. And it's all worked out for the best, but Jessica is right: you'll have to find it in your heart to forgive him eventually."

"Eventually is not today. I'm still furious with him. I promised Tristan I'd pay my father a visit when we go back to London. But I won't give him the satisfaction of my forgiveness before then. He should stew over every misdeed that led to the current strain in our relationship."

Jessica hugged Charlotte and everyone followed suit, closing the four of them in a tight circle. It was funny how Jessica had never been surrounded by very many female friends in the past and now she had three she trusted as implicitly as she did Tristan, Leo, and Hayden. Life had a comical way of working out in the end.

"This really is the happiest day of my life," Jessica said after a moment.

"You'll want to tell Hayden your good news," Genny said.

Jessica turned toward the mirror and pulled her veil down over her face. "I'll tell him later. Just think of the dinner conversation we can have on the topic. Right now, Hayden is as anxious to be married as I am."

"Then let's go meet your soon-to-be husband," Bea said, taking Jessica's arm. While her father wasn't here to hand her over to Hayden, Bea, whom Jessica had known the longest, was here for her. And this day wouldn't be complete without any of the women in the room. Their stories were all intertwined, and one marriage might not have happened without each of the others.

"Shall we, then?" Jessica said, and walked out of the bedchamber she'd been assigned while at Tristan's and down the stairs toward the back garden, where Hayden waited for her with the vicar.

* * *

Hayden checked his watch again. Jessica was taking her sweet time, not that he minded; he just wanted to finally celebrate their union properly with their friends.

She'd made him wait longer than he'd anticipated for the wedding despite not having banns read to honor their upcoming nuptials. She insisted on a proper wedding dress, which meant they had to find a dressmaker, then they had to ship in lace for the veil or something of that sort. Jessica had managed to delay the actual ceremony for two weeks.

Jessica had always danced to her own tune, and he supposed the more he rushed her the slower she would finish the task at hand. He'd have to exercise more patience for his tenacious wife.

"You've looked at your watch every minute for the past ten minutes," Tristan said. "Time will not move faster, no matter how much you will it."

"It's easy enough for you to stand patiently by when it's not the woman you love delaying your big moment."

"Jez will be down soon enough. You know how women get when they are left together for too long." Leo was spinning Rowan around in a circle.

"I wouldn't do that, Leo. He's liable to throw up after all the punch he had at lunch."

Leo laughed. "I'll be sure to turn him the other way."

Ronnie pulled on Hayden's sleeve, drawing his attention to something other than his late bride. "Uncle Hayden, can you spin me around?"

He went down on bended knee. "I don't think that wise."

"Oh, come now, Hayden," Leo said as he stood Rowan on wobbly legs. "Here, Ronnie, we'll give you a go-around. Don't tell your aunt Bea. She'll have my head for rumpling up your clothes before the ceremony."

Hayden shook his head as he stood next to the vicar again.

"Ah-hem."

Hayden knew that throat clearer and chuckled when Bea gave Leo a look of pure annoyance. He would feel the full brunt of her wrath later.

"I forgot myself," Leo said to Bea apologetically.

Tristan jostled his arm into his friend's side with a laugh. "Serves you right."

Tristan's gaze was soon drawn away when his wife, Charlotte, walked down the garden path in a yellow day dress that she looked radiant in. Hayden knew what that glow on a woman meant. He looked at Tristan again, wondering if his friend was aware of the state of his new bride.

"Will the groom please turn and face the front?" Charlotte asked once she stood next to her husband.

Hayden and Jessica had decided on a semi-traditional wedding, which meant he wouldn't be able to see his bride until they'd finished their vows.

Hayden turned, smoothing his hands down over his vest and jacket, nerves assailing him for the first time since Jessica had agreed to be his wife.

The shuffle of more feet came down the path—the other women, he assumed. It was hard not to turn to see Jessica, but he managed. Barely.

The vicar droned out the service for their union. Hayden didn't hear a word as he reached back to find her hand. Jessica's lace-gloved fingers grazed his palm before he caught her and spoke out his portion of the vows. Jessica repeated them.

"You have declared your consent before God. May the Lord in his goodness strengthen you and fill you both with his blessings forevermore," the vicar concluded.

Finally Hayden turned to his bride.

Jessica's hand shook in his, testament that her nerves were in line with his.

Hayden carefully lifted her veil. "I love you, Jess."

Jessica had tears of joy in her eyes. She threw her arms around his shoulders and kissed him for all their friends to see just how much they loved each other.

There were claps and whistles from Tristan and Leo. The women were sighing and crying about the beautiful ceremony.

When they parted, Hayden wiped her tears away with his thumbs. "You are the most beautiful woman in the whole world, my darling scandalous duchess."

"I love you, Hayden. Thank you for opening my eyes once and for all." And then Jessica kissed him again, as he held her tight in his arms. Their display of love and affection for each other was met with more cheers from their friends.

Finally, he'd taken his bride.